*The shadow of the Ripper falls upon London once again....*

THE AUTUMN OF 1888 WAS KNOWN AS THE AUTUMN OF TERROR. Jack the Ripper was out there somewhere, in the fog, waiting with his knife. He could strike anywhere, at any time. The thing about autumn this year was that everyone knew precisely when the Ripper was going to strike, if he kept up with the schedule he'd set so far. The next date was September 30. That was when Jack the Ripper struck twice, so it was referred to as "the Double Event." The Double Event was a big part of the reason Jack the Ripper was seen as so amazingly scary—he managed these brutal and somewhat complicated murders right under the eye of the police, and no one saw a thing.

On that point, the past and the present were exactly alike.

## OTHER SPEAK BOOKS YOU MAY ENJOY

| | |
|---|---|
| *Hold Still* | Nina LaCour |
| *Let It Snow* | John Green, Maureen Johnson, and Lauren Myracle |
| *Looking for Alaska* | John Green |
| *Nightshade* | Andrea Cremer |
| *Ripper* | Stefan Petrucha |
| *Shelter: A Mickey Bolitar Novel* | Harlan Coben |
| *Trance* | Linda Gerber |
| *Walk of the Spirits* | Richie Tankersley Cusick |
| *Wintergirls* | Laurie Halse Anderson |

THE
NAME
OF THE
STAR

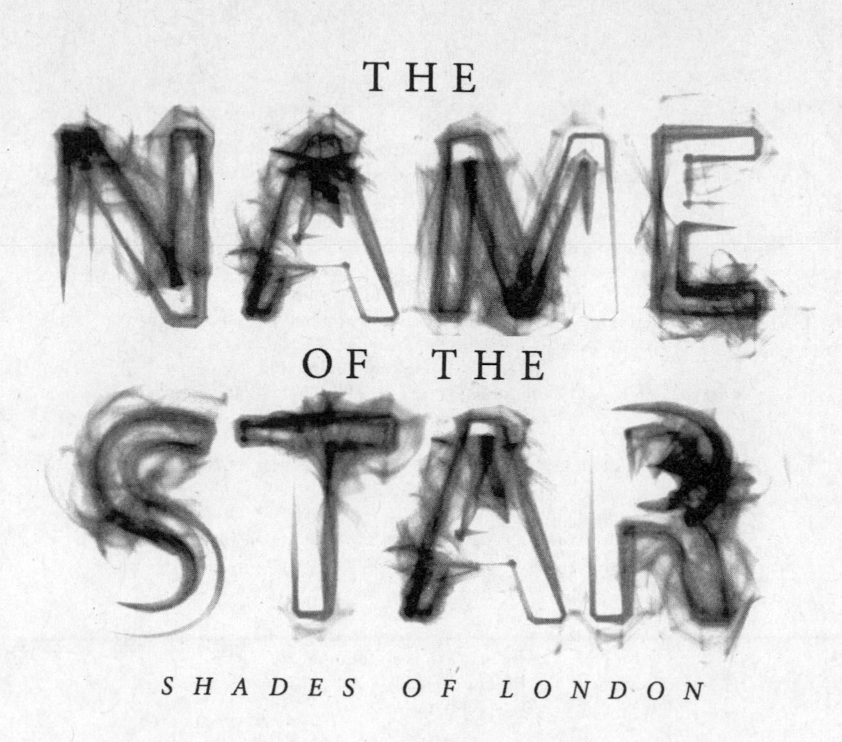


*SHADES OF LONDON*

# maureen johnson

**speak**
An Imprint of Penguin Group (USA) Inc.

SPEAK
Published by the Penguin Group
Penguin Group (USA) Inc., 345 Hudson Street, New York, New York 10014, U.S.A.
Penguin Group (Canada), 90 Eglinton Avenue East, Suite 700, Toronto, Ontario, Canada M4P 2Y3
(a division of Pearson Penguin Canada Inc.)
Penguin Books Ltd, 80 Strand, London WC2R 0RL, England
Penguin Ireland, 25 St Stephen's Green, Dublin 2, Ireland (a division of Penguin Books Ltd)
Penguin Group (Australia), 250 Camberwell Road, Camberwell, Victoria 3124, Australia
(a division of Pearson Australia Group Pty Ltd)
Penguin Books India Pvt Ltd, 11 Community Centre, Panchsheel Park, New Delhi – 110 017, India
Penguin Group (NZ), 67 Apollo Drive, Rosedale, Auckland 0632, New Zealand
(a division of Pearson New Zealand Ltd.)
Penguin Books (South Africa) (Pty) Ltd, 24 Sturdee Avenue, Rosebank,
Johannesburg 2196, South Africa

Penguin Books Ltd, Registered Offices: 80 Strand, London WC2R 0RL, England

First published in the United States of America by G. P. Putnam's Sons,
a division of Penguin Young Readers Group, 2011
Published by Speak, an imprint of Penguin Group (USA) Inc., 2012

3 5 7 9 10 8 6 4



THE LIBRARY OF CONGRESS HAS CATALOGED THE G. P. PUTNAM'S SONS EDITION AS FOLLOWS:
Johnson, Maureen, date.
The name of the star / Maureen Johnson. p. cm.—(Shades of London ; bk. 1)
Summary: Rory, of Bénouville, Louisiana, is spending a year at a London boarding school
when she witnesses a murder by a Jack the Ripper copycat and becomes involved with
the very unusual investigation.
ISBN 978-0-399-25660-8 (hc)
[1. Boarding schools—Fiction. 2. Schools—Fiction.
3. Murder—Fiction. 4. Witnesses—Fiction. 5. Ghosts—Fiction.
6. London (England)—Fiction. 7. England—Fiction.] I. Title.
PZ7.J634145Nam 2011 [Fic]—dc22 2011009003

Speak ISBN 978-0-14-242205-2

Designed by Marikka Tamura
Text set in ITC New Baskerville

Printed in the United States of America

*For Amsler.*

*Thanks for the milk.*

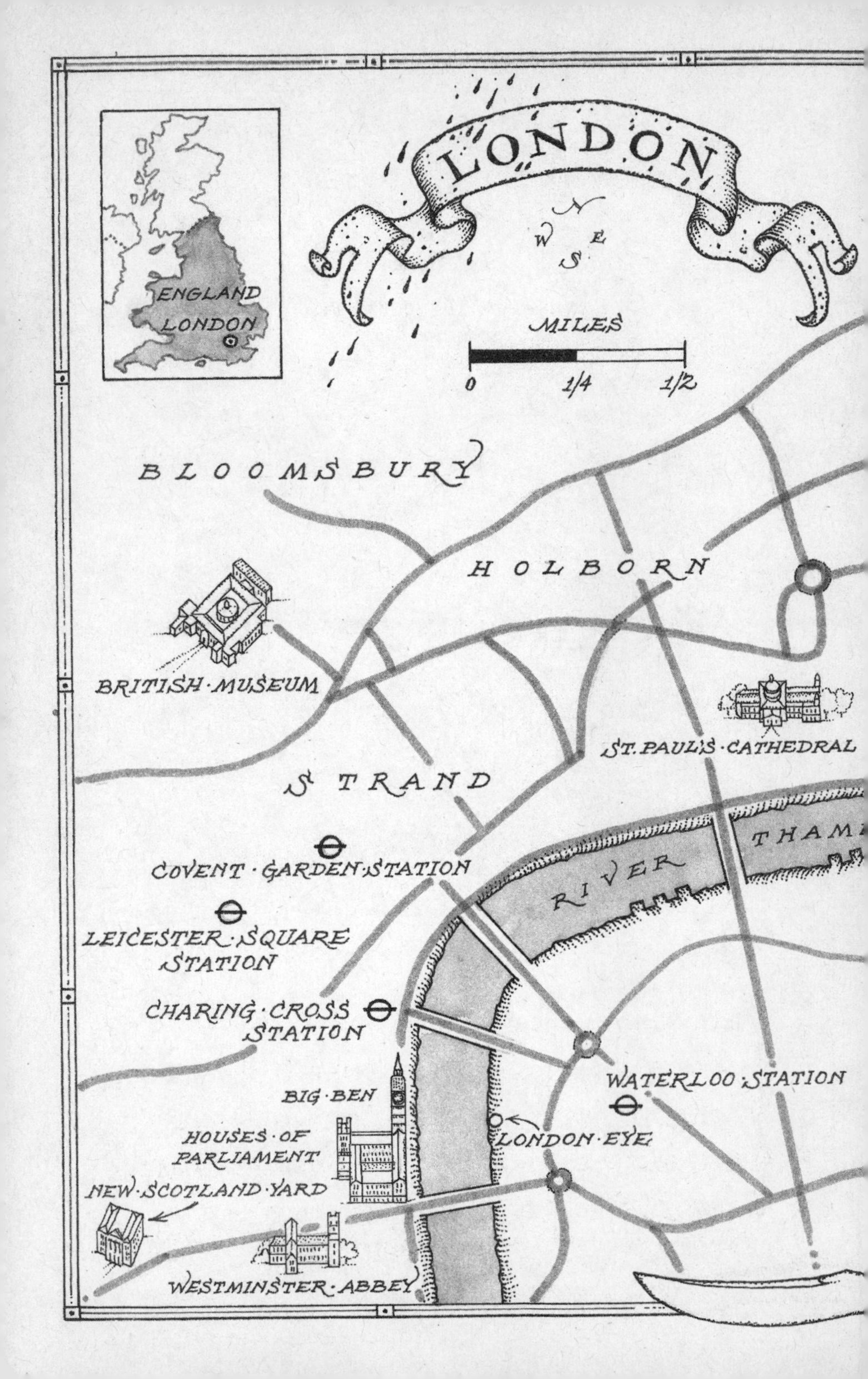
LONDON
N
W E
S
MILES
0
1/4
1/2
ENGLAND
LONDON
BLOOMSBURY
HOLBORN
BRITISH·MUSEUM
ST. PAUL'S·CATHEDRAL
STRAND
COVENT·GARDEN·STATION
RIVER THAM
LEICESTER·SQUARE
STATION
CHARING·CROSS
STATION
WATERLOO·STATION
BIG·BEN
LONDON·EYE
HOUSES·OF
PARLIAMENT
NEW·SCOTLAND·YARD
WESTMINSTER·ABBEY

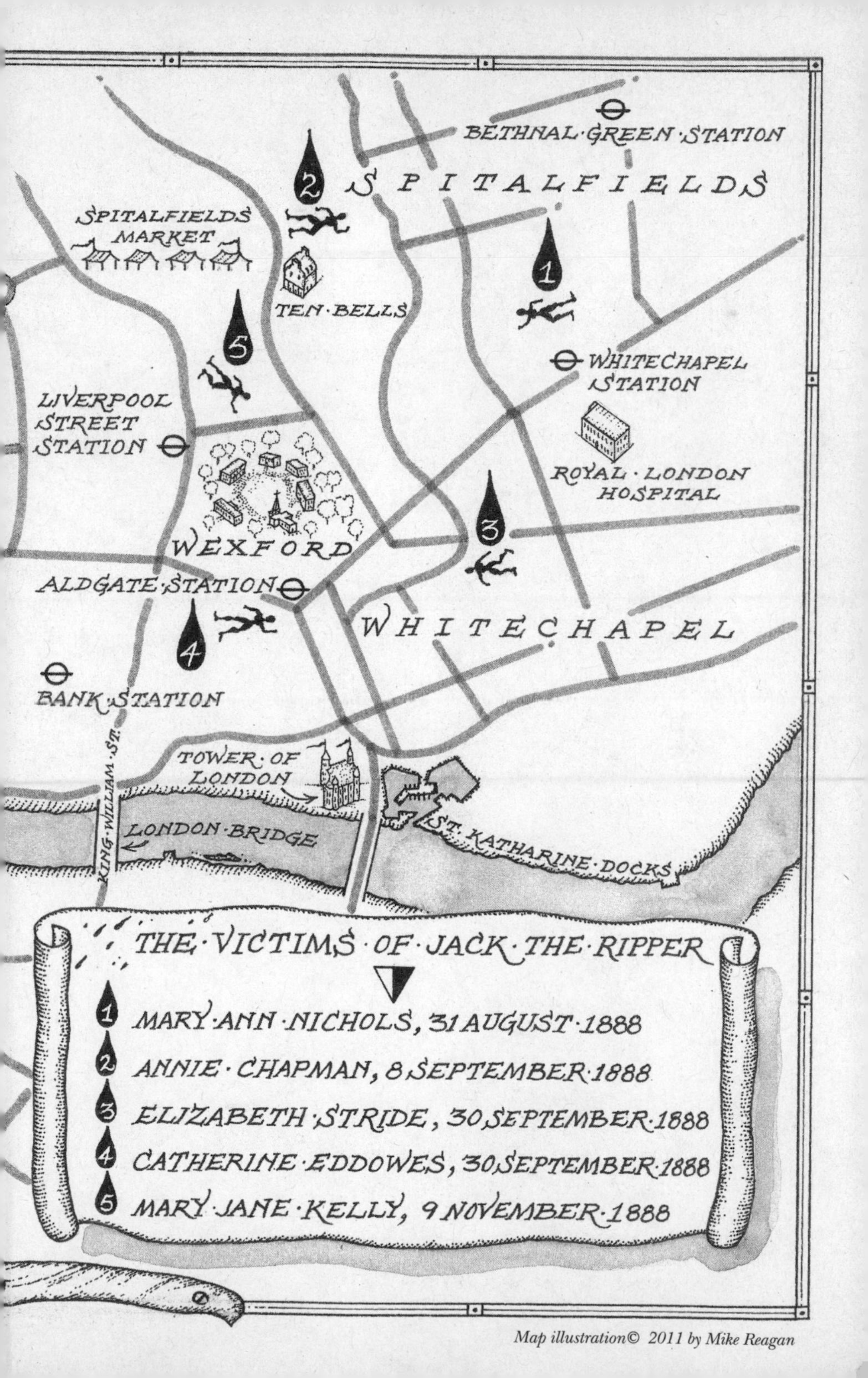
BETHNAL·GREEN·STATION
SPITALFIELDS
SPITALFIELDS MARKET
TEN·BELLS
WHITECHAPEL STATION
LIVERPOOL STREET STATION
ROYAL·LONDON HOSPITAL
WEXFORD
ALDGATE·STATION
WHITECHAPEL
BANK·STATION
KING·WILLIAM·ST.
TOWER·OF LONDON
LONDON·BRIDGE
ST. KATHARINE·DOCKS
THE·VICTIMS·OF·JACK·THE·RIPPER
1 MARY·ANN·NICHOLS, 31 AUGUST·1888
2 ANNIE·CHAPMAN, 8 SEPTEMBER·1888
3 ELIZABETH·STRIDE, 30 SEPTEMBER·1888
4 CATHERINE·EDDOWES, 30 SEPTEMBER·1888
5 MARY·JANE·KELLY, 9 NOVEMBER·1888

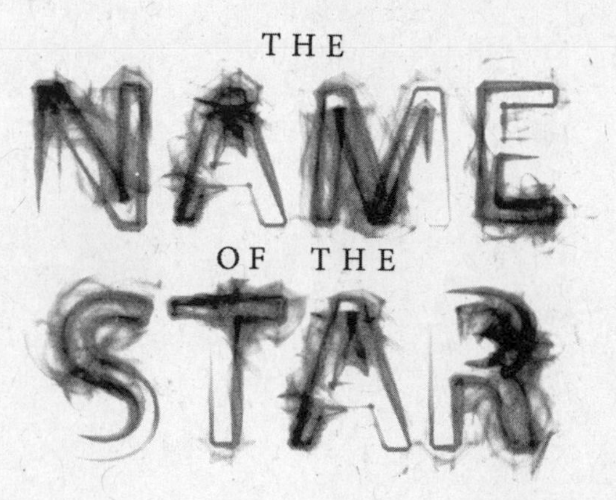
THE
NAME
OF THE
STAR

## DURWARD STREET, EAST LONDON
## AUGUST 31
## 4:17 A.M.

THE EYES OF LONDON WERE WATCHING CLAIRE JENKINS.

She didn't notice them, of course. No one paid attention to the cameras. It was an accepted fact that London has one of the most extensive CCTV systems in the world. The conservative estimate was that there were a million cameras around the city, but the actual number was probably much higher and growing all the time. The feed went to the police, security firms, MI5, and thousands of private individuals—forming a loose and all-encompassing net. It was impossible to do anything in London without the CCTV catching you at some point.

The cameras silently recorded Claire's progress and tracked her as she turned onto Durward Street. It was four seventeen A.M., and she was supposed to have been at work at four. She had forgotten to set her alarm, and now she was running, trying to get to the Royal London Hospital. Her shift usually got the fallout from last night's drinking—the alcohol poisonings, the falls, the punch-ups, the car accidents, the occasional knife fight. All the night's mistakes came to the early-shift nurse.

It had been pouring, clearly. There were puddles all over the place. The one mercy of this doomed morning was that there was only the slightest drizzle now. At least she didn't have to run through the rain. She got out her phone to send a message to let them know she was close. The phone emitted a tiny halo that encircled her hand, giving it a saintly glow. It was hard to text and walk at the same time, not if she didn't want to fall off the pavement or walk into a post. Am running lake . . .

Claire had tried to type the word *late* three times, but it kept coming up as *lake*. She wasn't running *lake*, she was running *late*. She refused to stop walking and fix it. There was no time to waste. The message would stand.

. . . Be there in 5 . . .

And then she tripped. The cell phone took flight, a little glowing ball of light, free at last before it clattered to the sidewalk and went out.

"Bugger!" she said. "No, no, no . . . don't be broken . . ."

In her concern over the fate of her phone, Claire first didn't take notice of the thing she had tripped over, aside from faintly registering that it was somewhat large and weighty and it gave a little when her foot struck it. In the dark, it appeared to be a strangely shaped mound of garbage. Something else put in her way this morning to impede her progress.

She knelt down and felt along the ground for the phone, sinking her knee directly into a puddle.

"Wonderful," she said to herself as she scrabbled around. The phone was quickly recovered. It appeared to be dark and lifeless. She tried the power button, not expecting any result. To her delight, the phone blinked on, casting its little light around her hand once again.

This was when she first noticed that there was something sticky on her hand. The consistency was extremely familiar, as was the faint metallic smell.

Blood. Her hand was covered in blood. A *lot* of blood, with a faintly jelly-like consistency that suggested congealing. Congealing blood meant blood that had been here for several minutes, so it couldn't be her own. Claire shifted around, holding up her phone for light. She could see now that she had tripped over a person. She crawled closer and felt a hand, a hand that was cool, but not cold.

"Hello?" she said. "Can you hear me? Can you speak?"

She got up alongside the figure, a smallish person dressed entirely in motorcycle leathers, wearing a helmet. She reached up to the neck to feel for a pulse.

Where the neck was supposed to be, there was a space.

It took her a moment to process what she was feeling, and in desperation she kept reaching around the edge of the helmet to get to the neck, trying to get a sense of the size of this wound. It went on and on, until Claire realized that the head was barely attached at all, and that the puddle she was kneeling in was almost certainly not rainwater.

The eyes saw it all.

# The Return

**Then shall the slayer return, and come unto his own city, and unto his own house, unto the city whence he fled.**

***—Joshua 20:6***

# 1

If you live around New Orleans and they think a hurricane might be coming, all hell breaks loose. Not among the residents, really, but on the news. The news wants us to worry desperately about hurricanes. In my town, Bénouville, Louisiana (pronounced locally as Ben-ah-VEEL; population 1,700), hurricane preparations generally include buying more beer, and ice to keep that beer cold when the power goes out. We do have a neighbor with a two-man rowboat lashed on top of the porch roof, all ready to go if the water rises—but that's Billy Mack, and he started his own religion in the garage, so he's got a lot more going on than just an extreme concern for personal safety.

Anyway, Bénouville is an unstable place, built on a swamp. Everyone who lives there accepts that it was a terrible place to build a town, but since it's there, we just go on living in it. Every fifty years or so, everything but the old hotel gets wrecked by a flood or a hurricane—and the same bunch of lunatics comes back and builds new stuff. Many generations of the Deveaux family have lived in beautiful downtown Bénouville, largely because there is no other part to live in. I love where I'm from, don't get me wrong, but it's the kind of town that makes you a little crazy if you *never* leave, even for a little while.

My parents were the only ones in the family to leave to go to college and then law school. They became law professors at Tulane, in New Orleans. They had long since decided that it would be good for all three of us to spend a little time living outside of Louisiana. Four years ago, right before I started high school, they applied to do a year's sabbatical teaching American law at the University of Bristol in England. We made an agreement that I could take part in the decision about where I would spend that sabbatical year—it would be my senior year. I said I wanted to go to school in London.

Bristol and London are really far apart, by English standards. Bristol is in the middle of the country and far to the west, and London is way down south. But really far apart in England is only a few hours on the train. And London is *London.* So I had decided on a school called Wexford, located in the East End of London. The three of us were all going to fly over together and spend a few days in London, then I would go to school and my parents would go to Bristol, and I would travel back and forth every few weeks.

But then there was a hurricane warning, and everyone freaked out, and the airlines wiped the schedule. The hurricane teased everyone and rolled around the Gulf before turning into a rainstorm, but by that point our flight had been canceled and everything was a mess for a few days. Eventually, the airline managed to find one empty seat on a flight to New York, and another empty seat on a flight to London from there. Since I was scheduled to be at Wexford before my parents needed to be in Bristol, I got the seat and went by myself.

Which was fine, actually. It was a long trip—three hours to New York, two hours wandering the airport before taking a six-hour flight to London overnight—but I still liked it. I was awake all night on the flight watching English television and listening to all the English accents on the plane.

I made my way through the duty-free area right after customs, where they try to get you to buy a few last-minute gallons of perfume and crates of cigarettes. There was a man waiting for me just beyond the doors. He had completely white hair and wore a polo shirt with the name *Wexford* stitched on the breast. A shock of white chest hair popped out at the collar, and as I approached him, I caught the distinctive, spicy smell of men's cologne. Lots of cologne.

"Aurora?" he asked.

"Rory," I corrected him. I never use the name Aurora. It was my great-grandmother's name, and it was dropped on me as kind of a family obligation. Not even my parents use it.

"I'm Mr. Franks. I'll be taking you to Wexford. Let me help you with those."

I had two incredibly large suitcases, both of which were heavier than I was and were marked with big orange tags that said HEAVY. I needed to bring enough to live for nine months. Nine months in a place that had cold weather. So while I felt justified in bringing these extremely big and heavy bags, I didn't want someone who looked like a grandfather pulling them, but he insisted.

"You picked quite the day to arrive, you did," he said, grunting as he dragged the suitcases along. "Big news this morning. Some nutter's gone and pulled a Jack the Ripper."

I figured "pulled a Jack the Ripper" was one of those English expressions I'd need to learn. I'd been studying them online so I wouldn't get confused when people started talking to me about "quid" and "Jammy Dodgers" and things like that. This one had not crossed my electronic path.

"Oh," I said. "Sure."

He led me through the crowds of people trying to get into the elevators that took us up to the parking lot. As we left the building and walked into the lot, I felt the first blast of cool breeze. The London air smelled surprisingly clean and fresh, maybe a little metallic. The sky was an even, high gray. For August, it was ridiculously cold, but all around me I saw people in shorts and T-shirts. I was shivering in my jeans and sweatshirt, and I cursed my flip-flops—which some stupid site told me were good to wear for security reasons. No one mentioned they make your feet freeze on the plane and in England, where they mean something different when they say "summer."

We got to the school van, and Mr. Franks loaded the bags in. I tried to help, I really did, but he just said no, no, no. I was almost certain he was going to have a heart attack, but he survived.

"In you get," he said. "Door's open."

I remembered to get in on the left side, which made me feel very clever for someone who hadn't slept in twenty-four hours. Mr. Franks wheezed for a minute once he got into the driver's seat. I cracked my window to release some of the cologne into the wild.

"It's all over the news." Wheeze, wheeze. "Happened up near the Royal Hospital, right off the Whitechapel Road. Jack the Ripper, of all things. Mind you, tourists love old Jack. Going to cause lots of excitement, this. Wexford's in Jack the Ripper territory."

He switched on the radio. The news station was on, and I listened as he drove us down the spiral exit ramp.

*". . . thirty-one-year-old Rachel Belanger, a commercial filmmaker with a studio on Whitechapel Road. Authorities say that she was killed in a manner emulating the first Jack the Ripper murder of 1888 . . ."*

Well, at least that cleared up what "pulling a Jack the Ripper" meant.

*". . . body found on Durward Street, just after four this morning. In 1888, Durward Street was called Bucks Row. Last night's victim was found in the same location and position as Mary Ann Nichols, the first Ripper victim, with very similar injuries. Chief Inspector Simon Cole of Scotland Yard gave a brief statement saying that while there were similarities between this murder and the murder of Mary Ann Nichols on August 31, 1888, it is premature to say that this is anything other than a coincidence. For more on this, we go to senior correspondent Lois Carlisle . . ."*

Mr. Franks barely missed the walls as he wove the car down the spiral.

*". . . Jack the Ripper struck on four conventionally agreed upon dates in 1888: August 31, September 8, the 'Double Event' of September 30—so called because there were two murders in the space of under an hour—and November 9. No one knows what became of the Ripper or why he stopped on that date . . ."*

"Nasty business," Mr. Franks said as we reached the exit. "Wexford is right in Jack's old hunting grounds. We're just five minutes from the Whitechapel Road. The Jack the Ripper tours come past all the time. I imagine there'll be twice as many now."

We took a highway for a while, and then we were suddenly in a populated area—long rows of houses, Indian restaurants, fish-and-chip shops. Then the roads got narrower and more crowded and we had clearly entered the city without my noticing. We wound along the south side of the Thames, then crossed it, all of London stretched around us.

I had seen a picture of Wexford a hundred times or more. I knew the history. Back in the mid-1800s, the East End of London was very poor. Dickens, pickpockets, selling children for bread, that kind of thing. Wexford was built by a charity. They bought all the land around a small square and built an entire complex. They constructed a home for women, a home for men, and a small Gothic revival church—everything necessary to provide food, shelter, and spiritual guidance. All the buildings were attractive, and they put some stone benches and a few trees in the tiny square so there was a pleasant atmosphere. Then they filled the buildings with poor men, women, and children and made them all work fifteen hours a day in the factories and workhouses that they also built around the square.

Somewhere around 1920, someone realized this was all kind of horrible, and the buildings were sold off. Someone had the bright idea that these Gothic and Georgian buildings arranged around a square kind of looked like a school, and bought them. The workhouses became classroom buildings. The church eventually became the refectory. The buildings were all made of brownstone or brick at a time when space in the East End came cheap, so they were large, with big windows and peaks and chimneys silhouetted against the sky.

"This is your building here," Mr. Franks said as the car bumped along a narrow cobblestone path. It was Hawthorne, the girls' dorm. The word WOMEN was carved in bas-relief over the doorway. Standing right under this, as proof, was a woman. She was short, maybe just five feet tall, but broad. Her face was a deep, flushed red, and she had big hands, hands you'd imagine could make really big meatballs or squeeze the air out of tires. She had a bob haircut that was almost completely square, and was wearing a plaid dress made of hearty wool. Something about her suggested that her leisure activities included wrestling large woodland animals and banging bricks together.

As I got out of the van she called, "Au*ror*a!" in a penetrating voice that could cause a small bird to fall dead out of the sky.

"Call me Claudia," she boomed. "I'm housemistress of Hawthorne. Welcome to Wexford."

"Thanks," I said, my ears still ringing. "But it's Rory."

"Rory. Of course. Everything all right, then? Good flight?"

"Great, thank you." I hurried to the back of the van and tried to get to the bags before Mr. Franks broke his spine in three places hauling them out. Flip-flops and cobblestones do not go well together, however, especially after a rain, when every slight indentation is filled with cold water. My feet were soaked, and I was sliding and stumbling over the stones. Mr. Franks beat me to the back of the car, and grunted as he yanked the bags out.

"Mr. Franks will bring those inside," Claudia said. "Take them to room twenty-seven, please, Franks."

"Righto," he wheezed.

The rain started to patter down lightly as Claudia opened the door, and I entered my new home for the first time.

# 2

I WAS IN A FOYER PANELED IN DARK WOOD WITH A mosaic floor. A large banner bearing the words WELCOME BACK TO WEXFORD hung from the inner doorway. A set of winding wooden steps led up to what I guessed were our rooms. On the wall, a large bulletin board was already full of flyers for various sports and theater tryouts.

"Call me Claudia," Claudia said again. "Come through this way so we can have a chat."

She led me through a door on the left, into an office. The room had been painted a deep, scholarly shade of maroon, and there was a large Oriental rug on the floor. The walls and shelves were mostly covered in hockey awards, pictures of hockey teams, mounted hockey sticks. Some of the awards had years on them and names of schools, telling me that Claudia was now in her early thirties. This amazed me, since she looked older than Granny Deveaux. Though to be fair, Granny Deveaux had permanent makeup tattooed on her eyes and bought her jeans in the juniors department at Kohl's. Whereas Claudia, it was clear, didn't mind getting out there in the elements and perpetrating a little physical violence in the name of sport. I could easily picture her running over a muddy hillside, field hockey stick raised, screaming. In fact, I was pretty sure that was what I was going to see in my dreams tonight.

"These are my rooms," she said, indicating the office and whatever splendors lay behind the door by the window. "I live here, and I am available at all times for emergencies, and until nine every evening if you just want to chat. Now, let's go through some basics. This year, you are the only student coming from abroad. As you probably know, our system here is different from the one you have at home. Here, students take tests called GCSEs when they are about sixteen . . ."

I did know this. There was no way I could have prepared to come here without knowing this. The GCSEs are individual tests on pretty much every subject you've ever studied, ever. People take between eight and fourteen of these things, depending, I guess, on how much they like taking tests. How you do on your GCSEs determines how you're going to spend your next two years, because when you're seventeen and eighteen, you get to specialize. Wexford was a strange and rare thing: a boarding "sixth-form college"—*college* here meaning "school for seventeen- and eighteen-year-olds." It was for people who couldn't afford five years in a fancy private school, or hated the school they were in and wanted to live in London. People only attended Wexford for two years, so instead of moving in with a bunch of people who had known each other *forever*, at

Wexford, my new fellow students would have been together for a year at most.

"Here, at Wexford," she went on, "students take four or five subjects each year. They are studying for their A-level exams, which they take at the end of their final year. You are welcome to sit for the A levels if you like, but since you do not require them, we can set up a separate system of grading to send back to America. I see you'll be taking five subjects—English literature, history, French, art history, and further maths. Here is your schedule."

She passed me a piece of paper with a huge grid on it. The schedule itself didn't have that day-in, day-out sameness I was used to. Instead, I got this bananas spreadsheet that spanned two weeks, full of double periods and free periods.

I stared at this mess and gave up any hope of ever memorizing it.

"Now," Claudia said, "breakfast is at seven each morning. Classes begin at eight fifteen, with a lunch break at eleven thirty. At two forty-five you change for sport—that's from three to four. Then you shower and have class again from four fifteen until five fifteen. Dinner is from six to seven. Then the evenings are for clubs, or more sport, or work. Of course, we still need to put you into your sport. May I recommend hockey? I am in charge of the girls' hockey team. I think you'd enjoy it."

This was the part I'd been dreading. I am not a very sporty person. Where I come from, it's too hot to run, and it's generally not encouraged. The joke is, if you see someone running in Bénouville, you run in the same direction, because there's probably something really terrible right behind them. At Wexford, *daily* physical activity was required. My choices were football (a.k.a. soccer, a.k.a. a lot of running outdoors), swimming (no), hockey (by this they meant field, not ice), or netball. I hate all sports, but basketball I at least know something about—and netball was supposed to be the cousin of basketball. You know how girls play softball instead of baseball? Well, netball is the softball version of basketball, if that makes any sense. The ball is softer, and smaller, and white, and some of the rules are different . . . but basically, it's basketball.

"I was thinking netball," I said.

"I see. Have you ever played hockey before?"

I looked around at the hockey decorations.

"I've never played it. I really only know basketball, so netball—"

"Completely different. We could start you fresh in hockey. How about we just do that now, hmmm?"

Claudia leaned over the desk and smiled and knitted her meaty hands together.

"Sure," I heard myself say. I wanted to suck the word back into my mouth, but Claudia had already grabbed her pen and was scribbling something down and muttering, "Excellent, excellent. We'll get you set up with a hockey kit. Oh, and of course you'll need these."

She slid a key and an ID across the desk. The ID was a disappointment. I'd taken about fifty pictures of myself until I found one that was passable, but in transferring it to the plastic, my face had been stretched out and had turned purple. My hair looked like some kind of mold.

"Your ID will get you in the front door. Simply tap it on the reader. Under no circumstances are you to give your ID to anyone else. Now, let's look around."

We got up and went back into the hallway. She waved her hand at a wall full of open mailboxes. There were more bulletin boards full of more notices for classes that hadn't even started yet—reminders to get Oyster cards for the Tube, reminders to get certain books, reminders to get things at the library.

"The common room," she said, opening a set of double doors. "You'll be spending a lot of time here."

This was a massive room, with a big fireplace. There was a television, a bunch of sofas, some worktables, and piles of cushions to sit on on the floor. Next to the common room, there was a study room full of desks, then another study room with a big table where you could have group sessions, then a series of increasingly tiny study rooms, some with only a single plush chair or a whiteboard on the wall.

From there, we went up three floors of wide, creaking steps. My room, number twenty-seven, was way bigger than I'd expected. The ceiling was high. There were large windows, each with a normal rectangular bit and an additional semicircle of glass on top. A thin, tan carpet had been laid on the floor. There was an amazing light hanging from the ceiling, big globes on a seven-pronged silver fixture. Best of all—there was a small fireplace. It didn't look like it worked, but it was incredibly pretty, with a black iron grate and deep blue tiles. The mantel was large and deep, and there was a mirror mounted above it.

The thing that really got my attention, though, was the fact that there were three of everything. Three beds, three desks, three wardrobes, three bookshelves.

"It's a triple," I said. "I was only sent the name of one roommate."

"That's right. You'll be living with Julianne Benton. She does swimming."

That last part was delivered with a touch of annoyance. It was becoming very clear what Claudia's priorities were.

She then showed me a tiny kitchen at the end of the hall. There was a water dispenser in the corner that had cold or boiling filtered water ("so you won't need a kettle"). There was a small dishwasher and a very, very small fridge.

"That's stocked daily with milk and soya milk," Claudia said. "The fridge is for drinks only. Make sure to label your drinks. That's what the pack of two hundred blank labels on your school supply list is for. There will be a selection of fruit and dried cereal here at all times, in case you get hungry."

Then it was a tour of the bathroom, which was actually the most Victorian room of them all. It was massive, with a black-and-white tiled floor, marbled walls, and big beveled mirrors. There were wooden cubbies for our towels and bath supplies. For the first time, I could completely imagine all my future classmates here, all of us taking our showers and talking and brushing our teeth. I would be seeing my classmates dressed only in towels. They would see me without makeup, every day. That thought hadn't occurred to me before. Sometimes you have to see the bathroom to know the hard reality of things.

I tried to dismiss this dawning fear as we returned to my room. Claudia rattled off rules to me for about another ten minutes. I tried to make mental notes of the ones to remember. We had to have our lights out by eleven, but we were allowed to use computers or small personal lights after that, provided that they didn't bother our roommates. We could only put things up on our walls using something called Blu-Tack (also on the supply list). School blazers had to be worn to class, official assemblies, and dinner. We could leave them behind for breakfast and lunch.

"The dinner schedule is a bit strange tonight, since it's just the prefects and you. The meal will be at three. I'll send Charlotte to come get you. Charlotte is head girl."

Prefects. I had learned this one. Student council types, but with superpowers. They who must be obeyed. Head girl was head of all girl prefects. Claudia left me, banging the door behind her. And then, it was just me. In the big room. In London.

Eight boxes were sitting on the floor. This was my *new stuff,* my clothes for the year: ten white dress shirts, three dark gray skirts, one gray and white striped blazer, one maroon tie, one gray sweater with the school crest on the breast, twelve pairs of gray kneesocks. In addition, there was another box of PE uniforms, for the daily physical education: two pairs of dark gray track pants with white stripes down the side, three pairs of shorts of the same material, five light gray T-shirts with WEXFORD written across the front, one maroon fleece track jacket with school crest, ten pairs of white sport socks. There were shoes as well—massive, clunky things that looked like Frankenstein shoes.

Obviously, I had to put on the uniform. The clothes were stiff and creased from packing. I yanked the pins from the shirt collars and pulled the tags from the skirt and blazer.

I put on everything but the socks and shoes. Then I put on my headphones, because I find that a little music helps you adjust better.

There was no full-length mirror to gauge the effect. Using the mirror over the fireplace, I got a partial look. I still really needed to see the whole thing. That was going to require some ingenuity. I tried standing on the end of the middle bed, but it was too far over, so I pulled it into the center of the room and tried again. Now I had the complete picture. The result was a lot less gray than I'd imagined. My hair, which is a deep brown, looked black against the blazer, which I liked. The best part, without any question, was the tie. I've always liked ties, but it seemed like too much of a Statement to wear them. I pulled it loose, tugged it to the side, wrapped it around my head—I wanted to see every variation of the look.

Suddenly, the door opened. I screamed and knocked the headphones off my ears. They blasted music out into the room. I turned to see a tall girl standing in the doorway. She had red hair in an incredibly complicated yet casual-looking updo, and the creamy skin and heavy showers of golden freckles to match. What was most remarkable was her bearing. Her face was long, culminating in an adorable nub of a chin, which she held high. She was one of those people who *actually* walks with her shoulders back, like that's normal. She was not, I noticed, wearing a uniform. She wore a blue and rose skirt with a soft gray T-shirt and a soft rose linen scarf tied loosely around her neck.

"Are you Au*rora*?" she asked.

She didn't wait for me to confirm that I was this "Aurora" she was looking for.

"I'm Charlotte," she said. "I'm here to take you to dinner."

"Should I"—I pinched a bit of my uniform in the hope that this conveyed the verb—"change?"

"Oh, no," she said cheerfully. "You're fine. It's just a handful of us, anyway. Come on!"

She watched me step awkwardly from the bed, grab my ID and key, and slip on my flip-flops.

# 3

"So," Charlotte chirped, as I stumbled and slid over the cobblestones, "where are you from?"

I know you're not supposed to judge people when you first meet them—but sometimes they give you lots of material to work with. For example, she kept looking sideways at my uniform. It would have been so easy for her to say, "Take a second and change," but she hadn't done that. I guess I could have demanded it, but I was cowed by her head girl status. Also, halfway down the stairs, she told me she was going to apply to Cambridge. Anyone who tells you their fancy college plans before they tell you their last name . . . these are people to watch out for. I once met a girl in line at Walmart who told me she was going to be on *America's Next Top Model.* When I next saw that girl, she was crashing a shopping cart into an old lady's car out in the parking lot. Signs. You have to read them.

I was terrified for a few minutes that they would *all* be like this, but reassured myself that it probably took a certain type to become head girl. I decided to deflect her attitude by giving a long, Southern answer. I come from people who know how to draw things out. Annoy a Southerner, and we will drain away the moments of your life with our slow, detailed replies until you are nothing but a husk of your former self and that much closer to death.

"New Orleans," I said. "Well, not New Orleans, but right outside of. Well, like an hour outside of. My town is really small. It's a swamp, actually. They drained a swamp to build our development. Well, attempting to drain a swamp is pretty pointless. They don't really *drain.* You can dump as much fill on them as you want, but they're still swamps. The only thing worse than building a housing development on a swamp is building it on an old Indian burial ground—and if there *had* been an old Indian burial ground around, the greedy morons who built our McMansions would have set up camp on it in a heartbeat."

"Oh. I see."

My answer only seemed to increase the intensity of the smug glee waves. My flip-flops made weird sucking noises on the stones.

"Your feet must be cold in those," she said.

"They are."

And that was the end of our conversation.

The refectory was in the old church, long deconsecrated. My hometown has three churches—all of them in prefab buildings, all filled with rows of plastic chairs. This was a *Church*—not large—but proper, made of stone, with buttresses and a small bell tower and narrow stained-glass windows. Inside, it was brightly lit by a number of circular black metal chandeliers. There were three long rows of wooden tables with benches, and a dais with a table where the old altar had been. There was also one of those raised side pulpits with its own set of winding stairs.

There was a small group of students sitting toward the front. Of course, none of them were in uniform. The sound of my flip-flops echoed off the walls, drawing their attention.

"Everyone," Charlotte said, walking me up to the group, "this is Aurora. She's from America."

"Rory," I said quickly. "Everyone calls me Rory. And I love uniforms. I'm going to wear mine *all the time.*"

"Right," Charlotte said, before my quip could land. "And this is Jane, Clarissa, Andrew, Jerome, and Paul. Andrew is head boy."

All the prefects were casually dressed, but in a dressy way. Like Charlotte, the other girls wore informal skirts. The guys wore polo shirts or T-shirts with logos I didn't recognize, and looked like people in catalog ads. Out of all of them, Jerome looked the most rock-and-roll, with a slightly wild head of brown curls. He looked a lot like the guy I liked when I was in fourth grade, Doug Davenport. They both had sandy brown hair and wide noses and mouths. There was something easy-going about Jerome's face. He looked like he smiled a lot.

"Come on, Rory!" Charlotte chirped. "This way."

By now I resented almost everything that came out of Charlotte's mouth. I definitely didn't appreciate being beckoned like a pet. But I didn't see any other course of action available, so I followed her.

To get to the food, we had to walk around the raised pulpit to a side door. We entered what had probably been the old offices or vestry. All of that had been ripped out to make a compact industrial kitchen and the customary row of steam trays. Tonight's dinner consisted of a chicken casserole, vegetarian shepherd's pie, a pan of roasted potatoes, green beans, and some rolls. There was a thin layer of golden grease over everything except the rolls, which was fine by me. I hadn't eaten all day, and I had a stomach that could handle any amount of grease I could get inside it.

I took a little bit of everything as Charlotte looked over my plate. I met her eye and smiled.

When we returned, the conversation had rolled on. There was lots of stuff about "summer hols" and someone going to Kenya and someone else sailing. No one I knew went to Kenya for the summer. And I knew people with boats, but no one who "went sailing." These people didn't seem rich—at least, they weren't a kind of rich I was familiar with. Rich meant stupid cars and a ridiculous house and huge parties with limos to New Orleans on your sixteenth birthday to drink nonalcoholic Hurricanes, which you swap out for real Hurricanes in the bathroom, and then you steal a duck, and then you throw up in a fountain. Okay, I was thinking of someone very specific in that case, but that was the general idea of rich that I currently held. Everyone at this table had a measure of maturity I wasn't used to—*gravitas*, to use the SAT word.

"You're from New Orleans?" Jerome asked, pulling me out of my thoughts.

"Yeah," I said, hurrying to finish chewing. "Outside of."

He looked like he was about to ask me something else, but Charlotte cut in.

"We have a prefects' meeting now," she informed me. "In here."

I wasn't quite done eating dessert, but I didn't want to look like I was thrown by this.

"I'll see you later," I said, setting down my spoon.

Back in my room, I tried to choose a bed. I definitely didn't want the one in the middle. I had to have some wall space. The only question was, did I go ahead and take the one by the super-cool fireplace (and therefore lay claim to the excellence of the mantel to store my stuff), or did I take the high road and choose the other side of the room?

I spent five minutes standing there, rationalizing the choice of taking the one by the fireplace. I decided it was fine for me to do this as long as I didn't take the mantel *right away.* I would just take the bed and not touch the mantel for a while. Gradually, it would become mine.

That important issue resolved, I put on my headphones and turned my attention to unpacking boxes. One contained the sheets, pillows, blankets, and towels I'd had shipped over from home. It was strange to have these mundane house things show up here, in this building in the middle of London. After making up my bed, I tackled the suitcases, filling my wardrobe and the drawers. I put my photo collage of my friends from home above my desk, plus the pictures of my parents, of Uncle Bick and Cousin Diane. There was the ashtray shaped like pursed lips that I stole from our local barbecue place, Big Jim's Pit of Love. I got out my collection of Mardi Gras beads and medallions and hung them from the end of my bed. Finally, I set up my computer and placed my three precious jars of Cheez Whiz safely on the shelf.

It was seven thirty.

I knelt on my bed and looked out the window. The sky was still bright and blue.

I wandered around the empty building for a while, eventually ending up in the common room. This would probably be the only time I had this room to myself, so I flopped on the sofa right in front of the television and turned it on. It was tuned to BBC One, and the news had just started. The first thing I noticed was the huge banner at the bottom of the screen that read **RIPPER-LIKE MURDER IN EAST END**. As I watched, through half-open eyes, I saw shots of the blocked-off street where the body was found. I saw footage of fluorescent-vested police officers holding back camera crews. Then it was back to the studio, where the announcer went on.

*"Despite the fact that there was a CCTV camera pointed almost directly at the murder site, no footage of the crime was captured. Authorities say the camera malfunctioned. Questions are being raised about the maintenance of the CCTV system . . ."*

Pigeons cooed outside the window. The building creaked and settled. I reached over and ran my hand over the heavy, slightly scratchy blue material on the sofa. I looked up at the bookcases built into the walls, stretching to the high ceiling. I had done it. This was actually London, this cold, empty building. Those pigeons were English pigeons. I had imagined this for so long, I didn't quite know how to process the reality.

The words **NEW RIPPER?** flashed across the screen over a panoramic shot of Big Ben and Parliament. It was as if the news itself wanted to reassure me. Even Jack the Ripper himself had reappeared as part of the greeting committee.

# 4

I WOKE UP THE NEXT MORNING TO FIND TWO STRANGERS in my room—one mom-looking type, and the other a girl with long, honey-blond hair wearing a sensible gray cashmere sweater and a pair of jeans. I rubbed my eyes quickly, reached around myself to make sure I was wearing something on both the top and bottom of my body, and discovered that I had slept in my uniform. I didn't even remember going to bed. I just rested my eyes for a minute, and now it was morning. Jet lag had gotten me. I pulled the blanket up over me and made a noise that resembled "hello."

"Oh, did we wake you?" the girl said. "We were trying not to."

This is when I noticed the four suitcases, two laundry baskets, three boxes, and cello that were already in the room. These people had been politely creeping around for some time, trying to move in around my sleeping, uniformed body. Then I heard the racket in the hallway, the sounds of dozens of people moving in.

"Don't worry," the girl said. "My dad hasn't come in. I don't want to disturb you. You keep sleeping. Aurora, isn't it?"

"Rory," I said. "I fell asleep in my . . ."

I let the sentence go. There was no need to point out the obvious.

"Oh, it's fine! It won't be the last time, believe me. I'm Julianne, but everyone calls me Jazza."

I introduced myself to Jazza's mom, then headed down to the bathroom to brush my teeth and try to make myself generally more presentable.

The halls were swarming. How I'd slept through this invasion, I wasn't entirely sure. Girls were squealing in delight at the sight of each other. There were hugs and air kisses, and lots of tight-lipped fights going on with parents who were trying not to make a scene. There were tears and good-byes. It was every human emotion happening at the exact same time. As I slithered down the hall, I could hear Claudia's voice booming from three flights down, greeting people with "Call me Claudia! How was your trip? Good, good, good . . ."

I finally got to the bathroom and huddled by a window. Outside, it was a bright, clear morning. There were really only three or four parking spots in front of the school. The drivers had to take turns and keep their cars in nearly constant motion, dropping off a box or two and then continuing around to let the next person have a space. The same scene was going on across the square at the boys' house.

I had planned much better entrances. I had scripted all kinds of greetings. I had gone over my best stories. But so far, I was zero for two. I brushed my teeth and rubbed my face with cold water, finger-combed my hair, and accepted that this was how I was going to meet my new roommate.

Since she was actually from England and able to come to school in a car, Jazza had way more stuff than me. *Way* more stuff. There were multiple suitcases, which her mom kept unpacking, piling the contents on the bed. There were boxes of books, about six dozen throw pillows, a tennis racquet, and a selection of umbrellas. Her sheets, towels, and blankets were all nicer than mine. She even brought curtains. And the cello. As for books, she easily had two hundred of them with her, maybe more. I looked over at my cardboard boxes and my decorative beads and ashtray and my one shelf of books.

"Can I help?" I asked.

"Oh . . ." Jazza spun around and looked at her things. "I think we've . . . I think we've brought it all in. My parents have a long drive back, you see, and . . . I'm just going to go out and say good-bye."

"You're done?"

"Yes, well, we'd been piling some things in the hall and bringing them in one at a time so we wouldn't disturb you."

Jazza went away for about twenty minutes, and when she returned, she was red-eyed and sniffly. I watched her unpack her things for a while. I wasn't sure if I should offer my help again because the things looked kind of too personal. But I did anyway, and Jazza accepted, with many thanks. She told me I could use anything I liked, or borrow clothes, or blankets, or whatever I needed. "Just take it" was Jazza's motto. She explained all the things that Claudia didn't, like where and when you were allowed to use your phone (in your house and outside), what you did during the free periods (work, usually in the library or in your house).

"You lived with Charlotte before?" I asked as I made up her bed with a heavy quilt.

"You know Charlotte? She's head girl now, so she gets her own room."

"I had dinner with her last night," I said. "She seems kind of . . . intense."

Jazza snapped out a pillowcase.

"She's all right, really. She's under a lot of pressure from her family to get into Cambridge. I'd hate it if my family was like that. My parents just want me to do my best, and they're quite happy wherever I want to go. Quite lucky, really."

We worked right up until it was time to get ready for the Welcome Back to Wexford dinner. It wasn't the cozy affair of the night before—the room was completely full. And this time, I wasn't the only one in a uniform. It was gray blazers and maroon striped ties as far as the eye could see. The refectory, which had looked enormous when only a handful of us were in it the night before, had shrunk considerably. The line for food snaked all the way around to the front door. There was just enough room on the benches for everyone to squash in. There were a few more choices at dinner—roast beef, lentil roast, potatoes, several kinds of vegetables. The grease, I was happy to note, was still present.

When we emerged with our trays, Charlotte half stood and waved us over. She and Jazza exchanged some air kisses, which nauseated me a bit. Charlotte was sitting with the same group of prefects. Jerome moved over a few inches so I could sit down.

We had barely applied butts to bench when Charlotte started in with the questions.

"How's your schedule this year, Jaz?" she asked.

"Fine, thank you."

"I'm taking four A levels, and the college I'm applying to at Cambridge requires an S level, plus I have to take the Oxbridge preparation class to get ready for the interview. So I'm going to be quite busy. Are you taking that class, the Oxbridge preparation class?"

"No," Jazza said.

"I see. Well, it's not strictly necessary. Where *are* you applying to?"

Jazza's doelike eyes narrowed a bit, and she stabbed at her lentil roast.

"I'm still making up my mind," she said.

"You don't say much, do you?" Jerome asked me.

No one in my entire life had ever said this about me.

"You don't know me yet," I said.

"Rory was telling me she lives in a swamp," Charlotte said.

"That's right," I said, turning up my accent a little. "These are the first shoes I've ever owned. They sure do pinch my feet."

Jerome gave a little snort. Charlotte smiled sourly and turned the conversation back to Cambridge, a subject she seemed pathologically fixated on. People went right back to comparing notes about A levels, and I continued eating and observing.

The headmaster, Dr. Everest (it was immediately made clear to me that he was known to all as Mount Everest, which made sense, since he was about six foot seven), got up and gave us a little pep talk. Mostly it boiled down to the fact that it was autumn, and everyone was back, and while that was a great thing, people better not get cocky or misbehave or he'd personally kill us all. He didn't actually say those words, but that was the subtext.

"Is he threatening us?" I whispered to Jerome.

Jerome didn't turn his head, but he moved his eyes in my direction. Then he slipped a pen from his pocket and wrote the following on the back of his hand without even glancing down: *Recently divorced. Also hates teenagers.*

I nodded in understanding.

"As you are probably aware," Everest droned on, "there's been a murder nearby, which some people have taken to referring to as a new Ripper. Of course, there is no need to be concerned, but the police have asked us to remind all students to take extra care when leaving school grounds. I have now reminded you, and I trust no more need be said about that."

"I feel warm and reassured," I whispered. "He's like Santa."

Everest turned in our general direction for a moment, and we both stiffened and stared straight ahead. He chastised us a bit more, giving us some warnings about not staying out past our curfew, not smoking in uniform or in the buildings, and *excessive* drinking. *Some* drinking seemed to be expected. Laws were different here. You could drink at eighteen in general, but there was some weird side law about being able to order wine or beer with a meal, with an adult, at sixteen. I was still mulling this over when I noticed that the speech had ended and people were getting up and putting their trays on the racks.

I spent the night watching and occasionally assisting Jazza as she began the process of decorating her half of the room. There were curtains to be hung and posters and photos to be attached to the walls with Blu-Tack. She had an art print of Ophelia drowning in the pond, a poster from a band I'd never heard of, and a massive corkboard. The photos of her family and dogs were all in ornate frames. I made a mental note to get more wall stuff so my side didn't look so naked.

What she didn't display, I noticed, was a boxful of swimming medals.

"Holy crap," I said, when she set them on the desk, "you're like a fish."

"Oh. Um. Well, I swim, you see."

I saw.

"I won them last year. I wasn't going to bring them, but . . . I brought them."

She put the medals in her desk drawer.

"Do you play sports?" she asked.

"Not *exactly*," I said. Which was really just my way of saying "hell, no." We Deveauxs preferred to talk you to death, rather than face you in physical combat.

As she continued to unpack and I continued to stare at her, it occurred to me that Jazza and I were going to do this—this sitting-in-the-same-room thing—every night. For something like eight months. I had known my days of total privacy were over, but I hadn't quite realized what that meant. All my habits were going to be on display. And Jazza seemed so straightforward and well-adjusted . . . What if I was a freak and had never realized it? What if I did weird things in my sleep?

I quickly dismissed these things from my mind.

# 5

LIFE AT WEXFORD BEGAN PROMPTLY AT SIX ON Monday morning, when Jazza's alarm went off seconds before mine. This was followed by a pounding on the door. The pounding went down the hall, as every door was knocked.

"Quick," Jazza said, springing out of bed with a speed that was both alarming and unacceptable at this hour.

"I can't run in the morning," I said, rubbing my eyes.

Jazza was already putting on her robe and picking up her towel and bath basket.

"Quick!" she said again. "Rory! Quick!"

"Quick what?"

"Just get up!"

Jazza rocked from foot to foot anxiously as I pulled myself out of bed, stretched, fumbled around filling my bath basket.

"So cold in the morning," I said, reaching for my robe. And it really was. Our room must have dropped about ten degrees in temperature from the night before.

"Rory . . ."

"Coming," I said. "Sorry."

I require a lot of *things* in the morning. I have very thick, long hair that can be tamed only by the use of a small portable laboratory's worth of products. In fact—and I am ashamed of this—one of my big fears about coming to England was having to find new hair products. That's shameful, I know, but it took me years to come up with the system I've got. If I use my system, my hair looks like hair. Without my system, it goes horizontal, rising inch by inch as the humidity increases. It's not even curly—it's like it's possessed. Obviously, I needed shower gel and a razor (shaving in the group shower—I hadn't even thought about that yet) and facial cleanser. Then I needed my flip-flops so I didn't get shower foot.

I could feel Jazza's increasing sense of despair traveling up my spine, but I *was* hurrying. I wasn't used to having to figure all these things out and carry all my stuff at six in the morning. Finally, I had everything necessary and we trundled down the hall. At first, I wondered what the fuss was about. All the doors along the hall were closed, and there was little noise. Then we got to the bathroom and opened the door.

"Oh, no," she said.

And then I understood. The bathroom was completely packed. Everyone from the hall was already in there. Each shower stall was already taken, and three or four people were lined up by each one.

"You have to hurry," Jazza said. "Or this happens."

It turns out there is nothing more annoying than waiting around for other people to shower. You resent every second they spend in there. You analyze how long they are taking and speculate on what they are doing. The people in my hall showered, on average, ten minutes each, which meant that it was over a half hour before I got in. I was so full of indignation about how slow they were that I had already preplanned my every shower move. It still took me ten minutes, and I was one of the last ones out of the bathroom.

Jazza was already in our room and dressed when I stumbled back in, my hair still soaked.

"How soon can you be ready?" she asked as she pulled on her school shoes. These were by far the worst part of the uniform. They were rubbery and black, with thick, nonskid soles. My grandmother wouldn't have worn them. But then, my grandmother was Miss Bénouville 1963 and 1964, a title largely awarded to the fanciest person who entered. In Bénouville in 1963 and 1964, the definition of *fancy* was highly questionable. I'm just saying, my grandmother wears heeled slippers and silk pajamas. In fact, she'd bought me some silk pajamas to bring to school. They were vaguely transparent. I'd left them at home.

I was going to tell Jazza all of this, but I could see she was not in the mood for a story. So I looked at the clock. Breakfast was in twenty minutes.

"Twenty minutes," I said. "Easy."

I don't know what happened, but getting ready was just a lot more complicated than I thought it would be. I had to get all the parts of my uniform on. I had trouble with my tie. I tried to put on some makeup, but there wasn't a lot of light by the mirror. Then I had to guess which books I had to bring for my first classes, something I probably should have done the night before.

Long story short, we left at 7:13. Jazza spent the entire wait sitting on her bed, eyes growing increasingly wide and sad. But she didn't just leave me, and she never complained.

The refectory was packed, and loud. The bonus of being so late was that most people had gone through the food line. We were up there with the few guys who were going back for seconds. I grabbed a cup of coffee first thing and poured myself an impossibly small glass of lukewarm juice. Jazza took a sensible selection of yogurt, fruit, and whole-grain bread. I was in no mood for that kind of nonsense this morning. I helped myself to a chocolate doughnut and a sausage.

"First day," I explained to Jazza when she stared at my plate.

It became clear that it was going to be tricky to find a seat. We found two at the very end of one of the long tables. For some reason, I looked around for Jerome. He was at the far end of the next table over, deep in conversation with some girls from the first floor of Hawthorne. I turned to my plate of fats. I realized how American this made me seem, but I didn't particularly care. I had just enough time to stuff some food down my throat before Mount Everest stood up at his dais and told us that it was time to move along. Suddenly, everyone was moving, shoving last bits of toast and final gulps of juice into their mouths.

"Good luck today," Jazza said, getting up. "See you at dinner."

The day was ridiculous.

In fact, the situation was so serious I thought they had to be joking—like maybe they staged a special first day just to psych people out. I had one class in the morning, the mysteriously named "Further Maths." It was two hours long and so deeply frightening that I think I went into a trance. Then I had two free periods, which I had laughingly dismissed when I first saw them. I spent them feverishly trying to do the problem sets.

At a quarter to three, I had to run back to my room and change into shorts, sweatpants, a T-shirt, a fleece, and these shin pads and spiked shoes that Claudia had given to me. From there, I had to get three streets over to the field we shared with a local university. If cobblestones are a tricky walk in flip-flops, they are your worst nightmare in spiked shoes and with big, weird pads on your shins. I arrived to find that people (all girls) were (wisely) putting on their spiked shoes and pads there, and that everyone was wearing only shorts and T-shirts. Off came the sweatpants and fleece. Back on with the weird pads and spikes.

Charlotte, I was dismayed to find, was in hockey as well. So was my neighbor Eloise. She lived across the hall from us in the only single. She had a jet-black pixie cut and a carefully covered arm of tattoos. She had a huge air purifier in her room, which had gotten some kind of special clearance (since we couldn't have appliances). Somehow she got a doctor to say she had terrible allergies, hence she would need the purifier and her own space. In reality, she used the filter to hide the fact that she spent most of her free time smoking cigarette after cigarette and blowing smoke directly into the purifier. Eloise spoke fluent French because she lived there a few months out of every year. As for the smoking, she never actually said, "It's a French thing," but it was implied. Eloise looked as dismayed as I did about the hockey. The rest looked grimly determined.

Most people had their own hockey sticks, but for those of us who didn't, they were distributed. Then we stood in line, where I shivered.

"Welcome to hockey!" Claudia boomed. "Most of you have played hockey before—we're just going to run through some basics and drills to get back into things."

It became pretty obvious pretty quickly that "most of you have played hockey before" actually meant "every single one of you except for Rory has played hockey before." No one but me needed the primer on how to hold the stick, which side of the stick to hit the ball with (the flat one, not the roundy one). No one needed to be shown how to run with the stick or how to hit the ball. The total amount of time given to these topics was five minutes. Claudia gave us all a once-over to make sure we were properly dressed and had everything we needed. She stopped at me.

"Mouth guard, Aurora?"

Mouth guard. Some lump of plastic she had left by my door during the morning. I'd forgotten it.

"Tomorrow," she said. "For now, you'll just watch."

So I sat on the grass on the side of the field while everyone else put their plastic lumps in their mouths, turning the space previously full of teeth into alarming leers of bright pink and neon blue. They ran up and down the field, passing the ball back and forth to each other. Claudia paced alongside the entire time, barking commands I didn't understand. The process of hitting the ball looked straightforward enough from where I was, but these things never are.

"Tomorrow," she said to me when the period was over and everyone left the field. "Mouth guard. And I think we'll start you in goal."

Goal sounded like a special job. I didn't want a special job, unless that special job involved sitting on the side under a pile of blankets.

Then we all ran back to Hawthorne—and I mean ran, literally—where everyone was once again competing for the showers. I found Jazza back in our room, dry and dressed. Apparently, there were showers at the pool.

Dinner featured some baked potatoes, some soup, and something called a "hot pot," which looked like beef and potatoes, so I took that. Our groupings were becoming more predictable, and I was starting to understand the dynamic. Jerome, Andrew, Charlotte, and Jazza had all been friends last year. Three of them had become prefects; Jazza had not. Jazza and Charlotte didn't get along. I attempted to join in the conversations, but found I didn't have much to share until the topic came around to the Ripper, when I dove in with a little family history.

"People love murderers," I said. "My cousin Diane used to date a guy on death row in Texas. Well, I don't know if they were dating, but she used to write him letters all the time, and she said they were in love and going to get married. But it turns out he had, like, six girlfriends, so they broke up and she opened her Healing Angel Ministry . . ."

I had them now. They had all slowed their eating and were looking over.

"See," I said, "Cousin Diane runs the Healing Angel Ministry out of her living room. Well, and also her backyard. She has a hundred sixty-one statues of angels in her backyard. Plus she has eight hundred seventy-five angel figurines, dolls, and pictures in the house. And people go to her for angel counseling."

"Angel counseling?" Jazza repeated.

"Yep. She plays New Age music and has you close your eyes, and then she channels some angels. She tells you their names and what colors their auras are and what they're trying to tell you."

"Is your cousin . . . insane?" Jerome asked.

"I don't think she's *insane,*" I said, digging into my hot pot. "This one time, I was over at her house. When I get bored there, I channel angels, so she feels like she's doing a good job. I go like this . . ."

I took a big, deep breath to prepare for my angel voice. Unfortunately, I did so while taking a bite of the hot pot. A chunk of beef slipped down my throat. I felt it stop somewhere just under my chin. I tried to clear my throat, but nothing happened. I tried to cough. Nothing. I tried to speak. Nothing.

Everyone was watching me. Maybe they thought this was part of the imitation. I pushed away from the table a bit and tried to cough harder, then harder still, but my efforts made no difference. My throat was stopped. My eyes watered so much that everything went all runny. I felt a rush of adrenaline . . . then everything went white for a second, completely, totally, brilliantly white. The entire refectory vanished and was replaced by this endless, paperlike vista. I could still feel and hear, but I seemed to be somewhere else, somewhere without air, somewhere where everything was made of light. Even when I closed my eyes, it was there. Someone was yelling that I was choking, but the words sounded like they were far away.

And then arms were around my middle. There was a fist jabbing into the soft tissue under my rib cage. I was jerked up, over and over, until I felt a movement. The refectory dropped back into place as the beef launched itself out of me and flew off in the direction of the setting sun and a rush of air came into my lungs.

"Are you all right?" someone said. "Can you speak? Try to speak."

"I . . ."

I could speak, and that was all I felt like saying at the moment. I fell against the bench and put my head on the table. There was a pounding of blood in my ears. I looked deep into the markings of the wood and examined the silverware up close. My face was wet with tears I didn't remember crying. The refectory had gone totally silent. At least, I think it was silent. My heart was drumming in my ears so loudly that it drowned out anything else. Someone was telling people to move back and give me air. Someone else was helping me up. Then some teacher (I think it was a teacher) was in front of me, and Charlotte was there as well, poking her big red head into the frame.

"I'm fine," I said hoarsely. I wasn't fine. I just wanted to leave, to go somewhere and cry. I heard the teacher person say, "Charlotte, take her to the san." Charlotte attached herself to my right arm. Jazza attached herself to my left.

"I've got her," Charlotte said crisply. "You can continue eating."

"I'm coming," Jazza shot back.

"I can walk," I croaked.

Neither one of them loosened their grip, which was probably for the best, because it turned out my ankles and knees had gone all rubbery. They escorted me down the center aisle, between the long benches, as people turned and watched me go. Considering that the refectory was an old church, our exit probably looked like the end of a very unusual wedding ceremony—me being dragged down the aisle by my two brides.

# 6

The san was the sanatorium—basically, the nurse's office. But since Wexford was a boarding school, there was a little more to it than just an office. There were a few rooms, including one full of beds where the really sick people could stay. The nurse on duty, Miss Jenkins, gave me a once-over. She took my pulse and listened to my chest with a stethoscope and generally made assurances that I had not choked to death. She told Charlotte to take me back to my house and make sure I relaxed with a nice cup of tea. Once at home, Jazza made it clear that she was taking over. Charlotte turned on her heel in a practiced way. Her head bobbed when she walked. You could see her updo bounce up and down.

I kicked off my shoes and curled up in bed. Though the offending beef was long gone, I rubbed at my throat where it had been. The feeling was still with me, that feeling of having no air, of not being able to speak.

"I'll make you some tea," Jazza said.

She went off and made me the tea, and I sat in my bed and gripped my throat. Though my heart had slowed to normal, there was still a tremor running through me. I picked up my phone to call my parents, but then tears started trickling from my eyes, so I shoved the phone under my blanket. I bunched myself up and took a few deep breaths. I needed to get this under control. I was fine. Nothing had happened to me. I couldn't be the pathetic, weepy, useless roommate. I had wiped my face clean and was smiling, kind of, when Jazza returned. She handed me the tea, went to her desk and got something, then sat on the floor by my bed.

"When I have a bad night," she said, "I look at my dogs."

She held out a picture of two beautiful dogs—one smallish golden retriever and one very large black Lab. In the picture, Jazza was squeezing the dogs. In the background, there were green rolling hills and some kind of large white farmhouse. It looked too idyllic for anyone to actually live there.

"The golden one is Belle, and the big, soppy one is Wiggy. Wiggy sleeps in my bed at night. And that's our house in the back."

"Where do you live?"

"In a village in Cornwall outside of St. Austell. You should come sometime. It's really beautiful."

I slowly sipped my tea. It hurt my throat at first, but then the heat felt good. I reached over and got my computer and pulled up some pictures of my own. First, I showed her Cousin Diane, because I had just been talking about the angels. I had a very good picture of her standing in her living room, surrounded by figurines.

"You weren't lying," Jazza said, leaning on the bed and looking closely. "There must be hundreds of them!"

"I don't lie," I said. I flicked next to a picture of Uncle Bick.

"I can see the resemblance," Jazza said.

She was right. Of all the members of my family, I looked most like him—dark hair, dark eyes, a very round face. Except I'm a girl, and I have fairly ample boobs and hips, and he's a man in his thirties with a beard. But if I wore a fake black beard and a baseball cap that said BIRDBRAIN, I think people would immediately know we were related.

"He looks very young."

"Oh, this is an old picture," I said. "I think this was taken around the time I was born. It's his favorite picture, so it's the one I brought."

"This is his favorite? It looks like it was taken in a supermarket."

"See that woman kind of hiding behind the pile of cans of cranberry sauce?" I asked. "That's Miss Gina. She runs the local Kroger—that's a grocery store. Uncle Bick's been courting her for nineteen years. This is the only picture of the two of them, which is why he likes it."

"What do you mean, 'courting her for nineteen years'?" Jazza asked.

"See, my uncle Bick—he's really nice, by the way—he runs an exotic bird store called A Bird in the Hand. His life is pretty much all birds. He's been in love with Miss Gina since high school, but he doesn't really know how to talk to girls, so he's just been . . . staying around her since then. He just tends to go where she goes."

"Isn't that stalking?" Jazza said.

"Legally, no," I replied. "I asked my parents this when I was little. What he does is creepy and socially awkward, but it's not actually stalking. I think the worst it ever got was the time he left a collage of bird feathers on the windshield of her car . . ."

"But doesn't he scare her?"

"Miss Gina?" I laughed. "No. She has a whole bunch of guns."

I made that last part up just to entertain Jazza. I don't think Miss Gina has any guns. I mean, she might. Lots of people in our town do. But it's hard to explain to someone who doesn't know him that Uncle Bick is actually harmless. You only have to see him with a miniature parrot to know this man couldn't harm anything or anyone. Also, my mom would have him locked up in a flash if she thought he was actually up to something.

"I feel quite boring next to you," Jazza said.

"Boring?" I repeated. "You're English."

"Yes. That's not very interesting."

"You . . . have a cello! And dogs! And you live in a farmhouse . . . kind of thing. In a village."

"Again, that's not very exciting. I love our village, but we're all quite . . . normal."

"In our town," I said solemnly, "that would make you a kind of god."

She laughed a little.

"I'm not kidding," I said. "My family—I mean, my mom and dad and me—are the normal people in town. For example, there's my uncle Will. He owns eight freezers."

"That doesn't sound *so* odd."

"Seven of them are on the second floor, in a spare bedroom.

He also doesn't believe in banks, so he keeps his money in peanut butter jars in the closet. When I was little, he used to give me empty jars as gifts so I could collect money and watch it grow."

"Oh," she said.

"Then there's Billy Mack, who started his own religion out of his garage, the People's Church of Universal People. Even my grandmother, who is almost normal, poses for a formal photograph each year in a slightly revealing dress and mails said photo to all her friends and family, including my dad, who shreds it without opening the envelope. This is what my town is like."

Jazza was quiet for a moment.

"I very much want to go to your town," she finally said. "I'm always the boring one."

From the way she said it, I got the impression that this was something Jazza felt deeply.

"You don't seem boring to me," I said.

"You don't really know me yet. And I don't have all of this."

She waved at my computer to indicate my life in general.

"But you have all of this," I said. I waved my arms too in an attempt to indicate Wexford and England in general, but it looked more like I was shaking invisible pom-poms.

I sipped my tea. My throat was feeling more normal now. Every once in a while, I would remember what it was like not being able to breathe and that strange whiteness . . .

"You don't like Charlotte," I said, blinking hard. I had to say something to get all that stuff out of my head. It was probably a little abrupt and rude.

Jazza's mouth twitched. "She's . . . competitive."

"That seems like a polite word for what she is. Is that how she got to be head girl?"

"Well . . ." Jazza picked at my duvet for a moment, pinching up little bits of fabric and letting them go. "The house master or mistress chooses the prefects. Claudia made her head girl, which she deserves, I suppose . . ."

"Did you apply?" I asked.

"You don't apply. You just get chosen. You don't have to be unpleasa—I mean, I like Jane a lot. And Jerome and Andrew are good friends of mine. It's just Charlotte, well . . . everything was a bit of a competition. Who studied more. Who was better at sport. Who dated whom."

Aside from being the kind of person who used "whom" correctly while gossiping, Jazza was also the kind of person who seemed pained about speaking badly about another person. She squeezed up her fists a few times, as if gossip required physical pressure to leave her body.

"When we first arrived, I was seeing Andrew for a while," Jazza said. "Charlotte had no interest in him until I did. But she could never let something like that go. She dated him after we broke up, then she broke up with him instantly, but . . . she has to . . . well, I don't have to live with her anymore. I live with you."

Jazza let out a light sigh, like a demon had been released.

"Do you date someone now?" I asked.

"No," she said. "I . . . no. Maybe at uni. This year, all I'm concentrating on is exams. What about you?"

I mentally paged over the short and terrible history of my love life in Bénouville. My life had been about school too. It had taken a lot of work to get into Wexford. And I wasn't sure if a few make-outs with friends in the Walmart parking lot constituted dating. Now that I thought about it, maybe I had been waiting too—waiting to come here. In my imagination, I'd always envisioned some figure by my side at Wexford. That prospect seemed unlikely after my display tonight, unless English people were really into people who could eject food from their throats at high velocity.

"Me too," I said. "Studying. That's what this year is about."

Sure, we both meant that to an *extent*. I had come to study. I did have to apply to college while I was here. I really was going to read those books on my shelf, and I really was excited about the prospect of my classes, even if it appeared that said classes would probably kill me. But neither of us was telling the entire truth on that count, and we both knew it. There was a look, an almost audible click as we bonded over this mutual lie. Jazza and I *got* each other. Perhaps she was the figure by my side that I'd always imagined.

# 7

THE NEXT DAY, IT RAINED.

I began the day with double French. At home, French was one of my strongest subjects. Louisiana has French roots. Lots of things in New Orleans have French names. I thought French was going to be my best subject, but this illusion was quickly shattered when our teacher, Madame Loos, came in rattling off French like an annoyed Parisian. I went right from there to double English Literature, where we were informed that we would be working on the period from 1711 to 1847. What alarmed me about that was its specificity. I didn't even think it was that the material was necessarily much harder than what I had in school at home—it was more that they were so adult about it. The teachers spoke with a calm assurance, like we were all fully qualified academics, and everyone acted accordingly. We would be reading Pope, Swift, Johnson, Pepys, Fielding, Coleridge, Wordsworth, Richardson, Austen, the Brontës, Dickens . . . the list went on and on.

Then I had lunch. It continued to rain.

After lunch I had a free period, which I spent having a panic attack in my room.

I thought for sure that they would cancel hockey. In fact, I asked someone what we did when our sports hour was canceled because of the weather, and she just laughed. So it was off to the field in my tiny shorts and fleece, with my mouth guard, of course. The night before I had to put it in a mug of boiling water to make it soft and mold it to my teeth. That was a pleasant feeling. At the field, I was greeted with the goalkeeper equipment. I'm not sure who designed the field hockey goalie's uniform, but I'd guess it was someone who decided to merge his or her love of safety with a truly macabre sense of humor. There were swollen blue pads for my shins that were easily twice the width of my leg. There was another set for the upper thigh. The arm pads were like massively overinflated floaties. There were chest pads with an oversized jersey to go over them and huge, cartoonish shoe objects for my feet. Then there was a helmet with a face guard. The overall effect was like one of those bodysuits you can get to make you look like a sumo wrestler—but far less elegant and human. It took me fifteen minutes to get all this stuff on, and then I had to figure out how to walk in it. The other goalie, a girl named Philippa, got hers on in half the time and was running, wide-legged, onto the field while I was still trying to get the shoes on.

Once I did that, my job was to stand in the goal while people hit hockey balls at me. Claudia kept yelling at me to repel this onslaught using my feet, but sometimes she would tell me to use my arms. All the while, rain poured onto the helmet and streamed down my face. I couldn't move, so the balls just hit me. When it was all over, Charlotte came up to me as I was trying to get out of the padding.

"If you want some help," she said, "I've been playing for a long time. I'd be happy to run drills with you."

What was especially painful about this was that I think she meant it.

At home, I had the third-highest GPA in my class, and literature was my thing. I would do the reading for English first. The essay I had to read was called "An Essay on Criticism" by Alexander Pope.

The first challenge was that the essay was, in fact, a very long poem in "heroic couplets." If something is called an essay, it should be an essay. I read it twice. A few lines stood out, like "For fools rush in where angels fear to tread." Now I knew where that came from. But I still didn't really know what it was about. I looked online first, but I quickly realized I had to up my game a little here at Wexford. This was a place for some book learning. So I went to the library.

Our school library at home was an aluminum bunker thing that they had attached to the school. It had no windows and an air conditioner that whistled. The Wexford library was a proper library. The floor was made of black-and-white stone. There were two levels of stacks—big, wooden ones. Then there was a massive work area, full of long wooden tables that had dividing walls, so you could have your own little space to sit in, with a shelf, a light, and plugs for your computer. The wall in front of you was even covered in cork and had pins, so you could tack up notes as you worked. This part was very modern and shiny, and it made me feel like a real person to sit there and work, like I really was one of these academics of Wexford. I could pretend, at least, and if I pretended long enough, maybe I could make it into a reality.

I took a seat at one of the empty cubicles and spent several minutes setting it up. I plugged in my computer. I pinned my course syllabus to the cork wall and stared it down. Everyone else in this room was calmly carrying on. No one had, to my knowledge, read their course assignments and tried to escape through a chimney. I had been admitted to Wexford, and I had to assume that they didn't do that just to be funny.

Wexford had a large assortment of books on Alexander Pope, so I headed off to the Literature Ol–Pr section, which was on the upper level and in the back. When I got to the aisle, I found a guy lounging right in the middle of it, on the floor, reading. He was in his uniform, but wore an oversized trench coat on top of it. He had really elaborate, bleached-blond, sticky-uppy hair formed into spikes. And he was singing a song.

*Panic on the streets of London,*
*Panic on the streets of Birmingham . . .*

Sure, it was very romantic to lounge around in the literature section with big hair, but he was doing this in the dark. All the aisles had lights on timers. When you went into the aisle, you turned on the light. It clicked itself off after ten minutes or so. He hadn't bothered to do this and was reading with just the scant amount of light coming from the window at the far end of the aisle. He didn't move or look up, even when I had to stand right next to him and reach over him to get to the books. There were about ten books of collected works of Alexander Pope, which I didn't need. I had the poem—I needed something to tell me what the hell it meant. Next to those were several books about Alexander Pope, but I had no idea which one I wanted. They were also very large. Meanwhile, the guy kept singing.

> *I wonder to myself,*
> *Could life ever be sane again?*

"Excuse me. Could I ask you to move a little?" I said.

He looked up slowly and blinked.

"Are you talking to me?"

There was a dim confusion in his eyes. He tucked in his knees and spun around on his butt so that he was facing up at me. Now I understood what people meant by bluebloods—he was the palest person I had ever seen, a genuine grayish-blue in the light of the aisle.

"What are you singing?" I asked. I hoped he would take that as "please stop singing."

"It's called 'Panic,'" he said. "It's by the Smiths. There's panic on the streets now, isn't there? Ripper and all that. Morrissey's a prophet."

"Oh," I said.

"What are you looking for?"

"A book on Alexander Pope, and I—"

"For what?"

"I have to read 'An Essay on Criticism.' I read it, I just don't . . . I need a book about it. A criticism book."

"Then you don't want these," he said, standing up. "They're

all rubbish. You'll do far better with something that puts Pope's work into context. See, Pope was talking about the importance of good criticism. All those books are just biographies with some padding. You want the general criticism section, which is over here."

It seemed to take extraordinary effort for him to stand up. He pulled his coat tight and shied away from me a little. Then he gave a little jerk of his spiky head to indicate that I should follow him, which I did. He maneuvered around the gloomy stacks, turning abruptly a few aisles down. He didn't turn on the light when we went in—I had to switch it on. He also didn't need to scan for the section or book he was looking for. He walked right to it and pointed to the red spine.

"This one. By Carter. This one talks about Pope's role in shaping the modern critic. And this one"—he indicated a green book two shelves down—"by Dillard. A little basic, but if you're new to criticism, worth a read."

I decided not to be resentful of the fact that he assumed I was "new to criticism."

"You're American," he said, leaning against the shelf behind us. "We don't normally get Americans."

"Well, you got me."

I wasn't sure what to do next. He wasn't talking; he was just staring at me as I held the book. So I flipped it open and started looking at the contents. There was an entire chapter on "An Essay on Criticism." It was twenty pages long. I could read twenty pages if it helped me look less clueless.

"I'm Rory," I said.

"Alistair."

"Thanks," I said, holding up the book.

He didn't reply. He just sat down on the floor and folded his trench-coated arms and stared up at me.

The aisle light clicked off as I left, but he didn't move.

It was going to take some time before I understood Wexford and its ways.

# 8

When you live at school, you get close to people really quickly. You never get away. You eat every meal with them. You stand in the shower line with them. You take class and play hockey with them. You sleep in the same place. You begin to see the thousand details of everyday life that you never catch when you just see people during school hours. Because you're there constantly, school time moves differently. After only one week at Wexford, I felt like I'd been there for a month.

I realized I was popular back in Bénouville, I guess. I mean, not homecoming queen material, because that always went to a Professional Pageant Quality person. But my family was Old Bénouville, and my parents were lawyers, which meant that I was basically always going to be okay. I never felt out of place. I never lacked friends. I never walked into a class without feeling like I could speak up. I was of the place. I was home.

Wexford was not my home. England was not my home.

I was not popular at Wexford. I wasn't unpopular either. I was just there. I wasn't the brightest, though I managed to hold my own. But I had to work harder than I'd ever worked. I often didn't know what people were talking about. I didn't get the jokes and the references. My voice sometimes sounded loud and odd. I got bruised from the hockey balls *and* the hockey ball protection I wore.

Some other facts I picked up:

Welsh is an actual, currently used language and our next-door neighbors Angela and Gaenor spoke it. It sounds like Wizard.

Baked beans are very popular in England. For breakfast. On toast. On baked potatoes. They can't get enough.

"American History" is not a subject everywhere.

England and Britain and the United Kingdom are not the same thing. England is the country. Britain is the island containing England, Scotland, and Wales. The United Kingdom is the formal designation of England, Scotland, Wales and Northern Ireland as a political entity. If you mess this up, you will be corrected. Repeatedly.

The English will play hockey in any weather. Thunder, lightning, plague of locusts . . . nothing can stop the hockey. Do not fight the hockey, for the hockey will win.

Jack the Ripper struck for the second time very early on September 8, 1888.

That last fact was hammered home in about seventeen thousand ways. I didn't even watch the news and yet, news just got in. And the news really wanted us to know about the eighth of September. The eighth of September was a Saturday. And I had art history class on Saturday. This fact seemed much more relevant to my life, being unused to the idea of Saturday class. I had always assumed the weekend was a holy tradition, respected by good people everywhere. Not so at Wexford.

But our Saturday classes were our "art and enrichment classes," which meant that they were supposed to be marginally less painful than the classes during the week, unless you hated arts or enrichment, which I suppose some people do.

Even though Jazza tried to wake me up on her way to the shower, and again on her way to breakfast, she succeeded only when she returned to the room to get her cello for music class. I fell out of bed as she hauled the massive black case out of the room.

I wasn't alone among the Saturday late starters. I'd already developed the habit of throwing my skirt and blazer over the end of my bed at night, so all I had to do in the morning was grab a clean shirt, pull on the skirt, shoes, and blazer, and scoop my hair up into any formation that looked reasonably like a hairstyle. I showered at night, and like Jazza, I had given up on makeup. My grandmother would have been appalled.

So I was ready in five minutes and flying down the cobblestones to the classroom building. Art history was in one of the big, airy studio rooms on the top floor. I took a seat at one of the worktables. I was still wiping the crap out of the corners of my eyes when Jerome took the seat next to me. This was the first class I had with a friend, which wasn't that shocking, considering that my friends numbered exactly two at this point. Out of everyone I'd seen, Jerome looked the most out of place in his uniform, certainly compared to the other prefects. His special prefect tie (their ties had gray stripes) was crooked and not quite tightened at the neck. His blazer pockets bulged with stuff—phone, pens, some notes. His hair was the most unkempt—but in a good way, I thought. It looked like he had trimmed his loose curls to just the regulation level, and maybe half an inch beyond. They fell just over his ears. And you could tell he just shook it out in the morning. His eyes were quick, always scanning around for information.

"Did you hear?" he asked. "They found another body around nine this morning. It's the Ripper, definitely."

"Good morning," I replied.

"Morning. Listen to this. The second victim in the Jack the Ripper murders in 1888 was found in the back of a house on Hanbury Street, in the back garden by a set of steps at five forty-five in the morning. That house is gone now, and the police were all over the location where it stood. This new victim was found behind a pub called the Flowers and Archers, which has a back garden very much like the description of the Hanbury Street murder. The second victim in 1888 was a woman called Annie *Chapman.* The victim this time was named Fiona *Chapman.* All of the wounds were just like Annie Chapman's. The cut to the neck. The abdomen opened up. The intestines removed and put over her shoulder. Her stomach taken out and put over the opposite shoulder. The murderer took the bladder and the—"

Our teacher came in. Of all the teachers I'd had so far, this one looked the mildest. The male teachers all wore jackets or ties, and the women tended to wear dresses or serious-looking skirts and blouses. Mark, as he introduced himself, wore a plain blue sweater and a pair of jeans. He looked to be in his midthirties, with tortoiseshell glasses.

"The police aren't even trying to deny it anymore," Jerome said quietly, right before Mark took roll. "There's definitely a new Ripper."

And with that, art history began. Mark was a full-time conservationist at the National Gallery, but he was coming in to teach us about art every Saturday. We were, he informed us, going to begin with paintings from the Dutch Golden Age. He distributed some textbooks, which weighed about as much as a human head (a guesstimate on my part, obviously, but once the Ripper was mentioned, body parts tended to come to mind).

It became immediately clear that even though this was a Saturday class under the general label of "art and enrichment," this was not just a way of killing three hours that might otherwise have been spent sleeping or eating cereal. This was a class, just like any other, and many people in it (Mark checked) were planning on taking an A level in art history. More competition.

On the positive side, Mark informed us that on several Saturdays we would be going to the National Gallery to see the paintings up close. But today was not one of those days. Today we were going to look at slides. Three hours of slides isn't as horrible as it sounds, not when you have a reasonably interesting person who really likes what he's talking about explaining them. And I like art.

Jerome, I noticed, was a careful note taker. He sat far back in his chair, his arm extended, writing quickly in a loose, relaxed hand, his eyes flicking between the slide and the page. I started to copy his style. He took about twenty notes on each painting, just a few words each. Every once in a while, his elbow would make contact with my arm, and he'd glance over. When class was over, we fell in step beside each other as we walked to the refectory. Jerome picked up right where he left off.

"The Flowers and Archers isn't far from here," he said. "We should go."

"We . . . should?"

Again, I knew many students at Wexford could legally drink, because you only had to be eighteen. I knew that pubs would be a part of life here somehow. But I hadn't expected someone, especially a prefect, to invite me to one. Also, was he asking me out? Did you ask people to crime scenes on dates? My pulse did a little leap, but it was quickly regulated by his follow-up.

"You, me, Jazza," he said. "You should get Jazza to come, otherwise she'll start stressing from day one. You're her keeper now."

"Oh," I said, trying not to sound disappointed. "Right."

"I have desk duty at the library until dinner, but we could go right after. What do you think?"

"Sure," I said. "I . . . I mean, I don't have plans."

He put his hands in his pockets and took a few steps backward.

"Have to go," he said. "Don't tell Jazza where we're going. Just say the pub, okay?"

"Sure," I said.

Jerome gave a slouchy, full upper body nod and walked off to the library.

# 9

It didn't take a great deal of insight to know that Jazza was not going to want to go to a crime scene that evening. She was, to use the vernacular, a normal person. She was at her desk eating a sandwich when I returned.

"Sorry," she said, turning as I came in. "My cello practice ran late, and I didn't feel like going over to the refectory. On Saturdays I sometimes treat myself to a sandwich and a cake."

"Treat myself" was a little Jazza-ism I loved. Everything was a tiny celebration with her. A treat was a single cookie or a cup of hot chocolate. She made these things special. Even my Cheez Whiz had become a little treat. It was more precious now.

Something was beeping on my bed. I still wasn't used to the unfamiliar ring and alerts of my English phone. I hadn't even gotten into the habit of carrying it with me because there was no one likely to call me, except my parents. They had been scheduled to arrive in Bristol that morning. That's who the message was from. I noticed an alarmed frequency in my mother's voice.

"We think you should spend the weekends up here, in Bristol," she said, once we'd gotten the basic hellos out of the way. "At least until this Ripper business is over."

Alarming though Wexford could be at times, I had no desire to leave it. In fact, I was certain that if I did, I would miss crucial things—all the things that would allow me to adapt and last the entire year.

"Well, I have class on Saturday morning," I said, "then we eat lunch. And doesn't it take, like, hours to get there? So I wouldn't even get there until Saturday night, and then I'd have to leave in the middle of Sunday . . . and I need all that time to do work. Plus, I have to play hockey every day, and since I don't know how to play, I have to do extra practice . . ."

Jazza didn't look up, but I could tell she was listening to every word of this. After ten minutes, I had convinced them that it wasn't a good idea to leave, but I had to swear up, down, and sideways to be careful and to never, ever, ever do anything on my own. They moved on to describing their house in Bristol. I was scheduled to see it for the first time during a long weekend break in mid-November.

"Your parents are alarmed?" Jazza asked when I hung up.

I nodded and sat down on the floor.

"Mine are as well," she said. "I think they want me to come home too, but they aren't saying. The trip to Cornwall would be too long, anyway. And Bristol is just as bad. You're right."

This confirmation made me feel a bit better. I hadn't just been making things up.

"What are you doing tonight?" I asked her.

"I thought I'd stay in and work on this German essay. And then I really need to put in a few hours of cello practice. I was in terrible shape this morning."

"Or," I said, "we could go out. To . . . a pub. With Jerome."

Jazza chewed a strand of hair for a moment.

"To a pub? With Jerome?"

"He just asked me to ask you."

"Jerome asked you to ask me to go to a pub?"

"He said it was my job to convince you," I explained.

Jazza spun around in her chair and smiled broadly.

"I *knew* it," she said.

Jazza and Jerome, I supposed, had had an ongoing flirtation, and now they had me to bring their love to life. If that was going to be my role, it was better if I accepted it. Or, at least, looked fake cheerful about it.

"So," I said. "You and Jerome? What's the story?"

Jazza cocked her head to the side in a decidedly birdlike fashion.

"No," she said, laughing. "Don't be disgusting. Me and Jerome? I mean . . . I love Jerome, but we're friends. No. He's asking you out."

"He's asking me out by asking me to ask you?"

"Correct," she said.

"Wouldn't it have been easier just to ask me?"

"You don't know Jerome," Jazza said. "He doesn't do things the easy way."

My spirits perked right up again.

"So," I said, "do you want to go, or . . ."

"Well, I should," she said. "Because if I don't, he might

get nervous and not go. He needs me there for support."

"This is complicated," I said. "Are all English people like you guys?"

"No," she said. "Oh, I *knew* it! This is perfect."

I loved the way she said *perfect. Pahh-fect.* It was *pahhfect.*

In order to go out, Jazza worked without pause the entire afternoon. I sat at my desk pretending to do the same, but my mind was wandering too much. I spent about two hours online quietly trying to look up what you were supposed to wear to a pub, but the Internet is useless for things like that. I got a terrible range of advice, from American travel sites (who advocated a wardrobe of non-wrinkle travel basics and a raincoat) to a bunch of English sites about how all girls at all pubs wore skirts that were too short or heels that were too high and how they all fell over drunk in the street—which prompted another half hour of angry searching about misogyny and feminism, because that kind of thing drives me nuts.

My problem sets, sadly, did not do themselves during this time. Nor did my reading read itself. I tried to tell myself that I was learning about culture, but even I wasn't going to be fooled by that. It was five o'clock before I knew it, and Jazza stirred and said something about getting dressed. On Saturday nights, you could wear whatever you wanted to dinner. This would be the first time I would greet Wexford as a whole in some Actual Clothes.

Since I still didn't know what to wear, I delayed a bit by switching on some music and watching Jazza change. She put on jeans; I put on jeans. She put on a light blouse; I put on a T-shirt. She put her hair up; I put my hair up. She skipped the makeup, but there, I diverged. I also wore a black velvet jacket. This was a present from my grandmother, one of the few things she'd ever gotten me that I wasn't skeeved to wear in public. Since I'm pretty pale—years of excessive sunscreen and being slowly bled to death by swamp mosquitoes—the rich black looked dramatic. I added some red lipstick, which may have been a touch too far, but Jazza said I looked nice, and she seemed to mean it. I also wore a star necklace, a gift from Cousin Diane.

The refectory was only three-quarters full, if that. Lots of people, Jazza explained, just skipped Saturday dinner entirely and started their evenings early. I got to look at the clothing choices of those who had stayed, and was happy to see that I had been wise to copy Jazza. Nobody was wearing anything too fancy—jeans, skirts, sweaters, T-shirts. Jerome was dressed in a brown hoodie and jeans. We ate quickly and headed out. I was shivering in my jacket. They didn't even need jackets. It was also still quite bright, even though it was after seven. We walked for several blocks, Jazza and Jerome chatting about things I neither knew nor understood, when Jazza began to look around in confusion.

"I thought we were going to the pub," she said.

"We are," Jerome replied.

"The pub is that way," she said, pointing in the opposite direction. "Which one are we going to?"

"The Flowers and Archers."

"The Flowers and . . . oh. No. No."

"Come on, Jazzy," Jerome said. "We have to show your roommate here around."

"But it's a *crime scene.* You can't go into a *crime scene.*"

Even as she said this, we caught the first glimpse of it all. The news trucks came first, their satellites extended. There were maybe two dozen of those. There was a whole section of sidewalk filled with reporters talking at cameras. Then there were the police cars, the police vans, and the mobile crime scene units. Then there were the people, so many people. Some sort of cordon had obviously been put up, so the people grouped around it. There had to be a hundred or more, just watching and taking pictures. We made it to the back of the crowd.

"Just let me get some pictures, and we'll go to a real pub," Jerome said, zipping off and squeezing through.

I stood on my toes a little to try to catch sight of the Flowers and Archers. It was just an ordinary-looking pub—black, large windows, cheerfully painted wooden arms over the door, a blackboard sign out front advertising a special. Only the dozens of police officers swarming around it like ants gave any indication of the terror that had occurred here. I suddenly felt uncomfortable. An unpleasant chill went up my back.

"Come on," I said. "Let's stand back."

I almost walked straight into a man who was standing right behind us. He was dressed in a suit with a slightly too-large jacket. He was completely and smoothly bald. His lack of hair highlighted his eyes, which were feverishly bright. When I apologized, the eyes grew wider, in what appeared to be shock.

"Not at all," he replied. "Not at all."

He stepped aside to let me pass, smiling widely.

"People are treating this like it's a party," Jazza said, looking at the people standing around with bottles of beer, taking photos on their phones and holding up video cameras. "Look how happy everyone seems."

"Sorry," I said. "Jerome said not to tell you. And I forgot when you started explaining all of the asking-out stuff."

"It's all right," she said. "I should have realized."

Jerome jogged back, beaming.

"I got right up to the front of the tape," he said. "Come on. Proper drink now."

We went to a pub a few streets over, closer to Wexford. The pub did not disappoint. It was everything the Internet had promised—big wooden bar, a decent crowd, pint glasses. Of the three of us, only Jerome was over eighteen, plus Jazza said he owed us for taking us to the murder site—so he was put in charge of buying all the drinks. Jazza wanted a glass of wine, but I wanted a beer, because that is what I'd heard you were supposed to drink at a pub. Jerome duly went off to the bar. All the inside seats were taken, so we went outside and stood at a small table under a heat lamp. The diameter brought us face-to-face with each other, our skin glowing red under the light. Jazza made short work of her glass of wine. A pint of beer, as it turns out, is a lot of beer. But I was determined to get it down.

Jerome had more to tell us about the events of the day. "The victim," he said, "not only had the same last name as the victim in 1888, she was the same age, forty-seven. She worked for a bank in the City, and she lived in Hampstead. Whoever this murderer is, he went to a lot of trouble to get the details right. Somehow, he got a woman with the right name of the right age to a pub nowhere near her house, and over a mile away from her work. At five in the morning. They're saying it doesn't look like she was bound or brought in with any struggle."

"Jerome is going to be a journalist," Jazza explained.

"Just listen," Jerome said, pointing at the roof, just above the door. "Look up. It's a CCTV camera. Most pubs have them. On that stretch alone, by the Flowers and Archers? I counted five cameras there. On Durward Street? At least six on the path the victim was walking along. If they don't have footage of the Ripper, then something is seriously wrong with the system."

"Jerome is going to be a journalist," Jazza said again. She was tipsy, rocking a little to the music.

"I'm not the only one who's noticed this!"

I looked up at the camera. It was a fairly large one, long and thin, its electronic eye pointed right at us. There was another one next to it pointing in the other direction, so that both halves of the pub garden were covered.

"I'm not a prefect," Jazza said suddenly.

"Come on, Jazzy," he said, tucking up under her arm.

"*She* is."

Jazza was talking about Charlotte, obviously.

"And what else is she?" Jerome asked.

Jazza didn't offer any reply, so I chimed in with, "A bitchweasel?"

"A bitchweasel!" Jazza's face lit up. "She's a bitchweasel! I love my new roommate."

"She's a bit of a lightweight," Jerome explained. "And never let her have gin."

"Gin bad," Jazza said. "Gin make Jazza barf."

Jazza sobered quickly on the way home, which was exactly when I felt the fizziness in my own head. I started to tell Jerome some of the stories I'd been telling Jazza the other night—Uncle Bick and Miss Gina, Billy Mack, Uncle Will. When he dropped us off on the steps under the large WOMEN sign over our door, he had a strange and unreadable look in his eye.

Charlotte was sitting at the desk in our front lobby, a checklist and a Latin book in front of her.

"Nice night?" she asked as we came in.

"Wonderful," Jazza said, a little too loudly. "And you?"

For the first time, as I walked up the winding stairs, I felt like I was coming home for the night. I looked down the long stretch of our hallway, with its gray carpets and odd bends and multiple fire doors breaking the path, and it all seemed very familiar and right.

The rest of the night was cozy. Jazza settled down with her German. I replied to some e-mails from my friends back home and noodled around on the Internet for a while and thought about doing French. Nothing disturbed my peace of mind until I was pulling the curtains for the night. As I did, something caught my eye. I had already yanked the curtain shut before my brain registered that it had seen something it didn't like, but when I opened it again, there was nothing out there but some wet trees and cobblestones. It had started to rain. I stared for a moment, trying to figure out what I'd seen. Something had been right below—a person. Someone had been standing in front of the building. But that was no surprise. People stood in front of the building all the time.

"What's the matter?" Jazza asked.

"Nothing," I said, pulling the curtain shut again. "Thought I saw something."

"This is the problem with all of this media coverage of the Ripper. It makes people afraid."

She was right, of course. But I noticed she pulled the curtains on her side more tightly closed as well.

## GOULSTON STREET, EAST LONDON
## SEPTEMBER 8
## 9:20 P.M.

VERONICA ATKINS SAT AT HER DESK IN HER TOP-FLOOR flat, overlooking the Flowers and Archers. She tucked one foot up on her chair and rotated slowly back and forth, then blindly reached around into the mess of bottles and cans and dirty mugs to put her hand on her current cup of tea. Veronica was a freelance IT consultant and graphic designer. Her flat was her studio. The front room, the one that looked out over the Flowers and Archers, contained her worktable.

Of course now was the deadline to get this website done, one of her biggest and most lucrative jobs of the year. The contract had no provision for lateness due to the fact that *the Ripper* chose to strike directly across the street, *at her pub*. In fact, she had installed the CCTV cameras at the pub after they had been robbed last year. Because she was friendly with the owner, she'd done it for a fraction of the normal cost. In return, he provided her with free drinks. Earlier in the day, she'd watched the police remove the recorder. They would be watching the results of *her* work . . .

Didn't matter. Nor did the sirens, the noise of the ever-increasing numbers of police going in and out of the mobile lab parked outside of her building, the helicopter that flew overhead constantly, the police who came to her door to ask if she'd seen anything. Normally, she could wander out in her bleach-stained TALK NERDY TO ME T-shirt, her old track-suit bottoms, her slippers, her pink and bleached blond hair piled into a messy knot on top of her head and secured with a plastic clamp meant to tie back computer wires. This was completely acceptable attire for grabbing a double espresso at Wakey Wakey. Today, she couldn't even step outside because the whole area was roped off and all the world's press was standing at the end of the road.

Nope. No excuses. Either she finished today, or she didn't get paid.

As a concession to the event, she had the news on her muted television. Every once in a while, she would glance over and stare at aerial views of her own building, long shots of the front of her house. Once, she even caught a glimpse of herself in the window. She resolutely ignored the two dozen messages from friends and family, begging to know what was going on.

But then something caught her attention. It was a new banner at the bottom of the news screen. It read: **CCTV FAILURE.** She quickly turned up the sound in time to catch the gist of the report.

"*. . . as in the first murder on Durward Street. This second failure of CCTV to capture any useful images of the individual dubbed the New Ripper calls into question the effectiveness of London's CCTV system.*"

"Failure?" Veronica said out loud.

The website instantly faded in importance.

No. She had not failed. She had to prove those cameras had not failed. It took a moment of thought, but then she remembered that the footage was backed up to an online server, and she had the documentation around somewhere. She got down on the floor, threw open a document file, and dumped out the contents. This was the box where she stuffed manuals and warrantees for all her equipment. Toaster oven, no. Kettle, no. Television, no . . .

Then, she found it. The paperwork for the cameras, with the access codes scribbled in pen on the front.

Of course, this meant she had to watch the footage.

She went to the kitchen, opened up a cabinet, and pulled out a bottle of whiskey—the good stuff, a birthday gift from a Scottish ex-boyfriend. This was the stuff she touched only on very special occasions. She poured herself a heavy shot into a juice glass and drank it all in one go. Then she pulled her curtains shut and sat in front of her computer. She went to the site, entered the codes, and was granted access. She clicked through the options, selecting Playback.

According to the news, the murder had occurred between five thirty and six in the morning. She set the playback time to start at 6:05. Then, with a deep breath, she hit Play, and then Rewind.

The footage was shot in night vision mode, which gave it a strange green-gray cast. And the first thing she saw was the body. It lay there alone on the concrete patio by the fence. It was strangely peaceful, if you ignored the gaping wound in the abdomen and the dark pool around it. Veronica swallowed hard and tried to control her breathing. Failure, her arse.

She could have stopped right there, could have immediately called the police, but something compelled her to keep watching. Horrible as it was, there was something compelling about being the first person to see the killer. He (or she) had to be on here.

She would be a hero—the person who recovered the footage. The person who caught the Ripper on film.

Veronica slowed it down, reversing gingerly. She watched the eerie sight of the blood seeping back into the body. The time markers ticked back. At 5:42 A.M., some of the dark objects around the woman began to move. Now Veronica could see what they were—intestines, a stomach—tucked neatly back into a gaping abdomen. Then the abdomen itself was carefully sealed up with the flash of a knife. The woman sat up, then rose from the ground in a sudden and unnatural way. The knife sealed a wound on her neck. Now she crashed into the fence. Now she was flailing. She was walking backward out of the garden.

Veronica paused the image at time stamp: 5:36 A.M.

The cameras had not failed, but her mind was slowly grasping what they had captured. And what they had captured made no sense. She became bizarrely calm, and played back the footage in the right order. Then she rewound and played it back again. Then she went to the kitchen and poured herself another juice glass full of whiskey. She threw up into the sink, wiped her mouth, and drank a glass of water.

She couldn't keep this to herself. She would go mad.

# Persistent Energy

**Instead of describing a 'ghost' as a dead person permitted to communicate with the living, let us define it as a manifestation of a persistent energy.**

***—Fred Myers, Proceedings of the Society for Psychical Research 6, 1889***

# 10

THE AUTUMN OF 1888 WAS KNOWN AS THE AUTUMN of Terror. Jack the Ripper was out there somewhere, in the fog, waiting with his knife. He could strike anywhere, at any time. The thing about autumn this year was that everyone knew precisely when the Ripper was going to strike, if he kept up with the schedule he'd set so far. The next date was September 30. That was when Jack the Ripper struck twice, so it was referred to as "the Double Event." The Double Event was a big part of the reason Jack the Ripper was seen as so amazingly scary—he managed these brutal and somewhat complicated murders right under the eye of the police, and no one saw a thing.

On that point, the past and the present were exactly alike.

The police had nothing. So, to help them, thousands more people joined the ranks of amateur detectives. They flew in from around the world.

There was, the news reported, a 25 percent increase in tourism during the month of September. Hotels in London were getting unprecedented numbers of reservations. And all those people came to hang out in our neighborhood, to crawl over every inch of the East End. You couldn't walk anywhere without someone taking pictures or making a video. The Ten Bells, which is the Ripper pub where the victims used to drink, was just a few streets over and had lines of people waiting to get in that stretched down the block. Hundreds of people shuffled past our buildings every day on any one of the ten Jack the Ripper walking tours that crossed our campus (until Mount Everest complained, and they rerouted around the corner).

The Ripper shaped our school life as well. The school had sent out letters to all our parents assuring them that we would be kept under nonstop lock-and-key surveillance, so really, school was the best place for us to be, and it was best to proceed as normal and not disrupt anyone's studies. On the night following the second murder, they changed all the rules about leaving school grounds. We had to be present and accounted for by eight o'clock every night, including weekends. We could be in our houses or the library. Prefects were stationed in both of these places, and they had clipboards with all our names. You had to check out with the prefect at your house, then check in with the prefect at the front desk of the library, then vice versa when you went home.

This caused major outrage, as it effectively killed all social life for the month of September. Everyone was used to being able to go to the pub on the weekends, or to parties. All that was over. In response, people started stocking their rooms with large amounts of alcohol, until an additional set of rules gave the prefects the power to do spot checks. Huge quantities were confiscated, making many people wonder what Everest was doing with all that booze. Somewhere on the school grounds, there was a Big Rock Candy Mountain of alcohol—a magical closet filled to the ceiling.

During that precious hour or so between dinner and eight o'clock, everyone would run out to whatever shop was still open to get their provisions for the night, whatever they might be. Some people got coffees. Some people got food. Some people ran to Boots, the pharmacy, to get shampoo or toothpaste. Some people ran to a pub for an incredibly fast round of drinks. Some people would vanish completely for the hour to make out with a significant other. Then there was an insane influx—the run back to Wexford. You would see this rush coming around the corner at 7:55.

There were two people not complaining about the new rules—the inhabitants of Hawthorne room twenty-seven. For Jazza, this was life as normal. She was perfectly content and cozy at home, working away. And while I occasionally scratched at the window and looked longingly outside, I appreciated the new rules for the one benefit they accidentally conferred—the curfew was a great equalizer. The entire social dynamic had altered. There was no question of who was going to what party or what club or pub. We were all inmates of Wexford. During those three weeks, it became my home.

Jazza and I developed our rituals. I'd put the Cheez Whiz on the radiator right before dinner. I developed this little trick by accident, but it worked amazingly well. Around nine at night, it would be perfect, warm and runny. Every night, Jazza and I had a ritual of tea and biscuits and rice crisps with Cheez Whiz.

I had lucked out on the roommate front. Jazza, with her wide eyes, her adorable caution, her relentless determination to do the nice thing. Jazza missed her dogs and taking long, hot baths, and she promised to take me home with her to where she lived, out in the wilds of Cornwall. She liked to go to bed at ten thirty and read Jane Austen with a cup of tea. She didn't care if I sat up, screwing around on the Internet or desperately cramming English literature into my brain or fumbling my way through French essays until three in the morning. In fact, those new rules probably saved my academic life as well. There was nothing to do but study. On Friday and Saturday, we'd get mildly drunk on mugs full of cheap red wine (supplied by Gaenor and Angela, who managed to stash theirs so cleverly that no one could find it) and then run in circles around the building.

That's how September went. By the end of it, everyone on my floor knew about Cousin Diane, Uncle Bick, Billy Mack. They had admired the pictures of my grandma in her negligee. I learned that Gaenor was deaf in one ear, that Eloise had once been attacked on the street in Paris, Angela had a skin condition that made her itchy all the time, Chloe down the hall wasn't a horrible snob—her father had recently died. When a little tipsy, Jazza did complicated dance routines with props.

People got more and more bitter about these rules as we approached the twenty-ninth. In response to the police request that everyone stay either at home or in a group, it was now a city-wide party. Pubs were offering two-for-one drinks. Betting shops had odds on where bodies would be found. Regular programming on BBC One had been replaced by all-night news coverage, and the other stations were running every kind of Ripper or murder mystery show they had. People were throwing lock-in parties in their houses to watch. The Double Event night was bigger than New Year's and we were not going to be a part of it.

On the morning of the twenty-ninth, there was an uncertain sky on the edge of rain. I trudged over to the refectory, limping a bit because of a brief romance my thigh had with a flying hockey ball during one of the rare moments I wasn't guarding the goal in my head-to-toe padding. I guess I wasn't overly concerned about the Ripper. In my mind, Jack the Ripper was a ridiculous creature that always lived in London. On that day, though, I saw the first signs of people really flaking out. I heard someone say that she didn't even want to go outside. Two people left school entirely for a few days. I saw one of them pulling her bag along the cobblestones.

"People are being serious," I said to Jazza.

"There's a serial killer out there," she said. "Of course people are serious."

"Yeah, but what are the chances?"

"I'll bet all the victims thought that."

"But still, what are the chances?"

"Well, I imagine they are several million to one."

"Not that high," Jerome said, coming up behind us. "You're only dealing with a small part of London. And while there might be a million or more people in that area, the Ripper is probably focusing on women, because all of the original victims were women. So halve that—"

"You really need another hobby," Jazza said, opening the door to the refectory.

"I have plenty of hobbies. Anyway, the Ripper never showed

any interest in kids or teenagers, so I don't think we have anything to worry about. Does that make you feel better?"

"Not particularly," Jazza said.

"Well, I tried."

Jerome stepped aside to let me go in first. We got in line and loaded our plates. We had barely started eating when Mount Everest rumbled in with Claudia and Derek, the housemaster of Aldshot, in tow.

"They don't look happy," Jerome said.

He was right. There was a frazzled gloom around all three of them. They walked up to the dais in formation, Everest moving to the front, and Claudia and Derek flanking him with their arms folded across their chests, like bodyguards.

"Everyone!" he said. "Silence. I have an announcement to make."

It took a moment for word to spread to all parts of the refectory that it was time to shut up.

"This evening," he began, "as you all know, there is going to be a great deal of police activity in London because of the Ripper situation. Therefore, we are altering the schedule for today. All school activities after four P.M. are canceled so that teachers may return home."

A cheer broke out.

"Settle down!" he said. "Dinner will be moved up to five P.M. so that kitchen staff can also return home before dark. All students will return to their houses after dinner and will remain there for the night. All other buildings will be off-limits and locked, including the library."

A low groan went around the room.

"I want to convey the seriousness of this," Everest added.

"*Anyone* who attempts to leave school grounds faces the possibility of expulsion. Is that understood?"

He waited until he got a grumbled yes.

"I will meet with all prefects now, in my office."

Jerome took a second to shove some extra food into his mouth before rising. At the end of our table, I saw Charlotte bounce up.

"This means I won't have that extra hockey practice this afternoon," I said to Jazza. "No hockey. *No hockey.*"

I banged my spoon on the table for emphasis, but she didn't get excited.

"I wish I'd gone home," Jazza said, poking at her food.

"It's going to be great," I said, shaking her arm. "No hockey! And I totally think my new shipment of Cheez Whiz might get here today."

True enough. I'd told all my friends I was out, and I fully expected to find a pigeonhole full of whizzy goodness this afternoon. But not even the promise of Cheez Whiz could remove the frown from Jazza's face.

"It's creepy," she said, rubbing her arms. "All of this has just made things . . . I don't know. Everyone's afraid. One man has made the entirety of London afraid."

There was nothing I could do. Jazza just didn't see the positive side of this. So I continued eating my sausages and let her have her moment. I was already thinking about the joy I'd feel in not walking to the hockey field and not standing in the goal and not getting hit with hockey balls. As a swimmer, it was a bliss she could never know.

# 11

THE POLICE ENCOURAGE LONDONERS TO USE EXTRA *caution this evening. The public are advised to walk in pairs or groups. Avoid areas of low lighting. Most important, don't panic—carry on your lives as normal. As they said in the Second World War, 'Keep calm and carry on'. . ."*

So we were inside again, and like everyone else in London—and around the world, probably—we were all gathered around the television. The common room was packed to capacity. Most people had work they were doing, or they had their computers on their laps. We had hours to wait for news to report anything of interest, so newscasters were filling the time with statements like that. *Keep calm and carry on.* Also, stay in and hide because the Ripper is coming.

Luckily, we all had his schedule. Like an evil Santa, there was no doubt when he did his work. On the night of the Double Event, the first attack occurred in a dark alley somewhere around twelve forty-five A.M. on the morning of the thirtieth. The victim was named Elizabeth "Long Liz" Stride. Her throat was cut, but she wasn't, like the other victims, disemboweled. For some reason, the Ripper left the scene and hurried about a mile away, to a place called Mitre Square. There he murdered and completely mutilated a woman named Catherine Eddowes in five or ten minutes flat. They knew that because a policeman walked through Mitre Square at one thirty, and nothing was going on. When he walked through again fifteen minutes later, there were the gruesome remains.

As for the route: Liz Stride was murdered on Berner Street, now called Henriques Street. From there, he hurried west to Mitre Square. Mitre Square was a mere ten-minute walk from Wexford.

Up until now, the Ripper hadn't really freaked me out much. But with every passing hour, it started to have more of an effect on me. Two people were going to get murdered tonight, right around where I was sitting. And the whole world was going to sit and watch, just like we were.

The first news broke at 12:57. We all knew it was coming, but it was still a shock when the news anchor touched his ear and listened for a moment.

*"Just coming in . . . The body of a woman has been found on Davenant Street, just off Whitechapel Road. Details are still coming in, but the first report indicates it was found in a car park or possibly outside of a petrol station. We can't confirm either story. The police are now spreading out and covering everything within a mile radius. Two thousand police officers and special constables have been deployed into the streets of East London. Let's go to the interactive map . . ."*

They had instantly created a live map with the murder scene and a circle radiating out from it in red. Our school was smack in the middle of this red section. The entire common room fell silent. Everyone looked up from what they were doing.

*"I can now confirm that the body of a* man *has been found on Davenant Street, in a small private car park. Witnesses who found the body say that the victim had a wound to the neck. Though we have no further details at this time, that is consistent with the Ripper murders. I have with me Dr. Harold Parker, professor of psychology at University College, London, and technical adviser to the Metropolitan Police."*

The camera panned over to a bearded man.

*"Dr. Parker,"* the anchor asked. *"What's your first reaction to this information?"*

*"Well,"* the doctor began, *"the first thing of note here is that the victim is a man. All the Ripper victims of 1888 were female prostitutes. However, it should also be noted that the third Ripper victim, Elizabeth Stride, was the only one who had no mutilations. Only her neck was cut. If this turns out to be the work of the new Ripper, it suggests a different pathology. This Ripper doesn't care about the sex or the profession of the victim—"*

"I can't watch this anymore," Jazza said. "I'm going upstairs."

Jaz got out of her chair and stepped over the various people sitting on the floor around us. I didn't want to stop watching, but she was clearly upset, and I didn't want to leave her alone.

"I hate what they're doing," she said as I followed her. "I hate the show they're making of all of this. It's horrible, and it's frightening, and people treat it like it's reality television."

"I think they're just reporting it because people want to know," I said, following her a few steps behind.

"I don't have to watch it, though."

My Cheez Whiz had, sadly, not arrived. I offered to make Jazza some tea instead, but she didn't want any. She planted herself on her bed and started refolding her laundry. We had a service at Wexford where they came once a week and took away our laundry bags, and when we returned in the afternoon, we'd find them outside our door, our clothes clean and folded. But Jazza always shook out her things and refolded them in her special way. I sat on my own bed and took out my computer, but before I could even open it, my phone rang. It was Jerome. I'd recently given him my number in art history so that we could meet up to work on a project. This was the only time he'd ever called.

"You guys should come over," he said as soon as I answered. He sounded very excited.

"Over where?"

"Aldshot. Where else? We can go on the roof."

"What?"

"Come on," he said. "It's all kicking off. We can get an amazing view from the roof. I know how to get up there."

"You're insane," I said.

"Who is it?" Jazza asked.

I cupped my hand over the phone.

"It's Jerome. He wants us to go over to Aldshot. To the roof."

"Then you're right," she replied. "He *is* insane."

"Jazza says you're—"

"I heard her. But I'm not insane. Leave Hawthorne the back way and cut around to the back of Aldshot. No one is going to catch you. Everyone's been checked in for the night."

I repeated the message. Jazza glanced over from her folding. Her expression conveyed the idea that she still wasn't very impressed with the suggestion.

"Say this," Jerome said. "Say these exact words. Say 'she'd

never think you had the guts to do it, which is why you should.' "

"What does that mean?" I asked.

"Just say it."

I repeated the message exactly as he said it. The words had a strange, almost magical effect. Jazza seemed to lift up off the bed a bit, her eyes aglow.

"Have to go for a moment," Jerome said. "Text me when you're coming. This is a once-in-a-lifetime chance. We'll be able to see everything from up there, and no one will know, I promise."

He hung up. Jazza was still suspended there, half sitting and half standing on the edge of the bed.

"What kind of voodoo was that?" I asked. "What did that mean?"

"He means," Jazza said, "that Charlotte would never suspect I had the guts to use the exit."

"The exit?"

"There's a way to get out. The ground-floor bathrooms. There are bars over the windows, but one of the windows . . . the screws that hold the bars on have been loosened. All you have to do is open the window, reach outside and give them a little turn, and they fall right out. Then you can push the bars back enough to get out of the window. I know about them because Charlotte was the one who developed that system. She loosened the screws. We can't, though. We'd get expelled."

"They said anyone caught *leaving* school grounds might be expelled," I said. "It *is* school grounds."

"Yes, but *we* can't be in Aldshot," Jazza said, her voice getting lower and lower. "That's just as bad. Well, not *just* as bad, but bad . . ."

Maybe it was simply that I had flown all the way to England and then been locked in a building for a month. I really, somewhat bizarrely, wanted to see Jerome. Jerome with his floppy curls and goofy Ripper obsession.

Jazza prowled the space between her bureau and the closet, stoking some internal fire. I had to add more fuel, and quickly.

"Who's most likely to catch us? Charlotte. And is Charlotte going to report her own vandalism? Is she really going to rat on someone using the exit *she* made?"

"Possibly," Jazza said.

"Let's set that possibility aside, then," I replied. "Come on. You know it would burn her if you had the guts to use it and she didn't. And you've been good forever. No one is going to suspect you of doing this. So you *have* to."

Some emotion took Jazza over for a moment. She got up and clenched her hands together, then studied the arrangement of her books with great intensity.

"All right," she said. "Let's do it. Let's do it now, before I back out. Tell him we'll be there in fifteen minutes."

First, there was feverish changing. We pulled off our pajamas and threw them to the floor. I put on my Wexford sweats, while Jazza put on a pair of black yoga pants and a dark hoodie. We both tied our hair back and wore sneakers. Action wear.

"Wait," Jazza said as we were about to step out the door. "We can't wear the shoes. We were just downstairs in socks. It's going to look like we're up to something. In fact, we should put our pajamas back on. We'll change downstairs in the toilets."

So we pulled off those clothes and put the pajamas back on and stuffed our sneaking clothes into our bags, because it was perfectly normal to carry your bag around the building for your books or your computer. We crept downstairs, though there was no crime in going down the stairs. Everyone, including Claudia, was riveted to the news, so we were able to slip by the common room door and continue on to the end of the hall, to the bathroom. The bathroom on this floor wasn't as big as our bathroom, because it didn't have showers, and it wasn't designed for thirty girls to get ready at the same time. This was the bathroom you used when you were in the common room and didn't feel like going up the stairs. It had one stall, which was unoccupied. Jazza and I changed quickly. Jazza went into the stall, opened the window, and climbed onto the toilet seat so she could work her arm through the bars at the right angle.

"I can feel it," she whispered. "I can twist it off."

She scrunched up her face as she worked. I heard the tiniest, tiniest *tink* as the screw hit the sidewalk below.

"That's one," she said. She turned gingerly on the seat and started working on the other. *Tink* again.

The bars were one large unit, all attached together. Jazza pushed them out. There was an opening of about a foot and a half for us to squeeze through, and a short drop to the ground.

"Ready?" she asked.

I nodded.

"You first," she said. "Because this is your idea."

We awkwardly switched positions. I got up on the seat and stuck my head outside, taking a deep breath of the cold London air. Once I went out this window, I was breaking the rules. I was risking everything. But that was the point, really. And who cared what we did when there was a killer out there? We were only going a few feet to another building, anyway. Mentally, I was already rehearsing my "but it wasn't off the grounds" defense.

I got up on the sill and put my legs through the opening. It was an easy jump to the ground, barely a jump at all. For a moment, I thought Jazza wasn't going to come, but she got up the courage and did the same thing.

We were out.

# 12

IT HAD TURNED INTO A CRISP, PERFECT AUTUMN night. The sky was clear, and I could smell leaves in the air, and just a little bit of burning wood. We couldn't walk through the square, obviously; we'd be seen by someone looking out one of the windows. So we had to run over a street and come around the long way, using off-school property. We'd approach Aldshot from behind. It would take about ten minutes to go this way, and we were now definitely breaking the rules, but we'd started this thing, and we had to continue it.

Once we were clear of the building and around the corner, we slowed to a fast walk.

"Rory," Jazza said breathlessly. "Is this stupid, what we're doing? Not because of the school thing, but because of, you know, the Ripper thing. What with him being out right now, killing people."

"We're fine," I said, blowing on my hands as we

hurried along. "We are literally walking around a corner. Together."

"This *is* stupid, though. Isn't it?"

"What you need to remember is that you are doing the interesting thing, and Charlotte is not. And if we get caught, I will claim I made you go. At gunpoint. I am American. People will assume I'm armed."

We walked faster, speeding down one of the small residential streets that backed up to Wexford. Inside many of the flats, I could see lights and a few parties of people drinking. You could see the reflection of televisions in so many of those windows—the now-familiar bright red and white logo of BBC News shining out into the dark. We made a sharp left at the shuttered shoe repair shop and ran the last block to approach Aldshot from behind.

Aldshot was the twin of our building, except that it had the word MEN carved in bas-relief over the front door. Even without that hint, you could tell that this building was full of guys. Hawthorne had distinctive and pretty curtains in many windows, the occasional plant on the windowsill, or some other decorative item. Even the light was different, because of all the lamps girls brought in, with paper shades diffusing and coloring the light. In Aldshot, no one changed the curtains, so they were all the standard grayish green. The decorations on their windowsills tended to be stacks of bottles or cans or—in fancy cases—books. The lights were all the standard issue. Weird how two identical buildings could be so different.

I could already see our point of access—it was a fire escape door, which had been propped open an inch or so by a small book wedged in the opening. We made it across the street and pressed ourselves against the side of the building, then we crept along, under the ground-floor windows. I reached forward and carefully opened the door, and we slipped inside. We were in the cold, fluorescent-lit concrete stairwell. I closed the door softly.

"We did it," Jazza whispered.

"Seems that way."

"Now we just wait here?"

"I guess."

"I don't feel very hidden."

"Me either."

We quietly approached the inner door that led to the ground floor of Aldshot. I could hear male voices and a television. Jazza and I huddled together, unsure what to do next, until we heard a door open on the floor above us. Jerome's curly head peered down at us over the railing, and he waved us up.

"I disabled all the alarms," he said. "Prefect secret. Everyone's downstairs watching."

He looked very satisfied with himself. He took us up two more flights, until we reached another door. This one was a lot more serious-looking, with a bar across it and a huge **DO NOT OPEN: DOOR ALARMED** sign in red. Jerome pushed this open with a bold stroke. The Klaxon I had been expecting didn't sound. We were suddenly on the wide roof of Aldshot in the bright cold, nothing but the sky above us.

"My God," Jazza said, cautiously stepping out. "I did it. We did it. We really did it."

We all took in the freedom for a moment. Jazza stood back, but Jerome and I went up to the edge. Below, I got a good view of our square, the halls, and all the streets around. Everything was lit—every streetlight, every window, every shop. The tall buildings of the City—the financial district of London that was right next to our neighborhood—were beacons, filling the air with even more light. London was awake, and watching.

"It's great, isn't it?" he asked.

It was great. This, I realized, is what I came for. This view. This night. These people. This feeling buzzing through the air.

"I suppose it's safe up here," Jaz said, coming a little closer and hugging herself for warmth. "The building is locked, and it's not easy getting up here. Plus, there's police all round. And helicopters."

She pointed at the bright lights of the helicopters drifting above like oversized bees. There were at least three we could see from where we were standing. The dragnet was on.

"Safest place in London right now," Jerome said. "As long as we don't fall off."

Jazza backed up a few steps. I peered down carefully. It was a sheer drop down to the cobblestones. When I looked up again, Jazza had wandered off to examine the view from the other side. It was just Jerome and me facing the square and the sky.

"Worth it?" he asked, smiling.

"So far," I said.

He laughed a little, then took a few steps back and sat down.

"It's almost time," he said. "And we don't want anyone to see us."

I sat next to him on the cold roof. He had everything ready—several windows on his computer open to various news and Ripper sites.

"You really like this, don't you?" I asked.

"I don't like people getting murdered, but . . . yeah, people are going to ask us where we were when this happened. This is going down in history. I want to be able to remember where I was and have that somewhere be cool. Like on the roof."

Just the way he looked, the wind lifting up his hair a little, his profile in the low light . . . Jerome was different to me now. He was more than just the friendly and somewhat strange guy I'd gotten to know. He was smart. He was adventurous. He'd been chosen to be a prefect, which had to mean something. I felt the *like* blossom in me.

"What happens now?" Jazza asked, coming over and joining us.

"We wait," Jerome said. "Catherine Eddowes was killed sometime between one forty and one forty-five. It's going to happen soon."

1:45 arrived. Then 1:46, 1:47, 1:48, 1:49 . . .

The newscasters spun on and on, filling time by showing the same film of police cars going through the streets. I started to feel weird waiting on the roof for someone to die. It was obvious that the news people had run out of ways of saying "nothing has been found." They returned to descriptions of the third body. The early reports confirmed that this was indeed a third Ripper murder. This was the quickest one, just a slash to the neck.

Two o'clock. Five past two. Jazza got up and began to hop on the balls of her feet and hug herself for warmth. I watched her gleeful pride slipping away with every passing minute.

"I want to go back," she said. "I can't stay up here anymore."

Jerome looked to her, then over to me.

"Do you want to stay, or . . ."

There was just a touch of sadness in his voice. This made me go tingly all over. But there was no way Jazza wanted to go back by herself, and really, neither did I.

"No," I said. "We should go back together."

"That's probably the best idea," he said.

He escorted us back down the fire stairs, to the back door.

"Be careful," he said. "Text me when you're there safe?"

"Okay," I said. I smiled a little. I couldn't help it.

The door shut, and we were once again outside in the cold. I didn't want to take the long way around, for several reasons—not the least of which was the fact that the Ripper was actually in East London somewhere. Cutting through the square was the safest and most direct route—but it also was the one that increased our chances of getting caught by several orders of magnitude. We'd be approaching Hawthorne straight on. Still, I thought we could do it.

There were lights along the sides of the square, but we could probably stay hidden by keeping near the trees where it was always dark and shady. Even if Claudia were staring out of the window, she'd need night vision goggles to see us creeping along under the trees' cover. I wouldn't have put it past Claudia to have night vision goggles, but again, she was probably watching the news with everyone else. That's where we had last seen her. The common room was in the back of the building.

Jazza stared at the square, making the same mental calculations.

"Really?" she asked.

"It's about fifty feet. Come on. Tree to tree, like a spy!"

"I don't think that's how spies work," she said, but she followed me as I bolted into the dark of the square. We made ridiculous dodges from tree to bush to tree, the leaves crunching under our shoes. When we reached the other side, we had to make the dash across the cobblestone street in front of Hawthorne, then sneak under the windows to the back of the building. The bathroom lights were off. As far as I could remember, we'd left them on. Someone had come in since. We'd managed to close the window as we got out, but we left it open just a crack on the bottom so we could push it back up again. I boosted Jazza up, and she squirreled under the bars and inside. I was about to do the same when I realized someone was next to me. It was a man, bald and dressed in a slightly oversized gray suit.

"Should you be doing that?" he asked politely.

"It's okay," I said quickly, once I swallowed a scream of surprise. "I go here."

"I take it you're not supposed to be out."

There was something strangely familiar about the man, something I couldn't quite place. It was something about his eyes, his bald head, his outfit. And he was creepy. Maybe it was just because he was some middle-aged man standing around school grounds, talking to underage girls. That would do it. That's the technical definition of *creepy*.

Jazza appeared at the window.

"Now!" she whisper-shouted, reaching down for me.

"Good night, girls," the man said, walking on.

I scraped up one of my knees on the bricks getting in, but I made it, tumbling into the stall. We quickly pulled the bars back into place and shut the window. We changed back into our pajamas frantically. There was still a lot of noise coming from the common room. We looked at each other, then began our slow walk down the hall. The idea was to casually pass the door. As we did, I glanced inside. The bottom of the screen read **NO FOURTH BODY FOUND**. Jazza kept on going, slipping along in her fuzzy socks.

And then we walked right into Claudia, who was adjusting a notice on the board in the front hall.

"Going to bed?" she asked.

"Yup," I said.

Jazza started hurrying up the steps, but I pinched the back of her fleece to slow her. Casual. Innocent. That's how we had to look. We said nothing until we were safely in our room. We both went right for our beds without switching on the lights, as if light made you louder.

"I think . . . it's okay," I said, sticking my legs straight up in the air and creating a teepee out of my blanket.

Silence from Jazza's side of the room, then a pillow made contact with my legs, knocking down my teepee. Jazza had a strong throwing arm. Then I heard a smothered giggle and what sounded like some kicking feet. I threw the pillow back and heard a little high-pitched squeal as it made contact.

"Why did I go up on that roof?" she whispered happily. "I hope Charlotte finds out. I really do. I hope she hears, and I hope she swallows her own tongue."

Even through the dark, I knew she was smiling. I pulled out my phone and sent Jerome a text.

The eagle has landed, I wrote. Operation successful.

His reply came a moment later: Understood.

Then a moment after that: Still no body.

Then a moment after that: He's hidden this one well.

Then: See you tomorrow.

Which was completely unnecessary, because *of course* he was going to see me tomorrow. He saw me every day. It was the kind of thing you said when you wanted to say something and that was the best you could do just to keep talking, keep the conversation going.

I decided to do what they always say in romance columns—I didn't reply. I grinned stupidly at my own suavity.

"Who were you talking to when you were out there?" Jazza asked.

"That guy," I said.

"What guy?"

Jazza was instantly on the alert, sitting bolt upright.

"The one who said good night to us."

"I didn't see anyone," Jazza said.

This made no sense. There was no way Jazza could have missed him.

"Who was it?" she asked urgently. "Someone from school?"

"No," I said. "Just some guy on the street."

"Are you joking? Because it's not funny."

"I'm not," I assured her. "He was just some random guy."

She slowly relaxed and settled back down.

"So," she said. "You and Jerome?"

"What about us?" I asked as I looked up at the long rectangles of light coming in through the window and stretching along the wall. We hadn't bothered to shut the curtains.

"Well?"

"Well what?"

"Do you like him?" she asked.

"He hasn't done anything," I said.

"But do you like him?"

"I'm thinking about it," I replied.

"Well, don't think too hard." Then I heard the giggling again, and another pillow made contact with the wall above my head and landed on my face.

"No danger of that," I said.

# 13

THE NEXT MORNING STARTED WAY TOO EARLY, WITH someone pounding wildly at our door.

"You get it," I mumbled into my pillow. "My legs fell off."

Grumbling and confusion from Jaz as she fell out of her bed and shuffled to the door. Charlotte was there, wrapped up in a fuzzy blue robe, looking shockingly awake.

"There's a school meeting in the dining hall at six," she said. "Twenty minutes."

"School meeting?" I repeated.

"You don't have to put on your uniform. Just be over there."

Meeting in twenty minutes, at six A.M., that meant it was . . . morning math, morning math, morning math . . . five forty. The sun wasn't even up. We had only gone to bed about three or four hours before.

"What *is* this?" I asked as I fumbled around, looking for my shoes.

"I have no idea," Jazza said. She didn't have time to mess around with her contacts, so she slapped on her glasses.

"Are they really going to have some assembly at six in the morning?" I asked. "Isn't that a crime against humanity?"

"We have to be in trouble. Someone did something. We did something."

"They're not having an assembly at six in the morning to yell at us, Jaz."

"You don't know that."

It looked like the zombie apocalypse in the hall, everyone shambling toward the steps, looking confused, blank, dead-eyed. One or two people had put on their uniforms, but mostly people wore sweatpants or pajamas. Jazza and I were of the pajama variety, with our PE fleeces on top for warmth and snuggle factor. Outside, it was one of those drizzly, it's-raining-even-though-it's-not-raining English days I'd been getting used to. The cold and wet woke me up a little, but it was mostly the sight of the police . . . that, and the small white tent and work lights that had been erected in the middle of the green, and the people in the sterile suits that were coming in and out of it.

"Oh, my God," Jazza said, grabbing my arm. "Oh, my God, Rory, that's . . ."

It was one of those forensic tents, is what it was, like you saw in crime shows and news bulletins. Everyone processed this fact at the exact same moment. There was one large intake of breath, then a teetering hysteria that Claudia tried to short-circuit by waving us into the dining hall with huge, semaphore-like motions.

"Come on," she said. "Come on, girls, come on, come on."

We allowed Claudia to herd us into the dining hall, which

was full of people who had all just received this jolt of adrenaline. There was a lot of noise, people running from table to table, a lot of phone checking. All the faculty who lived nearby were there as well, sitting up on the dais, looking as surprised as the rest of us. When everyone had been shoved inside, the door was slammed shut loudly, and Mount Everest gave us an "all right, all right, quiet down," which had very limited effect.

"This is Detective Chief Inspector Simon Cole," he yelled over the noise, "and he needs to speak with you. You will give him your full attention."

There was the man from the news, the suited and serious-faced chief inspector, flanked by two uniformed officers. This was the real thing. That brought the silence down.

"At two fifteen this morning," the inspector began soberly, "a body was found in your school green. We believe this relates to an ongoing investigation, which you are probably aware of . . ."

He didn't say "Ripper." He didn't need to. A shock wave passed over the room—waves of people inhaling all at once, then a buzzing murmur and a scraping of benches as people turned around to look at each other.

"Was it someone from Wexford?" a guy shouted.

"No," the inspector said. "It was not someone from your school. But this area is now a crime scene. You will not be permitted to cross the square while our forensic team is working. There will be a police presence here for several days. Today, several detectives will be stationed in the library, ready to take statements from any of you who saw anything out of the ordinary last night. We want to know if you saw or heard anything at all, no matter how unimportant it seems. Any people you saw. Any strange noises. Nothing is too trivial."

Mount Everest jumped in again.

"Any of you who might be afraid of coming forward to the police because you were violating a school policy *at the time* . . . you will not be punished. Come forward and tell the police everything you know. There will be no repercussions from the school if you aid the police. Everyone will stay on school grounds today. We will arrange for breakfast items to be brought to your houses, so there will be no breakfast in the refectory today, in order to limit the amount of traffic through the green this morning. Lunch will go on as normal. If you have something to tell the police, step forward. And remember, there is *no reason for alarm.*"

We were dismissed. We'd only been there for a few minutes, but everything had changed. Everyone was awake and unsure. There was a lot of low, confused mumbling. But unlike every other time the entire school was assembled, no one was snickering or talking too loudly. Several more police were already by the refectory door, eyeing us all as we passed out of the building.

I realized I was shaking when I stepped back inside Hawthorne. At first I thought I was cold, but it didn't stop, even after I sat on the radiator for five minutes. Jazza was acting the same way, sitting on the heater on her side of the room. We sat there, in the half dark, perched awkwardly for several minutes.

"What about the guy?" I finally asked her.

Jazza looked at me, judging whether or not I was being serious.

"Jaz, he was right behind me. He said good night. You're sure you didn't see or hear him?"

"I didn't," she said. "I swear."

I bit my lip and ran through the memory again. It still didn't make any sense, Jazza not seeing or hearing the guy. I knew I hadn't imagined it.

"I suppose I just wasn't paying attention," she said after a moment. "I was only looking at you. I was nervous. If you feel you have to . . ."

She trailed off as the implication of this hit her.

"If you feel you have to say something, you should," she said, more firmly. "Even if it means . . ."

"They said we wouldn't get in trouble."

"Even if it did," she said.

It took me about ten minutes to get up the courage to go downstairs. Before I could leave the building, I had to check in with Call Me Claudia. She was in her office on the phone, roaring away to some equally loud friend of hers about what had happened the night before.

"Yes, Aurora?"

"I . . . saw something."

Claudia considered me for a moment.

"Last night?" she asked.

"Last night," I repeated. I left the rest of the sentence alone while she considered this.

"Well, then," Claudia said. "You'd better go over to the library."

The activity outside had already increased. Police officers in fluorescent green jackets with reflective stripes were all over the place, putting up even more blue and white crime scene tape, marking off paths around the grounds. I continued past them, taking the long way around to the library. Two uniformed officers were stationed outside the doors. They admitted me. Another officer talked to me when I entered and escorted me to one of the worktables, where various people—I assumed more police officers—had already set up shop. These people were in normal clothes, suits and business wear. I was placed at a table, and a tall black woman with closely cropped hair and rimless glasses sat down across from me. She looked like she was in her twenties, but she wore a no-nonsense navy blue suit with a white blouse that made her seem older and more serious. She set down a few forms and a pen.

"I'm DI Young," she said politely. "What's your name?"

I told her my name.

"American or Canadian?" she asked.

"American."

"And you saw or heard something last night?"

"I saw a man," I said.

She pulled out one of the forms and put it on a clipboard, so I couldn't see what she was writing.

"A man," she said. "Where and when was this?"

"I think it was two . . . just after two. It was right when everyone was looking for the fourth body. The fourth murder was supposed to be at one forty-five, right? Because we waited for a few minutes before we came back . . ."

"Came back from where?"

"We snuck out. Just to go over to Aldshot. Just for a little while."

"Who is we? Who was with you?"

"My roommate," I said.

"And her name is?"

"Julianne Benton."

DI Young wrote something else on her form.

"So you and your roommate snuck out of your building . . ."

I wanted to tell her to keep it down, but you can't tell the police not to broadcast your business so you don't get in trouble.

". . . and you saw a man just after two in the morning. Is that correct?"

"Yes."

She made another note.

"And you're sure of the time?"

"Well," I said, "the news kept saying that the fourth victim in 1888 was found at one forty-five. We were on the roof watching the news on Jerome's computer—"

"Jerome?" she asked.

Now I'd gotten Jerome into it.

"Jerome," I repeated. "He lives in Aldshot."

"Exactly how many of you were there?"

"Three," I said. "Me, Jazza, and Jerome. We went to see Jerome in his building, and then the two of us came back."

More writing.

"And you were watching the news at one forty-five."

"Right. And they . . . I mean, I guess, you . . . didn't find a body. So we waited for a while, about ten minutes or so, then Jazza wanted to go home, because it was creepy. So we ran across the square—"

"You crossed *the square* at two in the morning?"

"Yes," I said, shrinking in my chair.

Detective Young pulled her chair in a little closer, and her expression grew a bit more serious. She nodded for me to go on.

"We had just gotten to the back window of Hawthorne and were climbing in, and this guy walked around the corner of the building. And he asked if we were supposed to be doing that—climbing back in the window. And I said it was okay, because we went there. He was creepy."

"Creepy how?"

The more I thought about it, the less I could explain *why* the guy was so creepy, aside from the fact that he was hanging around the school. There was just something about him that made my brain twitch and gave me the very strong feeling that he shouldn't be there. The guy was just wrong in every way . . . but that is not an explanation.

There's something witnesses do that my parents had explained to me many times. Once witnesses find out that what they've seen might be important—that it might have something to do with a crime—their brains get out the crayons and start coloring things in, making things seem moody and suspicious and full of meaning when it's entirely possible that nothing was going on. The noise in the night that you thought was a car backfiring is now clearly a gunshot. That guy you saw at the store at two in the morning buying lots of trash bags? At the time, you thought little of him. But now that he's on trial for killing someone and chopping up the body in the tub, you remember that he was nervous and sweaty and shifty and maybe even splattered with blood. And you won't be lying, either. The mind does this. It constantly rewrites our memories to accommodate new facts. This is why police and lawyers break people down to make sure witnesses report the facts and nothing but the facts.

In short, I felt I should have been better at being questioned by the police. I'd practically been *trained* for this. What I'd seen was a guy walking past our window. He could have been completely innocent. But still, all I had was "creepy." If pushed, I could add "icky." Out of place. Incorrect.

"Just . . . creepy."

"Then what happened?" she asked.

"He said something about how we shouldn't be out, and then Jazza came to the window and helped me inside."

"And what happened to the man?"

"He walked away."

"What did he look like?" she asked.

"He was, I don't know . . ."

What did people look like? Suddenly I didn't know how to describe anything.

"He was in a suit. A gray suit. And it was kind of weird . . ."

"In what way?"

"It just looked . . . weird. Old—"

"He was an old man?"

"No," I said quickly. "His suit looked kind of old . . . ish."

"In what way? Was it very worn?"

"No," I said. "It looked new, but old. Just . . . I . . . I don't know much about suits. Not super old. Not, like, historic. Kind of like . . . something on *Frasier*? Or *Seinfeld* or something? You know, the show? It was like a suit out of a nineties sitcom. The jacket was kind of long and big."

She hesitated, then wrote this down.

"Right, then," she said patiently. "How old would you say he was?"

I imagined Uncle Bick, without his beard, maybe forty pounds lighter, in a suit. That was about right. Uncle Bick was thirty-eight or thirty-nine.

"Thirties, maybe? Forty?"

"All right. Hair color?"

"No hair," I said quickly. "Bald."

We ran through every option—tall, short, fat, thin, glasses, facial hair. In the end, I painted a portrait of a man of average height and weight, with no facial hair or distinguishing characteristics, who was bald and wore a suit that seemed to me a little out of date. And since it was dark and "crazy" isn't an accepted eye color, I couldn't help much on that front either.

"Stay here for just a moment," she said.

She went away. I shivered and looked around. A few of the officers who were working in the library glanced over at me as I sat alone at the table. No one else, it seemed, had come in to report anything. It was just me. When she returned, she was wearing a tan raincoat and she had Inspector Cole with her. Up on the dais, Inspector Cole looked much younger. Up close, I could see fine wrinkles around his eyes. He had a steady, unwavering stare.

"We'd like you to show us exactly where you saw this man," she said.

Two minutes later, we were on the sidewalk outside Hawthorne, staring up at the bathroom window. The screws were still on the ground. It was only now that I realized that we'd left our entire building vulnerable. A sloshy, queasy feeling came over me.

"So," DI Young said, "show us exactly where you were."

I positioned myself right under the window.

"And where was the man?" she asked.

"Right about where you are," I said.

"So, quite close. Within ten feet."

"Yes."

"And your roommate?"

This was the first time DCI Cole had spoken to me. He was staring at me unblinkingly, judging me, his hands deep in the pockets of his coat.

"Was right here," I said, pointing up at the window.

"So she saw him as well."

"No," I said. The queasy feeling got worse.

"She didn't see him? But she was right in the window, wasn't she?"

"I guess she was just looking at me."

DCI Cole bit his upper lip with his lower teeth, looked from me to the window and back again, then waved DI Young to the side and spoke to her quietly. Then he walked away without another word.

"Let's go back inside and go through this again," she said.

So I returned to the library with Detective Young. I was given a cup of coffee once we sat down, and another officer came over and sat with us. I never got his name, but he typed a lot into a laptop as I spoke. The questions were more detailed this time. How did we get out of the building? Had we been drinking? Did anyone see us leave?

"We want to do an E-fit," Detective Young finally said. "Do you know what that is?"

I shook my head wearily.

"It's a way of producing digital images of suspects based on witness reports. Those pictures you see on the news? Those are E-fit pictures. We're just going to go through your story one more time. You provide us with all the details you can remember. We enter them into a program that creates a digital image of a face, which we can then refine until it looks like the man you say you saw. All right?"

I didn't like the way she said "you *say* you saw," but I nodded. I was pretty sure at this point that if I went through this again, my head would explode. Nothing seemed real anymore. But they weren't going to let me go until I did this. So we went through it a third time, this time concentrating solely on the man. We went into even deeper detail—the size of his eyes (medium), the depth of his eyes (deep, I guessed), wrinkles (none, really), the size of his lips (normal), the shape of his eyebrows (slightly arched), his weight (normal, maybe a little thin). It was only when we got to the color of his skin (white) that something stood out.

"He seemed very . . . gray," I said. "Kind of pale. Or sick."

"So he was a Caucasian man with a pallor?"

It was more than that, though. His skin and his eyes didn't match. His eyes were so bright and clear to me, but the rest of him . . . the rest of him hardly seemed to matter. It was like I forgot the rest of his body.

The E-fit produced something that looked like a cartoon, specifically, like an older, more evil Charlie Brown. In reality, the man's head wasn't so smooth. Not that it was lumpy, either, but skulls have textures that are hard to explain.

Detective Young looked at the image with a resigned expression.

"All right," she said. "For now, you should go back to your

building. But make sure to stay around today. Don't leave the campus area."

By the time I stepped outside, it was fully daylight and there were television trucks all over the square, pulling up on the sidewalks, taking up every available space. Police officers in bright neon Windbreakers were moving around them, telling drivers to move, pointing camera people away from the school. A female reporter immediately descended on me.

"Were you in there talking to the police?" she asked.

"I just saw a guy," I mumbled.

"You saw someone?"

"I—"

"What exactly did you see?" Suddenly, there were two cameras in my face, blinding me with their lights. I was about to answer when two police officers hurried over, one sticking her hand over the camera lens.

"You lot, you stop filming *now*," she barked. "I want to see all your footage—"

"We have every right—"

"You," the other officer said to me, "get back to your house."

As I hurried off, the cameras followed me, and the reporter called, "What's your name? Your name?"

I didn't answer. Call Me Claudia was standing in the door of Hawthorne, and this time, I was happy to see her. As I left, I was sure that the cameras trained on my fleeing figure got some really excellent footage of my butt hustling through the rain in my alligator pajamas.

# 14

Jazza was pacing our room when I returned. She had her pink piggy mug out, which was the tea mug she reserved for times of extreme stress.

"Is everything all right?" she asked. "You were gone for ages!"

"It was fine," I said. "They just asked me a lot of questions."

Jazza didn't ask if I'd said anything about her. Instead, she waved me over to the window.

"I can't believe this is happening. Just look out there."

We both knelt on the spare bed we had pushed against the wall and were using as a sofa. It was right under our middle window. Through the rain-streaked glass, we saw the white-suited figures coming in and out of the white tent. More lights were set up. More people arrived. More cameras and police and police tape.

This activity remained the focus of the next few hours, with the occasional break to drink tea. Since the view from our room was so good, lots of people from the other side of the hall came in to have a look. The view out the windows was actually a lot more interesting than the news—in fact, it *was* the news. The news cameras filmed our buildings and the little tent until the police moved them back and set up a cordon around the campus, stranding us on a little island of activity.

Eventually, we all found ourselves crowded into the common room, staring at the television. Every once in a while, the news would fill us in on some aspect of what was going on outside. The victim was female again. Her name was Catherine Lord. She worked at a pub in the City. She had last been seen leaving after they closed at midnight. A coworker had walked her to her car. CCTV had caught her car pulling away. Footage from various traffic cameras tracked her from there. She had not driven home. Instead, she had driven to the location of the fourth murder. Her empty car had been found three streets away from Wexford, and while there was a partial CCTV record of her walking away from it, no one could explain what she was doing or where she was going. The news showed a picture of her, taken earlier that evening. Catherine Lord had been beautiful, with bright strawberry blond hair, and she looked barely older than us. She wore a white Victorian-style dress with a tight bodice and lots of lace. Her pub had been hosting a Ripper night special, and she and all the other bar staff were in costume. The news couldn't get enough of this—a pretty girl in a Victorian dress. The perfect victim.

*That girl* had died just outside my door. It was possible she was still in that white tent. Her dress would no longer be white.

"Julianne," Claudia said, appearing at the door, "come here, please."

Jazza looked at me, then stood and went out of the room. She was still gone when we were all taken over to lunch as a group soon after. It was absolutely pouring now, but that didn't slow down any of the activity outside. The police had moved the media away. We could see them all huddled down at the end of the street, held off by a few police officers. They had their cameras trained on us, beckoning us to come closer. To combat this, the school was making a bunch of teachers stand out in the rain and haul anyone back who wanted to go be on television. The police had more or less taken over the streets and the square. It was now a given that we would only be permitted to go from our dorms to the dining hall or library. Any attempt to walk in any other direction was met by flailing arms and a shooing motion.

The dining hall staff, to their credit, had risen to the occasion and had cooked not only for us, but for the police outside. There were extra urns of hot coffee and tea, trays of muffins and sandwiches, as well as the usual offerings. Today, it was some kind of limp pasta with a pink sauce, a stewlike thing of lamb and peas, and a tray of hamburgers. I had no appetite at all, but I grabbed one just to have something on my tray. Andrew and Jerome were already there, and they waved me over to sit with them.

"Where's Jazza?" Andrew asked.

"Talking to Claudia, or . . . someone. I'm not sure."

Jerome looked at me. He had undoubtedly already done the "we crossed the square at the same time the murder happened" math, or maths as they insisted on calling it here. He looked at my untouched burger, and I think he knew—not exactly what had happened, but certainly that something wasn't good.

Jazza joined us a few minutes later.

"All right?" Jerome asked.

"Fine," she said, a fake breeziness in her voice. "It's all fine."

After a half hour, we were all herded up again, the girls first. Outside, the police parade was still going on. A third mobile forensics unit van had joined the two that had been here most of the morning, and there were police with plastic rain slickers on walking the green in a long line—about thirty of them—taking every step together, examining the ground as they went.

As we came up to Hawthorne, there was a policeman standing in the middle of the road outside. He was tall and very young-looking, with black glasses. His face was long and thin, with pronounced cheekbones and long hollows under them. Even though he had the fluorescent green police jacket and the signature high black helmet and all the stuff that said POLICE, he didn't seem like a policeman. His black hair was just a little too long, his face a little too fresh, his bearing a little too self-conscious.

"Miss Deveaux?" He said my name elegantly, like someone who knew French and knew where the proper emphasis should be. He said my name way better than I did, that was for sure. And his voice was surprisingly deep.

"Um," I said. I had gotten a lot less articulate since I woke up that morning. He didn't seem to care what I replied. He knew exactly who I was, and he barreled right on.

"And you're Julianne Benton? Her roommate?"

"Yes," Jazza said, in her smallest of tiny voices.

"You were together last night at two A.M.?"

"Yes," we said, at the same time.

"You saw a man?" he asked me.

"Yes. I told—"

"And you didn't," he said to Jazza. It wasn't a question. "You're sure?"

"No, I . . . no."

"Even though he was directly in front of you?"

"I . . . No. I . . . No . . ."

Jazza was fumbling. The way this guy was saying it, it was like she had failed a test.

"Both of you," he said. "Don't speak to anyone from the press. If they approach you, walk away. Don't give your name. Do not repeat anything you told the detective this morning. If you need assistance, phone this number."

He handed me a small piece of paper with a phone number written on it.

"Phone it any time you need assistance, day or night," he said. "And if you ever see that man again, even if you just *think* you see him, you call that number."

He turned and walked away. Jazza and I wasted no time in running into the building, right up the stairs, and into our room. I slammed the door behind us.

"What happened?" I asked.

"They just took me and . . . they asked me about what we did . . . and I told them about how we went out and went to the roof . . . and they didn't care about that, really . . . They wanted to know about the man . . . but I didn't see the man . . .

I don't know how I didn't see him, but I didn't, and that's all they wanted to know about, and I couldn't tell them anything so . . . oh, God."

She dropped onto her bed. I sat next to her.

"It's fine," I said. "You did fine. They promised we wouldn't get in trouble."

"I don't care about that! I don't understand how I didn't see him. And who was that? That policeman? He didn't look like a policeman. He looked our age. Can you be our age and be a policeman? I suppose you can, but . . . he doesn't look like one, does he? Though, I suppose . . . I suppose policemen don't look like any particular kind of person, but still. He doesn't look like one, does he?"

No. He didn't look like a policeman. Policemen were supposed to look . . . not like him. He did look young. More than that, he looked a little too well kept, with fancy designer glasses and smooth, pale skin.

Jazza took the card from my hand and examined it.

"This is a mobile number," she said. "Shouldn't a police card have the number of a main switchboard or something? Shouldn't you just dial 999 if there's a problem? I'll bet you he's a reporter. He has to be a reporter. It's illegal to masquerade as a policeman."

None of this was helping my queasy feeling. I began to pace.

"I think you should go back to the library and report what just happened," she said.

"I don't really want to go back out there right now."

We had a few moments of independent fretting, then Jazza got up with a determined look on her face.

"If Claudia suspects something, that we went out, she might tell Charlotte. Charlotte's her minion."

"So? Charlotte doesn't know we went out."

"But she knows about the window bars in the toilet. Come on."

I followed Jazza back downstairs, where she proceeded to the bathroom in what I suspect was supposed to be a very stealthy way. It was a little more rabbitlike, with quick moves and nervous glances. She dashed into the bathroom and, once she checked to make sure it was empty, went right to the window, opened it, and gave the bars a shake. They were firmly bolted again.

Jazza gripped the bars until her knuckles went white and closed the window.

"I hate her," she said.

Even I wasn't sure that it was fair to blame Charlotte for the fact that someone had become aware of the window bars. But Jazza needed to blame Charlotte. It was important for the balance of her mind. Someone had to be blamed if we went down for this, and I was glad it wasn't me.

"We're having tea," she said calmly. "And we are not going to get upset. I am going to make the tea."

With that, she strode back upstairs. She grabbed two mugs off the shelf above her desk and two tea bags from her jar of special tea bags. I left her to it, pulled my robe on over my clothes, and went to the window. Outside, the line of police was still marching down the green. They stretched from one side to the other, no more than two feet apart. The only area they avoided was the part with the white tent, which had its own staff searching the ground. They were quite literally looking at every single inch of the green.

Last night felt like it had happened years before.

And then I noticed that right below our building, down on the cobblestone street, was the young policeman. He was staring right at my window, right at me. Jazza was right. He couldn't be a policeman. He looked really young. Yet, there he was, standing around in the middle of half the police in London. You would think that they would notice if there was a fake policeman in their midst.

I made eye contact with him, making sure he knew I saw him. He quickly walked away.

# 15

THE WHITE TENT WAS THERE ALL DAY SUNDAY. It glowed at dusk, when it was illuminated by dozens of high-powered work lights. The press was there too, hovering on the edges of campus, watching. The school sent around an e-mail saying how really, really safe it all was, even though there was a homicide investigation going on on the green at that very second, and several psychologists were being called in to talk to anyone who felt like they needed support.

And people were freaked out, but they showed it in weird ways. Back at home, people would have been weeping and doing a lot of very public group hugs. At Wexford, some people just aggressively pretended nothing was happening. Eloise, for example, sat in her room and smoked and read French novels. Charlotte patrolled the halls, poking her big red head into our rooms. Angela and Gaenor drank their way through a small crate of wine bottles they'd smuggled in, staggering into our room at points with mugs full of red wine. One of them hung a pink bra from our lighting fixture. I left it there. It was a nice bra.

At night, you could hear high-pitched nervous chatter through our halls. No one could sleep, so everyone talked. I think things were largely the same over at Aldshot. Most of the guys showed up at breakfast with red eyes with deep shadows under them, indicating either lots of reading or lots of booze.

My parents tried to put me on a train to Bristol, but I insisted that I had to stay, that we were perfectly safe. And we were, really. We were knee-deep in police and all of our movements were recorded. They eventually accepted this, but they also called every two hours or so. My entire family called. Uncle Bick and Cousin Diane called several times. Miss Gina called. And then there were the e-mails. Everyone from Bénouville wanted the story. I spent most of Sunday holding a phone in one hand and typing with the other.

I didn't mention to anyone that I had actually *seen* the killer. It was hard to keep this fact quiet. I had the best gossip on the planet, and yet I could say nothing. I was still the Only Witness in the Case, and at any moment, Scotland Yard was going to yank me in and quiz me for hours. Then everyone would know who I was. I'd be all over the news.

I waited for them to come and ask me more questions. But no one came. The news never mentioned a witness. And we never heard a word from Claudia about what we may or may not have been up to on the night of the murder. Wexford was true to its word. If they knew we'd gone to the roof, they were giving us a pass.

Classes were canceled on Monday morning, by which point there was a definite funk in the air in Hawthorne. I don't want to say the building stank, but there was a closeness. The heaters were on full blast, the air was thick with moisture and stress hormones. On Monday afternoon, they allowed us to go to class and to the library, but our movements were strictly controlled. We had to stick to the cobblestone path at all times. They put up nylon barriers on the edge of the green so that we couldn't see the tent as easily—but we still had a pretty clear view from any second-story window.

I had a free period, so I went over to the library, just to get out of the building. I thought I went quickly, but by the time I got there, all the carrels were taken, as were all the chairs around the room and all the spots on the floor next to the electrical outlets.

I decided to go upstairs, and I made my way back to the literature section. I peered down each one until I found Alistair. He was there—same magnificent hair, same big trench coat and Doc Martens boots. He had only changed positions. Now he was sitting in the windowsill, still mostly in the dark.

"Mind if I sit here?" I asked. "There's nowhere downstairs."

"Do what you like," he said, not looking up.

I hit the switch at the end of the aisle and took my place on the floor. The floor was cold, but at least it was somewhere to sit, and somewhere not totally on my own. After ten minutes, the light automatically clicked off. I looked over to see if Alistair was going to get up and turn it back on, but he just kept on reading. I peeled myself from the floor and flicked the switch.

"It's bad for your eyes," I said. "Reading in the dark."

Alistair smirked a little. I didn't know why. There was nothing funny about eyestrain. I hadn't been there very long when Jerome appeared at the end of the aisle, his computer under his arm.

"Jazza said you were over here," he said. "Can I talk to you? I need to show you something."

Jerome was so preoccupied that he didn't even acknowledge Alistair's presence.

Jerome led me to one of the tiny study rooms that lined the first floor. All the rooms were occupied, but he found one containing three year twelves who were all playing video games.

"Out," he said, opening the door. "We need this room."

There were cries of protest, but Jerome pushed the door open wider.

"Study use only," he said. "Out."

"Using your prefect powers for evil?" I asked as they shuffled past us. One of them was considerably taller than Jerome and looked down at him with palpable disdain, but Jerome didn't care. He was already setting up his computer.

"Shut the door," he said. "Sit down."

There were three chairs and a tiny table in the room. The room wasn't wide enough for a fourth chair. It wasn't really wide enough for the little table. I slipped in next to Jerome, who was logging on and pulling up a site.

"I have to warn you," he said. "This is disturbing. But you should see it. Everyone's going to see it soon enough."

He was on a site called Ripperfiles. In the middle of the front page was a video screen. He hit the Play symbol.

The footage was in night vision, which meant that it had a

greenish-gray cast, with bright white highlights. The first frames were of a garden and a patio with a few empty tables. I realized immediately that this had to be the Flowers and Archers.

After thirty seconds or so of this, a gate opened. Someone walked into the garden, very straight-backed and stiff. It was a woman. She was wearing a skirt and a coat. She crossed from the left of the frame to the right, until she was positioned almost perfectly in the eye of the camera, then she turned slowly.

Her eyes said it all. They were huge points of white light. She stood there, utterly unmoving except for a light heaving of constrained cries. Her attention seemed focused on something in front of her, just out of view. Then she jerked to the side, toppling against the fence and bouncing to the ground. She began to fight, arms flailing. It was only then that I realized that she wasn't looking at someone outside of the camera's range. There was simply no *murderer* there. The victim was well in the center of the yard, so her assailant should have been fully visible. But there was no one. She flailed at the air. Then there was a flash, a little glint of something streaking across the screen, and she went still. Her legs suddenly jerked up, so that the knees were bent and the heels placed on the ground. Then the knees were knocked open. Then a glint again.

Jerome reached over and hit Pause.

"You don't want to see the rest," he said. "I'm sorry I saw it."

"I don't get it," I said. "What was that?"

"That was the footage from the pub. It wasn't destroyed."

"But it can't be."

"It is. A member of this site got it straight from the backup server. This is it."

"It's obviously just someone acting out the crime."

"Honestly," he said, "it's real. This site . . . These people are serious. Obviously, something's been done to the footage to remove the assailant, but no one can figure out what. This has been passed around to all kinds of technical experts, and no one can figure out what's been done to it. This video? It's going to be all over the place. Every conspiracy nut in the world is going to go crazy for this."

The image was still frozen there—the woman on her back, the strange glint hanging in the air. Jerome closed the computer partway.

"The other night," I said. "When we were sneaking back in. I saw someone."

"You're a witness?" he asked.

"I was," I said. "They made me do something called an E-fit."

"You did an *E-fit*?"

I explained to Jerome about the man—how he had appeared from around the corner, how he had seen me climbing back into the window. Jerome was completely staggered by this. His jaw dropped open slightly. He was fairly loose-jawed to begin with—hence his power to declare Total War on his food, his easy smiles, his ability to talk for ages. We had probably been this close before, shoved together on the benches of the refectory, but I became acutely aware that we were alone in this little study room. Study closet, really. And we were closer now than I remembered. We must have been moving together while I was watching the video.

"It's been weird," I said. "Jazza didn't see him. She was inside. I was still out on the sidewalk, so . . . they're only talking to me. But I think they think I'm crazy. Or lying. They haven't been in touch."

"I'm sure they'll get in touch when they catch him," he said. "Then they'll probably bring you in to identify him."

That made sense. There was no point in contacting me until they had something to ask me.

We were so close now that I couldn't look directly at him, not at his eyes, anyway. This is when it finally dawned on me that he hadn't brought me in here for the sole purpose of watching a video of someone being murdered (though that was probably *part* of the reason).

Also, it was very warm in the little study closet.

To be honest, I'm not sure which one of us did it first, but it was a done deal as soon as I managed to pull my gaze back from his chin to his eyes.

## BBC TELEVISION CENTRE,
## SHEPHERD'S BUSH, WEST LONDON
## OCTOBER 2
## 1:45 P.M.

THE BBC IS USED TO DEALING WITH FREAKS, CRANKS, and psychos. Bomb threats are not uncommon. Nor were threats to James Goode, host of *Goode Evening*, the nightly news roundup and opinion show. A major newspaper's readers' poll had recently voted James the fifteenth-most famous person in Britain, third-most annoying, and number-one "celebrity you would least like to date." It was estimated that 42 percent of his audience tuned in just to hate him, a behavior he actively encouraged.

So when the associate producer of *Goode Evening* returned from lunch to find the brown-paper-wrapped parcel on his desk, he was puzzled. No one in the office claimed any knowledge of having accepted its delivery. The mailroom had no record of it. Someone had been in the office at all times, and yet no one had seen a person walk in and deliver a box. It simply appeared, with the words "Mr James Goode, BBC Centre" written on it in a harsh black scrawl. It had no stamps, no delivery stickers, no bar codes or tracking numbers. It was utterly anonymous.

Which meant that this was a serious breach of security. The producer was already reaching for the phone when James himself came strutting into the office.

"We have a problem," the producer said. "Breach of security. I think we have to get everyone out."

"What?" James Goode said the word in the same way normal people usually said things like "you burned my house down?" But the producer was used to this.

"This box," he said. "No one saw it come in. No postage, no delivery markings, didn't come through the mailroom. We have to—"

"Don't be stupid," James said, taking the box.

"James—"

"Be quiet."

"James, really—"

But James was already attacking the packaging tape with a pair of scissors. The producer set down the phone softly, closed his eyes, and quietly prayed that he wouldn't explode in the next few seconds.

"I don't want people calling health and safety for every little thing," James went on. "That's precisely the kind of behavior I . . ."

He silenced himself, which was not normal James Goode behavior. The producer opened his eyes to find James reading a piece of yellow paper.

"James?"

James hissed him silent as he reached into the box gingerly to move aside some wrapping. He started visibly and pushed down the flaps of the box, hiding the contents.

"Listen to me," James said intently. "Get news on the phone. Tell them to get a camera up here now and that I'm going to need to be on the air in fifteen minutes."

"What? What are you doing?"

"I have the next piece of the Ripper story. And tell them to be *quiet* about it. Lock the door. No one else comes into this office."

Fifteen minutes later, after a protracted argument with the news department, there was a camera in the *Goode Evening* office and a news producer with a headset talking rapidly to the newsroom. James was sitting at his desk. His awards had been hastily shoved together on the windowsill just behind him, crushed together to fit in the frame. In front of him was the box.

"Are you ready yet?" he snapped. "How bloody difficult is it to stop them jabbering on for two minutes? I'm trying to *hand* them a story. Tell them to stop doing the bloody weather and—"

"We're live in ten," the person from news said. "And nine, eight, seven . . ."

James composed himself for the countdown and was ready at one.

"Ladies and gentlemen," he said, "just after two in the afternoon, I received this package here in my office at BBC Centre."

He indicated the box, then held up the piece of yellow paper.

"Inside I found this note, which, as you will hear, I have been instructed to read. I am following the instructions in an attempt to save lives . . ."

He began to read.

*From hell.*
*Mr Goode, I send you half the Kidne I took from one man prasarved it for you tother piece I fried and ate it was very nise. I may send you the bloody knif that took it out if you only wate a whil longer.*

The camera panned over to show the contents of the box. Nestled in a wad of bubble wrap was a brownish-red object sealed in a plastic zipper-top bag. The object was about the size of a human fist, and there was no mistaking that it was some kind of an organ.

The camera jerked back to James, who continued reading.

*I hav already chose my next acquatence and I am eager for the 9th of november as I am hungry and hav the itch. Please show my lovly Kidne on your show Mr Goode and read my note or I may hav to come quick and take more. . . .*

The screen abruptly switched back to the newsroom. Someone, somewhere at the BBC, had pulled the plug. The anchor apologized for the graphic footage.

Inside his office, James Goode went on. The last sentence of the letter was the money sentence, the one he had practiced reading with the most care, the one he had memorized and could say looking right into the camera. This was, he knew, the sentence no one would ever forget. This was his moment.

He read it, unaware that it was being heard only by himself and the two other people in the room.

# The Star That Kills

**In our lifetime those who kill**
**the newsworld hands them stardom**
**and these are the ways**
**on which I was raised.**

***—Morrissey,***
***"The Last of the Famous***
***International Playboys"***

# 16

The police packed up by Wednesday morning, and the press left as soon as the white tent came down. Jerome's prediction about the video came true. By that afternoon, every news station on the planet was showing it. It was on the front page of every website. Even though hoaxes were an everyday occurrence, this video was proving hard to dismiss. Video experts had all had a look at it. Facial recognition software confirmed that the woman in the footage was the victim, Fiona Chapman. No one could explain the fact that the killer couldn't be seen. And it was physically impossible that he was just avoiding the camera. Somehow, he had accessed the footage on both the hard disk and the server and erased himself. Some people thought he had special military cloaking technology.

Three students had been pulled from school. Teachers wanted to be able to leave the school grounds before it got dark at five. In the air, there was a deep sense of unease, everywhere.

As for the mad make-out session with Jerome, I wasn't sure what it meant. It could have been a part of the general insanity. It could have been stress that kicked our hormones into gear like that. But the fact is, when you live with someone—or on the same campus, I mean—and you have a mad make-out session, you have two choices. You can either indicate that you enjoy your mad make-out sessions and intend to indulge in them at every given opportunity (i.e., Gaenor and Paul, her year twelve boyfriend, known to make out while eating shepherd's pie, which is not a euphemism), or you do not acknowledge the make-out session, or indeed any physical attraction. There is no middle ground, not at boarding school. I told Jazza, of course. But no one else. Jerome seemed to be doing the same thing. In fact, I was pretty sure he hadn't told Andrew.

On Wednesday night, Jazza and I sat on our respective beds doing homework while the news played on my computer. After the video came out, watching the news became a matter of habit. The topic, as ever, was the Ripper—in this case, the letter that had been received at the BBC the day before.

*"This letter,"* the newscaster said, *"of course, is based on the famous 'From Hell' letter that was received by Mr. George Lusk of the Whitechapel Vigilance Committee on October 16, 1888. It's the only letter out of the hundreds that came in that most Ripper experts think was actually from the killer. We now also know that there was more to the letter, which we didn't hear. To discuss this, we have Mr. James Goode."*

"Oh, God," I said. "Please. Not again. Not again with this guy."

This guy, James Goode, had seemed to be on about half of all the television shows I saw in England before this happened. Now his smug face was on TV all the time, on every station.

*"James, many people are saying that you should have turned the package over to the police immediately,"* the interviewer said, *"not shown the contents on the air."*

*"People have a right to know,"* James replied, leaning back. *"And we arranged it so that one very critical piece of information was left out. Only Scotland Yard and I know the full contents of the message."*

*"You're saying you intended for your own broadcast to be cut off so abruptly?"*

*"Of course I intended it."*

"Who is this jackass?" I asked. "Why is he always on TV?"

"James Goode? I don't know. He was a journalist, and they gave him a show. Everyone hates him, but he's really popular, which makes no sense, I suppose."

"He's a jackass," I repeated, and Jazza nodded sagely.

*"It's always been a subject of debate whether or not the original 'From Hell' letter of 1888 was a hoax. That letter, like your letter, contained half a human kidney, which could have come from the fourth victim, Catherine Eddowes. Of course, now we possess the capability to determine these things for certain. It has been confirmed that the kidney sent to you was the left kidney of the fourth victim, Catherine Lord. Why do you think you were chosen, James? Why you, and not the police?"*

*"I suppose the killer wanted to send a message,"* James said. *"He wanted to make sure the kidney was seen by as many people as possible, and he knew I had the pull to make that happen."*

*"And of course the one thing this last murder has shown is that the killer probably has extensive medical knowledge. This was always a matter of debate in the case of the first Ripper, but this time, there is a consensus amongst the medical professionals involved that this murderer almost certainly has some medical training. The kidney was*

*removed with great skill. We have an image of the kidney taken from that broadcast. Viewers are advised that the following image is quite graphic, and—"*

"I am getting so sick of looking at this kidney," I said.

"It's a farce," Jazza replied. "They act like they're shocked and horrified, and then they show it off twenty times a day."

"Have you seen the singing kidney video?" I asked.

"Ugh. No."

"It's really funny. You should watch it."

"Can you switch it off?"

The computer was at the end of my bed. I closed it with my socked foot and continued reading my selections from *The Diary of Samuel Pepys* (which is pronounced *Peeps*, not *Peppies*, something I found out the hard way in class)—specifically, a section in which he describes the Great Fire of London. There was a knock at our door. Charlotte opened the door when we called.

"Benton, Deveaux, you're wanted downstairs."

In Hawthorne-speak, *downstairs* meant Call Me Claudia's apartment, and last names meant the business was in some way official.

"What for?" Jazza asked.

"Sorry. No idea."

She and her hair left us. Jazza shoved her German off her lap and spun toward me.

"Oh, God . . . ," she said.

"It's fine," I said. "It's fine. She would have killed us by now if she wanted to."

"She was probably waiting until the police left."

"Jazza."

"Why else would she want us?"

"Jazza," I said again.

"What do we do?" she said, rocking on the edge of her bed. "Rory? What do we do?"

"We go down."

"And?"

"And . . . she says stuff," I said. "I don't know. We just go."

We gathered ourselves together, put on our most innocent faces, and walked downstairs as a united front. Claudia called us inside on the very first knock.

"Ah, girls . . ."

I immediately relaxed. It was a cheerful "ah, girls." Not an "I'm going to murder you now with a hockey stick" kind of "ah, girls." She gestured for us to take a seat in one of her floral chairs. Jazza swallowed so hard I heard it.

"You're getting a roommate tomorrow," she said. "Her name is Bhuvana Chodhari. Late admission."

"Why is she moving into our room?" I asked. "Eloise has a room all to herself."

"Eloise has severe allergies. She needs an air purifier in her room."

This was so obvious and outrageous a lie that I almost laughed out loud. Eloise didn't have allergies. She smoked more than a tire fire.

"Your room was originally a triple," Claudia went on. "There's plenty of space. If you have anything in the third wardrobe, you need to get it out tonight. That will be all, I think."

We returned to our room and shut the door.

"She knows," Jazza said.

I nodded.

"This totally blows," I added.

After briefly analyzing the dimensions, we concluded that there was no way this room was a triple. At most it was maybe four feet wider than the rooms around it, and it did have an extra window, but that was it.

"You never know," Jazza said. She had recovered from the initial shock and was trying to be the ever-bright-and-cheery one. "She may be lovely. I mean, I like having just the two of us in here, but it might not be bad."

"We're losing our sofa."

I looked mournfully at the extra bed we had turned against the wall and loaded down with Jazza's two hundred cushions.

"We hardly ever use it," Jazza babbled on. "And it could have been worse. It could have been so much worse."

But I think she felt the same way I did. This was our room, our little peaceful spot in the universe, and we'd lost it because we'd snuck out. I fell silent and looked up at the sky through the panes of the window. It was getting dark so much earlier. It came on fast here. The trees were black outlines against the dark lavender of the London night sky.

"Crap," I said.

# 17

THE NEXT MORNING, WE TOOK A FINAL LOOK AT OUR room as it was before we headed off to breakfast. When I returned to do a book switch-out after lunch, our room had a new occupant. Bhuvana was stretched out on the bed, talking on the phone. She gave me a little wave and a smile and wrapped up her conversation. She seemed fine with the position of the bed and had redecorated it with a huge pink and gray duvet and a stack of metallic silver and pink pillows. There were bags everywhere—suitcases, duffel bags, shopping bags.

Bhuvana was, as her name suggested, of Indian descent. She had very straight, very black hair, with one bright streak of artificial cherry red on the right side. It was cut into a severe line just at the shoulders, and she had razor-straight bangs. Along with the fact that she wore a lot of black eyeliner and long, dangling gold earrings, she reminded me of pictures of Cleopatra. She clearly wasn't from India, though. Her accent was as British as they come—fast, urban, kind of Cockney, I guess. I could barely understand her at points.

"Aurora, yeah?" she said as she hung up the phone. She bounced off the bed to embrace me and give me two air kisses.

"Rory," I corrected her. "You're Bhuvana?"

"Boo," she corrected me right back. "Only my gran calls me Bhuvana."

"Only my grandma calls me Aurora."

So we had that in common. Boo was several inches taller than me. She too had put her uniform on right away, but she wore it with a swagger, her tie slightly undone and jerked to the side.

"Did your parents just . . . drop you off?" I asked, looking at the stuff piled around the floor.

"Well, I live in London," she said breezily. "I was in Mumbai visiting family, yeah? And I got sick, which is why I'm late for term. So, yeah, got catching up to do."

Boo's things looked like they had been hastily packed—everything randomly shoved into bags. Clothes, mugs, wires, pictures, trinkets. Her clothes were definitely more interesting than ours. Boo tended to lean toward the sparkly, the stretchy, and the dance-friendly.

"I've never boarded before," she said, shoving handfuls of red and purple lace underwear into a drawer. "This is all new to me. Never been away from home."

"Me neither," I said.

"Let's see . . ." She pulled out a wrinkled schedule from her pocket and passed it over to me. I pulled out my own wrinkled schedule from the front pocket of my bag. They were completely identical.

"I guess we do the same stuff," Boo said, smiling. "Looks like we have hockey now."

She produced a hockey stick from the rubble, as well as a proper mouth guard—a fancy, fitted one, not the kind you boiled, like mine. She also had the shoes and the pads and a bag to carry them all.

Once we arrived at the field, Claudia gave Boo a short test to determine her level of experience, and it was clear from her reaction that Boo was the girl she had been waiting for all her life. Boo was an athlete. She was fast, she was strong, she was coordinated. She ran up and down the field with that stick like a thing born to run up and down a field with a stick. She nailed me in the face guard with a ball. My new roommate was a champion.

"We play every day?" she asked excitedly as we returned to Hawthorne.

"Every day," I answered miserably.

"That's brilliant! We didn't have much sport at my old school. Sorry about your face. Is it all right?"

"It's fine," I said. And it was fine, even though the shock of the blow had sent me flying backward and it had taken two people to help me get up.

From there, we returned for our quick showers, then we had one hour of further maths, which Boo did not like at all. All the confidence of the field drained from her face. I walked her to dinner and introduced her around. Jazza, of course, was gushing and polite, but I could see her taking in the details—the earrings, the stripe in the hair, the sound of Boo's voice. I couldn't tell what Jazza was thinking, but from the wideness of her eyes, I sensed faint alarm. Boo was not like us. Boo didn't read Jane Austen in the tub or play cello for fun. Even with my limited knowledge of English accents, I could hear the rough edges of Boo's voice. Her accent was urban. She put "yeah" at the end of her sentences.

Boo, for her part, greeted everyone warmly, and she shared my love of meats. We got almost the same meal—sausages and mash with extra gravy. She wasn't a delicate eater. I liked that.

"You'll have to take those earrings off, Bhuvana," Charlotte said from across the table. "Earrings have to be close to the ear—studs or small hoops only. Sorry."

She didn't sound even remotely sorry. Boo eyed her, then removed the earrings and set them on the table next to her spoon.

"You're head girl?" Boo asked, picking up her knife and chopping up a sausage.

"Yes. You can come to me any time you like to help you get settled in."

"I'm all right," Boo said. "I have these two."

She indicated Jazza and me as if we had been friends all our lives.

"And it's Boo," she added. "Not Bhuvana. Boo."

Boo didn't exactly flex her muscles or punch her fist into her palm, but there was a certain pulling back of the shoulders that suggested that Boo was used to dealing with things in a very different way than Charlotte was used to. It wasn't hard to imagine Boo grabbing hold of Charlotte's updo and putting her face down in a plate of mashed potatoes. It was not difficult to imagine this *at all.*

"Boo," Charlotte repeated coolly. "Of course."

Back in our room, Boo continued to unpack. Jazza watched in silence, staring at the pile of heels and sneakers Boo had just dumped out of a plastic bag.

"So, yeah, I was in Mumbai, and I got *really* sick . . ." She pulled an electric kettle out of a pile of clothes.

"We're not really supposed to have that in here," Jaz said worriedly.

"It's just a kettle," Boo replied with a smile. "I've got to have my tea."

"Well, me too, but—"

"I'll hide it, then."

Boo shoved the kettle on the windowsill and half covered it with Jazza's lovingly hung curtain.

"But it's the electricity, I think," Jazza went on. "I think that the—"

There was a pounding at our door—the kind of heavy *thump, thump, thump* you might get during a friendly police raid when they come at your door with a battering ram. Jazza jumped a little and mouthed "the kettle, the kettle!" but Boo was already opening the door. Call Me Claudia was standing there, resplendent in a bright plaid dress.

"Bhuvana!" she boomed. "Call me Claudia. Settling in all right?"

"Brilliant, yeah," Boo said.

"Coming in midterm can be quite difficult. I assume you two will do everything to help her along?"

Jazza and I nodded and mumbled our yeses. Claudia lingered for a moment, a widening smile on her face. She was staring at Boo as if Boo were the source of true Enlightenment.

"Excellent hockey skills," Claudia said. "Truly excellent."

"I was captain of mixed hockey at my old school, yeah."

"Excellent. Well, finish settling in. You know where I am if you need me."

Boo closed the door behind Claudia. "See?" she said. "No problem with the kettle! So what do you lot do around here?"

"We study," Jazza said. "And there's tea and cereal down the hall."

"For fun?" Boo said.

Jazza was stumped.

"We can't go out much," I said. "Studying. Stuff like that."

"What school were you at before here?" Jazza asked politely.

"Just the local sixth form. But it's not that good and they thought I was advanced and all, and my gran is paying, so they moved me here."

Boo dumped out an entire bag's worth of sequined pillows. Jazza's gaze moved over all of Boo's things, the electronics and clothes and accessories. I did the same, trying to figure out what she was looking for—and I saw soon enough. Something was missing. Books. There were no books at all.

"What subjects are you taking?" Jazza asked.

"Oh, same as Rory. French and, um . . ."

Boo flopped down on the ground and stretched herself long across the floor to reach the front pocket of her bag and plucked out the already crinkled schedule. She rolled onto her back to read.

". . . further maths, literature, art history, and normal history."

"Are you doing A levels in all of those?" Jazza asked.

"What? Oh, yeah. Well, maybe. Yeah. Some of them."

Jazza and I sat on our beds on opposite sides of the room

judging our new roommate, who was now doing some leg stretches and flashing us her blue lace underwear in the process. Boo went right on talking, unaware or unconcerned by any awkwardness. Mostly, she talked about television shows I didn't know or had only heard of in passing.

There was nothing wrong with Boo. She was certainly friendly, and I was in no position to judge anyone for their attitude toward their work. Wexford wasn't the toughest school in England, but it wasn't the easiest either. Boo's attitude toward her classes just wasn't quite right. You didn't just show up a month late, then roll around on the floor, barely aware of what subjects you were taking.

But then, I realized, I had no idea what happened in England. Maybe it was completely normal to do just that. I was the outsider, not Boo. I'd built up an illusion in this room with Jazza—an illusion that this was home, that I understood the rules here. Boo, quite accidentally, made me remember that I understood very little, and at any moment, the rules could change.

# 18

GATORS ARE JUST SOMETHING YOU HAVE TO ACCEPT where I come from. Most don't go anywhere near the houses, even though there are lots of delicious children and dogs there. Every once in a while, though, an alligator has a lightbulb moment and decides to take a stroll and see the world a bit. One day when I was eight or so, I opened the back door, and I saw this thing way at the end of the yard. I remember thinking it was a big black log—so, of course, I went down to look at it, because what's more exciting than a big log, right? I know. Children are stupid.

I had gotten about halfway down the yard when I realized the log was moving toward me. Something in the primitive part of my brain immediately said, "Alligator. Alligator. ALLIGATOR." But for a second, I couldn't move. I had to stand there and watch the thing come toward me. It looked genuinely happy, like it couldn't believe its luck. It started slowly, waddling its way closer to get a better look. And there I was, with my brain still saying, "ALLIGATOR. ALLIGATOR." Something finally clicked, and I started running like hell toward the house, screaming one of those high-pitched screeches only kids can do.

Okay, maybe it didn't get *that* close and it didn't move *that* much, but it still came toward me, and if you've been chased by an alligator at any distance or speed, I don't think people should get all "But how *far* was it? And how fast was it going?"

And I'm not saying that having Boo Chodhari in my room was *exactly* like having an alligator in my yard, but there were certain similarities. It broke the illusion that this space was our own. It wasn't. The school was just an environment—a little ecosystem—over which we had no control.

My initial assessment was correct—Boo and Jazza were not exactly the best match. Both of them were nice, and both of them tried, but they were simply too different. There were no fights, but they didn't say much to each other, which was out of character for both of them. And Boo was always around. Always. If I went to study, she went to study. If I went to the bathroom, she needed to "do her teeth" or sit on the radiator and talk and file her nails. And her stuff . . . Her stuff was everywhere. Bras, shirts, papers, cords . . . There was a path of stuff from Boo's bed to the closet to the door. We had to make our beds and keep things generally kind of tidy. Charlotte could enforce this. Before Boo came, Charlotte never bothered to check our room, because it was always fine. But now she was stopping by once, sometimes twice a day to get Boo to pick her crap up off the floor. This did not breed warm feelings between the two of them.

Also, Boo carried two phones with her at all times. Two. She tried to hide this fact at first, but I'd see her with them both. One was a very new, very shiny phone. The other was older, with actual buttons instead of on-screen ones. I finally asked her why, and she said that she reserved one phone for guys she'd just met. "So they don't have your regular number, yeah? They have to earn the regular number, once I make sure they're not creepers."

And though she dutifully sat with us in our room and in the library or the common room, and she carried around books and opened them, Boo did absolutely no work whatsoever. In fact, she had the power to diminish the concentration of anyone sitting near her. You'd realize that she was humming under her breath or tapping her long nails on the table, or you'd hear the sound of a soap opera or reality show leaking from her headphones, and your own attention would dissipate.

Jazza quickly became obsessed with observing all Boo's study habits and reporting them to me. The days got shorter. The air got colder and crisper, and my knowledge of Boo Chodhari's every study habit grew exponentially.

"Has she even started on that essay you have for English literature?" Jazza asked me over breakfast on the three-week anniversary of Boo's arrival. Boo generally didn't make it to breakfast. That was the only time I didn't see her.

"I have no idea," I said, drinking my lukewarm juice. "I haven't started it yet."

"I just don't understand her," Jazza said. "She didn't even bring any books with her. She does literally no work. Literally.

She missed a month of school. And why does she always carry those two phones? Who carries *two phones*?"

I continued eating my all-sausage breakfast, letting Jazza get it out of her system.

"It's you she likes," Jazza said. "She always has to go where you go."

"We're in the same classes."

"Your roommate again?" Jerome said as he joined us. This was not a new topic for breakfast.

"I'm finished now," Jazza said.

Jerome started violently slicing apart his fried eggs. It was fascinating to watch him eat. He chowed down with the speed and force of a well-organized military campaign. He didn't so much have breakfast as defeat it.

"Bit of news," he said. "Someone's donated a pile of money for a Bonfire Night party. No one's going to be allowed out, so they're doing something here."

"What's Bonfire Night?" I asked.

"Remember, remember the fifth of November?" Jerome said.

"Nope," I replied. "I have no idea what you're talking about."

"Guy Fawkes Night," Jazza explained, sighing at the change in subject. "Fifth of November, 1605. A group of people led by Guy Fawkes had a plan to blow up the Houses of Parliament, the Gunpowder Plot. But he failed and was executed. So on the fifth of November, we burn things."

"And blow things up," Jerome added, throwing down his fork. "Fireworks are very important. Anyway, it's going to be a dance, and it's fancy dress. Kind of a belated Halloween thing."

"Formal?" I said.

"Fancy dress means costumes," Jazza said.

It was clearly one of those mornings when I was particularly American. That happened sometimes.

"Thursday the eighth is the final Ripper night. So they're having an early Bonfire Night party the Friday before, and then they're going to lock us in until the Ripper stuff is over. Hope you like being indoors, because we'll be in all week."

"I don't care," Jazza said. "Just as long as it ends."

"Who knows?" Jerome said. "Maybe this Ripper wants to keep it going. No reason for him to stop. Maybe he wants to be the new and improved Ripper."

Jazza shook her head and got up to refill her tea.

"What if he does that?" I asked Jerome. "What happens?"

"Well, then the police have no idea when he'll strike or where or how many times, and everyone freaks out every single day. I don't think the eighth of November is the thing to worry about—it's what comes after. I think that's when whatever this is really starts."

"But you're an insane conspiracy nut," I pointed out.

"Granted."

Jerome and I had reached that point where I could say things like that. It was only a slight exaggeration. I ripped off a piece of my doughnut and threw it at him. He had eaten everything on his plate and had no food to fire back with, so he crumpled his napkin and chucked it at my head. Charlotte gave us a reproachful look from the end of the table.

"Don't make me use my powers on you," he said quietly.

"I'd like to see you try."

I sent a low-flying piece of doughnut just inches over the table surface, right at his prefects' tie.

"Jerome . . . ," Charlotte said.

"Yes?" he replied, not looking over.

"You know you shouldn't be doing that."

"I know many things, Charlotte."

He turned and gave her a smile and gave me a little shiver. It was pleasantly evil. I remembered now—Charlotte and Andrew had once gone out. Andrew and Jerome were best friends. Jerome probably *did* know many things. Charlotte simply turned away, as if she had forgotten what was going on.

"Okay," I said very quietly. "Your powers are a little hot."

It was as open a declaration as I'd ever made. I waited to see how he would respond. He looked down at his plate, still smiling.

"What's going on now?" Jazza said, setting down her tea and throwing a leg over the bench.

"We're annoying Charlotte," I said.

"Finally," Jazza replied in a low voice, "a hobby of Jerome's I can fully support. Carry on."

I didn't even mean for it to, but Jazza's commenting got to me. I started to watch Boo when we sat in the library together that afternoon during our free period. We sat across from each other at a table in the corner, our laptops back to back. I was trying to cram in the writing of the aforementioned essay. This was the first major assignment I'd had for literature—seven to ten pages on any work of my choice that we'd already read. I was doing mine on Samuel Pepys's diary, mostly because that was the reading I understood the best. Boo had her computer open, but she was reading a gossip site. I could see the reflection in the window.

"What are you working on?" I asked quietly.

"What?" she said, pulling off her headphones.

"What are you working on?"

"Oh. Just reading."

"What are you doing your essay on?"

"Not sure yet," she said, yawning.

I gave up and went to get a book. Boo followed me, dawdling along behind me, staring at the books like they were very interesting objects from some other universe. As I made my way to the criticism section, I saw Alistair sprawled in the middle of an aisle, reading. He had his book on the floor and was idly turning the pages with one hand.

"Hi," I said, switching on his light.

"Hello."

Boo regarded Alistair with surprise. She immediately walked up to him.

"Oh . . . hello. I'm Bhuvana. Everyone calls me Boo."

"Boo?"

Boo burst out laughing. Alistair and I just stared at her.

"Sorry," she said. "I am called Boo. That's always funny, though."

Alistair nodded dismissively and turned back to his book.

"It's nice to meet you," Boo said. "Really."

"Is it?" he asked.

"This is Alistair," I explained to Boo. Then to Alistair I said, "I need a good book on Samuel Pepys."

"McCalistair. The one with the blue cover and the gold lettering."

I scanned the shelf for a book that fit this description.

"Rory and I are roommates," Boo said. "I'm new."

"Well done," Alistair replied. "So there are two of you now."

"Three," I said. "We have a triple."

I found the book and held it up to him for confirmation. He nodded. It was huge—a two-hander with a layer of dust on top. I thought we were done, but Boo sat down on the floor next to Alistair.

"Is this your favorite spot?" she asked.

"It's private," he said.

"You go," she said, waving me off. "I'm going to talk to Alistair for a while."

I had serious doubts about how well that would go down with Alistair, but he raised no objection. If anything, he seemed slightly curious about Boo and her incredibly forthright approach to conversation. Whatever the case, if it gave me five minutes away from her, I was taking it.

I went back downstairs to my table and opened the book. It had a pronounced old book smell, and pages that had been allowed to turn very slightly golden, but not brown with age. Alistair had given me a serious book, one that covered every aspect of Samuel Pepys's life. It was time to be a serious student, so I found the section of the book devoted to the section of the diary I was reading at the moment and tried to develop an interest. But what I was really watching was the light in the aisle upstairs. It clicked off, and neither Boo nor Alistair emerged, and Boo didn't switch it back on. They had to be talking, or . . .

It was hard to imagine Boo and Alistair instantly making out, but that actually made a lot more sense than the idea of them having a long conversation. Alistair liked books and emo eighties music and being poetic—and Boo liked the opposite of all of those things.

Her notebooks were there, just inches away from me. I hesitated for a moment, then, using my pen, dragged the one marked Further Maths over to me, keeping one eye on the balcony in case Boo emerged. I flipped open the notebook. Not many pages had been used. The ones that had were covered in doodles and song lyrics and the occasional equation for what looked like good measure. There was no work in it at all, not a single effort to solve a single problem set. I closed the book and pushed it back.

Since I'd already violated her privacy, I decided there was no reason to stop there. I pulled over the history notebook. Same thing. A few scribbled notes, some doodles, but nothing usable. Boo *really* wasn't trying, to an alarming extent. Jazza was right. Chances were, Boo would be kicked out soon enough, and we'd get our room back. I wasn't proud of this thought, but it was the reality.

Boo came out of the aisle above, and I dropped the heavy research book on top of her notebook as she passed along the balcony toward the stairs. Once she was on the stairs, her view was blocked, and I shoved the notebook back to about the place where I'd found it. Boo wasn't exactly meticulous, so I didn't think she'd notice if it was an inch or two out of place.

She dropped down in her seat and put her headphones back on. I kept my eyes on the book, as if I'd been reading all along. She had her laptop open, like she was working, but I could see her screen's reflection in the window. She was watching a soccer match online. We were pretending for each other.

There was something very weird about Boo Chodhari, something more than the fact that she wasn't doing any work for school. I wasn't sure what it was, but I had a strong feeling I should be watching her a lot more carefully.

# 19

SATURDAY MORNING, I HEADED OFF TO ART HISTORY with Boo at my side. Jazza had gone home for the weekend. Boo and I were on our own for a few days. I had been assigned the task of reporting back every single thing Boo did in her absence. I hadn't told Jazza about the library incident yet, mostly because it really didn't make me look good. In boarding school, you have to respect other people's privacy. I couldn't just say that I'd been looking at Boo's notes. That violated the unspoken code.

"I still can't believe this," Boo groaned as we walked over to the classroom buildings. "Class on Saturday mornings. Isn't that against the law or something?"

She pronounced the word *something* like *somefink.*

"I don't know," I said. "Probably not."

"I'm going to look it up, because I think it is. Child welfare or somefink."

In the classroom, everyone was milling around

with coats on. Today we were taking one of the trips Mark had promised us on the first day.

"Everyone have their Oyster cards?" Mark asked. "Good. So, we'll walk over to the Tube together. If we get separated, go to Charing Cross. The museum is right there. We'll meet in room thirty in one hour's time."

Jerome lingered with his hands in his pockets, waiting for me to walk with him. I hadn't taken the Tube yet since my arrival, so I was nerdily excited about this. Our lives at Wexford were very contained. I was finally going to *London,* even though I'd been in London the whole time. There was the famous sign—the big red circle with the blue line through it. The white-tiled walls and the dozens of electronic ads that kept time with you as you went down the escalators, changing their displays so you could watch an entire commercial. The floor-to-ceiling ads for albums and books and concerts and museums. The whoosh of the white trains with the red and blue sliding doors. Boo put her earbuds in immediately and slipped into a daze once on the train. I sat next to Jerome and watched London go by, station after station.

When we got off, we were on Trafalgar Square, the massive plaza with Nelson's Column and the four big stone lions. The National Gallery was just behind them, a palace-like structure on its own island of cobbles and stone.

"Today," Mark said, when we finally assembled in room thirty, "I want you to get the feel of the galleries by doing something quite simple and, I think, fun. I want you to partner up and choose one object or subject, then find five treatments of that subject in paintings by five different artists."

"Partners?" Jerome asked.

"Sure," I said, trying to smile in a relaxed way.

I don't think Boo actually knew we were partnering up. She hadn't taken her earbuds out and was now looking at the assignment sheet with a baffled expression. I hurried Jerome out of the room before she noticed where we had gone. Around us, I could hear other people making their choices—horses, fruit, the Crucifixion, domestic bliss, windmills, the Thames, business transactions. None of these things seemed very interesting.

"So what do you think we should do?" Jerome asked.

We had stopped by *The Rokeby Venus,* which is a huge painting by Diego Velázquez of a woman lounging around, admiring her face in a mirror held by Cupid. But the picture is painted from behind, so the focus of the painting is mostly her butt.

"I suggest we do ours on 'five treatments of the human butt,'" I said.

"Agreed," he said, smiling. "Bottoms it is."

For the next hour, we went around the National Gallery assessing butts. There are a lot of naked butts in classical paintings. Big, proud, classical butts everywhere, sometimes draped with a little cloth for flavor. We favored the bigger butts with the most detail. We gave points for best cracks, best dimpling, and best smiley curvature around the upper thigh. We differed on only one issue: I liked the reclining butts, Jerome liked the action butts. Butts leading people into battle, butts about to get on a horse, butts giving speeches, butts looking dramatic. Those were his kind of butts. I liked the way the more relaxed butts squished on one side, and the cheeky over-the-shoulder look most of their owners gave. "Behold," they seemed to say. "Amazing, isn't it?"

Within an hour, we had three excellent butts on our list. We made notes about the paintings, the periods, the colors, the context, all that. We had just gone back into one of the smaller galleries, one full of tiny paintings, when I felt Jerome standing much closer to me than he really needed to.

"Now, that," he said, "is a fine butt."

I looked around. This was primarily a fruit room, with a few paintings of angry priests thrown in for kicks. Only one painting was blocked from my view by a woman standing right in front of it. The woman was wearing a very form-fitting knee-length skirt with a red swing jacket with cropped arms. The jacket stopped right at her waistline, so her butt was well displayed. She even wore seamed black stockings and low, thick heels. Her bobbed hair was elaborately arranged in tight curls, close to the head.

From the loopy smile on his face and the way he was craning his neck a little, I finally figured out that he meant my butt, not hers. It took me a second to realize Jerome could come out with a line that bad—and mean it. I wasn't even sure how my butt looked in my Wexford skirt. Gray, I guessed. Kind of woolly. But there was a goofy sincerity to his effort that made me flush. We were going to public kiss. Actually here, in this museum, in front of real people and possibly our classmates.

"Sorry," he said. "I had to say it."

"It's okay," I said, stepping closer. "But I think she heard you."

"What?" he asked.

We were pretty much face-to-face now, whispering to each other.

"I think she heard you."

"Who heard me?"

"The *lady.*"

"What *lady?*"

We were chest-to-chest and stomach-to-stomach. I had my hands on his waist. He put his hands on my hips as well, but he wasn't making a kissing face. He was making a "what are you talking about?" face, which is squishier.

The woman turned and looked at us. She had to have heard everything we were saying about her. For someone so dressed up, her face was remarkably plain. She wore no makeup and her skin was dull. More than that, she looked extremely unhappy. She walked out of the gallery, leaving us alone.

"We chased her off," I said.

"Yeah . . ." Jerome detached his hands from my hips. "Still not following you."

Just like that, the moment blew away. There would be no kiss. Instead, we were both confused.

"You know what?" I said. "I'm going to go to the bathroom for a second."

I tried not to run through the maze of rooms, past the pictures of fruit and dogs and kings and sunsets, past the art students doing sketches and the bored tourists milling around trying to look interested. I needed the bathroom. I needed to think. I was getting dizzier by the second. First, I saw a man standing in front of me that my roommate didn't see. Second, I had just seen a woman standing in front of a painting, and

Jerome hadn't seen her. The first time kind of made sense. It was Ripper night, we were rushing back, we were scared of getting caught, it was dark. Yes, Jazza could have missed him. But there was no way Jerome could have missed what I was talking about today—which meant either we didn't understand each other at all, or . . .

Or . . .

I found the bathroom finally, and it was empty. I looked at myself in the mirror.

Or I was crazy. Healing Angel Ministry crazy. I certainly wouldn't be the first in my family to see people or things that weren't there.

No. It had to be simpler than that. We had to just be misunderstanding each other. I paced the bathroom and tried to come up with some interpretation of his words that made it all make sense, but nothing camc to mind.

Boo came in.

"You all right?" she said.

"Uh . . . yeah. Fine."

"You sure?"

"I just . . . I must not be feeling well. I'm just a little confused."

"Confused how?"

"It's nothing," I said.

I went into one of the stalls and locked the door. Boo stood outside.

"You can tell me," she said. "Honestly. You can tell me anything, no matter how weird it sounds."

"Just leave me alone!" I snapped.

Nothing for a moment, then I saw her feet backing away

from the stall. She paused by the door, then I heard it open. I looked out to see if she had gone. She had. I emerged and went to the sinks.

"I misunderstood," I said aloud to myself. "That's all. I don't get the English stuff yet."

With that, I splashed some water on my face, fixed on a smile, and stepped out. I would find Jerome. I would make him explain to me what I was missing. We would laugh, then we would kiss with tongue, and all would be well.

As I walked back through the galleries, I saw Boo on the phone, pacing. She never spoke to anyone that intently. Then she hung up and dodged around a group of tourists and headed toward the lobby. Little threads began to connect themselves in my head. I didn't know what this all added up to, but something was coming together. A strange and sudden impulse came over me.

While we were technically in class, Mark wasn't watching us—and when the class was over, we were free to leave on our own. And I couldn't stay here anymore, anyway.

So I followed her.

She stood on Trafalgar Square, just under the museum steps, and made another phone call. I watched this from above, from the raised entrance of the museum. Then she hurried to the entrance of Charing Cross Tube. I went down the stairs after her, tapping my Oyster card on the turnstile, and followed her down the escalators to the tracks. She got on a Northern Line, the black line, and rode the train two stops. At Tottenham Court Road, she switched to the Central Line going east—that was the way back to school. Our stop was Liverpool Street. But at Bank, she switched again, to the District Line, still going east. To keep out of her sight, I had to stay at the far end of the cars and hope she wasn't paying too much attention. Luckily for me, Boo was Boo, head down, looking at her phone, adjusting her music.

She got off at Whitechapel and stepped out onto the incredibly busy road full of market stalls and small restaurants of all kinds—Turkish, Ethiopian, Indian, American fried chicken. Across the street was the Royal London Hospital—a name I vaguely recognized from some news report. Whitechapel was Ripper central. I let her get a little bit ahead of me, but not too far or she'd be swallowed up in the crowd. I had to push my way along to keep her in my sights, weaving around the vendors who sold shopping bags and African masks and umbrellas. It was a busy Saturday afternoon, and the street was packed. The air was thick with the smells of shops selling grilled halal meat and spicy Caribbean chicken and goat. I got stuck several times behind people with bags or Styrofoam containers of food and had to use all the meager skills I had developed dodging hockey balls in the goal to get through. (Despite the fact that Claudia told me every day that dodging the balls was *not the point* of being in goal, it was the only lesson I learned.)

Boo walked quickly, turning off Whitechapel and heading down a side road, turning again and again, so quickly that within five minutes I knew I could never find my way back on my own. Boo began to wave frantically at someone over in the playground across the street. I looked over and saw a young woman dressed in a brown wool suit. It looked like an old-fashioned kind of uniform—a female soldier's uniform, but not a modern one. Her dark brown hair was tightly made up in a retro style, medium length and done up in tight curls around the edges, under her hat. She was picking up trash from the playground and throwing it away. No one got that dressed up in some kind of 1940s outfit to clean streets.

Boo glanced both ways and ran across the street, barely missing a car. I stepped behind a big red mailbox and watched her talking to the woman, guiding her over to a more secluded spot. After a minute or two, a police car came down the street. It slowed and pulled up next to the playground. Out of it stepped the young policeman from the day of the murder, the one Jazza thought was a reporter.

I felt myself go cold all over.

"What the hell?" I said out loud.

Now it was the three of them—the woman in the brown wool uniform, the young policeman, and my roommate—all in a very animated conversation. It was like the entire world was colluding to make me feel insane, and it was doing a *really good job.*

I tried to make sense of the scene. The policeman had to be a real policeman. If he was a reporter, as Jazza suspected, he couldn't go around in a disguise *all the time.* He wouldn't have a police car. Boo had come into the school right after the murders. Boo went everywhere I went. As for the woman in the uniform, I had no idea who she was, and I didn't care. The fact that Boo and the policeman were talking together in secret was enough.

And then, one of the many other people coming down the street walked through the woman in the uniform.

*Through* her.

In response to this, the woman simply turned and glanced over her shoulder with a kind of "Well, that was rude" look. This was all I needed to see. There was something wrong with me, no question. I couldn't stay there hiding behind a mailbox. The little green man came up on the street-crossing sign, so I crossed, my head swimming. I walked right at them. I needed help. I could feel my knees weakening with every step.

"There's something wrong with me," I said.

The three of them turned and stared at me.

"Oh, no," the policeman said. "No . . ."

"I didn't!" Boo said. "She must have followed me."

"Are you all right?" the woman asked, striding toward me. "You need to sit down. Come on, now."

I allowed the woman to guide me to the ground. Boo came over and squatted by my side.

"It's fine, Rory," she said. "You're okay."

The police officer kept back.

"She needs our help," Boo said to him. "Come *on,* Stephen. It was bound to happen."

The woman in the uniform was still hanging over me.

"Just breathe evenly," she said. She had one of those voices that you don't argue with, or even question.

"You're fine, Rory. Honestly. You're fine. We're going to help you. *Aren't we?*" Boo looked at Stephen as she said this.

"And do what exactly?" he finally said.

"Take her back to yours," Boo said. "Talk to her. Jo, help me get her up."

Boo helped me up on one side while the soldier woman took the other. Boo did most of the lifting. The policeman, Stephen, opened the door to the police car and waved me into the back.

"It wasn't supposed to happen like this," he said. "But you had probably better come with us now. Come on."

"Give her a paper bag to breathe into," the woman in the uniform called to Boo. "Works wonders."

"I'll do that," Boo called. "See you later, yeah?"

As a small crowd of interested onlookers stopped to watch, I allowed Boo and the policeman to put me in the back of the police car.

# 20

So I got to ride in a London police car.

"My name is Stephen," the policeman said as he drove. "Stephen Dene."

"Rory," I mumbled.

"I know. We met."

"Oh, yeah. Are you actually a cop?"

"Yes," he said.

"So am I," Boo added.

Stephen was taking us right into the center of town. We went around Trafalgar Square, weaving our way around double-decker buses and cabs. We passed the National Gallery, where my day had started, and continued up the road, coming to a stop just a short distance beyond it. Stephen and Boo got out, and Stephen came and opened my door. He offered me his hand to help me out, but I rejected it. I needed to walk on my own. I needed to concentrate on a task, or I would lose my rapidly slipping grasp on reality.

We were on a very busy street, full of theaters and shops and people.

"It's this way," Stephen said.

They guided me to a small alley. There was a pub hidden down there, and the stage exit of a theater. Then we passed under a brick arch, and the alley got narrower, and suddenly we were on a street that was like something out of Dickens and really out of place with the area around it. Cars couldn't come down this way—the path was only about six feet wide. The houses were all made of brown brick, with old gaslights in front, huge windows with black panes, and shiny black doors with big brass knockers. You could tell that it used to be a little street of shops, and these were all the old shop windows. The sign on the wall said Goodwin's Court.

Stephen stopped in front of one of the doors and opened it by entering a code into a number pad. The building was small and quiet, with a very modern but plain entryway and a stairwell that smelled strongly of new carpet and paint. A series of lights came on automatically as we went up the steps to the third floor, where there was just one door. I could hear a television on inside—some kind of sports coverage. Cheering.

"Callum's home," Boo said.

Stephen made an affirmative sound and opened the door. The room we walked into felt large, considering the smallness of the street. It was sparsely furnished with two old sofas, a few lamps, and a battered table covered in papers and files and mugs. Everything looked like the cast-off pieces from someone's grandmother's house—one floral sofa, one brown. Floral mugs. The rest was IKEA or cheaper. I could tell that the place itself—its size, its newness, its careful maintenance—was well above the price range of its occupants.

The occupant was sitting on one of the sofas, watching a soccer game on television. I saw the back of a head, with black, closely cropped hair, then a heavily muscled arm with a tattoo of some kind of creature holding a stick. The owner of the hair and arm raised himself up from a slouched position to peer over the sofa. It was a guy, one in a tight polo-neck shirt that stretched across his chest. He was probably about my age. It also appeared he knew exactly who I was, because he said, "What's she doing here?"

"Change of plan," Stephen said, tearing off his coat and throwing it over a chair.

"Kind of a *major* change of plan, wouldn't you say?"

"Turn the television off, will you? This is Callum. Callum, this is Rory."

"Why is she here?" Callum said again.

"Callum!" Boo said. "Be nice! She just found out about *you know what.*"

Callum held his bag of food out to me. "Do you want a chip?" he asked. When I shook my head, he dug in and retrieved a burger.

"Are you going to eat that now?" Stephen asked.

"I was eating when you came in! Besides, it's not going to help her, letting my food get cold. What are you going to do now, exactly?"

"We're going to explain," Stephen said.

"Well, this should be interesting."

"It wasn't my decision," Stephen said.

"She needs to know," Boo cut in.

Their conversation spun around me. I didn't even try to follow it. Callum switched off the television, and I was planted on one of the sofas. Boo sat with Callum, and Stephen got a kitchen chair and sat directly in front of me.

"What I'm about to tell you is going to be a little hard to accept at first," he began.

I giggled. I didn't mean to. Stephen looked over his shoulder at the others. Boo nodded to me encouragingly. Stephen turned back and took a deep breath.

"Have you recently had a brush with death?" he asked.

"They should really include that question in job interviews," Callum said.

Boo elbowed him hard, and he shut up.

"Think," Stephen said. "Have you? Has anything happened to you?"

"I choked," I said after a pause. "A few weeks ago. At dinner."

"Since that incident, you've been seeing people . . . people that other people don't see. Am I correct?"

I didn't need to answer. They already knew.

"What's happening to you is a rare but far from unknown condition," he said.

"Condition? Like a disease?"

"Not a disease . . . more of an ability. It won't hurt you in any way."

Callum was about to interject again, but Boo reached over and punched the underside of his bag of fries.

"Shut it," she said.

"I didn't!"

"You were about to."

"Both of you," Stephen said, more seriously this time. "Stop. This isn't easy for her. Remember how it felt."

Callum and Boo stopped tittering and tried to look composed.

"What you're seeing—"

"Who," Boo cut in again. "Who she's seeing."

"*Who* you're seeing . . . those people are real. But they're dead."

Dead people you could see. That meant ghosts. He was saying I saw ghosts.

"Ghosts?" I said.

"Ghosts," he repeated. "That's the usual term."

"I know lots of people who say they can see ghosts," I said. "They're all crazy."

"*Most* people who claim to be able to see ghosts can't. Most of the people who claim they have seen ghosts simply have very overactive imaginations or are easily suggestible. But *some* people can, and we are some of those people."

"I don't want to see ghosts," I said.

"It's brilliant," Boo said. "Really. The woman you saw on the street. She's dead. She's a ghost. But she's not scary. She's lovely. She's a good friend of mine. She died in the war. She's so amazing. Her name is Jo."

"What I'm saying is," Stephen continued, "the ability is rare, but it's nothing to be concerned about."

"Ghosts?" I said again.

"This is going well," said Callum, shoving a handful of fries into his mouth. "I wish you'd done it this way with me."

"Let me explain," Stephen said, adjusting his chair a little to back up an inch or so. "The ability to do what we can do . . .

it's not understood very well, but we do know a few things. Two elements need to be in place. One, you have to have the underlying ability. Possibly it's genetic, but it doesn't appear to run in families. Two, you have to come very close to death during your adolescence. This part is key. No one develops the ability after eighteen or nineteen. You have to—"

"Almost die," Callum said. "We all almost died. We all had the trait. Now we all have the sight."

They gave me a few moments to process this information. I got up and went to the window. There wasn't much of a view. I could see the brown brick of the building a few feet away, and a pigeon roost on top of the opposite roof.

"I can see ghosts because I choked?" I finally said.

"Correct," Stephen replied. "Basically. Yes."

"But I'm not supposed to be worried about it?"

"Correct."

"So . . . if I'm not supposed to be worried about it, why am I sitting here with you? You said you were police. What kind of police? Why did the *police* come to tell me I could see *ghosts*? How can you even be police? You're, like, my age."

"No age requirements in our line of work," Callum said. "The younger the better, really."

"This is where it gets a little more complicated," Stephen said. "We didn't come to tell you that you can see ghosts. We happened to be working, and this happened to you today, and Boo thought you needed an explanation."

"Working on what?" I said. "What are you doing?"

"We're assisting with the investigation. You're a witness. It's standard procedure to watch over a witness."

Finally, I did the math. I was a witness. I could see ghosts. I had seen someone on the night of a Ripper murder, someone Jazza couldn't see, even though he was right in front of her. Someone whom no camera could film. Someone who left no DNA. Someone who walked away without a trace . . .

I had the not entirely unpleasant sensation of falling. Falling, falling, falling . . .

The Ripper was a ghost. I had seen the Ripper. The ghost Ripper.

"I think she's figured it out," Callum said.

"What the hell do you do?" I asked. "If he's a . . ."

"Ghost," Boo said.

"Then what do you do? You can't stop him. You can't catch him. He knows I saw him. He knows where I live."

"You need to trust us," Stephen said, holding up his hands. "You're actually the safest person in London right now. You need to go on with your life completely as normal."

"How do I do that?" I asked.

"You'll adapt," he said. "I promise. The initial shock wears off quickly. A few days, a week, and you'll be fine. We're all fine. Look at us."

I looked at them—Stephen, so young and so serious. Boo, smiling away next to me. Callum, keeping suspiciously quiet and shoving food into his mouth. They did look pretty normal.

"I'll be with you," Boo said. "I'm staying until this is all over. Nothing is going to happen to you."

"So I just go back?" I said.

"Correct," Stephen replied.

"And go to class, and play hockey, and talk to my parents—"

"Yes."

"But what are you going to *do*?"

"We can't tell you that," Stephen said. "I'm sorry. What we do is classified. You can't tell anyone that we've met. You can never discuss this conversation. You just have to trust us. We are police. We are looking after you."

"How many more of you are there?"

"The entire force is behind us," Stephen said. "The security services. There are people working on this at every level of government. You have to trust us."

I had never experienced this feeling before. My heart had been going fast all through this discussion, but now it slowed and I was almost sleepy. My system could take no more. I sat down on the sofa again and put my head back and stared at the ceiling.

"I need to go to bed now," I said. "I just want to go home."

"Right," Stephen said. "I'll take you two back."

Boo walked me to the door and out into the hall while Stephen got his coat and keys.

"I'm not one hundred percent sure that was a good idea," I heard Callum say.

# 21

AT THE END OF THE SCHOOL YEAR AT THE UNIVERSITY where my parents teach, you can see parakeets in the trees. This is because some students get pets during the year, and they think they're temporary, because some people are just like that. When they leave campus, they open up the cages and let the birds fly right out of the window.

My uncle Bick has a soft spot in his heart for the birds left behind. During exam week, he drives around looking for them. He really means well, but Uncle Bick can be a little scary looking, with his bushy beard and his battered truck with the WANT TO SEE MY COCKATOO? sticker on the back, cruising around slow by the dorms. Eventually, someone freaks out, and campus security gets called, and Uncle Bick gets pulled over and has to explain that he's just trying to rescue parakeets. Since they never believe him, he has them call my mom's office, because she is his sister and his lawyer and a Distinguished Member of the Faculty. Then my mom sits Uncle Bick down and explains where the state of Louisiana stands on Peeping Toms (a fine of five hundred dollars and up to six months in jail), and how it really isn't good for her career to have her brother repeatedly stopped on campus under suspicion of violating said Peeping Tom law—and then Uncle Bick rails on about the poor little parakeets and how something should be done. After about an hour of this, we all go out for pit barbecue at Big Jim's Pit of Love because there's just no point in talking about it anymore. This family ritual of ours signals the start of summer.

One year while out parakeet hunting, Uncle Bick caught a little green one he named Pipsie. Pipsie had clearly had a hard life. When Uncle Bick found her, she was sitting on a stop sign, tweeting her head off. She had a broken wing and was missing one foot. Other parakeets would have given up, but Pipsie was a survivor. She managed to get herself on top of that sign and get rescued. I don't know how. She couldn't fly.

Pipsie was undernourished and dehydrated, and her feathers were coming out. Uncle Bick nursed little Pipsie back to health with a care and devotion I couldn't help but admire. He'd sit for hours, dripping water into her beak through an eyedropper. He fed her mashed food from the end of a coffee stirrer. He bound up her broken wing until it healed.

"Look at how she adapts," he'd say whenever I came into the shop. "Look at her. She's a lesson to us all. We can all adapt."

Which is great, except . . . Pipsie didn't really adapt. Her wing healed crooked, so she could only fly about six inches off the ground in semicircular patterns. She fell off the perch all the time, so Uncle Bick just kept her in a box on the counter. One day, Pipsie got it in her tiny bird mind that she could fly again. She got up to the edge of the box and surveyed the landscape and spread her crooked wings and went for it. She fell off the counter and landed on the floor, just as the delivery guy swung the door open and rolled in three hundred pounds of birdseed on a hand truck.

This is all I could think about after Stephen told me to "adapt."

Stephen drove Boo and me back to school, dropping us off a few streets away so that no one would see us coming back to school grounds in a police car. It was only five o'clock. People were filing into the refectory for dinner. I was too nauseous to eat. Boo was starving, though, so we walked over to the local coffee place, where she could get a sandwich. I watched her devour a ham and brie.

"So," I said, "it's your job to hang around with me?"

"Pretty much," she said.

"How does this work?"

"Well, Stephen's an actual police officer with a uniform and everything. Callum works undercover on the Underground, because there's loads of ghosts down there. And I'm new. My first assignment was to come and watch over you."

"So you had something happen to you?" I asked. "That's why you're like this?"

"When I was eighteen, I was a bit of a club kid—"

"When you were eighteen? How old are you now?"

"Twenty."

"Twenty?"

"I'm a fake student," she said. "With a fake age. Anyway, my friend Violet and I were coming home from a club. She was driving. I knew she was drunk. I should never have gotten in the car. I should have stopped her. But I was kind of drunk myself, and I didn't always make the best decisions back then. We ran smack into a bollard. There was smoke, we were bloody, Violet was unconscious. I heard this voice telling me to keep calm, to get out of the car. I looked over, and it was Jo. She was standing there. I was crying, completely freaking out, but she talked me through it. We've been best friends since then. Actually, I tried to get her a phone for Christmas. She can carry things—not big things, but she can lift things like phones. But it's kind of hard owning things when you're a ghost. You don't have pockets or anything. And people would just see a phone floating around, which would be weird. She picks up trash because she likes to keep busy, and apparently people don't notice trash moving. They think the wind's blown it or someone's thrown it. You have to think about these kinds of things when you're a ghost."

"I don't know if I can do this," I said.

"Do what?"

"This *thing*. This thing that I am."

"Course you can. There's nothing to *do*, anyway. It's just natural, yeah?"

"How am I supposed to do all this work?" I said, running my hands through my hair. "This essay. I have to write it this weekend. I have to write an *essay* on Samuel *Pepys* and his stupid frickin' *diary* and I can see *ghosts*."

I walked around the room, picking up my things, putting them back down again, trying to establish some baseline of reality. Everything seemed the same. Same room. Same Boo. Same ashtray. Same unwashed mug with red wine residue in it.

Boo ate her sandwich and watched me.

"I've got it," she said, brushing the crumbs from her lap onto the floor. "The library."

As it was a Saturday night and just before dinner, there were only a handful of people in the library, and those who were weren't the kind who paid much notice to other people. They were all deep in their zones—headphones, computers, books. Boo walked the floor quickly, weaving in and out of all the stacks downstairs, then going upstairs and doing the same thing. Alistair was sprawled on one of the wide windowsills at the end of the literature section, authors Ea–Gr row. He had one leg stretched high, his Doc Martens boot planted flat against the side of the window, the other hanging down. He seemed to be the focus of Boo's search, because she walked right up to him.

"She knows now," Boo said.

Alistair lazily lifted his gaze from the book.

"Congratulations," he said drily.

I still had no idea what we were doing. My thoughts were moving very slowly. They both looked at me, and when I didn't respond, Boo explained.

"What we just talked about," Boo said. "Alistair is . . . like that."

"Like . . ."

And then I realized why Alistair was looking at me like I was so stupid. The eighties look he was rocking—that was no look. That was his actual hairstyle from the actual eighties.

"Oh, my God," I said. "You're . . ."

"Yeah! He's dead."

Boo said it like she was telling me it was his birthday. Alistair looked . . . like a person. The spiked hair and the rolled jeans and the big trench coat . . . I reached up and touched my own hair—longish, straight, very dark—and was suddenly very glad that I hadn't dyed it pink, like I'd been considering. Pink hair for a few weeks, fine. Pink hair for eternity, that I wasn't so sure about.

Which was not a good or decent thought to be thinking. I should have been thinking about the nature of life, the idea of dying at eighteen at school, the idea that for some people, death wasn't the end. But those were all big thoughts, too big for me right now. So I concentrated on his hair. His eternal hair. His eternal Doc Martens.

I started laughing hysterically. I laughed so hard, I thought I was pretty much going to throw up in the middle of the literature section. Someone came into the end of the aisle and stared at me in annoyance, but I couldn't stop. When I finally got it under control a little, Alistair slipped down from his perch.

"Come on," he said. "Might as well show you."

He walked us down to the ground floor, to the research section, by the librarian's desk. There was a shelf full of *The Wexford Register,* the school newspaper, bound in green leather.

"March 1989," he said.

Boo pulled the 1989 volume down and set it on one of the nearby tables. She flipped through to March. The paper looked weirdly cheap and cheesy, roughly typed. We found a large photo of Alistair on the front of the issue from March 17. He was smiling in the photo, his hair particularly large and obviously bleached blond even in black-and-white. The headline read "Wexford Mourns Death of Student."

"'Alistair Gilliam died in his sleep on Thursday evening,'" Boo read softly. "'He was the editor of the school literary magazine and was well-known for his love of poetry and the band the Smiths' . . . in your sleep?"

"Asthma attack," Alistair said.

I started to giggle again. It rose up in my throat. The librarian looked over with an annoyed expression and put his finger to his lips. Boo nodded, replaced the book, and we returned to the privacy of the upstairs stacks. After checking to make sure we were basically alone, she continued the conversation.

"You didn't die here," Boo said quietly. "So why do you come here?"

"Would you want to stay in Aldshot all the time? At least here I can read. Got nothing else to do. Read everything in here—twice. Well, most of it. Lots of it's shite."

"It's great how you can pick up the books and turn pages," Boo said.

"It took time," he said. "But what about you two? You usually don't come in pairs."

"You've met people like us before?" Boo asked.

"One or two over the years. But they're always alone, and always a bit mental."

Not a great endorsement of my kind. And from the way Alistair was looking at me, I could tell that he hadn't quite put me in the nonmental category yet.

"We're a bit special," Boo said. "I'm a police officer."

"You're a rozzer?" Alistair laughed properly for the first time.

"*Yes,* me," she said. "We're working on the Ripper case. The Ripper is . . . like you."

"What do you mean, *like me*? You mean dead?"

Boo nodded.

"Dead, but nothing like me. We're not all alike, you know."

"Course!" Boo said. "Sorry!"

"I'm not into killers," Alistair replied. "I was a vegetarian. Meat is murder, you know."

"I'm *really* sorry."

Boo reached out and touched his arm. He looked solid enough.

"How are you doing that?" I said. "I saw someone walk through that other woman."

"Oh," Boo said. "It depends on the person. Some people are really solid. Some are a bit more like air. Alistair is more solid. Can you pass through things? Doors, or walls?"

"I don't like to," he said. "I can. It takes time."

"The more solid, the longer it takes and the harder it is. The ones who are more like air, they can do that more easily, but they're not as physically strong. It's harder for them to move things. But all ghosts are people, and you just respect them, no matter what they're like, yeah?"

Alistair seemed mollified by this ghosts' rights speech.

"Rory is needed for the investigation, see?" Boo said. "And she's just found out what she can do, and it takes some time to adjust to that. She has this assignment to do, and obviously, she can't do it. So, I was thinking, maybe you could help?"

Alistair didn't, to my surprise, walk away or simply evaporate in disgust (because, for all I knew, he could do that).

"What is it?" he asked.

"Six to eight pages on the major themes of *The Diary of Samuel Pepys,*" I said automatically.

"*The Diary of Samuel Pepys* is massive," Alistair replied.

"Oh . . . I mean, just the part about the fire."

"The major theme of the part about the fire is the fire."

"Also . . . rhetorical technique, or something."

"Could you help us with that?" Boo asked. She had an alarmingly huge smile. "I mean, you're obviously clever, and we have a murderer to stop. Can you type, or—"

"I *don't* type."

"Or write," she said quickly. "Can you hold a pen?"

"I haven't practiced in a while," he replied. "I used to be able to do it. When do you need it?"

"Tomorrow morning?" I replied.

Alistair tapped his mouth with his fisted hand and thought for a moment.

"I want music," he said.

"Music!" Boo nodded. "We can get you music! What music do you want?"

"I want *Strangeways, Here We Come* by the Smiths and *Kiss Me Kiss Me Kiss Me* by the Cure—"

"Wait, wait . . ."

Boo hurried off. I heard her making her way down the steps. While she was gone, I just stared at Alistair and he stared back at me.

"Pen," she said as she returned. She held up a pen as proof. "Say those again."

Alistair repeated his album choices, and Boo wrote them down on her palm.

"And *London Calling,*" he added, leaning over to make sure

she was getting the names right. "I want *London Calling* by the Clash."

"I'll get you these albums tonight," she said, holding out her hand so he could see what she had written. "And something to play them on. Deal?"

"I suppose," he said. "Wait . . . I also want *The Queen Is Dead.* Also by the Smiths."

"Four albums," she said, holding up her palm to show him. "One paper. *Deal?*"

"Deal," he said.

"See that?" Boo asked when we were outside. "Not scary, is he? And your paper is sorted."

There was something in what she was saying. Alistair hadn't scared me. There was really nothing weird about the conversation at all, if you discounted the fact that we had discussed an article about his death.

"Are there any other ghosts around here?" I asked.

"Not that I've seen, but sometimes they're shy. A lot of them love attics, basements, underground areas. People scare them. Funny, isn't it? People are scared of ghosts, ghosts are scared of people, when there's no reason for any of it."

"Except that the Ripper is a ghost," I said. "There is no humanly possible way for me *not* to worry about that. And Jerome thinks I'm insane."

"Oh." Boo waved her hand dismissively. "He'll forget."

"I don't think he will."

"Course he will. And it's only Jerome."

My silence intrigued her.

"You?" she said. "And Jerome?"

I remained silent.

"Seriously? You and Jerome?"

"It's not . . . It's not a—"

"Oh," she said, smiling hugely. "Then don't worry. I'll fix it."

# 22

JEROME DIDN'T FORGET. OF COURSE HE DIDN'T FORGET. I saw an invisible woman and ran away from class. No one forgets that. And then I'd hidden myself away for the rest of the day, which didn't help.

When I walked into breakfast the next morning, I saw him sitting with Andrew. He raised his head when he saw me come in and nodded. Boo and I got into line. She filled up a plate with a full English—eggs, bacon, fried bread, mushrooms, tomatoes. Like me, she could put it away. That morning, though, I had no appetite. I took some toast.

"No sausage?" the lady behind the counter said. "Feeling ill?"

"I'm fine," I said.

"Don't worry so much," Boo said.

We took our seats, sitting on the opposite side of the table from Jerome and Andrew. They'd left space for us, as normal.

"Hi," I said.

Jerome looked over at me from the remains of his breakfast. "No sausage?" he asked.

Apparently my pork consumption habits were a matter of public record. Boo dropped down next to me, her spoon bouncing off her tray and clanking to the floor.

"Rory here," she said. "Sick all night. Crazy fever. Babbling her head off about ponies."

"Fever?" This caught Jerome's attention. "You were ill yesterday?"

"Mmmm," I said, glancing over at Boo.

"Babbling and babbling, like a babbling thing," Boo went on. "Madness. Wouldn't shut up."

"Have you been to the nurse?" Jerome asked.

"Mmmm?" I said.

"She's really fine," Boo said. "Probably some period thing. I go completely mental too. Period fever. It's the worst."

This effectively killed all conversation for a while. Boo charged right on, telling us a very long story about how her friend Angela was getting cheated on by her boyfriend, Dave. No one tried to interrupt her. I just got through my toast as quickly as I could and excused myself. Boo was right behind me.

"Fixed that," she said.

"You told him I had *period fever,*" I replied. "There's no such thing as period fever."

"No such thing as ghosts either."

"No, there is *really* no such thing as period fever. There's a difference between being a guy and being *an idiot.*"

"Let's get your essay," she said, looping her arm through mine.

Boo waltzed me into the library, and I allowed myself to be waltzed. Alistair was tucked into a deep corner in the extremely unpopular microfilm section, behind a machine. Boo had provided him with a tiny iPod, and he was listening to something, eyes closed. I guess the earphones didn't stay in his ears because he didn't really have ears, but he managed to hold them up. The music flowed out of them into the air. As we came up, he opened his eyes slowly.

"On the shelf," he said. "Between the bound copies of *The Economist,* 1995 and 1996."

I went to the spot he directed us to. There, between the books, were fifteen handwritten pages, with footnotes and comments scribbled in the margins. I had just pulled these out when Jerome approached us. Boo grabbed them from me.

"Sorry," he said, "but . . . can we talk?"

"Mmmm?" I replied. No guy had ever asked me if I wanted to talk, not like that. Not like a talk, talk kind of talk—if this was, in fact, a talk, talk "can we talk?" Or whatever.

"You go," Boo said, shoving the papers into her bag. "I'll see you later."

I walked toward Jerome slowly, afraid to look at him. I no longer knew how to behave. I had been assured that I wasn't insane, but that wasn't very helpful. There was a ghost ten feet away from us who had done my homework, and Jerome couldn't see him.

"You're welcome," Alistair called after me.

We stepped outside into the steel gray morning. I didn't care that I was cold.

"Where do you want to go?" he asked. There was something nervous about the way he was standing, his shoulders hunched and his hands deep in his pockets, his arms locked to his sides.

Lacking any better idea, I suggested Spitalfields Market. It was big, it was busy, it was cheerful, and it would distract me a little. It used to be a market for fruits and vegetables. Now it was a ring of boutiques and salons. In the middle was a loosely enclosed space, one half devoted to restaurants, the other to stalls full of everything from tourist junk to handmade jewelry. Shoppers buzzed all around us. The racks were heavy with Jack the Ripper merchandise—top hats, rubber knives, I AM JACK THE RIPPER and JACK IS BACK shirts.

"What's going on with you?" he finally asked.

What *was* going on with me? Nothing I could tell Jerome. I'd never be able to tell anyone what was going on with me, with the possible exception of Cousin Diane.

We had passed all the way through the market and were in the small courtyard on the side. We sat down on a bench. Jerome sat close, his leg almost against mine. I got the feeling he was keeping just a little space in case I turned out to be irredeemably insane. But he was giving me this chance now to explain. And explain I would, somehow. I would say *something.*

"Since the night, with the . . . with the Ripper . . . I've been . . . freaked out? A little?"

"That's understandable," he said, nodding. He was willing to try this out as an excuse for my behavior. I had to keep him talking about this topic—his favorite.

"Who is Jack the Ripper?" I said.

"What do you mean?" he asked.

"I mean, you read everything about Jack the Ripper—who is he? I think I'd feel better if I . . . understood what he was. What it was all about."

He moved a millimeter or two closer.

"Well, I suppose the first thing is that Jack the Ripper is kind of a myth," he said.

"How can he be a myth?"

"What's known for sure is this: there was a string of murders in the Whitechapel area of London in the autumn of 1888. Someone was killing prostitutes, in more or less the same way. There were five murders that seemed to have the same signature—slash to the neck, mutilations to the body, and in some cases, removal and arrangement of the internal organs. So those are known as the Jack the Ripper murders, but some people think there were four murders, some six, some more than that. The best guess is that there were five victims, and that's what the legend is built around. But that could be completely wrong. If you go to the Ten Bells Pub, for instance, they have a plaque on the wall commemorating six victims. So the facts of the whole thing are unclear, which is part of the reason it's almost impossible to solve."

"So this killer is following one version of the story?" I said.

"Right. He's not even following a very nuanced version of the story. It's pretty much the Wikipedia version or the version from the movies. The name. That's another issue. Jack the Ripper never called himself Jack the Ripper. Just like now, there were dozens of hoaxes. Loads of people sent letters to the press claiming to be the murderer. Only about three of these letters were considered to be even possibly real—and now the general opinion is that they're all fakes. One was the 'From Hell' letter, which is the one that James Goode got. Another was signed Jack the Ripper. That one was probably written by someone from the *Star* newspaper. The *Star* got famous because of Jack the Ripper. They took the stories of these murders and created one of the first media superstars. And they did a really good job, because here we are, over a hundred years later, still obsessed."

"But there have been other murderers since," I said. "Lots of them."

"But Jack the Ripper was kind of the original. See, he was around when the police force was fairly new and psychology was just starting out. People understood why someone might kill to steal something, or out of anger, or out of jealousy. But here was a man killing for seemingly no reason at all, hunting down vulnerable, poor women, cutting them apart. There was no explanation. What made him so terrifying was that he didn't need a reason. He just liked to kill. And the papers played the story up until people were mad with fear. He's the first modern killer."

"So who did it?" I asked. "They have to know."

"No," Jerome said, leaning back. "They don't know. They never will know. The evidence is gone. The suspects and witnesses are long dead. The vast majority of the original Jack the Ripper case files are gone. Keeping records for the long term wasn't considered that important back then. Things got thrown away. People took souvenirs. Papers got moved, lost. Lots of records were lost in the war. It's exceedingly unlikely that we will ever find anything that conclusively identifies Jack the Ripper. But that won't stop people from trying. They've been trying nonstop since 1888. It's the one magic case that everyone wants to solve and no one can. Pretending to be Jack the Ripper is pretty much the scariest thing you could possibly do because he's a total unknown. He's the one that got away with it. Does any of this actually make you feel better?"

"Not really," I said. "But it's . . ."

This time, it was definitely me. I leaned into him, and he put his arm over my shoulders. Then I put my head against his, and his curls pressed into my cheek. From there, it was a slow turn of the head until our faces were together. I started pressing my lips into his cheek—just a hint of a kiss, just to see how it went. I felt his shoulders release, and he made a little noise that was partly a groan, partly a sigh. He kissed my neck, up, up, up to my ear. My muscle control began to slip away, as did my sense of my surroundings. My body flushed itself with all the good chemicals that it keeps in reserve for making out. They make you stupid. They make you wobbly. They make you not care about Jack the Ripper or ghosts.

I reached up and ran my hand along the back of his neck, deep into his hair, then I pulled his face closer.

# 23

CLEARLY, JEROME AND I HAD A COMPLICATED THING going on. He told me scary Jack the Ripper facts, and I had the sudden need to make out with him until I ran out of breath. I would have continued indefinitely if Boo hadn't bounded up to us like a deranged puppy. Jerome and I detached so quickly that a thin bridge of saliva connected us for a glittering moment. I swung it away.

"Heya!" she said. "Sorry! I didn't realize you came here too! Came over for a coffee."

She held up a coffee as proof.

Jerome was so startled that he had a violent coughing fit.

"Well," he said when he recovered. "I . . . well. Hello."

"Hi," Boo said. She was still standing there, bouncing lightly on the balls of her feet.

"Yeah," he said. "I'd best get back. I have a physics lab to work on."

He got up abruptly and left.

"Sorry," Boo said. "It's my job to follow. And I wouldn't have interrupted, but I had an idea. You need a bit more practical experience. It'll help you. And since you don't have to do that paper and it's Sunday, we can go out."

Boo had an ability to attach herself to me and steer me around. Her grip was like iron. She began to move me out of the market and down the street, toward the Tube. About forty-five minutes later, for the second time in less than twenty-four hours, I turned up on Goodwin's Court. Boo half dragged me down the alley and pressed the silver buzzer on their front door.

"How do you even know they're home?" I asked.

"They'll be home," she said. "One of them's always here."

No answer. Boo buzzed again. There was a crashing noise, followed by an electronic squawk.

"What?" a male voice yelled.

"It's me!" Boo yelled back. "I have Rory with me!"

"You what?"

I thought it was Callum, but it was hard to tell.

"Let us up!" Boo yelled.

A mumbled something on the other end, and the intercom went dead.

"I don't think they like it when I come over," I said.

"Oh, they don't mind."

"I think they do."

Nothing from the door. Boo pushed the intercom again, and this time, the door buzzed open. Again, up the stairs with the automatic lighting. I could see that the staircase was very well maintained, with tasteful framed black-and-white photos up the staircase and a highly polished silver rail. The apartment on the first floor bore a small glass sign on the door: DYNAMIC DESIGN. Upstairs, Callum was at the door, dressed in the same snug shirt and a pair of shorts. He held a mug of something steaming hot.

"What are you doing?" he asked Boo in a groggy morning voice.

"Just bringing Rory round."

"Why?"

Boo ignored this and stepped past him, dragging me in with her.

"Where's Stephen?" Boo asked, taking off her coat and hanging it on the rickety coat stand by the door. Callum collapsed onto the brown sofa and regarded us both with tired eyes.

"Out getting the papers."

"What are you up to?" she asked.

"What are we always up to?"

He indicated the stacks of papers and folders scattered all over the table and the floor around it. Boo nodded, made a quick circuit of the room, and planted herself next to him. Stephen came in a moment later. He was dressed in a worn and slightly baggy pair of jeans. I'm not sure they were supposed to be baggy; I think he was just thin. With his striped black sweater, red scarf, and glasses, he really looked like a student, probably in the English department. Someone who quoted Shakespeare for fun and used Latin terms for things. He did not, under any circumstances, look like a cop. But as soon as he saw us, he got that look on his face—instantly focused.

"What's happened?" he asked.

"Nothing," Boo said. "I just brought Rory round."

"Why?"

No. They didn't want me here. Boo had not caught on to this.

"I was thinking," she said. "We should go ghost-spotting. Rory's never been."

Stephen stood there for a minute, gripping his newspaper.

"Can I speak to you in the other room for a moment?" he said.

Boo got up, and the two of them disappeared into another room. Callum continued to sip his tea and watch me. In the other room, I could hear a very animated conversation, one low voice (Stephen's) and one relatively higher voice (Boo's). I distinctly heard Stephen say, "We are not social services." The higher voice seemed to be winning.

"I didn't ask to come here," I said. "I mean, here, to this apartment. Today."

"Oh, I know." Callum stretched lazily and turned to watch the door where the conversation was going on. Last time, I had taken in the basics about Callum—he was black, he was shorter than Stephen, he was extremely well built, and he wasn't thrilled about my presence. All of those things remained true today. In the daylight and in slightly less shock, I could take in some more. Like Boo, Callum had an athlete's build—he wasn't huge, just well developed in what looked like a very deliberate way. His face was round, with wide, appraising eyes and a mouth that always seemed to be cocked in a half smirk. He had very thick, very straight eyebrows, one of which was sliced through by a scar.

"What's the thing on your arm?" I asked, pointing at his tattoo. "Is that some kind of monster?"

"It's a Chelsea lion," he said patiently. "For the football club."

"Oh."

I wasn't being stupid. It didn't look like a lion. It looked like a skinny dragon with no wings.

"So how do you like England so far?" he asked.

"It's kind of weird. You know. Ghosts. Jack the Ripper."

He nodded.

"Where are you from?" he said. "That accent?"

"Louisiana."

"Where's that again?"

"In the South," I said.

The conversation in the other room had gone down in volume.

"I don't even know why he bothered," he said, stretching again. "Boo was always going to win. Better get dressed."

He got up and went out of the room, leaving me alone. The apartment, I noticed, looked very much like Boo's part of the room—stuff everywhere. Maybe seeing ghosts made you give up on cleaning. I could see that certain parts of the room were reserved for certain activities. The coffee table was for eating—it was covered in tinfoil takeout dishes and mugs. The table by the window had a computer and lots of files, with boxes full of more files on the floor. The walls around the table were covered in notes. I had a look at them. They all seemed to relate to the Ripper—dates, locations. I recognized some of the names and photographs of suspects from 1888 from the constant news coverage. What was unusual, though, is that there were comments about these people—places of burial, locations of death, home addresses. It looked like Stephen and Callum and Boo had gone to these places and checked them out, adding notes like "uninhabited" or "no evidence of presence."

I moved away from the wall of notes when I heard someone returning. Stephen and Boo came back in, followed by Callum, who was now wearing jeans.

"Perhaps we should do an hour or two of ghost-spotting," Stephen said, not sounding very enthusiastic. Boo was beaming and doing some hamstring stretches.

"We should take her underground," Callum said. "It's easier there. It'll take five minutes, tops."

"Maybe in the train tunnels," Boo said. "But not on the platforms."

"I *work* there. I should know. I saw about fifty once."

"You never!"

"I did. Not all in one place, but all around one station."

"Around one station? So in the tunnels, then."

"*Some* of them were in the tunnels. But I'm telling you. Fifty."

"You're such a liar," Boo said with a laugh.

"There's one hanging around Charing Cross," Callum said. "I've seen her loads of times. Let's just take her there and get this over with."

"Fine," Stephen cut in. "Charing Cross."

My approval was not needed on the idea.

It was a cool day. The sun was out, and the leaves were just changing. The other three, being English and used to colder weather, wore no coats. I did, and I pulled it tight around me as we walked down the busy streets, past some West End theaters and pubs, around a church and through Trafalgar Square. There were loads of tourists on the square, taking pictures of each other climbing on the huge lions at the base of Nelson's Column, screaming as legions of pigeons swooped down at their heads. I didn't really feel like a tourist anymore. I wasn't sure what I was. I was definitely feeling increasingly self-conscious about being with these three, since I was a clear disruption to the routine and probably an annoyance, but feeling self-conscious was better than feeling crazy. They were ignoring me anyway and having a debate about paperwork.

"So then we fill out a G1 form . . . ," Stephen was saying.

"What I don't understand," Callum replied, "is why we call it G1, since we only have one form. Can't we just call it *the form*?"

"We only have one form now," Stephen said, not looking up. "We might have other forms in the future. Also, G1 is actually shorter than *the form*."

"Here's a better question," Callum replied. "Why have a form at all? Who's going to check? Who's going to care? No one knows we exist. No one wants to know we exist. We're not taking people to court."

"'Cause," Boo said. "We need a record. We need to know what we did. We need it to train other people to do this job. And ghosts are still people. They were someone. Just because they're not alive—"

"You know what? I think *being alive* should be a primary way of figuring out who is and who isn't a person. I think that should be question number one. Are you alive? If yes, go on to question two. If no, *you should not be reading this*—"

"Oh, that's *such* rubbish. One of my best friends happens to be a dead person."

"All I'm saying is," Callum said calmly, "since we can do this any way we want—and how often do you get that chance in life?—why did we choose to do this in a way that involves paperwork?"

"I can make a G2 if you want," Stephen said magnanimously. "Just for you. Special form for interdepartmental incidents involving both the police and the transport system. We'll call it Callum's Form. A Callum 2A could be for the Underground. You'd get a Callum 2B for any incidents on buses. Maybe a Callum 2B-2 is any incident that takes place at a bus shelter."

"I will kill you, you know."

"And if you do," Stephen said with a hint of a smile, "and I come back, I am going to haunt the hell out of you."

We'd reached the steps of the Charing Cross Underground station, and Stephen turned to me and re-included me in the conversation.

"Here's what you need to understand," he said in a slightly lecturing tone. "London is one of the world's oldest continually inhabited cities. We've had multiple wars, plagues, fires . . . and we keep building on top of old grave sites. Loads of buildings are built on old plague pits. The Tube system alone was responsible for disturbing *thousands* of graves. As far as we know, most ghosts tend to stay around the places they died, places that had some major significance in their lives, or, occasionally, the place where their body is buried. Their range varies. But the Tube has lots."

"Lots and lots and lots," Callum added as we reached the turnstiles.

Callum waved a pass that got him in for free. The rest of us tapped our Oyster cards, and the gates opened to admit us. I followed them to the escalators.

"The thing you have to remember," Boo said, "is that ghosts

are just people. That's it. They aren't scary. They aren't out to get you"—Callum made a strange noise—"they aren't spooky or weird, and they don't fly around with sheets on their heads. They are just dead people who've gotten stuck here for a bit. They're usually quite nice, if a little shy. Normally, they're lonely and they like to talk, if they can."

"If they can?"

"There's a lot to learn," Stephen said. "They take a lot of forms, some more corporeal than others."

"So, who becomes a ghost? Everyone?"

"No. It's fairly rare. From what we can tell, ghosts are people who just haven't . . . died completely. Their death process isn't complete, and they don't leave."

This I sort of understood. My parents work on a college campus, and I'd spent some time around it. Sometimes people graduate but they don't leave. They hang around for years, for no reason. I would think of ghosts like that, I decided.

"Ghosts look like people, so you often can't tell the difference," Boo said. "You have the ability to see them, but it doesn't mean you know what you're looking at."

"It's like hunting," Callum cut in.

"It is nothing like hunting." Boo elbowed him hard. "They're *people.* They look like living people, because you're used to seeing living people. You assume everyone you see is alive. You have to consciously start separating the living from the dead. It's tricky at first, but you get the hang of it."

"She's down here," Callum said. "I saw her on the Bakerloo Line platform."

We followed him down the steps to that platform. The London Tube had such a reassuring, almost clinical appearance—

white-tiled walls with black-tiled edges, neat and distinctive signage, the cheerfully colored map . . . signs showing the WAY OUT and barriers to keep people moving in the right directions . . . staff in purple-blue suits and computer screens showing the status of trains . . . big ad posters and electronic ad boards that flashed mini-commercials. It didn't look like something dug out of an old plague pit. It looked like a system that had been here for all of time, pumping people through the heart of the city.

A train had just come in, and the platform emptied out except for us and the handful of people who were too slow. Then I noticed the dark arches at each end of the platform, the openings for the trains leading to the tunnels—the wind that blew in with each train came from there. And when the train left, I noticed one woman in particular down at the far end of the platform. The toes of her shoes were just over the edge. She wore a black sweater with a thick cowl neck, a plain gray skirt, and a pair of gray platform shoes. Her hair was long and curled off her face in large wings. I guess what drew me to her—aside from the fact that she didn't get on the train and her vaguely retro outfit—was her expression. It was the expression of someone who had given up completely. Her skin wasn't just pale, it was faint and grayish. She was the kind of person you didn't see, alive or dead.

"That's her," I said.

"That's her," Callum confirmed. "She looks like a jumper to me. Jumpers do that a lot, stand on the edge and stare out. Never kill yourself in a Tube station. Tip number one. You might end up down here forever, staring at the wall."

Stephen coughed a little.

"Just giving advice," Callum said.

"Go talk to her," Boo said.

"About what?"

"Anything."

"You want me to walk up to her and say, 'Are you a ghost?'"

"I do that," she replied.

"I love it when you get it wrong," Callum said.

"Once. It happened *once.*"

"It happened twice," Stephen said, looking over.

Boo shook her head and waved me down to the end. I hesitated a moment, then followed a few steps behind until we were next to the woman.

"Hello?" Boo said.

The woman turned, ever so slowly, her eyes wide and sad. She was young, maybe in her twenties. Now I could see her frosted, silvery hair and a heavy silver pendant around her neck. It seemed to weigh her head down.

"We aren't going to hurt you," Boo assured her. "I'm Boo. This is Rory. I'm a police officer. I'm here to help people like you. Did you die here?"

"I . . ."

The woman's voice was so faint that it barely qualified as a sound. I felt it more than I heard it. It made me shiver, it was so soft.

"What? You can tell us."

"I jumped . . ."

"These things happen," Boo said. "Do you have any friends here in the station?"

The woman shook her head.

"There's a lovely burial site just a few streets over," Boo went on. "I'm sure you could meet someone there, make some nice friends."

"I jumped . . ."

"Yeah, I know. It's okay."

"I jumped . . ."

Boo glanced over at me.

"Yeah," she said. "You said. But can we—"

"I jumped . . ."

"Okay. Well, we'll come back and visit. Is that all right? You have friends. You're not invisible to everyone."

Callum looked very smug as we walked back.

"Jumper?" he asked.

"Yes," Boo said.

"Give me five pounds."

"We didn't have a bet, Callum."

"I just deserve five pounds. I can tell a suicide from fifty paces."

"Enough," Stephen said. "Rory, how did that go?"

"It was okay, I guess," I said. "Eerie. She just kept saying she jumped. And her voice was . . . cold. Like a cold breath in my ear."

"She was a quiet one," Boo said. "Not very strong. Scared."

"Why do they wear clothes?"

Callum and Boo laughed, but Stephen nodded.

"That's a very good question," he said. "They *should* be naked, or so you'd think, right? Yet they always come back clothed. At least every time I've seen them. This lends itself to the theory that what we're seeing is a kind of manifestation of a vestigial memory, perhaps even a self-perception. So what we're seeing is less of how they were, but more of how they perceived themselves, at least around the time of their death—"

"Skip this part," Callum said to him. Then to me, "Stephen talks like that sometimes."

We returned the way we came, back up the escalators and back into the daylight.

"Now," Stephen said, "you've seen one, and you've seen that there's no—"

But my mind was elsewhere.

"The clothes," I said. "The guy I saw, if he was the Ripper, he wasn't wearing old-fashioned clothes. Not, like, Victorian clothes."

I don't think Stephen had been concentrating too hard on me until I said that. I almost saw his pupils refocus.

"That's correct," he said.

"I told you," Boo said. "She's a quick one."

"So, this Ripper ghost whatever . . . he's not *the* Ripper. Not the Ripper from 1888."

"That's what we concluded from your description," Stephen said, sounding somewhat impressed. "So we stopped pursuing that angle."

"So how do you figure out who he is?"

That made Callum laugh and turn away, clasping his hands behind his head.

"Well," Stephen said, "we're using his choices of location, combined with your E-fit image . . ."

"But how do you find some random dead guy from whenever?"

Even Boo turned away now. "We have ways," Stephen said.

The bright look in his eye had gone out, and he stared at the people sitting on the lions. I had asked something they didn't want to be asked. I got the sense that the more I pressed this, the more unhappy and possibly unhinged I would become. I had to embrace the daylight, the sanity I had at this moment.

"Fine," I said, wrapping my arms around myself.

"We just wanted to give you some experience with your new ability," Stephen said. "But we have to get back to work. Boo will take you back."

"Wait," I said as Stephen and Callum turned to go, "one more question. If there are ghosts, does that mean there are . . . vampires? And werewolves?"

Whatever misery I had caused by my previous question, it was wiped out with this one. They all laughed. Even Stephen, who I didn't know could laugh.

"Don't be stupid," Callum said.

# 24

GHOSTS, ACCORDING TO THE INTERNET:

Souls, spooks, shades, poltergeists, revenants. Generally regarded to be people returned from the dead, though there are also ghost animals, and ghost ships, and even ghost trains and planes and articles of furniture and plants. Often known to linger around places they lived in or died in, looking sad. Both can and cannot be photographed, though when photographed, may appear as a blob or orb of light. Science rejects and confirms their existence. Can be contacted through mediums, who are all fakes.

In other words, the Internet was useless at teaching me anything, except that a lot of people had strong feelings about ghosts, and every culture in the world had something to say about them, through all of history. Also, a lot of people online who claimed to be ghost experts were clearly much crazier than anyone from my town, which was saying something.

What was reassuring, I guess, was the sheer *number*

of people who believed in ghosts and who claimed to have seen them. I certainly would never be lonely. And they couldn't *all* be crazy.

There were about a half-dozen television shows devoted to the subject of ghost-hunting. I watched a few of these. What I saw were crews of people sneaking around houses with night vision cameras, jumping at every noise and saying, "Did you hear that?" Replaying said noise over and over—and the noise was always a little bump or a door closing. Or they'd have some piece of machinery that they'd hold over a spot in the room and they'd say, "Yup, a ghost was here."

Not very impressive. Not one of them was seeing an actual, talking person. The shows, I concluded, were all bull, designed to entertain people who really liked to see things about ghosts, no matter how lame they were.

This little research project of mine, however fruitless, was good at keeping my mind level. I was doing something, and doing something was better than doing nothing. And here's an amazing fact about the human mind: it can cope with a lot. When something new enters your reality that you don't think you can deal with, your mind deals. It does everything it can to accommodate the new information. When the information is so big and so difficult to process, sometimes your brain skips stress and confusion and goes right to a happy island, a little sweet spot.

My new ability didn't interfere with my life. I got used to seeing Alistair—and after all, aside from his haircut, there was nothing odd about him. He was just a grumpy dude in the library. Though he was slightly less grumpy now that he had a bunch of albums and something to play them on. He secreted the iPod Boo had given him with his albums somewhere in the library and he made it clear that he was willing to trade homework for more music. We had found a currency that he accepted.

And I saw Boo every day—someone with the same ability that I had—and she wasn't even remotely bothered by it.

I didn't forget, exactly, but this new knowledge slipped to the back of my mind . . . and I adapted. I was able to move on to more pressing matters, like the upcoming fancy dress party. After several nights of discussion in our room, we had decided to go to the party as the Zombie Spice Girls. Boo was a natural for Sporty, since she could have thrown either one of us over a wall without breaking a nail. Jazza was going to be Ginger, because she had a red wig and a strong desire to make a dress out of a Union Jack flag. (Although it had been explained to me several times, since Jaz's uncle was in the navy, that it was called a Union Jack only when it was flown at sea. Otherwise it was just a Union flag. I was learning all kinds of things in London, mostly about ghosts and flags and disbanded girl groups, but still. Learning is good.) I, apparently, was a natural for Scary. I asked them if this was because my hair was dark, and they both just laughed, so I had no idea what that was about. Mostly, our costumes involved putting on some zombie makeup, tight clothes, and high platform shoes that Boo bought in a second-hand store. We had a plastic bone to represent Posh, and if anyone asked about Baby, we were just going to say we ate her.

Boo was down the hall getting some fake tattoos drawn on by Gaenor. Jazza was squeezing herself into her Union Jack dress, which she had made out of a decorative pillowcase. I was trying to tease out my hair as big as it could go.

"You never showed me your essay," she said, out of the blue. "The one on Pepys. You said you wanted me to read it over."

"Oh . . ." I rubbed the gray makeup hard into my face. "It wasn't as bad as I thought."

"What did you end up writing?"

I had no idea what I'd ended up writing. I'd typed it, but I'd barely read it. It had something to do with the concept of a diary kept for both public and private reading and how that affected the tone of the narrative. So I lied.

"I compared it to modern accounts of major events," I said. "Like Hurricane Katrina. He was writing about the Great Fire of London, which was where he lived. I wrote about how you talk about things that affect you personally."

That was actually a genius idea. I only ever have genius ideas after the fact. I should have just written the damn paper.

"You and Boo have been getting along a lot better this week," she said, doing a chest check. Her dress was really tight. This was a whole new Jazza coming out—almost literally. Normally, I would have started joking about this, but I smelled trouble. Those words meant, "You haven't told me anything about Boo this week, and now I am convinced you like her better than me."

"I've accepted her," I said as breezily as I could. "She's our pet."

Jazza gave me a slight sideways look as she pulled the dress up a little higher over her girlish assets. It was wrong to refer to Boo as a pet. That was normally the kind of thing Jazza would censure, but she said nothing.

"It could be worse," I said.

"Of course," Jazza said, going over to her bureau. "I'm not saying, you know, that I . . . but . . . I've . . ."

Boo returned, dressed in a shiny tracksuit with a lopsided ponytail. I was pretty sure those were just some of her actual clothes, and not something she had gotten as a costume.

"Watch this, yeah?" she said, immediately going into a handstand and walking a few steps. Then she tumbled over and crashed into Jazza's desk, almost knocking over her photos. "Haven't done that since I was fourteen."

Jazza looked at me through the mirror as she attached her false eyelashes.

There was a look on her face that suggested a rapidly dwindling patience level.

We had decided to stick together for at least a half hour, so that everyone could comprehend our group costume. We would share custody of Posh the Bone. The prefects had done a really good job transforming the refectory into a Halloween-ish party venue. Eating in here every day, I had forgotten that it was an old church. These decorations really brought that out—the candles in the stained-glass windows, the fake cobwebs strung everywhere, the low lighting. Charlotte, dressed in a very short-skirted policewoman's outfit, was leading the dancing brigade, jumping around at the front of the room, her long red hair flapping up and down like a matador's cape. She was head girl, and she would show us how to party if she had to.

I wasn't really sure why Charlotte had decided to come to the party as a stripper. I found myself at a loss for words as she complimented us on our costumes.

"You're a . . ." I tried to find the right thing to say. "Really . . . hot cop?"

"I'm *Amy Pond*," she said. "From *Doctor Who*. This is her kiss-ogram outfit."

It was a good moment to catch sight of Jerome. He was wearing normal clothes with loads of scribbled-on pieces of paper stuck all over them, and his hair sticking up, a coffee mug in his hand.

"Tell me what you want, what you really, really want," he said.

We had been planning for someone to ask us that.

"Braiiinnnnssss," we said in unison.

"It's both sad and incredibly impressive that you were all ready with that one."

"What are you?" I asked.

"I'm the Ghost of the Night Before Exams."

"And how long did it take you to come up with that?" Jazza asked.

"I'm a busy man," he replied.

We formed a group on the side of the dance floor—me, Jazza, Jerome, and occasionally Andrew, Paul and Gaenor. Boo, we quickly discovered, was very serious about her dancing. She was right up front, by the DJ stand, doing complicated moves and the occasional surprise handstand.

The room was hot—we were all sopping wet in no time. The stained-glass windows had a veneer of steam. And unlike American dances, they didn't screw things up with that awkward slow dance every five or six songs. This was all dance, with lots of remixes, like an actual club. My Scary Spice outfit, which consisted of a sports bra and oversized pants, was actually a blessing. I would have sweat through a shirt.

Jerome and I didn't dance together, exactly, but we did remain side by side. Every once in a while, he would (seemingly accidentally) touch my waist or my arm. Anything more than that would have been too much of a statement, but I felt I got the message. He also had prefect jobs to do, so he would regularly disappear to refill bowls of food or tend the bar. That was another strange thing—the bar. An actual bar, with actual beer. We had tickets that allowed us two pints each. I have absolutely no idea how this was managed. Jerome had tried to explain it to me—how even though the law was that you had to be eighteen to drink in a pub, the circumstances varied, and at a closed event with teachers somehow this was legal. I got one of my beers, but I was jumping around and sweating too much to drink it. I would have vomited instantly. But two beers seemed to be nothing to the average English student. Everyone else gulped them down, and I was pretty sure that the two-ticket rule was not being very strictly enforced.

As the night wore on, there was a not-unpleasant funk in the air, the scent of beer and dancing. I started to forget any time I wasn't at this place, with the lights strobing against the stained glass and the stone walls, the teachers in the shadows, checking their phones out of sheer boredom.

In fact, at first I thought he was a teacher. He came up behind Jazza. The suit, the bald head.

"What's the matter?" Jaz yelled happily.

Of course, she couldn't see him, even though he was right at her back, standing right up against her. He stroked her shoulder lightly with the tips of his fingers. I saw her twitch a bit and flick at her wig. He stepped around and placed himself between Jazza and me.

"Come outside," he said. "Do it now."

I began to back away, very slowly.

"Where are you going?" she yelled.

"Bathroom," I said quickly.

"Are you ill? You look—"

"No," I yelled back, shaking my head.

Leaving that room was the hardest thing I've ever had to do. I felt the heat of everyone at my back. Outside, it was cold—bright cold, a lifting cold. Every single streetlight was on. Every light in every window. Everything to battle against the dark of the sky, the dark that went up and up and up forever. This thin little halo so low to the ground. The wind was kicking up a fury, spinning leaves and trash around us, and I remember thinking, *This is it. I am walking into forever.* It was almost funny. Life seemed downright accidental in its brevity, and death a punch line to a lousy joke.

Our footsteps were so loud on the pavement. Well, mine were. I don't think he had any. And his voice didn't echo between the buildings. He walked me up to the road, and we walked along beside all the closed shops.

"Just fancied a chat," he said. "There aren't many people I can talk to. I'm not sure if you remember where we first met. It was at the Flowers and Archers. The night of the second murder."

I had no memory of this at all.

"It's quite an unusual ability, what you have," he said. "Part genetics, part dumb luck, something you can never talk about to any rational person. I remember the feeling."

"You were—"

"Oh, yes. I was like you. It's hard, I know. Upsetting. The

dead aren't supposed to be among the living. It offends the natural order of things. All I ever wanted to do in life was make sense of it. And now, here I am . . . part of the puzzle."

He smiled at me.

I was cold from the inside out. My *hair* was cold. My *thoughts* were cold. It was as if every cell in my body stopped doing its cellular duty and stiffened in place. My blood became still and had no life-giving power, and my breath crystallized and pierced my lungs like shards of glass.

"Have you ever met any more like us?" he asked. "Or are you all alone in the world?"

Some impulse told me to lie to him. Telling him that I did meet some people and that they were the *ghost police* . . . It seemed like I was asking for more trouble than I was already in.

"Just some weirdos," I said. "Back home."

"Ah," he said. "Some weirdos back home."

A leaf drifted down from a tree and started to pass slowly through his shoulder on its way to the ground. He flinched a bit and brushed it away.

"Your name—Aurora. It's very unusual. A family name?"

"My great-grandmother," I said.

"It's a name full of meaning. It's the name of the Roman goddess of dawn and of the polar lights."

I had Googled my own name before. I knew all this. But I decided not to interrupt him to tell him that I was aware.

"Also," he added, "of a collection of diamonds right here in London, the Aurora Pyramid of Hope. Lovely name. It's the largest collection of color diamonds in the world. You should see them under a UV light. Marvelous. Do you have any interest in diamonds?"

That's when I saw Boo. She was walking toward us very casually, like she didn't even see him, talking away loudly into her phone in what sounded like a pretend conversation. She must have seen me leave, or seen him. Whatever the case, she was here.

"That girl," he said. "I've seen you with her. I get the sense she annoys you."

"She's my new roommate."

Boo was doing a really good job at pretending she couldn't see him. She was waving at me and talking really loudly.

"Yeah, yeah," Boo was saying into the phone. "She's right here. You talk to her . . ."

"She's very loud," the man said. "That's something I find quite annoying, how everyone speaks so loudly all the time into their mobile phones. Those weren't around when I was alive. They make people so rude."

Boo reached out to me, both hands on her phone. She was gripping it strangely, fingers on the keypad.

He lurched forward and grabbed her by the wrists. In one fluid motion, he swung her into the road, directly into the front of a passing car. It was so fast—two seconds, three seconds. I watched her hit the car. I watched her break the front headlight and slide up over the hood and smack into the windshield. Then I watched her roll down as the driver skidded to a stop.

"Next time," he said, "tell the truth when I ask you a question."

He was right in my face. I felt no breath coming out of him because, of course, he didn't breathe. He was just cold. I kept absolutely still until he backed away and walked off. The driver's screaming stirred me to action. He was out of his car and standing over Boo, saying, "No, no, no . . ."

I stepped into the street, to where Boo was. My legs felt like they weren't quite connected to my body, but I kept moving forward and got down on the ground next to her. There was some blood on her face from where she'd been cut, but mostly, she looked like she was asleep. Her leg was at a terrible, unnatural angle.

"What was she doing?" the driver cried, grabbing his head. "What was she doing? She jumped—"

"Call for help," I said.

The man from the car was still clutching his head and having a meltdown, so I had to yell at him. He took out his phone, his hands shaking.

"Boo," I said, holding her limp hand, "you're going to be okay. It's all going to be okay. I promise. You are going to be fine."

I heard the driver giving the information about where we were, his voice cracking. People hurried up to us. Other people were on phones. But I kept my eyes on Boo, my hand on her hand.

"What happened?" the driver said. "Was she drunk? Did she jump? I don't understand . . . I don't understand . . ."

He was almost crying now. Of course he didn't understand. He'd just been driving his car down the street, and all of a sudden a girl on the sidewalk flung herself into the road. It wasn't his fault, and it wasn't her fault.

"Do you hear that?" I said to her, listening to the approaching sirens. "Help's almost here."

I heard someone running toward us and looked up to see Stephen. He got to his knees and examined Boo quickly. Then he took the phone that was still in Boo's grasp.

"Come on," he said, pulling me to my feet.

"I'm not leaving her."

"There's an ambulance and several police cars right behind us. You have to move. Now. *Now,* Rory. If you want to help her, walk with me."

I took one last look at my roommate lying in the road, then I let him lead me to the awaiting car, and we sped off, lights flashing.

## THE TEN BELLS PUB, WHITECHAPEL
## NOVEMBER 2
## 8:20 P.M.

DAMN, IT FELT GOOD TO BE A RIPPEROLOGIST.

That was the first time Richard Eakles had ever been able to say that, even to think it. Being a Ripperologist had never been cool. Since he was fifteen years old, Richard had been obsessed with Jack the Ripper. He read every book. He obsessed over every site. He was on the forums. By the time he was seventeen, he was going to conferences. And now, at twenty-one, he was a webmaster of Ripperfiles.com—the Ripper site and database widely regarded as the best in the world. Oh, some people—they need not be named—had laughed at his hobby before. No one was laughing now. Now he was needed. Ripperologists were the only ones who could help. Ripperologists had been conducting the Ripper investigation for over a hundred years.

In fact, tonight had been his idea. He'd posted it on the forum. Maybe they should have a conference, discuss theories? The idea took off like wildfire within the Ripperology community. Then everyone wanted in on the action. The BBC. CNN. Fox. Sky News. Japan News Network. Agence France-Presse. Reuters. The list went on and on. And it wasn't just the press that wanted in. Scotland Yard was going to be in attendance as well, and—some people said—MI5. Rippercon was the hottest ticket in London tonight, and he was one of the stars.

And they had the perfect venue, the Ten Bells, the famous pub located smack in the middle of the Ripper zone, a pub frequented by several of the victims back in 1888. These days the Ten Bells was overrun by students and tourist groups fresh off the Jack the Ripper tours. The students came for the cheap drinks and run-down sofas and chairs. The tourists came to take in the ornate original tiling and to drink real English beer in a real English pub where Jack the Ripper had probably *been.*

Tonight, though . . . it was a lot harder to get in. Satellite news vehicles lined the street. There were police and crowds of onlookers and people with cameras. At least a dozen news reporters were outside, giving reports. The pavement was ablaze in camera lights. Richard had to hold up the badge he wore around his neck and squeeze his way in.

Inside, it was even more intense. The Ten Bells was just a normal-sized pub, not the kind of place where you could really fit a major international news conference. The space behind the bar had been converted into a pit for the news cameras, all trained at the one small table at the front of the room, and the small screen and whiteboard that he had requested for his presentation. The windows had all been covered in heavy material so that no one could look inside.

He had done a little quick research online and found that when you went on camera, you weren't supposed to wear patterned clothing. It made the camera go crazy or some such. So he had settled for a plain black dress shirt over his black REMEMBER 1888 T-shirt. He took a moment to greet a few of the other prominent Ripper bloggers, who had been allowed to have the few remaining tickets, then took his place at the table. They really had assembled an amazing panel for tonight, the top Ripperologists from around the world. Three of them from England, two from America, one from Japan, one from Italy, and one from France—every one of them an expert on the case.

Since Richard had helped to put this event together, he was going to be speaking first. His presentation was the most general, but outsiders needed the basic facts.

After making sure that everyone was in place, Richard stood up and faced the crowd. God, it was hot in here. He was already sweating. He gripped the dry-erase marker tightly in his hand.

"Good evening," he said, trying to keep his voice steady. "Tonight's discussion will focus on the fifth canonical murder in 1888. We'll start with an overview of that night, then we'll go into some specifics, some theories, and some 3-D re-creations of the scene. So, let me begin . . ."

So many cameras. So many cameras pointing at him. His whole life had been building to this moment.

"Murder number five," he said. "Mary Jane Kelly. Last seen alive just after two in the morning on the ninth of November, 1888. Her body was discovered in her lodging rooms around ten forty-five the same morning by her landlord, who had come to collect her rent. Kelly was the only victim to be murdered indoors, and her body was considerably mutilated, most likely because the Ripper had the time and privacy to do things in the way that he . . . really wanted. Her clothes were folded neatly on a chair, and her boots placed by the fire. Hers was also the only crime scene to be photographed. We're going to put those photos up now. Please be warned that even though these photographs are of a very low quality by modern standards, they are still extremely graphic."

Richard gave the signal for the lights to be turned down. Even though he had seen this photograph hundreds—maybe thousands of times—it never failed to chill him. This was the photograph that showed just how brutal and terrible the Ripper was, why he needed to be identified, even though he was long dead. The skin of her thighs had been removed and set on a table next to the bed. Her internal organs had been removed, some set around her body in a pattern. Mary Kelly needed justice. Maybe, now that all this was happening, maybe now she would finally get it.

The crowd in the Ten Bells stared at the photograph. It had been shown around a lot in the last few weeks. No one was reacting with the appropriate horror as he ran through her extensive injuries. A few reporters and prominent bloggers took notes. The police sat and listened with folded arms.

"All right," Richard said, "we can bring the lights back up."

The lights didn't come back up.

"All right," he said, louder. "The lights, please."

Still no lights. In fact, everything in the room shut down. All the camera lights went out, as did the power on his computer. There were groans and yells as dozens of live-feed cameras went out at once, and people began bumping together in the intense dark.

Richard stayed where he was, by the board, wondering what to do next. Should he just keep talking? Or should he wait until they were on camera again? It was very difficult, this being in the middle of an international news story.

He felt the pen being removed from his hand and the brisk squeaky noise it made on the board. Someone was writing something on the board, but he couldn't see who. He stepped toward the board, toward the spot where the person had to be and felt around in the dark. There was absolutely no one there.

The pen was gingerly put back into his hand.

"Who are you?" he whispered. "I can't see you."

In reply, the unseen person shoved him forcibly up against the board, crushing his face into it. Then the lights came back on.

Richard heard a confused grumble pass around the room as they took in the sight of him splayed against the board, arms spread. As he backed up a few inches and tried to regain his poise, Richard saw something written on the board in large, bold letters:

**THE NAME OF THE STAR IS WHAT YOU FEAR**

# Inner Vileness

**Do we indeed desire the dead**
**Should still be near us at our side?**
**Is there no baseness we would hide?**
**No inner vileness that we dread?**

***—Alfred, Lord Tennyson,***
***"In Memoriam A.H.H.,"***
***part 51***

# 25

STEPHEN WAS DRIVING WITH A GRIM, FIXED INTENSITY. We sped past the school, past a huge cluster of news trucks and police cars surrounding Spitalfields Market. I had to sit in the back, because you can't sit in the front seat of a police car unless you're actually a police officer—so I must have looked like a criminal to anyone passing by. A young, crying criminal in zombie makeup.

"How did you know where we were?" I said, wiping my eyes with the back of my hand.

"She phoned me and said you had gone missing from the party, then again from the street once she found you."

"I want to go to the hospital."

"That's the last place you're going," Stephen said, glancing at me through the rearview mirror. "You're already in HOLMES."

"In what?"

"HOLMES. The Home Office Large Major Enquiry System. You're in the police database, that's what it means. You're a witness in the Ripper murders, and you're under protection by us. And the police establishment doesn't exactly know we exist. This all just got very, very complicated."

"Complicated?" I shot back. "Boo's back there in the road, possibly dead, and all you can say is that this is *complicated*?"

"I'm trying to keep you safe, to keep you both safe. There was nothing we could do to help her. The ambulance was right behind us. The best thing was to get you out of there." He took off his policeman's hat and wiped his forehead.

"Tell me one thing," he said. "Did anything happen to the Ripper?"

"What?"

"What happened to him after the accident?"

"He walked away," I said.

"Were there lights?" he said again, more urgently. "Sounds? Anything? Are you *sure* he walked away?"

"He walked away," I said again.

Stephen let out a loud, exasperated sound and switched on the car's lights and sirens. Then he hit the gas, and I was thrown back against the seat by the surge in speed. I could basically determine that we were going west, into the center of London. Within a few minutes, I realized that we were headed toward Goodwin's Court. When we got there, Stephen pulled the car over abruptly. I had to wait for him to let me out of the back, then he hustled me down the alley and into his building. The automatic lights clicked on as he hurried me up the stairs.

"I have to ring someone," he said, switching on the overhead light. "You should sit."

Stephen went down the short hallway and into the room next to the living room, leaving me alone for a moment. The apartment was cold, and it smelled stale. There was a bag of used takeout cartons by the door filled with the remains of Chinese food and fish-and-chips. Clothes were strewn about the sofas and chairs. There had been some kind of paperwork explosion over by the window—masses of manila folders turned open, pages piled and stacked and spread out. All the notes on the walls looked like they had been replaced with new ones.

I could hear Stephen through the thin wall. He was talking to someone very urgently.

"How's Boo?" I asked when he emerged.

"I don't know yet. I have someone at the hospital who'll send me a report. Your school has been told that you're with the police giving a statement. You need to sit. We have to talk."

"I don't want to sit. I want to see my roommate."

"She's not your roommate," Stephen said. "She's a police officer. And the one thing you can do to help her is to tell me what you know."

"She's *still* my roommate," I said.

Which was odd. Because not long before, I would have sold Boo to the lowest bidder. Now her welfare was the only thing that mattered.

"Do you want to help her?" Stephen asked. "Then you'll tell me everything."

He indicated the sofa. I sat. He pulled up one of the chairs and sat directly in front of me, leaning forward to look me in the eye, as if he could tell when I was leaving something out by studying my pupils up close. I had been grilled by the police before. At least that experience had prepared me for this.

"The school was having a dance—" I said.

"I know," he cut in.

"You told me to tell you everything," I snapped. "So are you going to listen or are you going to tell me what you already know?"

Stephen put up his hands, conceding the point.

"Go on," he said.

"We were having a dance," I said again. "And we were . . . dancing. Everything was fine. Then he appeared. He was just there . . ."

"He?"

"The man, the guy. The Ripper." Saying "the Ripper" made me queasy. I wiped my nose with the back of my hand. "He stood right in front of me. I mean . . . I could *feel* him. I could feel something. He told me to come outside with him . . . I didn't want to, but . . ."

Only now did it occur to me what might have happened if I hadn't gone. It was possible that he would have just walked away, that Boo would be fine right now. It was equally possible that he would have shoved a knife directly into Jazza's neck. And now that I had a chance to run over the possibilities, I felt myself begin to quake.

"He asked me if I knew where we'd met. I thought it was at school, but he said we met at the Flowers and Archers on the night of the second murder—"

"You were at the Flowers and Archers on the night of the second murder?"

"My . . . friend. Jerome. He wanted to go. We just went to the street, not to the pub. You couldn't get near the pub."

"I was there," Stephen said. "And you're saying he was too?"

"That's what he said. He said we met there, but I don't remember him."

"But he remembered you," Stephen said. "So you must have reacted to him in some way. Even just looked at him, moved around him. He knew you could see him."

"Well, yeah. He knows I can see him. He knows I have it. This thing. That we do. Because he had it too."

"He had the *sight*?"

Something on Stephen beeped. He slapped his pockets until he found his phone, then read a message. He grabbed the remote and switched on the television. The familiar red BBC logo lit up the room.

The newscaster was standing outside on the street bathed in the glow coming from dozens of cameras and their lighting equipment.

*". . . a very strange evening here at the Ten Bells, where the international Ripper conference was held this evening. Conference organizer Richard Eakles had just started his presentation when witnesses say there was a power cut. Eakles claims that while the room was in darkness, someone pushed him up against the board and wrote a message . . ."*

The image cut to a picture of the whiteboard, the words written in all caps, in a firm hand. THE NAME OF THE STAR IS WHAT YOU FEAR.

*"The meaning of the message is unclear,"* the newscaster went on, *"but some people have noted that the quote is similar to one from the Bible . . ."*

"That's from the book of Revelation," I said. "Our local seafood place puts up quotes from the book of Revelation every week. That's why we call it Scary Seafood. It's a quote about the third angel that comes at the end of the world. Something about the star being Wormwood."

There were piles of books along the walls. Stephen scanned through these for a moment, finally finding one he wanted in a large pile. He managed to extract it, but five or six books on top of it came tumbling down. He ignored this and started flipping through the onionskin pages.

"Where, where, where . . . here. 'And the third angel sounded, and there fell a great star from heaven, burning as if it were a lamp, and it fell upon the third part of the rivers, and upon the fountains of waters; and the name of the star is called Wormwood: and the third part of the waters became wormwood; and many men died of the waters, because they were made bitter.'"

On the news, they were back in the studio, and the newscaster was talking to a guest.

*". . . most people here feel that this incident was some kind of stunt, but some concerns have been raised that the real Ripper did somehow manage to leave this message. And if he did, it could have some serious implications. Sir Guy, what do you make of this?"*

*"Well,"* the guest said, *"I don't think we can rule this out as a threat of terrorism. The Bible quote clearly indicates poisoned water. I think we would be remiss if we didn't consider the possibility that this entire incident has been a form of terrorist attack, designed to cause London to . . ."*

Stephen turned off the television, and the room went quiet.

"Right," he said, after a moment. He left the room and went down the hall. He returned with some clothes and a rough red towel. "You can change into these. They'll be more comfortable."

Their bathroom was a pretty no-frills place, just two toothbrushes, two towels, two razors. I scrubbed my skin with a bar of hand soap, turning the makeup to a gray runny mess that stung my eyes and took ten minutes to rinse off. I left big gray streaks all over the towels. When I looked at myself in the mirror, my skin was pale and raw, my eyes were red, and my hair was wet and streaked with makeup and soap. The sight of my reflection almost brought me to tears for some reason. I had to sit on the edge of the bathtub and take a few deep breaths. Then I stripped off the costume and picked up the things Stephen had given me. One turned out to be a pair of sweatpants that said ETON down the leg. The lettering had been broken up from lots of washings and wearings; the words were cracked. Eton was a name I knew. There was also an oversized and overwashed polo-neck shirt from some event called the Wallingford Regatta. Stephen was well over six foot, and I just about made it to five foot four, so I had to roll up the cuffs of the sweats in order to walk.

As I picked up my clothes, I felt my phone in my pocket. I removed it and found that I had several messages from Jazza and Jerome, wanting to know if I was all right. I would answer them later. When I emerged, Stephen was in the kitchen, staring at the kettle as it boiled. He was staring at it so intently, in fact, I wondered if he wasn't controlling the boil with his mind.

"I'm making tea," he said, keeping his gaze on the kettle.

The kitchen was as plain as everything else in the apartment, but the appliances that were built in were high quality—all stainless steel and sleek. The counters were made of a sparkling granite, and the cabinets were smoked glass. The surroundings didn't match the small card table that served as a dining table, or the plastic folding chairs, or the mismatched mugs.

"I spoke to someone at the hospital," he said. "She's awake. They're x-raying her now. She seems to have several broken bones. They're not sure of the extent of it, but she's awake. That's something."

I took a seat at the table and pulled my feet up onto the chair. The kettle rumbled and clicked off. He dropped two tea bags into mugs.

"This is a nice place," I said, just to make it less quiet.

"We got it at a steep discount." He brought the mugs over to the table. Mine had a chip on the rim. "We could never afford to live around here, but . . . there was another inhabitant who was giving all the other tenants trouble. No one wanted to live here. We sorted it out."

"A ghost?"

He nodded.

I wrapped my arms around my legs and placed my forehead on my knees.

"You're the only police looking for the real Ripper, right?" I asked. "Because the regular police can't see him. What if you can't stop him?"

"We can," he said. He set a box of shelf-stable milk in front of me, punctuating his remark. He had said all he was going to say about that. We sat in silence for a few moments, looking at our tea but neither of us drinking it. We just let it steep, darker and darker, like our thoughts. The kitchen wasn't very well lit, so there was a closeness—a gloom around us.

"What happened to you?" I asked. "To make you like this?"

He tapped his mug with his spoon, considering his answer. "Boating accident. At school."

"Eton," I said, pointing at the leg of the pants. "That's where you went?"

"Yes."

"And how long have you been . . . this? A policeman, or whatever you are?"

"Two years."

Stephen removed the tea bag and set it on a lid from a takeout container. He seemed to be weighing something in his mind. He took a long breath and exhaled loudly.

"Everyone's always known that London is full of ghosts," he said. "It's a particularly haunted city. And in that spirit of organizing things and controlling the empire, it was decided—very quietly—that something needed to be done, some kind of watch needed to be kept. But belief in ghosts, and science, and law and order, these things didn't really go together. Back in 1882, a group of prominent scientists founded the Society for Psychical Research, probably the most respectable and serious attempt to study the subject of the afterlife. This was right in the middle of the development of the police force and the security service. The police system itself isn't that old. The London Metropolitan Police was founded in 1829, and the Security Services—which is MI5 and things like that—in 1909. So in 1919, with the help of the Society for Psychical Research, the Shades were born."

"The Shades?"

"It's another word for ghosts. MI5 are called the spooks, and we were a lot smaller and stranger. A shady little branch. I think they used to call us Scotland Graveyard as well. Anyway, we were around for years. Very secret. Never very large. But in the Thatcher years . . . someone got wind of the group and didn't like it. I don't know what happened . . . something political. But they shut it down in the early nineties. Two years ago, they decided to start it up again. They found me. I was the first one."

"How did they find you?"

"It's complicated," he said. "And classified."

"So, are you a cop? A real one?"

"I am," he said. "I was trained. The uniform is real. The car was issued to me."

There was a jingle of keys in the door, and Callum entered, wearing a London Tube uniform.

"What's going on?" he asked. "I got your message."

"There's been an accident," Stephen said.

"What sort of accident?"

"Boo—"

"Boo got hit by a car," I said. "The Ripper came after me. Boo tried to help, and he threw her in front of a car."

For a moment, Callum couldn't speak. He leaned against the counter and put his hand to his forehead.

"Is she—"

"She's hurt," Stephen said, "but she's alive. I had to get Rory away from the scene."

"Alive? Conscious alive? How alive?"

"She wasn't conscious at the scene," Stephen said.

Callum just stared at me.

"It's not her fault," Stephen said.

"I know that," Callum replied, but he wasn't acting like he knew that. "Please tell me she got him. Please tell me that. Please let that be the upshot of all this . . ."

"It sounds like she tried," Stephen said. "But no."

"It was a mistake to send her in alone," Callum snapped. "I told you it was a mistake. I told you we should have just stayed at the school."

"We needed to investigate—"

"Investigate what? What exactly have we come up with so far?"

"He spoke to Rory," Stephen said, his voice rising. "We learned a few things. We learned he had the sight when he was alive. That's probably why he's been trailing Rory. That's probably why he killed at Wexford. He found someone who could see him, who could hear him."

"Oh, good," Callum said. "Well, then. Sounds like we've solved it."

"Callum!" Stephen's voice went deep when he yelled. I could feel the sonic boom in my stomach. "You aren't helping. So either stop it now or go outside and walk it off."

For a moment, I thought they were going to have a fight—a real, physical one. Callum stood up, straightened, and stormed out of the room. I heard a door slam somewhere else in the apartment.

"Sorry," Stephen said quietly. "He'll calm down in a moment."

I could hear things being thrown around in the other room. Then the door opened again and Callum joined us, rattling the table and spilling our tea with the force of sitting down.

"So what do we know?" he asked.

"Someone is clearing up the red tape. He'll tell me when it's all right for me to take Rory back to Wexford. Until then, we should stay here with her."

"We should be out there, dealing with him."

"I'd like that too," Stephen said, "but we have no idea where he's gone. But in the meantime, we can work with what he's said this evening. He's been communicating."

Stephen quickly brought Callum up to speed on the various messages while I drank some tea and kept my head down. I was a little frightened of both of them at the moment. Boo was hurt because of me.

"There was something written on a wall after one of the Ripper killings in 1888," Stephen said. "After the fourth murder—a bit of anti-Semitic graffiti. Most people think it was a false lead, that it wasn't written by the Ripper at all—or if it was, it was probably written to lead the police down the wrong path. This message feels wrong . . ."

"Maybe he just wanted to turn up at that Rippercon thing," Callum said. "Do a signing for the fans."

"Possibly," Stephen said. "Everything he's done so far has been about attracting an audience. The very act of imitating Jack the Ripper is an attempt to get attention and cause fear. He commits murders in full view of CCTV cameras. He sent a message to the BBC to be read aloud on television. Tonight, he pulled Rory aside. And then he wrote a message right in front of half the world's press, directing us to a phrase from the Bible. It's all been very, very specific and theatrical."

"But everyone's going to think this Richard Eakles guy wrote that," Callum said. "Apart from us, no one's going to believe his story that an invisible man knocked him aside to write some weird, possibly Bible-related message. At least the one about Rory was clear."

"What *one about Rory*?" I said.

Callum backed away from the table a little and played with the edge of the plastic tablecloth. Stephen exhaled long and slow.

"There's one part of this we haven't mentioned," Stephen said, staring at Callum. "We didn't want you to be unduly alarmed. It's all under control—"

"What message about Rory?" I said again.

"The James Goode letter," he said. "There was one final sentence that confirmed in our minds that what you had seen was real. It wasn't read on the air. It said . . . *I look forward to visiting the one with the sight to know me and plucking out her eyes.*"

Both of them remained silent while I took this in. I stared into the depths of the teacup. I was from Louisiana. Bénouville, Louisiana. Not from here. I was from the land of hot weather and storms and big box stores, of freaks and crawfish and unstable McMansions. Home. I needed home.

"You are the only lead," Stephen said. "Every other avenue has been tried. The paper and the package that was sent to the BBC . . . analyzed over and over. Paper and box and wrapping from Ryman's stationers—one of thousands they sell every year. Not particularly helpful, as he obviously didn't buy it—an invisible man can't walk into a shop and buy a box—so we couldn't trace it at the point of sale. CCTV turned up nothing, as is now well-known. No physical evidence at any crime scene to tie back to the killer—again, obvious to us, baffling to the lab. We only had you. From you, we at least knew he wasn't the original Jack the Ripper, because of his appearance . . ."

I think he saw that none of this was helping, so he shut up.

"The plan is simple," he said. "You stay at Wexford, and we stay near you. Very near you. If he comes anywhere near you—"

"He came near me tonight," I said.

"So we double our protection," Stephen said. "It won't happen again. But now you know, and you have to listen to us, and you have to trust us."

"What can you do?" I said, my voice shaking. "If he comes near me, what can you do about it?"

Callum opened his mouth to speak, but Stephen shook his head.

"We take care of it," Stephen said. "The details are covered under the Official Secrets Act. You can be angry. You can be upset. You can be whatever you want. But the truth is, we're the only people who can keep you safe. And we will keep you safe. It's not only our job, but now he's hurt our friend, and that happens to bother us quite a lot."

"I could go home," I said.

"Running away won't help. Going home probably wouldn't even deter him, if he's serious. The ghosts we've encountered operate basically in the same manner as humans in terms of general locomotion. While most tend to haunt one place, there are plenty that have much larger territories. The Ripper seems comfortable moving around the East End. There's no reason I can think of that he wouldn't be able to travel."

He didn't sugarcoat it. The bluntness was oddly calming.

"So you stay where we can do something about it," he went on. "And you try to live your life as normally as you can."

"Like you two?" I asked.

It was a bit of a low blow, but Callum laughed.

"I think she's getting it," he said.

# 26

It was almost three in the morning when Stephen dropped me off at Wexford, but there were lots of lights on in the windows. I saw people looking out as I stepped from the police car.

"For the next few days, Callum and I will be keeping an eye on you," he said. "One of us will always be around. And remember, you have to say she stepped out into the road and didn't see the car."

Claudia threw open the door before Stephen hit the buzzer. I never thought I'd be happy to see her, but there was something reassuring about her indomitable presence. She checked me over with what seemed like genuine concern, then sent me upstairs while she spoke to Stephen. I gave him a final nod of good night from the steps.

Jazza was awake. Every light in our room was on, including my bedside light. The moment I stepped in the door, she sprang up and threw her arms around me.

"Is she okay?"

"I think so," I said. "Well, she's awake. She has some broken bones."

"What happened? You went to the toilet, and you never came back."

"I was just feeling a little sick," I said. "I went out for some air. I walked around the block. And . . . she followed me. She was on the phone. I guess she . . . she just didn't see the car."

"God, I feel so terrible. All those things I said about her. But she really is sweet. Oh, God, but she really doesn't pay attention, does she? Are you all right?"

"Fine," I lied. I mean, I was physically intact, but inside, I was quaking.

"I warmed your cheese for you," she said, pointing at the radiator.

"I love it when you talk dirty."

I was in no shape to eat any Cheez Whiz, so I went right to my bureau to get out my pajamas.

"Where did you get those clothes?" Jazza asked.

"Oh . . . they lent them to me."

I quickly removed the Eton sweats and shoved them into my laundry bag.

"The police lent you clothes from Eton?"

"I guess they had them around or something."

"Rory . . . you leave the party and Boo follows, then Boo gets hit by a car . . . I don't know. I don't want to pry, but . . . what's going on?"

For just a second, I thought about telling her. I wanted her to know. I imagined all the words coming out of my mouth, the whole ridiculous story.

But I couldn't do that.

"It's all just . . . a lot of bad luck."

Jazza slumped a bit. I wasn't sure if it was relief or disappointment. Luckily, we didn't have to talk about this anymore, because there was a knock and pretty much everyone from the hall came in to get the news.

When I closed my eyes that night, two things ran through my mind: the image of Boo on the street, and the Ripper himself.

No one understood. Not my classmates. Not my teachers. Not the police.

Jazza slept. I didn't.

They probably would have let me skip class the next morning, but there was no point. I'd been in my bed for hours, doing nothing but staring at the ceiling and listening to Jazza breathe and trying to distract myself from the endless, terrifying thoughts. At six, I got up and showered. I was sticky with sweat, a sweat that had nothing to do with being hot and everything to do with being awake so long. I yanked my uniform from the end of the bed, pulled a shirt from a hanger. I couldn't bother putting my hair up, or even brushing it. I just smacked it down with my hands.

I skipped breakfast and went right to art history. No one hid their interest when I walked into the room. I'm not sure if it was the news about Boo or my general appearance. At home, people would have asked. People would have been crawling all over me for information. At Wexford, they seemed to extract what they wanted to know by covert staring.

Mark, a Wexford outsider, was oblivious to the drama of the night before. "Today," he said cheerfully, "I thought we'd cover something topical. We're going to talk about depictions of violence in art. And where I'd like to start is by taking a look at an artist called Walter Sickert. Sickert was an English impressionist who painted urban scenes in the late nineteenth and early twentieth centuries. Sickert is often brought up when discussing Jack the Ripper. There are a number of reasons for this . . ."

I rubbed my head. There was no escaping the Ripper. He was everywhere.

"Sickert was obsessed with the Jack the Ripper crimes. He believed he had rented a room formerly occupied by Jack the Ripper, and he made a painting of it entitled *Jack the Ripper's Bedroom.* Some people even believe that Sickert was Jack the Ripper, but I'm not sure those claims have much to do with reality."

A painting appeared on the screen. It was a dark room, a bed in the middle. Plain, brooding, dark.

"Another reason," Mark said, "was the fact that in 1908, Sickert painted a series of paintings based on a real-life murder, the Camden Town Murder. The murder had taken place the year before, and the scene was similar to that of the last murder victim in the Jack the Ripper murders, Mary Kelly—certainly in the setting."

A click. A new painting. A woman lying on a bed, naked, her head turned away. A man sitting on the edge of the bed, mourning over what he had done.

"Art of a murder scene," Mark said. "Death is a common theme in painting. The Crucifixion has been painted thousands of times. The executions of kings. The killings of saints. But this painting is more about the murderer than the victim. It even encourages us to feel mercy for him. This painting from the series is called *What Shall We Do for the Rent?*"

Mark went on, telling us all about English impressionists and the brushstrokes and the light. I just kept staring straight ahead at the still figure on the bed—the shaded, almost forgotten figure of the woman.

I didn't have any mercy for the killer.

An hour and a half into class, we had a bathroom break. I was the first one out the door.

"I'm not going back in there," I said to Jerome. "I don't know if you can . . . prefect-arrest me or something. But I'm not going back."

"I'm not going to prefect-arrest you," he said. "But I should walk you back to your building. I'll tell Mark you were ill."

So Jerome walked me the thirty or so feet back to Hawthorne. We had just about reached the door when he stopped.

"Only a few more days," he said. "It's almost over."

Jerome hesitated, then put his hand on the side of my head, leaned down, and kissed me.

When I looked up, I just caught sight of Stephen. He was sitting on a bench in the square, pretending to read. He wore a sweater and jeans and a scarf, no uniform. He immediately removed and played with his glasses, turning away from the sight of the kissing. But he had seen it, and that felt weird. I stepped away from Jerome.

"Thanks," I said. I meant for the walk back to the building, but it sounded like I meant the kiss.

"Did you see the thing on the news?" Jerome asked. "About the message? How everyone thinks it's from the Bible, and it might be about terrorism? I don't think it is—neither do any of the people on the Ripper boards. The name of the star . . . it's not from the Bible—he means the name *Jack the Ripper.* That's the name of the Star."

"What?"

"Jack the Ripper never called himself Jack the Ripper. The name came from a letter sent to the Central News Agency. It was a hoax, and almost definitely written by a reporter from the *Star* newspaper. That was the paper that made the Ripper famous. The whole thing was kind of a media creation. When he says 'the name of the star is what you fear,' he means it—everyone's afraid of this idea of the Ripper, this thing that gets bigger and bigger because of the news. And he's the star of the show, right? It's a joke. It's a sick one, but it's a joke. It's bad, but . . . it's not terrorism or anything. At least, I don't think so. If that helps."

He raised his hand and walked back toward the classroom building. I had nowhere to be. I'd just ditched my only Saturday obligation, and everyone else was in class. All was quiet in Wexford's little square of London. I could hear various instruments being played in the music rooms. Jazza's cello was certainly among them, but I couldn't pick it out of the general noise.

I walked away from school and to the main shopping road, which was crowded with people out doing Saturday errands. I went into our local coffee shop, for lack of any better destination, and stood in the stupidly long line and ordered myself the first drink that came to mind. There were no tables to sit at, so I leaned at the bar by the window. Stephen came in and stood next to me.

"I heard what your friend said."

"Hi," I replied.

"It makes quite a bit of sense, actually. I should have thought of that. The *Star* newspaper. He's right. The name of the star is what you fear . . . People are scared of the name Jack the Ripper. He's not talking about the Bible at all. He's laughing at everyone for all the attention he's getting. He's laughing at the Ripperologists, the police, the media . . ."

I looked out at the street—what I'd come to know as a typical one in London. Most of the buildings very low, colorful shop fronts, lots of advertisements for cheap phones and good deals on drinks. The occasional red double-decker bus going by. The more than occasional tourist with a map, a camera, and one of those Jack the Ripper top hats they were selling at the souvenir stalls.

"But Callum had a good point last night," Stephen added. "We're the only people who know Richard Eakles didn't write that message on the board. I feel like . . . I feel like I'm being played with. Personally."

"What about Jo?" I asked. "Someone should tell her what happened."

The change in topic threw him.

"What?"

"Jo," I said again, "is Boo's best friend."

"Oh. Of course." He scratched his head. "Yes. Of course."

"So I want to go and talk to her."

"I suppose that's fine," he said. "Though I don't have the car with me. I don't drive it when I'm not in uniform."

We took the Tube together. Stephen didn't say much, and the trip wasn't long from Wexford. We found Jo down the street from the playground where I'd first seen her. She was wandering along, picking up trash.

"I'll let you . . . ," Stephen said. "Perhaps you should . . ."

It was the first time I'd seen him unsure of what to do.

"I'll do it," I said.

"I'll wait right here."

I came up behind Jo. She didn't turn. I guess she was used to people being close to her, or just going through her.

"Hi," I said. "It's me. Rory. You remember . . . from the other day?"

She turned in surprise.

"Of course!" Jo said. "Feeling better? That must have been a right old shock."

"I'm fine," I said, "but Boo . . ."

I stopped talking for a moment as a woman went by, pushing a stroller. She was so unbearably slow. I wanted to come up behind her and shove her along so I could continue talking. Jo stopped and let her get some distance on us.

"She was hit by a car," I said.

"Is she all right?"

"She's alive," I said. "Hurt. She's in the hospital. The Ripper did this to her. He came after me, and Boo protected me. That's how she got hit. He threw her in front of a car. I just thought . . . someone should tell you."

A lot of people, when they hear bad news, they take a deep breath, or they hyperventilate. Jo didn't do any of these things, because Jo didn't breathe. She bent down and picked up a used coffee cup. It seemed to take all her strength, so I took it from her and carried it the three feet to the trash can.

"You needn't do that," she said. "I can carry those. Sandwich wrappers, coffee cups, aluminum cans. I can lift them. One day, I saw a girl sitting at the café just up the road. She set her purse down next to her. A man came by and took it. She had no idea. I happened to be walking past, and I reached over and snatched it back from him and set it next to her. Now, that was hard, but I did it. She was never the wiser, but it gave him a good fright. This is my street. I keep it clean and safe."

She didn't show much emotion, but I got the sense that she dealt with her shock by keeping busy or talking. She needed someone to talk to.

"Did you live here?" I asked.

"No. I died right over there. Do you see that block of flats?" She pointed at a modern apartment building. "Those are quite new. Back in my day, this was a row of houses. That's where it happened. I didn't live here in my life, but after that, it became my home. Strange impulse, to stay where you died. I don't quite know why I do it . . ."

"What happened?" I asked. "If that's okay to ask."

"Oh, that's no bother," she said almost cheerfully. "Luftwaffe raid. Tenth of May, 1941. That was the last big night of the Blitz. That was the night the Germans hit St. James's Palace and the Houses of Parliament. I worked in communications, sending coded messages and reports on what was going on in London. We had a small telegraph office located quite near here. A bomb hit the end of the road and destroyed everything along this street, including most of these houses. I came out after the bombs fell. You could hear survivors under the rubble. I was helping get a little girl out from under a pile of the stuff when the rest of her house fell on us both. And that was it, really. Thirteen hundred people died that night. I was just one of them."

It was all very matter-of-fact.

"When did you know you were a ghost?"

"Oh, immediately," she said. "One moment I was helping the girl out of the rubble—the next, I was looking down at the rubble and watching someone lift me out of it, and it was abundantly clear that I was dead. It was a shock, of course. The bombing raids had stopped for a while, but there was so much destruction all around . . . there was so much to do. I would sometimes find someone who had been gravely injured, and they could see me, and I would sit and talk to them. I'd pick little things out of the rubble—photographs, things like that. I was still useful. I just refused to slip away. At first, it was difficult. For the longest time, weeks, I was too weak to do anything except linger on the spot where I died. I had no form that I could see. But I managed to pull myself away from the rubble. I suppose I made myself, really. You mustn't let these kinds of things get in your way. It's as Prime Minister Churchill said: 'Never give in, never give in, never, never, never, never—in nothing, great or small, large or petty.' A wonderful speech. He gave it after my death, but it was quoted all over. I've always gone by those words. They've gotten me through many years."

Jo's literal "never say die" attitude was somewhat overwhelming, but one thing was clear—she knew about fear. She knew what it felt like and how to deal with it.

"I'm afraid," I said. "I'm really afraid. The Ripper is . . . he wants me."

Now that I'd said it, it felt true and real. Jo faced me and looked me in the eye.

"Jack the Ripper was just a man. He wasn't magic. Even Hitler was just a man. This Ripper is nothing more than that."

"He's a ghost," I corrected her. "An incredibly powerful ghost."

"But ghosts are just people. We just seem more frightening, I suppose, because we represent something unknown. We can't usually be seen. We're not supposed to be here. And there are good people who can catch this Ripper."

"I know," I said, "but . . . they're all . . . really young. Like me."

"Who do you think goes into the army? Young people. This entire nation was defended by young people. Young people on the battlefield. Young people in airplanes. Young people in the headquarters, breaking codes. The number of people I knew who lied to sign up at fifteen and sixteen . . ."

She trailed off, watching a guy lingering around a bike that was clearly not his. She smoothed out the jacket of her uniform, though it wasn't wrinkled. It probably couldn't wrinkle.

"Thank you for letting me know," she said. "Not everyone considers me—worth informing. You're like Boo, very conscientious. She's a good girl. A bit of an ongoing project, but a good girl. Now I should go and see to that bicycle."

Jo marched across the street, barely checking to see if cars were coming her way. Halfway across, in the path of a tiny sportscar, she turned back.

"Fear can't hurt you," she said. "When it washes over you, give it no power. It's a snake with no venom. Remember that. That knowledge can save you."

With just an inch or so to spare, she stepped out of the path of the car and continued on her way.

# 27

I CAN BARELY REMEMBER WHAT I DID FOR THE NEXT few days. Classes were canceled all week. Callum and Stephen took turns keeping watch. And the days ticked by. November 4, November 5, November 6 . . . The news kept track even if I didn't.

On Wednesday, the seventh of November, I woke around five in the morning. My brain had suddenly clicked back on, and my heart was racing. I sat up and looked around the dark room, examining every formation. That was my nightstand next to my bed. There was my bureau. There was the wardrobe door, slightly open, but not enough for someone to hide behind. There was Jazza, asleep in her bed. I grabbed my hockey stick and stabbed around under my bed, but felt nothing. Then I realized that that wasn't a very good test for a ghost, so I stood up on the bed and jumped out as quietly as I could, then got down on the floor and looked underneath. No one was there. Jazza shifted, but she didn't wake.

I took my robe and bath basket and walked quietly down to the bathroom, where I examined every stall and every cubicle before taking my shower, and even then, I kept the curtain partway open. I didn't care if anyone walked in.

I went to breakfast as soon as it opened, long before Jazza was out of bed. I saw Callum standing on the corner, over by the refectory. He was wearing a dark blue London Underground suit with an orange Day-Glo vest over the jacket, and he had a clipboard. If he had planned on trying to blend in, that wasn't really working.

"What are you doing?" I said.

"Pretending to survey traffic patterns for a new bus route. I have a clipboard and everything."

"Did you guys make that up?"

"Course we made it up," he said. "It was the only thing we could think of to justify my standing in front of a school all day, and the clipboard was the only prop we had. And you shouldn't be seen talking to me, so keep moving."

He turned back to his clipboard, ending the conversation. I hurried away from him, feeling stupid.

I was the only person at breakfast at that hour. I tried to eat my normal plate of sausages but could only get down some juice and the bitter, lava-hot coffee. For entertainment, I read the brass plaques on the wall—names of former students and their various achievements. I looked at the stained-glass image of the lamb in the window above me, but that only reminded me that lambs are famous for being led to slaughter, or sometimes hanging out with lions in ill-advised relationships.

I had to know what they could do to stop the Ripper. I had to find out, or I would go insane. I got up, shoved my tray into the rack, and went back outside and right up to Callum.

"I just said—"

"I want to see what you do," I said.

"You're looking at it."

"No, I mean . . . I want to see how you take *care* of them."

He kicked at the cobbles.

"I can't do that," he said.

"So how am I supposed to stay sane?" I asked. "Don't you think I deserve to know what can be done? I'm defenseless. Show me."

"Do you have any idea how many forms I've had to sign saying that I'd never talk about this?"

"So you'd rather stand around here with a clipboard all day? If you don't show me, I will stand here and stare at you. I will follow you. I will do everything you don't want me to do. I am giving you no choice."

The corner of Callum's mouth twitched slightly. "No choice?" he said.

"You have no idea how reckless I can be."

He looked around, up and down the street, toward the square. Then he walked away for a few moments and made a call.

"Here's the agreement," he said when he walked back to me. "You don't tell anyone. Not Stephen. Definitely not Boo. No one."

"This never happened. I wasn't here."

"And it stays that way. I got a call from Bethnal Green station earlier. They're having a problem there. Come on, then."

We walked to Liverpool Street station. Along the way, I also counted the cameras—thirty-six that I saw, and probably loads more I didn't. Cameras attached to the corners of buildings, to traffic lights, in deep window wells and perched high on stone ledges, sharing poles with streetlights . . . so many cameras, and not one of them would do the slightest bit of good when it came to the Ripper.

At Liverpool Street, he flashed a badge to get into the station, and I tapped my Oyster card on the reader. By the time I was going through the gate, he was halfway down the escalator, and I had to hurry to keep pace with him.

"What do they think you do, exactly?" I asked when we got on the train.

"I'm officially employed by the London Underground. They think I'm an engineer. That's what my file says, anyway. It also says I'm twenty-five."

"Are you?"

"No. I'm twenty."

"So what do they do when they figure out you can't . . . engineer?"

"People get my name and number from other station managers, and they only call me when things are . . . *not right.* I show up, and the problem goes away. A lot of people, in my experience, really don't want to know the details. If they knew how many of their problems I fix, how many trains I keep on time . . . I'm probably the most important employee they have."

"And the most humble," I added.

"Humility is overrated." He smiled. "It's a big area to cover. There's a whole world down here. The Tube itself has about two hundred and fifty miles of track, but the majority of what I do concerns the parts that are actually underground, about one hundred and twelve miles of functional track, plus all the unused tunnels and service tunnels."

The train whizzed along. All I could see out of the windows

was dark, and occasionally the suggestion of the brick walls of the tunnel around us.

"This station we're going to is one I work at a lot. They know me. It was the site of the largest loss of life in any Tube station, anywhere on the network. It was used as an air raid shelter during the war. One night, they were testing antiaircraft weapons near here—a secret test. The people heard what sounded like an air raid and ran like hell for this station. Someone tripped and fell on the stairs, and soon hundreds of people were crushed in the stairwell. A hundred and seventy-three people died, and a lot of them seem to have stuck around."

With that, the recorded voice announced that we were pulling into Bethnal Green. When we got off, the station was extremely quiet. A man with a large belly and a face full of broken capillaries was waiting on the platform.

"All right, Mitchell," he said with a nod. "Who's she?"

"In training. She'll stay on the platform. What's the problem?"

"Eastbound track. They get to the train stop. Then they stop moving, no matter how fast they're going."

Callum nodded, like he knew exactly what this meant.

"All right. Normal rules apply."

"Right."

The man walked off, leaving us.

"What are the normal rules?" I asked.

"He walks away and has a tea break and doesn't ask any questions."

Callum set his bag down on the station platform and removed his jacket, then jumped up high, throwing the jacket over the CCTV camera pointed at the end of the track.

"Do the same with your coat to the one down there," he said, pointing me to a camera toward the middle of the platform.

I took off my coat and got under the camera. It was up pretty high, but I managed to get my coat over it after a few throws. Callum went to the far end of the platform, where there was a safety gate about chest high. It was loaded down with safety signs. Everything about this gate said, "No. Don't. Go back. Wrong. Death is certain beyond this point." Callum opened the gate, which gave access to a few steps that led down to the track level.

"So," Callum said, "the train stops are malfunctioning. The train stops are the controls at the beginning and middle of the track at every Tube station. If a train approaches at anything faster than ten miles an hour, the switch is tripped, and the train stops automatically. Now, this is really important. Look down. How many rails do you see?"

I looked down. I saw three rails—two of track, and a third, heavier one running through the middle. They were all resting on blocks of some kind, about two feet off the ground.

"Three," I said.

"Okay. Best bet, don't step on *any* of them. But the one you really can't step on is that third one, because you'll fry. The trick is you walk in the space between the rails. It's wider on this side. Walk really, really carefully. It's not complicated, but if you mess up, you'll die, so pay attention. You wanted to learn. This is how you learn."

Callum smiled slyly. I wasn't sure if he was joking. I decided not to ask. I followed him down the steps. The entrance to the Tube tunnel was in front of us—a semicircle of light black that led into an unknown pitch-black. Callum put a flashlight into my hand.

"Keep it pointed forward and down. Walk slow and steady and don't jump if you see a rat. They'll run from you, don't worry."

I did as he said, trying to act totally unconcerned about the electric rail or the rats or the dark. Once in the tunnel, the temperature immediately dropped a few degrees. About twenty feet in, there was a man. He was right between the rail and the sloping brick wall of the tunnel. He wore a rough work shirt and boots, loose gray flannel pants, no coat.

"I hate this station," Callum said under his breath.

When I shined my light directly onto the man, he was harder to see. He was so pale and fragile, he was like a trick of the light, a kind of visible sadness in the dark of the tunnel.

"Listen, mate," Callum said. "I'm really sorry. But you're going to have to stop messing with that switch. Just stay away from it, all right?"

"My family . . . ," the man said.

"A lot of times," Callum said, never taking his eyes off the man, "they don't even mean to do the things they do. Their presence just interferes with the electronics. I doubt he even knows he's been tripping the switch. You didn't even mean to do that, did you?"

"My family . . ."

"Poor bastard," Callum said. "All right, Ror. Come closer. Up here."

There was a shallow lip along the wall of the tunnel that Callum stood on so I could get closer to the man. As I did, the air got palpably colder and more sour. The man's eyes were milky. He had no pupils. His expression was impossibly sad.

Callum took the flashlight from my hand and replaced it with his cell phone. He had the same old model as Boo.

"Here's what I want you to do," he said. "Press down on the numbers one and nine. Press hard, and keep pressing."

"What?"

"Just do it. Go on. You have to be within a foot or so."

I positioned my fingers on the one and nine and was about to press when Callum reached over and moved my arms forward, so that my hands and the phone accidentally went right through the man's rib cage. I just felt the slightest sensation as I broke through him, like I'd put my fist through an inflated paper bag. This made me flinch for a second, but the man hardly seemed to notice that I had inserted myself into his chest cavity.

"Good," Callum said. "Now press, both at once, hard!"

I tightened my grip, digging my nails into the number pad. I immediately felt a change in the air around us—there was a very slight but steadily growing warmth, and my hands began to shake.

"Keep holding," Callum said. "It vibrates a little. Just keep pressing."

The man looked down at himself, at my hands clasped in a prayerlike position in his chest, shaking, holding the phone with all my might. A second or two later, there was a bright blip, like a lightbulb going out—except it was a huge lightbulb, the size of a person. There was no noise, but there was a light rush of air and a weird, sweet smell that I can only describe as burning flowers and hair.

And he was gone.

# 28

WE WERE IN A SMALL SQUARE OUTSIDE OF A CHURCH. The vicar was opening the door for the morning service and was unhappy to find me quietly being sick into a crisp pile of fallen leaves. It felt bizarrely good, vomiting in this clean, blowy air. It meant I was alive and not in the tunnel. It meant that smell was out of my nostrils.

"Feel better?" Callum asked when I stood up.

"What did I just do?"

"You took care of the problem."

"Yeah, but *what did I do*? Did I just kill someone?"

"You can't kill a dead person," Callum said. "Makes no sense."

I made my way over to a stone bench and collapsed onto it, turning my face up to get as much of the dampness as I could.

"But I just did *something*. He . . . exploded. Or something. What happened to him?"

"We have no idea," Callum said. "They just go away. You wanted to know. Now you know."

"What I know is that you fight *ghosts* with *phones*."

"It's called a terminus," he said.

The vicar was staring at us from the top of the steps. Though the throwing up had made me a little shaky, every step brought some strength back. Whatever I had expelled, I was glad it was gone.

"Stephen told me he was in a boating accident," I said. "What happened to you?"

Callum leaned back and stretched out his legs.

"We had just moved here from Manchester. My parents had split up a year before, and we were moving around a lot, house to house. My mum got a job down here, and we moved to Mile End. I was a good footballer. I was on track to go professional. I know a lot of people *say* things like that, but I really was. I was in training. I'd been scouted. A few more years, they figured, and I'd be up for it. Football was all I had and all I did. No matter where we went, my mum always saw to it that I had my training. So it was December. It was pissing down rain, freezing. The buses weren't running properly. A kid I went to school with had showed me this shortcut through this estate they were ripping down. You weren't supposed to go in there. They had fencing all around it and warning signs, but that wasn't stopping anyone."

"Estate? Like a mansion?"

"No, no," he said. "An estate is public housing. You call them projects or something like that. Some of them are rough places. This one was one of the worst—it had been ripped apart, was stinking, falling to pieces, completely dangerous in every way. So they moved everyone out and shut it down. They were building a block of fancy new flats in its place. So in I go, jogging through, no problem. Good shortcut home. And then . . . I see the wire. Severed. Live. On the ground. Sending out sparks. And here I was, standing in this lake-sized puddle not ten feet away from it. I saw the thing come off the ground. I saw it lift up and move. And then it bullwhipped into the water, and I felt the first shock hit . . . and then, I saw him. He had long hair and this weird yellow shirt with a big collar, some brown sleeveless jumper over it, bell-bottoms, and these shoes . . . red-and-white ones, with two-inch soles. He was like no one I'd ever seen before, right out of the seventies. He hadn't been there a second ago, but I could see that he was holding the wire and he was laughing. And then I realized that my legs were shaking. I fell to my knees. He kind of teased the wire over the water, and I was saying, 'No, no, don't.' He just kept laughing. I tried to move, but I fell into the water on my face. After that, I can't remember. I survived, of course. The whole thing was caught on CCTV, so someone in security saw it all happen. Of course, what they saw was me trespassing and then having some kind of seizure and falling into the water I was standing in. They found the wire when they got there, of course, and realized I'd been electrocuted. I told them about the other kid, but when they looked at the footage, I was alone. And that was the beginning . . ."

Callum looked up at the church spire. The vicar had given up his staring and left us alone.

"Something happened to me in that water," he said. "Something happened to my legs. Because after that day, I couldn't run right. I couldn't kick right. I lost all my nerve. The only thing I could do, play football, was taken from me. But then a few weeks later, a man showed up at my door to ask me if I wanted a job. He already knew everything about me—my family, my football. I needed some convincing it was all real, but then I agreed. First, they sent me off for some training, police stuff mostly. Then I met Stephen. He was in charge. We didn't get on at first, but he's all right, Stephen. Once he started training me, it was obvious why they picked him to be in charge."

"Why?"

"Because he's brilliant," Callum said. "Top marks at Eton. That's as clever as they get. But he's not a total wanker, like most of those people are—he's just a little special sometimes. Anyway, from there, I shadowed someone on the Underground for a while. They had me in as a trainee. Stephen taught me about the Shades, about the history, about the new plans for how everything was going to be run. When he thought I was ready, he gave me a terminus."

He held up the phone and looked at it with admiration.

"A terminus?" I said. "That's what it's called."

Callum nodded.

"The very first thing I did was go back to that building site. By the time I got there again, the new flats were up. Shiny glass ones, with a gym up top, all full of bankers. I had to look around for a little while, but I found him. I guess he didn't like the new building much. He was down in the car park, just wandering around, looking bored. I actually felt sorry for him for a second, poor bastard, doomed to walk around some car park, and whatever monstrosity comes next. He didn't recognize me. Didn't think I could see him. He paid me no mind as I walked right up to him, took out my phone, pressed one and nine, and fried him. He'll never hurt anyone again. But that's the first day I knew—this was my real calling. I don't know what I would do without it. It's the most important thing in my life. It gives you back some control."

"When Boo walked up to him, she had her phone out," I said, putting this together with the memory that was playing over and over in my mind. "I thought she was handing me her phone."

"She finally tried to use it," Callum said, stopping. "God . . ." He leaned over and put his head in his hands. "She doesn't believe in using the terminus," he explained. "We fight about it all the time."

I'd been so wrapped up in my own part of this that I hadn't really noticed how Callum and Stephen and Boo felt about each other. I saw they were upset, but . . . now it hit me. They were friends.

"So," he said, lifting up his head. "Now you know how we can take care of him. Do you feel better?"

I didn't answer, because I didn't know.

Jazza was out when I got home, so I was on my own, listening to people talking and laughing in the rooms around mine.

My desk was a nightmare—an altar to all the work I hadn't done over the last few days. It was amazing how quickly your academic future could crumble. A week or two and you were totally out of step. I might as well have missed the entire year.

I might as well have never come to Wexford. Of course, now I had bigger things to worry about, but I allowed myself a few minutes of panic to take in the enormity of how screwed I was, Ripper stuff aside. It was almost like a mental vacation from the stress of the ghosts and the sight and the murders.

The dark came fast, and I had to switch on my desk light. Then I heard people getting up and going to dinner. It was already five. I had no appetite, but I had to get out as well. I wasn't staying here by myself. When I got outside, Callum was gone and the police car had taken his place. Stephen sat in the driver's seat. He waved me over and opened the door. As soon as I got in, he drove around the corner, away from the prying eyes of people going to dinner.

"It's time to go over the plan for tomorrow," he said. "It's very simple. You stay at Wexford. We'll cover the building at all times. Boo's well enough to come. She can't walk, but she can be here, in a wheelchair. She can keep her eyes open. Tomorrow morning, I search your building from the top down. I've got special permission from the school. Once we're sure it's clear, you stay inside your building all night, with Boo. I'll be at the front of the building, and Callum will be at the back. He won't be able to get in without one of us seeing him. You'll never be alone, and you'll never be undefended. And you'll have this."

He held out a phone—specifically, Boo's phone, which was the same low-tech model they all carried. This one still had the white scratch marks on the black plastic from when it had skidded across the road after Boo's accident.

"I know you know what this is," he said.

"I have no idea what you're talking about," I replied.

"I followed you two," he said simply. "I saw you go into Bethnal Green station, and I saw your reaction when you emerged."

"You followed . . ."

"Callum's wanted to tell you from the start," he said. "I probably would have ended up telling you if he hadn't. I had a feeling it was going to happen. But now that you do . . ."

He held up the phone. "It's called a terminus. *Terminus* means end, or boundary stone."

"It's a *phone,*" I said.

"The phone is just a case. Any device would do. Phones are just the easiest and least conspicuous."

He removed the back of the phone and showed me the contents. Inside, where all the circuitry and computery bits were supposed to be, there was a small battery and two wires joined in the middle by some black electrical tape. He pried this up very, very carefully, and waved me in closer to look. There, wrapped in the fine ends of the wires, was a small stone of some kind—a pinkish one, with a twisting streak down the middle.

"That's a diamond," he said.

"You have phones full of *diamonds*?"

"One diamond each. These wires run a current through it. When we press the one and the nine at the same time, the current runs through the diamond and it emits a pulse that we can't hear or feel, but it . . ."

"Explodes ghosts."

"I prefer to think that it disperses the vestigial energy that an individual leaves behind after death."

"Or that," I said. "But diamonds?"

"Not as strange as it sounds," Stephen replied. "Diamonds make excellent semiconductors. They have many practical uses. These *particular* three diamonds are highly flawed, so they aren't really valuable to most people. But to us, they're priceless."

He carefully snapped the cover back onto the phone. Once he had made sure the phone was closed correctly, he handed it to me.

"They have names," he went on. "This one is Persephone."

"The queen of the underworld," I said. I used to have a book about myths when I was little.

"Described by Homer as the queen of the shades," Stephen said, nodding. "The one Callum carries is Hypnos, and the one I carry is Thanatos. Hypnos is the personification of sleep, and Thanatos is his brother, death. They get the poetic names for a reason. All secret weapons have code names for the files. What I've just given you is an official secret, so please be careful with it."

I looked at the phone in my hand. I could still smell that smell from the Tube tunnel. I could still feel that wind, see the light . . .

"Does it hurt them?" I asked.

"I have no idea," he replied. "That question has bothered me in the past, but not now. You need to take that, and if the time comes, you *need* to use it. Do you understand?"

"I'm never going to understand this," I replied.

"One and nine," he said. "That's all you have to remember."

I swallowed hard. There was still a burning in my throat from the vomiting.

"Go on," he said. "Try to get some rest. I'll be right here. Just keep that with you."

I got out of the car, gripping the phone. I tried to remember what Jo said about young people defending the country as I looked at Stephen. He looked tired and there was just a hint of five o'clock shadow along his chin. I had him. I had Callum. I had an old phone.

"Night," I said, my voice dry.

# 29

Again, I woke up around five in the morning. I'd gone to sleep with the terminus in my hand, but I'd let it go in my sleep. I had to look for it for a few seconds. It was under the duvet, down by my feet. I don't know what I'd been doing in my sleep to kick it down there. I dug it out and held it tightly, pressing my fingers on the one and nine. I practiced this several times, setting it down and grabbing it back up again as fast as I could, putting my fingers on the buttons. Now I understood why they used old phones—no smart buttons. When the time came, you had to find them and feel them under the pads of your fingers.

I got up and leaned against the heater under the window. Stephen's police car was parked just outside. It was the only thing I could see very clearly, since the sun wasn't up—it had yellow reflective squares all over the sides, alternating with blue, and orange and neon yellow on the back. English police cars were serious about being seen.

For everyone else at Wexford, this was just a normal Thursday—mostly. As on the last Ripper day, we would be on lockdown starting after an early dinner. A few police cars were now parked along the side of the building, and some news vans were joining them.

That afternoon, I went to the library. The carrels were all full—people seemed to be going on as usual, working away, cramming down the material for when classes started up again next week. I went directly upstairs, to the stacks. Alistair was in his usual position, draped all over the floor, book in front of him. Today, it was poetry. I could tell from the wide white margins on the page and his particularly languid pose.

I sat down nearby and put an open book on my lap, so I at least had the pretense of reading if anyone found me. We said nothing to each other, but he seemed fine with my presence. A few minutes later, though, a library assistant came by with the cart. He pointed to the book on the ground in front of Alistair.

"Is that yours?" he asked.

"No," I said.

I should have realized why he was asking, because he reached down and took it away, dropping it on the cart. Alistair looked sour as his reading material rolled off.

"What's your problem?" he asked. "You look miserable."

When Alistair said it, it almost sounded like a compliment.

"Is it bad?" I asked. "Dying?"

"Oh, please don't," he said, flopping flat on the floor.

"I'm afraid of dying," I said.

"Well, you probably won't for a while."

"The Ripper wants to kill me."

That made him pause. He lifted his head from the ground to look at me.

"What makes you say that?" he said.

"Because he said so."

"You serious?" he asked. "The Ripper?"

"Yup," I said. "Any advice? In case it happens?"

I tried to smile, but I know it didn't look like a smile—and there was no hiding the quake in my voice.

Alistair sat up slowly and tapped his fingers on the floor.

"I don't even remember dying. I just went to sleep."

"You don't remember it at all?"

He shook his head.

"I thought I was having a really strange dream," he said. "In my dream, the IRA had put a bomb in my chest, and I could feel it ticking, and I was trying to tell people it was going to explode. Then it went off. I saw the explosion come out of my chest. Then that part of the dream faded, and I was in my room, and it was morning. I was looking down at myself in bed. For all I know, this is all part of that dream. Maybe I'm still having it."

"Why do you think you came back?"

"I didn't come back," he said. "I just never left."

"But why? I mean, don't they say that ghosts come ba—stay around—because they have unfinished business or something?"

"Who says that?"

That was a good question. The answer was television shows, movies, and Cousin Diane. Not exactly the most reliable places to get information.

"I hated this place," he said. "All I wanted was to get out. Death should have taken care of that, and yet here I am. Over twenty-five sodding years at this sodding school. I don't know what to tell you. I don't know why I'm like this or what happens to other people. I just know I'm still here."

"Would you go, if you could?"

"In a second," he said, lying back down. "But that doesn't seem to be happening. I don't even think about that anymore."

I squeezed the terminus in my pocket. I could make Alistair's dream come true, right now. In a second. The enormity of it just made it funny. Don't want to exist anymore? Okay! *Zap.* Done. Puff of smoke and you're gone, like a magic trick. I ran my finger over the buttons. Maybe this was how I was meant to spend this day—setting someone free.

But this was Alistair, whom I'd come to think of as someone who went to my school—not just some shadow in a tunnel. Or what did they call it? A shade.

I took the terminus all the way out of my pocket and put it on my lap. I'm not actually sure what I would have done if Jerome hadn't appeared and sat down next to me. Luckily, he took my opposite side, or he would have ended up right on top of Alistair.

"What's that?" Jerome asked, nodding at the phone.

"Oh . . . Boo's phone."

"*That's* her phone? How old is that thing?"

He reached for it, but I moved it aside.

"Shouldn't you be studying?" I asked.

"I'm supposed to be meeting with my Latin group. But there are only five of us, and three left school."

"Chickens."

"*Audaces fortuna iuvat.*"

"What does that mean?" I asked.

"Fortune favors the brave," both he and Alistair said at the same time.

Jerome shifted around a bit so that we were arm to arm and leg to leg.

"Are you okay?" he asked. "Why are you up here sitting on the floor?"

"It's quiet," I said. "And I just like floors."

I think Jerome was prepared to take anything I said at that moment as a flirtatious remark. He had that look on his face that indicated that hormone levels were high and the time was right. Under any other circumstances, I would have been delighted. At the moment, I wasn't feeling much of anything. I'd exhausted my supply of emotions.

"Oh, God," Alistair said.

"Sorry," I replied.

"Sorry for what?"

That was Jerome.

"I thought I . . . scratched you," I lied. "With my nail."

"Just do it," Alistair said tiredly. "It happens all the time. I'm used to it."

"Are you all right?" Jerome asked, his face close to mine. He sounded so English. *Awl riiight.* I didn't answer. I kissed him.

Our previous making out had been a little frenzied. Today was different. We pressed our lips together and held them there. I could feel the warm air from his nose as he breathed in and out. We kissed each other's necks. I started to warm up a bit and gave in to the slow molasses that was creeping back through my veins. Kissing is something that makes up for a lot of the other crap you have to put up with in school, and as a teenager in general. It can be confusing and weird and awkward, but sometimes it just makes you melt and forget everything that is going on. You could be in a burning building or a bus about to fall off a cliff. It doesn't matter, because you are just a puddle. I was a puddle on the library floor, kissing the guy with the curly hair.

"Could you not roll on top of me, though?" Alistair asked. "I was here first."

When the bell went off, signifying what would have been the end of the period had it been a normal school day, we both jumped a little and blinked. Alistair had gotten up and moved away to another corner, and I heard some sniggering in our general direction. We emerged from the library bleary-eyed and collars crooked. The three police cars had turned into two police cars and four much larger vans. There were also people coming in twos and threes and fours carrying signs and candles.

"There's going to be a vigil tonight," Jerome said, adjusting his prefect's tie. "On the Mary Kelly murder site. It's just a few streets over. Supposed to be thousands of people."

The sun was already retreating, and the crowds were coming. The Ripper, the Ripper, the Ripper.

We went right next door to the refectory. Jerome held my hand. This did not go unnoticed. It wasn't mentioned either. But I saw it register. I was suddenly starving and took a heavy helping of fish pie. I ate with one hand, and with the other I held Jerome's hand under the table. There was just a trace of sweat on his brow. It made me proud. I caused that sweat.

And life was good for about half an hour.

"So there's some speculation on where tonight is going to

happen," Jerome said. "Because it's going to be indoors, right? A lot of people are saying hotel, because of all the tourists . . ."

My good mood exploded. Pop. Gone.

He went on for a good ten minutes about the various odds on locations for that night's murder. I took it as long as I could.

"I have to call my parents," I said, getting up. I shelved my tray roughly and joined the many people who were heading out.

The stupid misting rain had started up again. I could see it under the orangey glow of the lights along the green and in front of the school. Loads more people were around the school now, the people with their signs and the police officers and the handful of press people who had decided to use the previous murder site as a place to broadcast.

"Hey!" Jerome called. "Wait! Rory!"

"It's not a game," I said, turning around.

"I know that," he replied. "Look, I know you were a witness. I'm sorry."

"You don't know anything," I snapped.

I regretted it even as I said it, but the simple fact was—something had to give. The kissing had distracted me for a little while, but reality was back.

Jerome looked at me in confusion and shook his head, unable to come up with the words.

"I'm going back," he said. "I've got desk duty all night."

I watched him as he cut across the square, turning up the collar of his blazer against the rain and stopping only to adjust his messenger bag.

Stephen was standing by the door in his uniform. I noticed Callum as well, also in a police uniform. It took me a moment;

the helmet was low over his face. Usually, Stephen wore a police sweater, a dark V-neck with epaulettes on the shoulders. Tonight, he and all of the other officers, including Callum, were wearing heavy tactical vests covered in tiny pockets. Stephen gave me a nod as I went in.

There was a mild commotion in the common room. It turned out to be a group of people gathered around Boo, who had triumphantly returned in a wheelchair. It's not that Boo had been hugely popular or anything, but she *had* been hit by a car and she *had* come back in a wheelchair. That kind of thing draws a crowd. Jo, I noticed, was standing just behind the chair, her arms politely crossed. I didn't even go in to greet them. I went right upstairs.

I had promised my parents a call after dinner, so I went upstairs to take care of that. They extracted some very serious promises from me that I would remain in the locked building surrounded by all the police officers. Bristol, from the sound of it, was also under a state of high alert, as were most of the major cities. Would the Ripper suddenly cross the country? Would copycat killers join in? It seemed like people didn't want London to have all the fun. Everyone deserved to share the fear.

I got off the phone as soon as I could and shut my eyes. I heard Jazza come in.

"Did you see Boo?" she asked.

"Yeah," I replied.

"You didn't come in to say hello. And Jerome was wandering around out in front of the building looking upset."

"Argument," I said.

"You're not saying very much."

I felt her sit on the end of the bed.

"Everyone is scared, Rory," she said.

The impulse to scream was very great, but I held it down. Screaming at Jazza would be bad. I just kept my eyes closed and rubbed my face.

"You should go down and say hello," she said.

"I will."

Jazza was disappointed in me. I could tell from her light-as-air sigh and the way she got up and went out without saying another word. I'd managed a trifecta—Alistair, Jerome, Jazza. Really, the only three people at Wexford I had any special bond with. If this was going to be my last night, I'd done a great job so far.

The dark had come, and Ripper night was here.

# 30

It was a long night, and I wasn't sure what was worse—the terror I was just managing to keep at bay or the boredom. We sat in that study room for six straight hours. Boo tried to keep me entertained by reading to me about celebrities, mostly English ones that I'd only recently learned the names of. My butt went numb from sitting. My back hurt from the chair. The air in the tiny study room got stale, and I grew to hate the powder blue walls.

It seemed to me that things should be more dramatic—not just sitting around with the ever increasing weight of time on my shoulders.

"You can go to sleep if you want," Boo said, just after one in the morning. "Not to bed, but if you want to lie down."

"No." I shook my head. "I can't do that."

She rolled herself back and forth in her chair.

"You've seen Callum and me, yeah?" she asked.

I wasn't sure what this question meant. I'd seen Callum, and I'd seen Boo.

"Do you think . . ." Again, she said *fink* instead of *think*. "Okay. I . . . I really like him. I have for the whole time, yeah, but I've had no one to tell. One year with no one to tell. And maybe he just doesn't think we can date because we work together. The two of them, they take it harder, you know? They were more messed up by whatever happened to them. Callum's angry. And Stephen . . . well, Stephen is Stephen."

This sudden insight into Boo's love life was confusing.

"What does that mean?" I asked.

"He's smart—like, proper smart. He went to Eton. Proper posh. But something about him . . . I mean, I know something bad happened. I know he doesn't talk to his family. He doesn't do anything outside of this job. I mean, they must have picked him for a reason to be the person to restart it all. And I love Stephen. I do. I didn't ever think I'd have a friend as posh as him, you know? He's dead sweet. He just has no life. He reads. He makes phone calls. He sits in front of his computer. I don't know if he has hormones."

There was something in what Boo was saying. Of all the guys I'd ever met, Stephen seemed the most . . . I wasn't sure what the word was. But I took Boo's point. You never got the feeling that Stephen had *those* kinds of thoughts.

"Callum has hormones," Boo continued. "I've seen him in action when we've gone out—I mean, as friends. We go out and he meets someone almost as soon as we get in the door of the club or whatever. But he doesn't date anyone, ever. Maybe we can't. Maybe that's part of it. I mean, we can't say what we do. But that's what makes me perfect, you know? You need to help me with this, yeah? It's good to have a girl around."

She sighed and smiled a little.

"And you have hormones," she said. "You and Jerome, always snogging each other's faces off."

Jerome. He was just over in Aldshot, but he might as well have been on the moon. I could have texted him or called him or sent him a note, but this wasn't a night where I could have a conversation like that. So maybe there wouldn't be more snogging of faces.

"Yeah," I said sadly.

Another hour ticked by. Jazza knocked on the door and said she was going to bed. Charlotte came to tell us that biscuits were being passed around in the common room, and brought us a handful. Gaenor came in to talk to Boo. Jo came in every once in a while to tell us the building was clear.

I jumped when my phone buzzed. There were a few people who might text me at this hour—my friends from home (though they usually e-mailed) and Jerome.

Hello, the text read. I'm bored.

I shared the sentiment, but I had no idea who I was sharing it with. The number wasn't Jerome's. I had only five English numbers in my phone, and this wasn't any of them.

Who is this? I replied.

The phone buzzed again. Yet another number this time, and another message.

Everyone loves Saucy Jack.

"Is that Jerome?" Boo asked.

Saucy Jack. That was another Ripper nickname from the past, another fake signature. The phone buzzed again. Yet another number.

Come to the King William Street Tube station at four.

The room felt very cold all of a sudden. Boo must have known something was wrong, because she took the phone.

"King William Street?" she said, looking at the message. "That's not a station."

She was still holding the phone when another message came in. She read it without asking my permission, and I saw her expression grow dark.

"What is it?" I asked.

"I'm getting Stephen," she said. She was reaching for her own phone and tried to keep her grasp on mine, but I got it away from her.

I will kill tonight, the new message said. I will kill and kill and kill and kill again until I make my way to you. I will kill all along the path. I will draw a line of blood until I reach you. Come to me first.

At least that cleared things up. I almost appreciated how unambiguous it was.

Stephen was in the study room with us about a minute later. He took the phone out of my hand and quickly scanned through the text messages.

"All different numbers," he said. "Do you recognize any of them?"

I shook my head. He already had his own phone out and was making a call.

"I need a trace on some text messages . . ."

He rattled off the numbers from the messages and hung

up without saying good-bye. Boo was already on her computer.

"King William Street station," Boo said. "I looked it up. It's a disused Tube station just north of London Bridge."

Stephen looked over her shoulder at the entry on the station.

"What's this down here?" he said, pointing. "Also the scene of a failed drugs bust in 1993 that resulted in the death of six undercover police officers."

"Bit of a strange coincidence that he wants to meet Rory at an abandoned station where six police officers died, isn't it?" Boo asked.

"Very," Stephen said. "There's a link to an article. Click on that."

They were still scanning this when Stephen's phone started to ring. He answered it and listened, mumbling a few yeses, then hung up.

"They traced the texts," he said. "All different phones, all triangulated to a pub two streets over. There's a party in there tonight. We can trace all the owners, but that's irrelevant. He's just picking up phones. What matters is that he's close by."

"Which is fine," Boo said. "We're ready for him. This thing about the station . . . he can't mean it."

I pulled Boo's laptop over. They were reading from a "this day in history" news site. Down the left side of the page, there was a column of photographs, the faces of the victims.

At first I thought I was imagining things. I definitely wasn't feeling right in the head.

"I don't like it," Stephen said, taking off his helmet and setting it on the table. He rubbed his hands through his hair until it stuck up. "We know he's close to this building right now. Why tell her to go across town to some old station?"

"Maybe he wants her to come out, and he kills her when she does?"

"Possibly," Stephen said.

I ignored the casual way they were talking about my impending murder. My attention was still drilled on the screen. No. It wasn't my imagination at all.

"He wants me to go to where he died," I said.

Boo and Stephen both looked at me. I pointed to the fifth picture down the side of the screen.

"That's him," I said, pointing to the bald man smiling back at us. "That's the Ripper."

# 31

A LONG SILENCE GREETED THIS ANNOUNCEMENT.

I was still staring at the photo on the screen. The Ripper had a name—Alexander Newman. In life, he smiled.

"Rory," Stephen asked, "are you sure that's him?"

I was sure.

"She's right," Boo said, leaning in and staring at the photo. "I didn't even recognize him. I mostly remember him throwing me into the bloody road. But she's right."

"This changes things," Stephen said. "He's playing a game with us. It's just after two, so we have two hours."

He paced the study room for a moment. There was a knock on the door. He threw it open to find Claudia in the doorway.

"Yes?" he snapped.

"All right in here?" she asked.

"Just doing some follow-up questioning," he said.

Claudia didn't look convinced. Now that I thought about it—Stephen really did look young, and he'd been around a lot. I don't think she questioned that he was a policeman, but I'm not sure she was completely convinced that he was around the building purely for police reasons.

"I see," she replied. "Well, make sure to pop by on your way out, please."

"Yes, I will," Stephen said quickly. "Thank you."

He didn't exactly slam the door in her face, but he came fairly close.

"We do two things," he said. "We make him think that Rory will meet him. We'll draw him away from here. The second thing is, we get Rory out of this building without anyone noticing."

"Why?" Boo asked.

"Because," he said impatiently, "before, we thought he was just going to come here and we'd be waiting. But now I have no idea where he plans on going or what he plans on doing. So our move is, we confuse him. He's been in control of this situation for so long, I can't imagine he'll be pleased if he thinks he doesn't know what's going on for a moment. Is there any other way out of this building besides the front door?"

"The only other way I know is through the bathroom window," I said. "And they fixed the bars."

"You can't go out a window. This building is surrounded. The police would notice, even if the Ripper missed it. No other way?"

I shook my head.

"All right," he said. "The two of you stay here. I'll be back."

Stephen was gone for about ten minutes. Jo came by on a break from patrolling the building, and Boo told her what was going on, so she stayed with us. When Stephen returned he had a plastic shopping bag with him, which he tossed onto the table. The bag had one busted handle and looked dirty, like it had come from the trash. Inside, there was a lump of black and white cloth and a very bright green plastic object.

"Put that on," he said.

I dumped out the bag and found what had been inside was a bunched-up police uniform, complete with the vest.

"Where did you get this?" Boo asked.

"It's Callum's," he said.

"What's he wearing?"

"At the moment, not much of anything. Put it on."

I noticed Boo perk up a bit at this piece of information.

"I'll go and have a chat with your matron. Change. Put your clothes in the bag. Hurry."

Callum and I were of a similar height; the pants were a little long, but not insanely so. The shirt was much too large—Callum had big arm muscles and a chest that was wide in different places. The belt was heavy and loaded down with things like handcuffs, a flashlight, a baton, and what appeared to be Mace. The tactical vest was also massive and heavy, with a radio on the shoulder.

"Take my shoes," Boo said.

She was wearing a pair of black flats, something she could easily slip on. They were kind of sweaty inside and too large for me, but they were better than the pink dotted slippers I'd been wearing. Stephen knocked once, then opened the door while I was still making the final adjustments.

"What about me?" Boo said.

"You can't move with that leg. Plus, you're needed here with a terminus in case I'm wrong. And you have to do this . . ."

He took out his notebook and wrote something down, then passed it to her. "You figure out a way to get this message all over those cameras at the vigil. Quick as you can."

"I can help with that," Jo said.

The helmet didn't fit at all. It was one of those tall, distinctly English bobby helmets. It had a large silver badge on the front, topped with a crown. The helmet was heavy and instantly fell over my eyes.

"Just hold it in place by the brim," Stephen said. "It's the wrong headgear for female officers, so keep your head down."

"I don't look like a cop."

"It doesn't have to fool anyone close up," Stephen added. "All we have to do is walk out of the building and around the corner. I've sent Claudia off to check a window. We need to move."

Boo looked pained that we were leaving, but it was all happening very fast.

"You lot be careful," she said. "And don't do anything stupid."

"We'll see you in a few hours," Stephen said. "Stay alert. Keep Jo with you."

Getting out of Wexford was easy—it was only a few steps down the hall, then a few more steps to the front door. We walked past the common room so quickly that all anyone saw was two briskly moving, vaguely police-like figures.

Once we were outside, it felt like a very different game. There were four police officers out front. Most were talking to each other or staring at the people who were coming and going from the vigil. Still, one of them turned in my direction. I put my head down instantly, holding the stupid helmet in place. There was a radio attached to the shoulder of Callum's vest, so I pretended to be talking into that. I couldn't walk that steadily in Boo's slightly oversized shoes, and once again, the stupid cobblestones were my enemy. I felt the cuff that I had shortened by tucking it up the pant leg coming slowly undone. Stephen couldn't support me because that would have looked too odd, but he walked very close, so I could bump into him as a way of keeping from falling over. He walked me straight down the cobblestone street, which led past one of the classroom buildings, and then to the main shopping road. As soon as we were clear of the place, Stephen caught me by the arm to help me. He half dragged me down the street, turning abruptly at a small alley next to a building that was being refurbished and converted to fancy new apartments.

There was nothing there but trash—old office chairs and rolls of discarded carpet and a Dumpster filled with scrap wood and broken pieces of wall.

"It's us," Stephen said.

"Oh, thank God," said a voice.

Callum emerged from behind the Dumpster. Even with all that was going on, it was hard not to take notice of this: he wore only his underpants and his socks and shoes. The underpants were those tight kind—not tighty-whities, but the slightly longer-legged ones that looked kind of sporty. His legs were hairier than I would have expected, and he had a long tattoo of what looked like a vine running from somewhere just above the leg of the underwear to a few inches above his knee.

I don't think I hid my staring very well either.

"Go ahead and change," Stephen said, handing me the bag. "I'll go and get the car."

"Please be quick," Callum added. "This is not as fun as it appears."

I stepped over the boards and got myself behind the Dumpster. It was cold and dusty back there, and it only got colder and more unpleasant when I shed my outfit. I tossed out the clothes as I finished with them, so by the time I emerged, Callum was fully dressed, doing up the buttons and zippers. This was slightly disappointing.

Stephen pulled up at the end of the alley, and we got into the car. The spot was probably illegal, but being in a police car, he could do what he liked. He had opened a laptop that was attached to a center console in the front of the car, and it appeared he was going into a police database.

"There's an Alexander Newman in here," he said. "Says he died in 1993, which was the year of the King William Street incident, but his file doesn't mention it. Says he was Special Branch. Medical degree from Oxford. Trained as a psychiatrist at St. Barts Hospital, three years on the force . . . What was this man doing on a drugs squad?"

"Is this what we should be worrying about right now?" I asked.

"He wants you to go where he died," Stephen said, not turning around. "Clearly, this place has significance to what's going on. The more we know, the better we can determine what to do next—or what he'll do next. There's also something very strange about this case file. A case like that, six officers dead, there should be endless documentation. This file seems light."

"You just love the paperwork, don't you?" Callum asked.

"I'm saying that for a case of this magnitude, there should be hundreds of pages. But all that's in here are the general report, the coroner's report, and four officer statements. Basically all this says is that a firearms unit was dispatched to the scene to try to take control of the situation, but by the time they got there, all the officers were dead. According to this, there were four officers in the armed response vehicle."

He typed some more. I looked out of the window to the dark street we had parked on. Not a person in sight. There was a CCTV camera pointed right at us. That was almost funny now.

"It looks like one has died and two are retired. But one's still working—Sergeant William Maybrick. City of London Police, Wood Street. He'll be on duty tonight."

"How do you know?" Callum asked.

"Because everyone is on duty tonight," Stephen replied. "I think it's worth the time to go and find out what he knows. Sirens on, I can get there in five minutes."

# 32

ONE THING ABOUT STEPHEN—HE COULD REALLY drive. He power-shifted through the gears as we tore into the City, ripping past banks and skimming inches away from the cabs and very expensive-looking cars that still floated around the streets. I caught a part of some snarky remark Callum made about Stephen celebrating a lot of birthdays by doing racing track days. Stephen told him to shut up.

We came to an actual screeching halt in front of the station. Because we were in a police car, we got to pull right up front. The Wood Street police station looked like a fortress built entirely of blocks of white stone. There were a few windows, and a big set of brown wood double doors with a crest sculpted into the stone just above—two lions snarling at each other over a shield. Two old-fashioned lamps, ones that looked like converted four-sided gas lamps with the word POLICE on them, provided the only light or identification.

"How exactly are you going to get him to talk to you?" Callum asked as he unbuckled himself.

"We have ways," Stephen said.

"We? I am part of that we. I don't know our ways."

They got out and continued their conversation outside of the car, but I couldn't hear it that well. I wasn't sure what I was supposed to do. I was in the back, and I was dressed in my alligator pajamas. Getting out seemed like the logical idea, but the door didn't open. Stephen came back and released me. The three of us marched into the station. At the front desk, Stephen asked for Sergeant Maybrick in such a firm and entitled way that the front desk officer raised an eyebrow. He looked at Stephen, then at Callum, and finally at me. I seemed to be the weak link in this overall picture.

"And you are?" he asked.

"Just ring him."

"He's quite busy at the moment."

"This has to do with the Ripper case," Stephen said, leaning over the counter. "Time is somewhat of the essence. *Pick up that phone.*"

The word *Ripper* really had an amazing effect on people. The desk officer picked up the phone instantly. A minute later, a man emerged from the elevator down the hall. He was at least an inch or two taller than Stephen and probably twice his weight. There were sweat marks under the arms of his white uniform shirt, and the epaulettes on his shoulder had a lot more stripes than Stephen's.

"I understand you have some information for me?" he said.

His accent, I now could recognize, was Cockney—serious London.

"I need you to tell me everything you remember about the deaths of the six officers at King William Street in 1993," Stephen replied. Even to my ears, this demand sounded ridiculous.

"And who are you exactly, Constable?" the sergeant said.

Stephen took a notepad from his belt, opened it, scrawled something, and passed the paper to the sergeant.

"Ring this number," he said. "Tell them you have Constable Stephen Dene with you. Tell them I need you to give me some information."

Sergeant Maybrick took the paper and stared Stephen straight in the eye.

"If you're wasting my time, son—"

"Ring the number," Stephen said.

The sergeant folded the paper in half and sharpened the fold by running his fingers along it several times.

"Ellis," he said to the man behind the desk, "you see these three stay here."

"Yes, sir."

The sergeant stepped down the hall and took out his phone. Stephen folded his arms over his chest, but from the way he clenched and unclenched his fists, I could tell that he wasn't entirely sure this was going to work. The desk officer studied us. Callum turned toward the wall to hide his alarmed expression.

"What number is that?" he hissed in Stephen's direction.

"One of our overlords," Stephen whispered. "And he's not going to be happy I gave out his number."

The conversation was a brief one. Sergeant Maybrick marched back down the hall in our direction, past the curious desk officer.

"Outside," he said, walking right past us to the door.

Once outside, he moved away from the building. He had a coughing fit, then took out a pack of cigarettes and lit one.

"What are you?" he asked. "Special Branch? CID?"

"I'm not authorized to tell you that," Stephen said.

"Then I really don't want to know. You sure you want me to tell you this with her here?"

I guess my pajamas didn't inspire much confidence. Or the fact that I was hopping on my toes to keep warm.

"I do," Stephen said.

"King William Street was a nasty business, one I was glad to have behind me." Sergeant Maybrick shook his head and took a long drag of his cigarette. "Call came in that shots had been fired and officers were down. We didn't know what they were doing down there or why. Four of us responded in the ARV. We were directed to a building on King William Street—Regis House. There was a door in the basement that led to the old station. It's deep, no lift, long set of stairs. I remember sizing that situation up—four of us, walking into a completely unknown terrain, underground. If the shooter or shooters were still down there, they'd be cornered. They could pick us off on the stairs, or we could end up in a situation where they'd end up killing everyone. No good no matter how we looked at it. Absolute pitch-black down them steps, seemed to go on forever, round and round. Lost radio contact. We shouted that we were coming, flashed our lights—gave whoever was down there every chance to stand down. Dead silence."

He looked at me again before continuing.

"The platform area was divided into two floors during the war. So there was a set of steps and an office on the upper floor. The door was open. Once we cleared the general platform area, two of us went up the stairs and another two went into the tunnels. I found a woman, Margo Riley, first. She was at her desk. David Lennox was on the floor by the supply cabinet. Mark Denhurst was in one of the back rooms. Jane Watson died with a pipe in her hand, trying to fight, I suppose. Katie Ellis was near the entrance of the tunnels. All of them long dead before we arrived."

"And Alexander Newman?"

"We'd been told to look for six officers. We found five in more or less the same area. Newman was the one missing. We finally found him as well, deeper in the tunnels. Bullet to the head. Always bothered me. There was something not right about what I was seeing. It was only later that we found out it was an undercover operation, a drugs bust gone bad. The dealers had gotten access and were storing and moving cocaine through the old tunnels. It was a terrible scene, and strange. Not like any drugs bust I ever saw, and I've seen a few. There were no drugs around, no evidence of a firefight. It was some kind of office down there. It looked like a group of people killed while going about their business. And it looked to me . . ."

This time, his hesitation didn't seem to be connected to me. He smoked for a moment, then tossed the cigarette to the ground and stomped it out.

"It certainly looked to me like Newman was the doer. The others were unarmed and had all been shot. He had a gun in his hand and the wound in his head looked self-inflicted—but it was very dark. You don't want to accuse a fellow officer of something like that without proof, but . . . anyway, they got us out of there pretty quick. I don't even remember seeing the SOCOs down there. No one was taking pictures or anything. They got us out of there and told us to keep schtum, which I have until now. There was a rumor—just a rumor, mind you—that Newman had been sectioned at some point. We all suspected that he'd had some kind of breakdown, killed the others, maybe under the stress of working undercover for too long. The official story was drugs bust, and we never challenged it. Those officers were dead. Nothing was going to bring them back. Their families deserved peace. But that scene was wrong. I always knew it was wrong. You're telling me this has to do with the Ripper?"

"Is there anything else you remember about that night?" Stephen asked.

"Just that it was terrible," he said. "You don't see many like that, and you don't want to. Once in a lifetime is enough."

"Nothing else? Nothing strange?"

"I suppose," Maybrick said, "there was one odd thing. When we found Newman, he was holding a Walkman."

"A what?" Callum said.

"You're too young for that, I suppose," he said. "A Sony Walkman. A music player. Used to be the thing. Played tape cassettes. He wasn't just holding it—he was clutching it tight to his body. Strange thing to be clutching during a drugs bust or a mass shooting, at any rate."

Stephen's expression changed instantly. His eyebrows rose so much, they seemed to drag his entire face along for the ride.

"That means something to you?" the sergeant asked. "What's going on here? I deserve to know. I've got a lot of people out on the street tonight looking for this bastard."

"Thank you," Stephen said. The deep, serious voice was dropped. This was normal Stephen. In fact, there was a shake in his voice. "That'll be all."

There weren't a lot of options for places to huddle at three in the morning on Ripper night, so we sat in the police car a few streets over, the engine idling.

"I'm not sure what we just learned," Callum said. "I just know I feel sick."

For once, I wasn't the only one who was completely baffled and uninformed. Stephen had fixed his gaze straight ahead, at the back of a van.

"Stephen?" Callum said. "Tell me you aren't thinking what I'm thinking. Please tell me that."

"A Walkman," Stephen said quietly. "Before mobile phones, that would have been the perfect device. Same idea. A common object that anyone could be seen carrying. A few buttons to push to send an electrical current through the stones. A Tube station used as an office. A body found clutching a Walkman. They weren't undercovers—they were *us*. The squad wasn't disbanded because of funding—it was disbanded because one of us went insane and murdered everyone else."

Callum laughed darkly and dragged his hands over his face.

"A dead station," he said. "For the dead police. That's what they're called, the disused ones. Dead stations."

"He knows we exist," Stephen went on, his gaze still fixed. "All the messages. Murdering people in front of cameras. He wanted to make sure we knew he was a ghost. He wanted to get our attention. He knows us. He's one of us."

"This seems like an ambush," Callum said. "If you're right, he wants us to go to the place where he murdered the entire previous squad. I've been in those tunnels and old stations. If you don't know your way around, you're in trouble."

"If we don't go," Stephen said, "he's going to kill people. This is our one and only chance. And we have to decide now."

Callum exhaled loudly and banged his head against the headrest. In the distance, I could hear the *neer-ner-neer-ner-neer-ner* of sirens, police cars chasing a man they could never see, never catch.

"Can't you call someone?" I said. "Get someone to tell you what to do?"

"There is no one," Stephen said. "We have superiors, but no one can make this decision. There's too little time and too little information. It's up to us."

He opened the computer once again.

"King William Street station," he said. "Popular with urban explorers. They have drawings and photos up. Built in 1890, closed in 1900. During the Second World War it was converted into an air raid shelter . . . There are two access points. The main one is in the basement of a large office building called Regis House on King William Street, like the sergeant just said. That leads to the original spiral emergency staircase. You go down seventy-five feet to the tunnels. The other access point is at London Bridge station. The old King William Street tunnels are used for ventilation for that station. The only people who can get down there are London Underground engineers. The public can't go down there anymore, because it's full of live cables."

"My favorite words," Callum said. "Live cables."

"You can go in through London Bridge," Stephen said. "It sounds like you can cross under the Thames through a tunnel. I can go down the steps. We'll come at him from two directions and get him between us. I'm not saying this is completely safe, or that it's ideal. But we are quite literally the only people who can stop him, and this is the only time we've ever known where he plans to be. We signed up to this job for a reason."

"Because we're freaks," Callum said. "Because we're unlucky."

"Because we can do something other people can't."

"But they didn't tell us about this, did they? They didn't tell us that someone on the last squad went mental and murdered the others."

"Would you mention that?" Stephen asked simply.

I don't plan many sieges or raids, but even I know that it's bad when you are going somewhere through a basement, to a place seventy-five feet underground that most people aren't even aware of.

"I hate this plan," Callum finally said. "But I know you'll go down there alone if I don't go. So I guess I'm in."

"I have to go with you," I said.

It's not that I am extremely brave—I think I just forgot myself for a minute. Maybe that's what bravery is. You forget you're in trouble when you see someone else in danger. Or maybe there is a limit to how afraid you can get, and I'd hit it. Whatever the case, I meant what I said.

"Not a chance," Stephen said quickly. "We're hiding you somewhere along the way."

"You don't have a choice," I said. "Neither do I. He wants

me. He's going to come after me. And if you fail, he's going to get me eventually."

"She's right," Callum said.

"She's never done this before," Stephen said.

"*You've* barely done this before," I countered. "Look, Callum just said this sounds like an ambush. You can't just sneak in and hope you'll corner him. You need something to keep him busy."

"She's right," Callum said again. "I hate this entire conversation, but she's right."

"She's also unarmed," Stephen countered. "The other terminus is with Boo. She's going to need it if he decides to go into Wexford instead. We can't leave her helpless."

"Let me put this another way," I said. "I'm coming. I'm not asking permission. I can't live like this. I can't live not knowing how this ends."

As soon as I said those words, I knew I had hit on the reason for my sudden burst of pure courage. I couldn't go on this way—with this sight, knowing that some ghost could come after me. I was either going to stop this, or I was going to die trying.

Stephen put his head in his hands for a moment, then beat a terse rhythm on the steering wheel. Then he turned on the sirens again and hit the gas.

**WHITE'S ROW, EAST LONDON**
**NOVEMBER 9**
**2:45 A.M.**

IN 1888, MILLER'S COURT WAS A DARK OFFSHOOT OF Dorset Street, known as "the worst street in London." Room thirteen, at 26 Dorset Street, had its own entrance on Miller's Court. Room thirteen wasn't even a real room—it was just an old back parlor cut off by a thin partition, twelve feet square, with a broken window. Inside, there was a bed, a table, and a fireplace. It was here that, on the morning of November 9, 1888, the body of Mary Kelly was discovered. She was found by her landlord, who came by at ten forty-five to collect the rent. It was the only time the Ripper struck indoors and the only time the crime scene was photographed. The hideous images of Mary Kelly in room thirteen entered the annals of history.

Dorset Street was so irredeemable that in the 1920s, the buildings were all demolished to make room for the new fruit market being opened in Spitalfields. On the exact spot where room thirteen once stood, there was now a warehouse where trucks could deliver goods for the market. And at two A.M. on this November 9, over five thousand people had gathered there. They filled the narrow passage between the warehouse and the multistory car park and spilled out onto the streets around. Most of those people had come for an all-night vigil to honor all the Ripper's victims, both from 1888 and the present.

But there were other people there as well. There were dozens of news reporters babbling on to rolling cameras in dozens of different languages. There were dozens of police officers, uniformed and plainclothed, wandering the crowd. There were souvenir carts selling WELCOME BACK, JACK and I SURVIVED NOVEMBER 9TH AND ALL I GOT WAS THIS BLOODY T-SHIRT (complete with fake bloodstain) shirts. There were food and drink vendors selling hot chestnuts, sodas, tea, sausage rolls, and ice cream. In many ways, it looked like a carnival.

No one noticed who started passing out the flyers. They just started circulating through the crowd and were passed on automatically. They contained six words only—no call to action, no instructions. Just a strange, simple message.

Several minutes later, to bring the point home, a flood of flyers drifted from the sky. The drizzle dampened them and made them heavy and sticky, so some adhered to the walls as they came down. The crowd looked up at the multistory car park behind them. The flyers were still falling, but there was no one throwing them. They came and they came, handfuls at a time.

One of the vigil organizers peeled a flyer off the wall and read it.

"What is this?" she asked. "Is this some kind of sick joke?"

Because the car park was sitting more or less on the site of the fifth Ripper murder, it had been closed and locked down for the night. Several police officers patrolled the ground floor. No one could have gotten to the top. And yet that was where the flyers were coming from. There was a lot of talking into shoulder radios, and a team ran up to scout every level and find whoever was up there. Two more police officers were in the car park office, looking at the CCTV camera screens in confusion. They could see the flyers going out, but couldn't see the person tossing them. The reports were coming in: "Level one, clear." "Level two, clear."

Down in the street, the reporters stared up at the shower of paper. The cameras turned upward to get the shot. At least it was different, something to break up the monotony of waiting for this thing to happen, the endless newscaster drivel and footage of police cars cruising along.

Only one person in the crowd saw who was throwing the flyers. That person was seventeen-year-old Jessie Johnson, who, three days before, had gone into anaphylactic shock after eating a peanut. She saw the woman in the 1940s army uniform leaning over from one of the levels, tossing the papers into the air.

"She's there," Jessie said. "Right there."

Jessie's observations were lost in the mayhem as a helicopter appeared low overhead, drowning out everything with the sound of chopper blades and blinding everyone with its powerful searchlight. It scanned the top of the car park while the people below shielded their eyes and their candles and tried to continue with the vigil.

"We will never forget," the person at the microphone yelled, "that the victims have names, have faces . . . We will take this night back . . ."

Jessie watched as the woman in the uniform finished throwing the flyers and disappeared. A few minutes later, she walked briskly out of the car park, right past three police officers. Even as it was happening, Jessie was rewriting the story in her mind. It was too odd. The woman must have been a police officer or something like that. She had no idea that she had just seen the British army's last active soldier from the Second World War, still in her uniform, still defending the East End.

Jessie looked down at the flyers, which coated the street and were being read by thousands of people and filmed by dozens of television cameras. They read

**THE EYES WILL COME TO YOU**

# Terminus

**Men would be angels, angels would be gods.**

***—Alexander Pope,***
***"Essay on Man"***

# 33

WE WERE SITTING IN THE POLICE CAR ACROSS THE street from Regis House. It was one of countless large office buildings in the City of London, maybe ten stories, made of grayish-white stone, full of offices. The front was mostly made of glass, with a large circular overhang in black metal giving its name and address, 45 King William Street. We had dropped Callum off at London Bridge station a few minutes before. Right now, he was making his way under the Thames via a tunnel.

"We'll give him ten more minutes," Stephen said, glancing at the dashboard clock. It was three forty-five.

Stephen looked out the window and surveyed the street. King William Street led up to London Bridge, and there weren't many pubs or restaurants on this stretch. The street was deserted except for us. I watched the traffic lights change, the little man on the "walk" sign turn from green to red.

Once again, it was time to wait. All of London was waiting, silent, as if the population had collectively drawn its breath in anticipation. There wasn't enough air in the car for me. Something was pressing on my chest. Fear. I tried to keep Jo's words in my mind—fear couldn't hurt me. It was a snake with no venom.

This was no snake. This was a thousand pounds of pressure.

"Remember how I said I had a boating accident?" Stephen said, breaking my train of thought. "It's not true."

He adjusted something on his tactical vest nervously.

"When I first met Callum and he asked me what happened, I started to tell him the story, which starts in a boathouse. But then I changed my mind. He just assumed I had a boating accident, and I never corrected him. I've said boating accident ever since."

"So what really happened?" I asked.

"My family is fairly wealthy. They aren't kind, or functional. We may have had a lot of things growing up, but a warm family life wasn't one of them. When I was fourteen, my older sister died of an overdose. It appeared to be accidental—she was out partying in London. The autopsy showed she had large amounts of both heroin and cocaine in her system. She was seventeen."

This was the kind of thing you should say something in response to, but given our circumstances, I felt it was okay to remain silent.

"She died on a Saturday. By the following Thursday, my parents sent me back to school and they went to St. Moritz on a skiing trip to 'get their minds off things.' That was how my family dealt with the death of their daughter. They sent me off, and they skied. For three years, I just tried to block everything else out. I studied. I did sports. I was the perfect student. I never let myself stop for one second to think about what had happened. Years of just blocking it out. Then, when I was in my last weeks of school and had been accepted to Cambridge, I realized it was the first time I really had nothing to do, nothing to work toward. And I started to think—all the time. I couldn't stop thinking about her. And I got angry. And I got sad. All the things I thought I'd kept out of my mind, they were all there, waiting for me. I was captain of the rowing team, so I had access to the boathouse. One night in early June, I went in, got a rope, and threw it over one of the beams . . ."

He didn't need to go any further. I got the idea.

"You tried to kill yourself," I said. "You must have failed. Because you're here. Wait. You're not a ghost, are you? Because that would totally destroy my mind right now."

"I didn't fail," he said. "I was interrupted in the middle of the process."

He took the keys from the ignition and put them in a pocket on his vest.

"The thing they don't tell you about hanging is how much it hurts," he said, "and it's not quick. That's why it's such a horrible punishment. The merciful hangmen knew how to break a neck instantly, which is humane. When you hang yourself, though, the rope slices into your neck. It's agonizing. As soon as I did it, I could see what a mistake it was, but I couldn't get the rope off. You can't, once it tightens around your neck and your body weight pulls you down. You kick, you pull on the rope, you fight. I was about to give up when I saw someone walk up to me. Another student, but not someone I recognized. He said, 'You can see me, can't you?' And he just sort of watched me, curiously. Then he put the chair upright and walked away. I got my feet back on the chair and got the rope from around my neck and swore never, ever to take my life for granted again, no matter how bad things seemed."

A keening siren in the distance interrupted the conversation.

"It's all right," he said. "I accept what I did, and I won't do it again. I don't tell people mostly because . . . I can't. I can't tell most people 'I tried to kill myself because I couldn't deal with my sister's death, but I'm okay now because I was saved by a ghost.' "

"No," I said. "I can see where you're coming from with that. But how did you get from there to this? To the ghost police?"

"Another thing they don't mention—probably because it hardly seems relevant—hanging leaves some terrible bruising around the neck." He adjusted his collar, as if remembering. "There's no mistaking it. The next morning, I found myself called to the infirmary, where a psychiatrist was waiting to talk to me. I could have lied to him, but I was still pretty dazed. I told him exactly what I had seen. That afternoon, they transferred me to a private mental health facility where they medicated me and put me in therapy. Two days after that, someone came to offer me a job. She said that I wasn't crazy. I was *depressed*, but I wasn't crazy. And I was depressed for a good reason. She knew what had happened to my sister. What I had seen was real. I had an ability that made me rare and very special, and did I want to do something worthwhile with it? Did I want to make a difference? A week later, I was released from the hospital. I was taken to an office in Whitehall, where a different person explained the rules to me. I would be the first of a newly re-formed and highly specialized squad. Technically, I would be a police officer. I would be trained as such. I would be, to the outside world, a police constable. That's what I had to tell everyone I was. In reality, I would be the commanding officer of a new police squad."

Stephen squeezed the steering wheel so hard, his fingers went white. This was as close as I'd ever seen him come to an emotion.

"That's how they used to recruit, you see," he said. "They'd look through psychiatric records for high achievers who told a similar story—those who had had brushes with death at a young age and then reported seeing people who weren't there. We were drawn from mental hospitals. I'm the last of that breed. Boo and Callum were tagged at A&E after their accidents. They were both talking about these mysterious people they'd seen . . . Both had been in accidents. Both were athletes. Both were street smart, if not academic. Both were from London and knew their way around. They were identified, and I was sent to recruit them. I'm the last of the mad ones."

"You don't sound crazy to me," I said.

Stephen nodded and looked out the window at Regis House, then back at the clock.

"Three fifty-five," he said. "Callum's in by now. It's time to go."

Regis House was a building that should clearly have been locked at four in the morning, but the doors were open when we tried them. The lights in the lobby were on, and there was a security desk that looked like it was normally manned. The guard was ominously absent, the chair pushed back almost to the wall. We saw a half-empty mug of tea on the desk and a computer opened to the BBC news site. Stephen leaned over and looked at the screen.

"Last updated a half hour ago," he said.

I noticed a piece of paper on the desk, the following scrawled on it: "Take the lift down a level. Stairs are at the far end of the hall. Look for the black door."

Neither one of us discussed the fate of the guard. There was no point. We took the elevator, then the stairs down into the physical plant of the building—the room with the heaters and pipes and all the heavy stuff needed to run a place of that size. In the far corner of the room, there was a black door. It had a few safety and warning stickers on it, but nothing out of the ordinary. Nothing to suggest where it might lead. Stephen removed his reflective jacket and dropped it to the floor, then carefully tried the handle. The door opened. I felt a rush of cold air come through the crack.

"One question," I said. "Did you tell me all that because you think I'm going to die?"

"No," he said. "It's because you're doing something brave, and I felt I should too."

"I'll take that as a yes," I said.

Before I could hesitate another second, I put my hand on top of his and pulled the door open wider.

# 34

THE SPIRAL EMERGENCY STAIRS, MADE AROUND 1890, hadn't been improved since then. A string of yellow work lights wound down and down and down, with no bottom in sight. Somehow, this twisting, descending string of bare bulbs made it worse. They didn't produce that much light—just enough to show the old tile work, dirty and often missing in patches, and the rough and worn condition of the steps.

I stood there on the top step, my toes hanging over the edge, not ready to move. I could already feel the cold seeping in around my neck, freezing my hands on the old handrail. The air had a hard, mineral smell. The only warmth came from Stephen, who was right at my back.

Without my conscious effort, one of my feet moved, and suddenly I was going down the steps, away from the world, from everything that was safe. A few steps down, I heard the dripping for the first time. This got louder and louder as I went. The only other sound was a strange, faint whistling—the echo of air passing through from ventilation fans and air-conditioning units and the other tunnels that made up this vast network under the city. This was the true Underground. I started to get dizzy from the spiral, from the sameness of it all. Then the spiral stairs stopped and turned into a straight set of stairs, maybe twenty or twenty-five in all.

"Please come down," said a voice. "Be careful on the last steps. They aren't in very good condition."

I froze in position. Now my brain remembered that it was supposed to be afraid. Stephen was still just one step behind me—he put his hand on my shoulder.

"No point in stopping," the voice said.

He was right. I was so deep now that going back wasn't an option anymore. This was the point where Stephen had to let me go on my own. He nodded to me, removing the flashlight from his belt and gripping it together with his terminus.

I took these last steps very slowly. They widened as I got nearer to the bottom, and they ended in what must have been the old entryway, where you bought tickets. The old ticket stalls were boarded up. Some of the tiling had been stripped away from the walls. There were a lot of modern safety notices stuck around, along with much older notices about smoking and nerve gas. Two arches opened in front of me. Pointing at each one was a crumbling cartoon picture of a hand, a little bit of the original Victorian decoration to direct the flow of traffic on and off of the platform. They probably looked nice at the time, but now they were unspeakably creepy.

I couldn't see Stephen anymore—he was hiding just out of sight up the steps, waiting. I passed through the arch on the right and stepped onto the old platform. It was a large space, with a high vaulted ceiling. The sunken bit where the trains used to pass had been raised up to the platform level, so it was one large room. Part of the space had been converted into a two-level structure with a set of stairs. The rest was chopped up strangely. There were random walls and doorways and halls. The train tunnels were now dark passageways, leading on to more strangely shaped rooms in a place that wasn't supposed to have any rooms. Heavy bundles of wires, a foot thick or more, ran along the walls and the edges of the floor. There were some posters left over from the days when the station was a bomb shelter, filled with slogans like CARELESS TALK COSTS LIVES and cartoons of Hitler hiding under tables. There were notices about smoking and being courteous to your sleeping neighbors.

A figure emerged from behind one of the walls. Now I understood why people thought ghosts floated. They moved with a strange ease. It looked like they had normal arms and legs that made them walk and reach, but there were no muscles in those arms and legs—no weight, no blood, none of the things that gave ordinary humans their individual ways of moving.

Aside from his silent approach, Newman was disarmingly normal.

"Hi," I said.

"Don't stand there in the doorway," Newman said. "Come through."

"I'm fine here."

Newman was carrying what looked like an old-fashioned doctor's bag. I'd seen these bags. They were Ripper-style prop bags, sold at stands all over the city. He set it down on an old metal worktable and opened it up.

"Well done with your message," he said. "I'm not sure how you managed it, but it was very effective. 'The eyes will come to you.'"

He produced a long knife with a thin blade from the bag. He was still far away from me. I'm not good at measuring distances, but it was far enough that if he ran for me, I could still turn and make a break for the stairs. But he made no indication that he intended to run at me. He poked through his bag in a leisurely fashion.

"How many of them are there?" he asked.

"What?"

"Remember some time ago, when we met?" he asked. "When I threw your friend in front of a car? I asked you if you'd ever met anyone like us, and you told me that you knew some . . . I think your words were, 'some weirdos at home'? You were lying, weren't you?"

I didn't reply.

"There's no need to deny it," he said. "I certainly hope you didn't come down here alone. It would be terribly irresponsible to send you on your own. Whoever's out there—why don't you come out and play as well? We're all friends down here."

Nothing. Just the dripping noise.

"No?" he called. "Don't want to? Look around you. Do you see this? This is the old headquarters. A good place for us—the Shades. Scotland Graveyard. Not a hint remains of what went on down here, all the work we did. When the government decides it no longer requires your services, it makes you go away. If you don't come out of here, do you think you'll get any recognition for your bravery?"

Still nothing.

"I know this place better than almost anyone. I know all the ways in. I didn't see anyone come down with you, so I can only assume they are coming through the tunnel from London Bridge."

He extended his arm to his right, toward one of the yawning openings into the dark.

"The other way in is the way you came, Aurora, right down those stairs. And I watched you. You came alone. Unless there are people on those stairs, waiting to make their entrance. Don't wait too long, for her sake."

"Hey!" called a voice from another part of the station. "Jack the Wanker! Over here! I want your autograph!"

Callum stepped out of the darkness of the tunnel, holding out his terminus.

"Ah," Newman said. "You're young. Makes sense, I suppose."

"That's right," Callum called. "I'm a kid. Come see my toy."

"Here's something I know about your toys," Newman said. "There are three of them. Are there three of you? I certainly hope so."

"I don't need any help," Callum replied.

"Telephones," Newman said, stepping closer to Callum. "Very good. We had to carry torches and Walkmans. They even tried to put one in an umbrella. Very cumbersome. The telephone—that's very good."

As Newman was turned away, Stephen made a dash from the steps, across the small ticketing room, and threw himself against the wall between the arches, right next to me.

"You seem keen," Newman said to Callum. "It's a good thing

I have this knife. Which one of us do you think would win in the end? I can slash your throat as fast as you can turn that terminus on me. Should we try it and see?"

He whipped the blade in an arc in front of him and took a few more steps toward Callum, who didn't move an inch.

"Oh, I like you," Newman said, approaching Callum. "You're a brave one."

"Stop," Stephen said, pushing me aside and stepping into the doorway.

"Here we go," Newman said. He didn't sound at all alarmed. "Two. One more, surely."

"You can't take both of us," Stephen said. "Make a move for one, and the other will get you. You may be a strong ghost, but we're still stronger."

"The dead travel fast," Newman said.

"Not that fast," Callum said. "Believe me, I can outrun you."

"He can," Stephen confirmed.

"Well then," Newman said, with a smile. "I suppose I'd better give myself up."

"Just put the knife down," Stephen said.

"You know . . ." Newman stepped back a bit, toward the two-leveled structure in the middle of the platform. "I did learn something very useful during my time down here—"

And with that, darkness—a darkness so absolute, my eyes had never experienced anything like it. My brain had no idea what to make of it. Now I truly understood where we were. We were deep underground. I had no sense of space, no sense of distance, no perspective at all. I couldn't have found my way back to the steps. I didn't have my cell phone on me—that had been taken away when they were tracing the texts.

"The location of the light switch," he said. "Funny how frightening the dark is."

His voice bounced around in all directions, off the curved ceiling, off the bricks and the tiles. He could have been thirty yards away, or he could have been next to me. Two tiny points of light appeared—the glow of the phones. After a moment, this was joined by a thin beam of light from Stephen's direction, and then from Callum's. The flashlights.

"Two lights," Newman said. "Where's the third one? Come out, come out . . ."

I saw Callum's flashlight beam swing around wildly.

"Where'd he go?" Callum yelled. "You see him?"

"Just keep your terminus out," Stephen called to him. "He can't go near you. They're more powerful now than they used to be."

"Is that a warning for me?" Newman said. "I still see only two of you. There must be more."

"There might have been a larger squad if you hadn't murdered everyone you worked with," Stephen replied.

"It never had to happen that way. I never intended to kill anyone. It was all very unfortunate."

"Murdering five people you worked with was unfortunate? Taking on the role of Jack the Ripper was unfortunate?"

"A means to an end," Newman said.

I was pretty sure Stephen was trying to make him talk to get a sense of where he was, but it was still impossible to tell. The acoustics sent the sound of his voice in far too many directions. Stephen reached over and grabbed me, putting his arms around me. He maneuvered us both over to the wall, then slipped from behind me and pushed the terminus into my hands.

"Hold this," he whispered. "Keep pressing one and nine. *Do not stop.* Stay against the wall so he can't get behind you."

I wanted to ask him what he was doing, but I was too afraid to speak. I heard him move away, then there was silence. Nobody said a word. A full minute went by, maybe more, with nothing happening at all. I dug my fingers so hard into the number pad that I could feel my nails slicing into it. It provided a small ball of light around my hands, a glow extending six or eight inches at best.

The lights suddenly came back on. My pupils contracted in shock, and it took a moment before I could see clearly. I was against the wall by the entryway arches. Callum was flat against the opposite wall, where the platform area was. We stared at each other.

"Stephen!" he yelled.

"Here," Stephen said quietly.

Stephen was speaking from inside the ticket area, just behind me. The noise didn't bounce around so much in there. And from the calm way he spoke, I had a terrible feeling that something very bad had happened. Callum came running in my direction, and I slowly peeled myself away from the wall and looked through the arch.

Stephen was standing on the bottom step, where he had thrown the switch on a set of emergency lights. He was holding his right arm, up near the shoulder. Newman stood a few feet away from him, casually leaning against the old ticket booth.

"Stephen?" Callum asked.

"Someone," Newman said, "was going to go for the lights."

"Get him," Stephen said quietly. "Just get him."

"What the hell is happening?" Callum said.

"Allow me to explain what's going to happen," Newman replied. "Your friend has just been injected with an extremely large dose of insulin. Within a few minutes, he will begin to experience shakes and sweating. Then comes the confusion. The weakness. Then breathing will become difficult as the body begins to shut itself down. The dose I've given him is fatal without treatment, but easily reversible with a simple injection. I happen to have a syringe ready to go. I will trade it for all three termini. Give them to me, and he lives. Or we stand here and watch him die. And it won't take long. You won't have time to run up those steps and call for help. All three, now."

"Callum, get him," Stephen said again. But he already looked pale and was gripping the railing for support.

"You're a nutter," Callum said. There was a tremble in his voice.

"The real Jack the Ripper was insane," Newman replied. "No question. What I want is rational. The terminus is the only thing in the world that can hurt me. If I have them, I have no predators. I have nothing to fear. We all want to live without fear. Now put it down and kick it to me. Both of you. And whoever else is out there."

"Why don't you kiss my arse?" Callum snapped. "How about that for an idea?"

"How about you think of your friend's welfare?"

Callum shifted the grip of his terminus.

"We came down to finish this," Stephen said. "Just do it, Callum."

"You kill me," Newman said, "you kill him. Your choice."

Callum glanced over at me.

"No surrender?" Newman asked politely. "Maybe you want to be in charge? Maybe that's why you're willing to let him die."

"Callum!" Stephen said. "Rory! He's right there! *Do it.*"

"No," Newman said, pointing at Callum. "This one . . . I understand him completely. He won't let go of that terminus, not for you. Not for anything. I understand. It makes you feel secure, doesn't it? It gives you back your sanity. It gives you control. The sight is a curse, and the terminus is the only cure. I have sympathy for you. I do. That's why I'm here. That's all I want too."

There was no sarcasm, no little smile. I think he meant it, every word of it.

"All of this," Newman said. "The Ripper, this station . . . all of it was just my way of trying to draw out the squad. I developed a plan that brought you to a place I knew well. I always knew there'd be more of you than of me, more than I could fight off. So I developed a plan in which I could get what I needed and you could all just walk away. He doesn't have a lot of time, Callum."

Newman leaned against the ticket booth and considered us both. I realized that I was holding up my terminus as well, my fingers poised on the one and the nine. I had done it unconsciously. Callum and I were trapped, unable to move forward.

"I see the way you look," Newman said to Callum. "The way you hold on to that terminus for dear life. Did one of them get to you, too? Is that how you got the sight? Several of us had experiences like that. We were always a little different, a little more intense. I had my accident when I was eighteen. I'd been given a secondhand motorbike as a gift for getting into Oxford. It was 1978. I was at home, in the New Forest. Lots of dirt lanes to ride on, nothing but ponies in the way. Best summer of my life. Exams done, future ahead of me. It was a perfectly clear evening, the sun still out around nine o'clock, height of June—and I was riding back home from visiting my girlfriend, coming down a stretch of the road I knew perfectly well. Then suddenly, something swung at me, knocking me off the bike. I went flying backward, the bike into a tree. And when I looked up, there was a boy standing over me, laughing. My father's friends happened to be coming by on their way to the pub, found me and the crashed bike. I told them about the boy. I pointed at him. He was still laughing. They didn't see him, and I was taken off to the hospital. The doctors assumed, quite reasonably, that I'd been on the bike when it hit the tree and had suffered a head injury.

"I started seeing people—people that no one else could see. I was involuntarily admitted to a mental hospital for observation for a month. You all know the feeling, I'm sure. You know you're not insane, and yet the evidence that you are seems overwhelming."

I could tell Callum was listening very carefully to all of this, shifting his gaze between Stephen and Newman.

"As the summer went on, I realized that I had a decision to make. I was either going to remain in this hospital, or I was going to get on with my life. I decided the best thing to do was lie, tell the doctors I couldn't see or hear them anymore. They assumed I was recovering from my injury, and I was released. I decided, because of my problem, to become a psychiatrist. I was a medical student at Oxford, and when I was done there, I went on to St. Barts. St. Barts is in the old body-snatcher district. If there's one place you don't want to have the sight, it's in the old body-snatcher district, because that place is thick with them, and they aren't pleasant. But I finished my training, took my exams, and qualified as a psychiatrist. My first position was with the prison system, working with young offenders. It was good work for me—dealing with people who were young, misunderstood, angry. It was a good place to learn about evil. About fear. About what happens to people who are isolated and confined from a young age. And, it might not surprise you, I encountered four teenagers there who had our sight."

Stephen was trying to keep himself together, but he had to sit down on the steps. Callum too was struggling, but the things Newman was saying . . . I knew they resonated with him.

"Then one day a man came up to me in the street and asked me if I'd like to put my abilities to good use. I still don't know who he was—someone quite high up in the Met or in MI5, I suppose. It turns out they had started reviewing files at psychiatric institutions to see if anyone was reporting a very specific set of delusions—reporting that they could see ghosts after a near-death experience. A brilliant way of recruiting, really.

"I was taken to Whitehall, to a small office, and the Shades were explained to me. They knew what I was. They liked that I had worked in the prison system. They liked everything about me. They gave me the one thing I had wanted since my accident—a weapon. Something to protect me against these things I was seeing. They gave me some control over my life. The day I became a Shade, I was truly happy for the first time since I was seventeen. I'll bet it was the same for you.

"I knew we were doing the jobs of bin men, cleaning ghosts off Tube platforms and out of old houses, but I didn't care. For the first time in my life, I was happy. But I couldn't help my nature. The others—they were drawn from ordinary police stock. I was an academic. I was a doctor. A scientist.

"There used to be a form of treatment for schizophrenics called insulin shock therapy. The patients would be brought in over the course of several weeks and regularly put into insulin shock, going deeper and deeper each time. Eventually, they'd be put into daily comas and brought out again after an hour or so. Not a very pleasant process, and the results were debatable. But I saw another use for the procedure. I devised a series of experiments to test different areas of the brain, to try to determine which one caused people to develop the sight. But to do this, I needed to re create the conditions under which the sight develops. Namely, I had to bring the body into a state that mimicked the onset of death. Insulin shock therapy did just that. Paranormal neuropsychiatry, and I was the only person in the world qualified to practice it.

"My status as a Shade gave me unrestricted access, and they already knew me as a doctor. So I went back to the places I had worked before. My idea was simple. I would take the young people I'd met who had the sight, and I would say I was giving them experimental therapy. Getting insulin isn't difficult, nor is the process of putting someone into a diabetic coma. It's a bit of a risky procedure, but done carefully it causes no lasting harm. And I would be working on youths in the prison system, people already considered irredeemable. I performed my work for two years, taking the same subjects down about a dozen times each. I also conducted physical and psychological examinations.

"No one knew about this research of mine," he continued. "I had planned on revealing it only when I had a clear result, at which point I would certainly have been given a proper lab and resources to continue. Finding out what controls the ability to see the dead? That's a valuable asset. So I still did all of my normal duties—removing ghosts from buildings, getting trains working, all the mundane things they had us do. In my spare time, I did my real work. I had just located a fifth subject, a young girl. I began the process with her. To this day, I'm not sure what went wrong. I took her down—and she didn't come back up. That's when the powers that be discovered the work I'd been doing. They should have thanked me, despite the mistake. They didn't."

I was convinced now that Newman was telling us the truth. He may have been a murderer, and evil, but he was also honest. At least he was right now.

"The trouble with joining a secret government agency is that they can't really fire you. And they couldn't exactly put me on trial either. No . . . the whole thing had to be very quiet. I was removed from this station, my powers stripped, and my terminus was taken away. I came down here that day to talk to my fellow Shades, and to take a terminus. I needed it. I couldn't go back to the way it was before, having nothing to protect me. I brought the gun because . . . I had to get them to see sense, to give me one. But they wouldn't. They just wouldn't cooperate. I suppose they didn't think I'd shoot . . ."

"Callum!" Stephen said weakly.

"You can let him die," Newman said, "or you can save him, right now."

"Let me see it," Callum said. "Let me see the syringe."

"I can't do that," Newman said. "Not until you each set your terminus down and kick it over to me."

"You could be lying."

"But you know my history now. You know why I killed. You know what I want. I *want* you to save him. I want to protect those with the sight. I just also want to protect myself. There is absolutely no reason we can't all walk away from this."

Then he looked right at me.

"Aurora," he said. "You've been exceptionally brave, and you're not even on the squad. You've risked your life to save others. I swear to you—if you set that down and kick it to me, I will be as good as my word. Give it to me."

Stephen put his head down. I think he knew what I was about to do and he couldn't watch. I couldn't watch him die. I slowly put the terminus on the filthy floor and gave it a kick. It landed more or less by Newman.

Now that I'd surrendered, the entire burden was on Callum. He looked as sick as Stephen. He shifted his weight from foot to foot, as if preparing to make a dash. His body was ready, but his mind was not.

"Now you, son," Newman said.

"Don't call me *son*! Don't you *speak* to me."

Newman closed his mouth and raised his arms to the side, making himself a wide and open target.

"You decide," he said. "I accept my fate. If you can live with the death of your friend, I can accept my end here. It's been a noble fight for all concerned."

Stephen could no longer plead. He had slumped against the wall and his eyes were half closed. Callum raised himself up on the balls of his feet, knees flexed. He was going to do it. I was sure of it.

And then he just opened his hands and let the terminus go.

"Kick it here," Newman said quietly.

Callum delivered a perfect side-of-the-foot kick, sending it right to Newman. I'd never seen anyone that agonized. He rubbed his hands over his face and held them there in a prayer formation.

"Give us the medicine," he said.

"When I get the third one," Newman said.

His demeanor had changed also. His eyes had widened and there was an energy about him—he looked alive.

"The third one isn't here," Callum replied.

"Liar!"

It was a piercing yell, with an echo.

"It's not here," Callum said again, pulling his hands away from his face and sighing. "But if you save him, I'll take you to it."

"Oh no," Newman said. He began to pace. "He will die, do you understand? And it will be *your fault*. Do you hear me? *Your fault!*"

Newman was yelling to the third person he still believed was crouching in the darkness—maybe in the stairs, maybe in the tunnels. He snatched up the two termini at his feet and began to pace, looking through the archways, looking up the steps, searching for the last Shade. Stephen was going to die for nothing unless . . .

Unless someone could talk Newman down, someone he could believe. Someone who held no threat. Someone he'd talked to before. Someone like me.

"I'll take you," I said.

# 35

THERE WAS A SOUND FROM THE STEPS, ONE SMALL groan from Stephen as he heard me say these words. Newman stopped pacing and stared at me, a wild look in his eye. He went back to the ticket counter and smacked both of the termini down, hard, then cracked open their cheap casing like two plastic Easter eggs. He ripped out the wiry innards, plucking the diamonds from each one, and pushed the empty, broken phones to the floor. Once this was done, he retrieved his knife, which was sitting there on the counter. He crossed the room in a few long strides and came right up to my face.

"Are you lying to me?" he asked, digging the point into my chin.

"No," I said through clenched teeth. It was hard to talk. Newman pressed the knife even harder, forcing my mouth closed. I felt the tip of the blade slip into my flesh, digging a small hole. Up close, he had a rotten smell that burned the inside of my nose. He no longer looked completely in control of himself.

He twisted the knife once, then grabbed me by the hair and dragged me across the room toward the ticket booth.

"Reach in there," he said, pointing the knife at some old boards that sealed off the old ticket window.

The boards gave when I pushed at them, and I was able to get my hand into the opening, though I couldn't see what I was reaching for. What I felt mostly was grime and cobwebs, and I was certain I was thrusting my hand into a place that had long been a nest for rats and mice. I felt what seemed like pencils, and some little rock-like things that were probably petrified rodent turds, but then I hit something smooth and thin and plasticky. I carefully pulled this out of the opening. It was a syringe, capped and pristine, and full of something.

"Take the cap off and inject him," Newman said.

"Where?"

"In the upper arm."

I approached Stephen, who looked up at me with a sweat-slicked face.

"Don't do this," he said. "Don't let him have it."

I pulled the cap off the needle end and jammed it into Stephen's arm. It took a lot of force to get it through the sweater and the shirt and his skin. It didn't go in all the way on the first try, so I had to keep pressing down to get into the muscle.

"Sorry," I said.

The plunger was equally hard to depress, but I eventually got it down, and whatever was in the syringe was now in Stephen. As I pulled it out, Newman put me in a choke hold and held the knife up to my eye.

"Stay exactly where you are," he said to Callum. "If I so much as *think* I hear you following, I'll slice her open."

I had been alone with the Ripper before, but he had never *had* me before. When Jo touched you, it felt like a gentle breeze. The Ripper felt like he had the contained wind strength of a hurricane—or at least a pretty serious storm, one that could rip off a roof or pull up a tree. He dragged me backward up the steps until we reached the spiral section, then pushed me ahead of him.

"If I don't get my terminus, I won't hold myself back," he said. "The girl with the long hair, your friend in the window? The boy with the curly hair? They'll be scrubbing the walls for weeks, trying to get the blood off. And what I will do to you will be even worse. Do you understand?"

"Yes," I said. I was crying a little, but I wiped my face and started the climb. I stumbled frequently as we went up, and I'd feel the knife tap the middle of my back. Once we got to the basement, he locked the access door, sealing Stephen and Callum inside. He allowed me to walk on my own, knowing that his threat kept me tethered.

"Where is it?" he snapped as we got into the elevator.

"It's at Wexford," I said.

"I will lead, and you will follow."

It was eerily quiet outside. No cars. No sirens. No people. Just the Ripper and me, stepping out into the dark. He turned sharply when we stepped out of the building and headed toward the river. The building was very close to the Thames, and King William Street continued straight on to London Bridge—one continuous sidewalk. Newman walked to the middle of the bridge, and I stayed with him, fighting every impulse to start running and never, ever stop.

The Thames was well illuminated, lined with buildings and landmarks. This was the main alley of London, and all the lights were on tonight.

"Hypnos," he said, holding up one of the diamonds. "It has a faint gray hint to the flaw."

He held up the other for comparison.

"And this is Thanatos. A similar color, but slightly more greenish if you look at it. Persephone's flaw is distinctly more blue."

I could barely see the diamonds at all. The wind was blowing in my face, and I was much too frightened to process anything that detailed.

"They're all slightly different in their effect," he explained. "Hypnos is the fastest to take effect. Thanatos is a bit slower to take action, not by much. And Persephone, the one we will go and get now . . ."

He palmed the two diamonds and closed his fist around them.

". . . was the one I carried. Quite powerful. That's why I preferred her. Plus, it's a lovely name—Persephone. The goddess of the Underworld. Dragged down to hell, then dragged right up again."

Newman shook the two diamonds in his fist like they were dice, and then he drew his arm back and threw them. They vanished in midair before dropping into the river below.

"Two gone," he said. "One to go. Come along, Aurora."

He turned back and walked exactly the way we had just come,

back down King William Street. East London is old and confusing, full of tiny streets and bends and turns, but his stride was purposeful and sure and quick. We walked right through the center of the London financial district, past the disappointed remains of Ripper parties, all waiting for that one last body. We wove through crowds of people, one living person and one dead person. In the dark, no one noticed the knife making its way along the city streets, held by no one. Or if they did, they would put it down to a trick of the eye, or a reflection, or too much beer.

I almost had to run to keep up with Newman, and my thoughts were going even faster. Callum would try to follow us, but he would have to get out first, and he would make sure to get Stephen to safety. So he was way behind me. Boo would be awake and on alert, and Jo was still on the lookout somewhere in the building. But Boo was also in a wheelchair. I was taking the Ripper into my home, and the only person who could fight him off was helpless.

But I was still going, still following, because there was no other way.

Wexford was still somewhat awake. The lights were on in some of the windows. The line of police had thinned out. Now there was one car and no actual officers were in sight, but there were a lot of people passing through the square as the vigil ended.

"Where is it?" Newman asked as we reached the green.

"In my building."

"Where?"

"Someone has it. I can go in and get it and bring it out to you."

"Oh, I think we'll go in together."

I tapped my card against the reader by the door, and it beeped. I heard the click as the door opened. Only two people were left in the common room. Charlotte was one of them, asleep in the chair closest to the door. The other was Boo.

"Hello, Rory," Charlotte said, waking up with a yawn. "Still awake?"

Boo naturally fixed her sights on Newman.

"It's her," Newman said. "From the night we took a walk. She's one of them?"

In a second, Boo had her terminus out and up, pointed in his direction. Newman flicked the knife so she could see it and held it at the right side of my neck, the point digging a small hole into the flesh.

"The others are alive for now," he said. "Ask Aurora. I've kept my word. In exchange, I will have that terminus. You'll drop that to the floor or she will be the first to go. Then I'll do this one in the chair, and then I'll do you."

"You feeling all right?" Charlotte asked Boo.

Boo held up the phone and kept her fingers over the one and the nine, but she didn't press.

The pressure on my neck increased, and I felt a trickle of blood run down the side.

"You're in a *wheelchair*," Newman said. "You have no options."

Boo hesitated for another moment, then released it to the floor.

"You dropped your phone," Charlotte said. "Really, are you all right?"

"Shut up, Charlotte," Boo said, not taking her eyes off of me or Newman.

Charlotte turned around in her seat to see what was going on. She could make no sense of it, me standing so stiffly, Boo throwing her phone around. She got up and reached for the phone, which caused Newman to lurch forward. He grabbed a lamp from the side table and smacked it against Charlotte's head as she bent over. She made a little cry of surprise, and then he hit her again, and again, until she fell to the floor and was still. He gingerly took the terminus from her hand.

"There," I said. "You have it. I told you."

"So you did," he said.

I had no idea what came next, and I'm not sure he did either. He stared at the terminus in shock. There was blood coming out of a gash on Charlotte's head. I had no idea if she was alive. Newman watched the news for a moment, mesmerized by the footage of the police cars trolling the streets, still looking for him.

"We're left with a situation, aren't we?" he said. "Our agreement was I got the terminus, and your friend Stephen was allowed to live. I've honored that. But I've started a project—a great project—and that project needs to be completed. Saucy Jack must finish his work."

"But . . ."

"Aurora," he said patiently, "it's much too good a show to end. And really, you always knew. You didn't run from me—you faced me. We were always going to finish this."

This didn't upset me as much as it should have. It felt more like a dream. I knew precisely what he meant. Maybe we were always going to finish this. Maybe he was the person I'd always imagined by my side in England—a star-crossed pair, the slayer and the victim, tied together by fate. Or maybe I was just tired of running from him, tired of feeling that knife.

"Why?" Boo said.

"Why?" Newman said. "Because I can."

"But what will it do?"

Newman pointed to the television behind him.

"This story," he said, "it's captured imaginations. I chose Jack the Ripper for a very specific reason. Fear. Jack the Ripper is one of the most feared figures in history. Look at all of these people obsessed with him. It's been over a hundred years, and people are still trying to figure out who he is. He's every figure in the dark. He's every killer that got away. He's the one who kills and never explains why. In the grand scheme of things, he didn't even kill that many people. You know what I think it is? I think it's the name. And he didn't even come up with it—a newspaper did, based on a fake letter."

"The name of the *Star*," I said.

He smiled and nodded, looking genuinely pleased.

"The name of the *Star*," he repeated. "Very good! The *Star* newspaper. Of course now, there are much more effective means of delivering news—constant news, instantly updated. I am the story. I am the star. I am in control."

Newman had never seemed crazy to me before that moment, but something had peeled away, revealing the raw energy underneath. He had what he wanted, and he had nothing left to fear.

He was going to kill me.

I experienced a kind of tunnel vision, a hollow sound in my ears. I could see only him. He was flicking the knife, casually slicing into the top of one of the chairs.

"Will you at least leave Wexford?" I asked.

"It's a reasonable request." He shrugged.

"Rory!" Boo said. She tried to wheel over to me, but I put up my hand.

"Not here," I said. "Please. Not in front of her."

"Where then?"

"There's a bathroom down the hall."

I was saying these words as though they made sense.

"As good a place as any," he said. "I'll follow you this time."

There was no point in saying good-bye to Boo. I just nodded and walked out of the room and into the hall. I couldn't hear Newman behind me, but I could feel his presence. I opened the bathroom door and stepped inside. He followed and locked it behind us.

The slash came as soon as I turned around to face him. It was so fast that I didn't even have time enough to look down and see what the knife was doing to me. My shirt instantly filled with blood. I didn't feel anything. I just stared at the increasingly large red stain all over my front. I watched it lengthen and widen. I couldn't feel any pain, which seemed odd.

Standing up was suddenly an issue. My body was cold all over and my legs shook. I started to slide down the wall. As I sank down, my new angle provided me with a very good view of the blood pooling in my clothes, so I resolved not to look at that ever again. I focused on Newman, on the studious calm of his face.

"I'll tell you something interesting," he said, tapping the tip of the knife against the sink. "You changed my plan. What I wanted was to draw out the squad, to spot one of them. Instead, I found you. It was so much easier having a target, someone to speak to, someone for the Shades to focus on. So I'm going to reward you. I was holding a terminus when I died. My fingers were on the buttons. I suspect—I have no proof, but I suspect—that it had something to do with the way I am. I not only returned, I returned quite strong. And I was the only person in that station to return. I've always wanted to know if these things are connected. I've cut you, and now you'll bleed out. I had to do the abdomen. You would have lost consciousness and died within moments of my slashing the neck. I avoided the femoral artery as well. That's a good cut."

He backed up to the far wall and bent down and slid the terminus across the floor to me.

"Go on," he said. "Pick it up. Use it on yourself. Hold it as long as you can."

I took my hand off my abdomen and grabbed for it. I tried to find the one and nine, but there were spots in front of my eyes, and my fingers were slippery. Maybe I could get up. I decided to try. My hands, however, were too slick with blood. They skidded over the tiles. I had no grip—and moving made it worse. Moving made it hurt, a lot.

"Don't struggle," he said. "You'll bleed faster. Just rest and press the buttons. It's your best chance, Aurora. Let's find out what it can do. Let's see if we can make you into a ghost."

Something was happening to the door. The door was moving. No, the door was growing—the door was growing inward . . .

I had to be hallucinating.

No, the door was growing inward, in strange lumps. Then the lumps became things I recognized. The top of a head, with a hat. A knee, then a leg, a foot, a face. It was Jo, forcing herself through.

Even Newman didn't appear to expect this—some World War II woman soldier to come through the door.

"How the hell did you do that?" he asked. "It would have taken me ages to get through a door like that."

"Experience," she said. "And willpower. It's not pleasant."

Jo was closer to me than Newman was. She got to my side at once and plucked the terminus from my hand.

"I believe you took this from a friend of mine," she said, holding it up. "I understand you also threw her in the path of a car."

Newman stepped back toward the stall. He was trying to remain calm, but his composure was slipping.

"Who are you?" he said.

"Flight Sergeant Josephine Bell of the Women's Auxiliary Air Force."

"I don't think you know what that does," he said. "You should be careful."

"Oh, I think I know precisely what it does," Jo said.

There was no hesitation in her movement—it was swift and even in a way that no living person could manage. In the next moment, she was in the corner with Newman. I remember the light. Something like a tornado formed in the middle of the bathroom, and the stall door flew open. The floor shook from the force. There was a noise too—a rushing sound that was soon drowned out by the shattering of the mirrors above me. They blew out powdered glass in one massive cloud. It seemed to hold itself in the air for a moment before falling. And the smell—that sweet, burning smell—it filled the room. Then the light faded, and they were gone. Both of them.

# 36

AT HEALING ANGEL MINISTRY, COUSIN DIANE reads people's auras. She says the auras are the angels who hover behind you, who protect you, and that you can tell the kind of angel it is by the color. She has a chart. Blue angels deal with strong emotions. Red angels deal with love. Yellow angels deal with health. Green angels deal with home and family.

The ones you want to watch out for are the white light angels. They're at the top of the chart. The white light ones come when *big stuff* happens. If Cousin Diane sees a white light angel behind someone, she tends to check the newspaper for articles about accidents and obituaries.

"White light," she'll say, tapping the article. "I saw the white light, and you know what happens then." And what happens then is that someone gets hit by a bus or falls into an old sewage ditch and dies.

I was seeing white light now, everywhere, soft and bright and complete.

"Crap," I said.

In reply, the light faded just a bit. I wasn't dead. I was pretty sure of that. Of course, it was possible that I was dead, and I just had no idea. I didn't know what dead felt like.

"Am I dead?" I asked out loud.

There was no reply, except for the quiet beeping of some machine, and some voices. Things came into focus a little more sharply. There were edges now where wobbly blobs had previously been. I was in a bed, a bed with rails and white sheets with a light blue blanket on top. There was a television on a mounted arm that swung over to the side of the bed. There was a tube coming out of my arm. There was a window with a green curtain and a view of the gray sky.

The curtain next to me snapped back. A nurse with short blond hair came over to me.

"I thought I heard you say something," she said.

"I feel weird," I said.

"That's the pethidine," she replied.

"The what?"

"It's a medication that takes away pain and makes you drowsy."

She grabbed the IV bag that I now saw hanging over me and examined the level of its contents. After finishing her examination of the bag, she turned to my arm, checking the bandage tape that was holding the IV tube in place. As she leaned over me, I noticed there was a silver watch pinned to the front of her scrub shirt—not a normal one, like a wristwatch, but a specialized piece that looked like a medal. Like she was a soldier. Like Jo.

Jo . . .

It all started to roll back into my mind. Everything that had happened in the bathroom, the walk across London, the station. It all felt very distant, like it had happened to someone else. Still, a few loose tears trickled from my eyes. I didn't mean to cry them. The nurse wiped my face with a tissue and gave me a sip of water through a straw.

"There we go," she said. "Take a nice sip. No reason to cry. Nice, slow breath. Don't want to upset your stitches, now."

The water had a calming effect.

"You've had a rough night," she said. "There's a policeman here to speak to you, if you're feeling up to it."

"Sure," I said.

"I'll send him in."

She left me, and a moment later, Stephen appeared in the doorway. All of the things that identified him as a policeman were gone—the jacket, the sweater, the hat, the belt of equipment, the tie. All he had left was his white shirt, which was streaked with dirt and full of wrinkles and sweat marks. He was pale to begin with, but now there was a distinct blue-gray undertone to his skin. Now I remembered. It came back in pieces. The station. The needle. Stephen on the ground. He'd been dragged back from the point of death, and it showed.

"We were sent to the same hospital," he said.

He came to the bedside and looked me up and down, assessing the state of things.

"The wound," he said quietly, "it didn't penetrate your abdominal cavity. I'm sure it hurts quite a bit, but you'll be all right."

"I don't feel it," I replied. "I think I'm on some awesome drugs."

"Rory," Stephen said. "I don't want to put pressure on you in this condition, but they're coming."

"Who?"

No sooner had I said this than there was a crisp knock on the door. Without waiting for a reply, a man walked into the room. He had a youngish face and a head of what seemed to be prematurely gray hair, and he was dressed in plain but well-tailored clothes—black overcoat, blue shirt, black pants. He could have been a banker or a model of some idealized traveler like I'd seen in the airplane magazine. Somebody expensive and polite and almost deliberately forgettable, except for the gray hair. Another man followed him—older, in a brown suit.

The gray-suited man gently shut the door and came around to the side of the bed closest to the window, where he could address both Stephen and me.

"My name is Mr. Thorpe, and I am a member of Her Majesty's security service. My colleague represents the government of the United States. Forgive the intrusion. I understand you've both had a difficult evening."

The unnamed American man folded his arms over his chest.

"What's happening?" I asked Stephen.

"It's all right," Stephen said.

"We have some business to finish to clear this matter up," Thorpe continued. "We require assurance that this matter is at an end."

"It is," Stephen said.

"You're quite sure, Mr. Dene? Were you present?"

"Rory was."

"Miss Deveaux, can you say without question that the . . . person . . . known as the Ripper is no longer with us?"

"He's gone," I said.

"You're sure?"

"I'm sure," I said. "I saw it happen. Jo took the terminus and . . ."

"And what?"

I looked at Stephen.

"They're both gone," I said.

"Both?" Mr. Thorpe said.

"Another . . . someone we work with."

"One of *them*?" Mr. Thorpe said.

Just the way he said it made me hate him.

"The threat has been neutralized," Stephen said evenly.

Mr. Thorpe sized us both up for a minute. Before, someone like him would have scared me to death. Now, he was nothing. A man in a suit, living and breathing.

"You must understand . . ." Mr. Thorpe bent down to speak to me. He'd overdone it on the breath mints. " . . . that it's not in your best interests to discuss what happened to you tonight. In fact, we must insist that you do not. Not with your friends, your family, any religious counselors or mental health professionals. The latter would be most detrimental to you personally, as your account would be interpreted as delusional. Furthermore, you have become involved with an agency covered by the Official Secrets Act. You are bound by law to remain silent. We think it's best that you remain in the United Kingdom for the time being, while this affair is being sorted out. Should you choose to return to the United States, you will still remain bound by this law, due to the special relationship between our two countries."

Mr. Thorpe looked to the man in the doorway, who nodded back.

"You must realize talking about this won't help anyone," Mr. Thorpe said, softening his tone just a bit in a way that felt very deliberate. "The best thing you can do is return to school and continue with your life."

The brown-suited man took his phone from his pocket and started typing something in. He walked out of the room, still typing away.

"Constable Dene," Mr. Thorpe said as he straightened up, "we'll be in touch, of course. Your superiors are very pleased with your performance in this matter. Her Majesty's government thanks you both."

He didn't waste any more time on good-byes. He was gone as quickly as he had arrived.

"What just happened?" I asked.

Stephen pulled a chair over to my bedside and sat down.

"The cleanup is starting. They have to create a story the public can handle. The panic has to end. All the loose ends have to be tied."

"And I can never tell anyone?"

"That's the thing about what we do . . . We can't tell anyone. It would simply seem insane."

For some reason, this is what did it. This is what made all the fears of the last days and the last hours come to the surface. I let out a sob. It was so loud and sudden that Stephen actually startled and stood up. I began crying uncontrollably, heaving.

I don't think he knew what to do for a moment, it was such an onslaught.

"It's all right," he said, putting his hand on my arm and squeezing a bit. "It's over now. It's over."

My wailing drew the attention of the nurse, who snapped the curtain back.

"All right?" she asked.

"Can you do something to make her comfortable?" he said.

"Are you finished with your questions?"

"We're done," he said.

"It's been four hours since her last dose, so that's fine. Give me a moment."

The nurse went away for a moment, returning with a syringe. She injected its contents into a bit of tubing coming off my IV line. I felt a tiny rush of something cool coming into my vein. I took a few more sips of the water, gagging and coughing a bit before I could get them down like a normal person.

"Nasty wound," the nurse said quietly. "I hope you catch whoever did that."

"We did," Stephen said.

After a minute or two, I felt myself slowly calming, and I had a strong desire to close my eyes. The tears were still running down my face, but I was quiet. Stephen kept his hand on my arm.

I heard my door open again. I thought it was the nurse until I heard Callum say hello to Stephen and ask if I was okay. I managed to extract myself from the gooey pull of the drug-induced sleep. Callum was pushing Boo's chair. As soon as they were over the threshold, Boo took over, wheeling herself up to me and clonking into the side of my bed. Her eyes were solidly red and her face was streaked with the remains of her eye makeup. She grabbed my hand.

"I didn't think you'd come out of that room," she said.

"Surprise," I replied.

"I went into the toilets after they took you out. I saw the mirrors and the window. I smelled the air. And Jo . . ."

"I'm sorry," I said.

"I told her where you were," she said, fighting to keep her voice steady. "I saw her go in. That's what she's like, you know?"

Some heavy tears ran from her eyes. We all had a silent moment for Jo. Callum put his hand on Boo's shoulder. I had a feeling he was thinking about the fact that he was the only one out of us that had been unhurt. Stephen was barely upright, Boo was unable to walk, and I was flat out in a hospital bed. But he may have been in the most pain.

"We found the terminus as well," Callum finally said. "Boo managed to get it out before it was bagged up as evidence. It doesn't work anymore. I tried it. It's not just the battery in the phone. Something's happened to it."

He reached into his pocket and produced a diamond. It had gone a strange smoky shade, like lightbulbs do when they've blown out.

"One terminus down," Callum said. "Poor Persephone."

"Where are the others?" Stephen said, rubbing his eyes. "God, I'd forgotten . . ."

So had I. They didn't even know the worst of it yet.

"He threw them into the river," I said.

Two tiny diamonds somewhere in the Thames. One tiny diamond filled with smoke.

"That's us finished then," Callum said quietly.

"It's not," Boo said, dropping back into her chair. It almost got away from her, but Callum steadied it in time.

"No terminus?" he asked. "No us."

"There was a squad before the terminus," Stephen replied. "There will be one afterward. The Ripper is dead, and we're all still here."

The drugs were creeping into the edges of my thoughts again, but it was warmer and more pleasant now. Everything started to go a bit slower, and things were running together. The tubes were a part of my arm. The blanket was a part of my body. But I don't think it was the drugs that made me think that I was a part of the "we" now.

# 37

WHEN I WOKE AGAIN, IT WAS DAYLIGHT. I WAS uncomfortable. My stomach was itchy.

"You were trying to scratch at your stitches," someone said. The voice was American, and very familiar.

I opened my eyes to find Stephen, Callum, and Boo were gone. In their place, I found my mother.

"You were trying to scratch at your stitches," my mom said again. She was holding my hand.

"Where did the others go?" I asked. "Did you see them?"

"Others? No, honey. It's just us. We got on the first train. We've been here since this morning."

"What time is it now?"

"It's around two in the afternoon."

I desperately wanted to scratch at my stitches. She steadied my hand again.

"Dad's getting a coffee," she said. "Don't worry. He's here. We're here now."

My mom sounded so . . . Southern. So soft. So out

of place. My mom was home. This was an English hospital. She made no sense in this context.

My dad joined us a minute later, bearing two steaming cups. He wore his slouchy dad jeans and Tulane sweatshirt. My dad never went out in the Tulane sweatshirt. They both looked like they had dressed in the middle of the night, in whatever they could find.

"Hot tea," he said, holding up the cups. "It's just wrong."

I smiled a little. We were iced tea drinkers, all of us. We'd joked about how disgusting it would be to drink our tea hot, with milk. That is just not how we do it. We had iced tea with every meal. Unceasing rivers of iced tea, even for breakfast, even though I knew that unceasing rivers of iced tea will stain your teeth a fetching ecru color, like old lace. I liked mine disgustingly sweet, too—so extra dental care points there. Iced tea, my family . . .

"Dad," I said.

He put down the cups and they both just stood there, looking upset. The only thing I could think was that this is what people must see at their own viewings, when they're stuck in their coffins. All you can do is lie there while people stand over you and mourn. It was a little much to bear, and my memories were coming back faster and faster. There were things I needed to know—I needed updates.

"Can I see the news?" I asked.

I don't think my mom loved the idea, but she swung the television over and got the remote out from where it was tucked on the side of the mattress. The news station was, predictably, running the Ripper story. The bold words at the bottom of the screen told me everything: **RIPPER DIES IN THAMES**. I got the gist of the story fairly quickly. Police had been tracking suspect . . . suspect spotted at the Wexford School, just blocks away from the Mary Kelly murder site from 1888. The school, the location of the fourth murder, was speculated to be the intended site of the last murder as well. Police intervened when suspect tried to break into building . . . suspect ran . . . suspect jumped into Thames . . . body pulled out of Thames by divers . . . evidence confirms suspect was involved in all murders . . . name not yet released . . . police confirm the terror is over.

"The police kept the details about what happened to you out of the press," my father explained. "To protect you."

They had done exactly as Stephen said—they'd made a story that people could handle. They'd even put a body in the water for the police to fish out. I watched the footage of the divers bringing it up.

I turned the television off, and my mom pushed it to the side.

"Rory," she said, smoothing my hair back from my forehead, "whatever happened, you're safe now. We'll get you through this. Do you want to tell us about it now?"

I almost laughed.

"It's just like the news said," I replied.

That answer would hold water for a while—certainly not forever, but for a few days, while I recovered. I fluttered my eyes a bit and tried to look extra tired, just to steer them away.

"You're supposed to stay here for a few more hours at least," my dad said. "We have a hotel room for the night, where you can get some rest, then tomorrow we'll all go to Bristol. You're going to love the house."

"Bristol?"

"Rory, you can't stay here, not after this."

"But it's over," I said.

"You need to be with us. We can't . . ."

My mom gave a terse head shake, and my dad nodded and stopped talking. Silent communication. A united mental front. That was a bad sign.

"That's for now," my mom said carefully. "If you want to go home . . . we can do that. We don't have to stay in England."

"I want to stay," I said.

Another silent communication—just a look this time. Silent communications meant that they were serious and it was a done deal. I was going to Bristol. There was no fighting this one, really. There was no way they'd let me out of their sight now, not after I'd been slashed open in the school bathroom. I would be watched carefully for a while, and if I appeared in any way bonkers because of this, we would be on a plane back to New Orleans in a minute and I would be in a psychologist's office the minute after that.

Which was all really undesirable right now. England was my new home. England was where the squad was, where I was sane. This was all too complicated for me to figure out right now.

"Can I have another shot?" I asked. "It hurts."

My mom hurried off to find someone. She returned with a new nurse, who gave me another injection into my IV. This was the last, she told me. I would be given some painkillers to take with me when I left.

I spent the afternoon drifting in and out of sleep and watching television with my parents. There were still a lot of Ripper roundups, but some stations had decided it was okay to start running non-Ripper-related programs. Normal life was taking over again on midday television—trashy talk shows, and antiques shows, and shows about cleaning. English soap operas I couldn't understand. Endless commercials for car insurance and strangely seductive commercials for sausages.

Just after four, I saw two very familiar figures in the doorway. I knew they would come eventually. What I didn't know was what to say to them. Their version of reality and mine had diverged. There was formal handshaking with my parents, then they came to the bedside and smiled slightly fearful smiles—the kind of look you give when you have absolutely no idea what to say.

"How do you feel?" Jazza asked.

"Itchy," I said. "Kind of high."

"Could be worse," Jerome said, trying to smile.

My parents must have realized that my friends needed a minute to say whatever it was they wanted to say. They offered teas and coffees all around and excused themselves. Even after they were gone, the awkward silence reigned for a few moments.

"I need to apologize," Jazza finally said. "Please let me."

"For what?" I asked.

"For . . . well . . . it's just . . . I didn't . . . Well, I believed you, but . . ."

She collected herself and started again.

"The night of the murder, when you said you saw someone and I didn't. For a while I thought you made it up, even when the police were around you last night. All along you were a witness—and then he came after you. I'm sorry. I'll never . . . I'm sorry . . ."

For a second, I was tempted—I just wanted to spill the entire thing, start to end. But no. Mr. Thorpe was right. I couldn't do that, ever.

"It's okay," I said. "I would have thought the same thing about me."

"Classes are still canceled," Jerome said. "But we were stuck there until they chased the news people away. It's a circus. Wexford, site of the final Ripper attack . . ."

"Charlotte," I said suddenly. "I forgot Charlotte. Is she okay?"

"Yes," Jerome said. "She needed some stitches."

"She's acting like she was as hurt as you," Jazza said in disgust.

Charlotte had been beaten over the head with a lamp by an invisible man. I was prepared to give her a pass.

"You're famous," Jerome said. "When you get back . . ."

Something in my expression made him stop.

"You're not, are you?" he asked. "They're taking you out of school, aren't they?"

"Is Bristol nice?" I asked them.

Jerome exhaled in relief.

"It's better than Louisiana," he said. "That's what I thought you were going to say. Bristol is reachable by train."

Jazza had remained quiet through all of this. She took my hand, and she didn't have to say a word. I knew exactly what she was thinking. It wouldn't be the same, but I was safe. We were all safe. We'd survived the Ripper, all of us, and whatever happened now could be dealt with.

"There's just one thing I wish," Jazza said after a moment. "I wish I could have seen her get hit with that lamp."

# 38

So my uncle Will has these eight freezers up in his spare bedroom. It took a lot of effort to get those freezers up the steps, and I think he had to reinforce the floor. He keeps them filled with every kind of provision you can imagine. One is filled with meat. Another with vegetables and frozen dinners. I know one has things like milk and butter and yogurt. I think he even has frozen peanut butter in plastic jars, and frozen dried beans, and frozen batteries because he read somewhere that freezing them makes them last longer.

I don't know if you're supposed to freeze things like peanut butter and batteries, and I know for certain that I don't want to drink three-year-old frozen milk, but I know why he does it. He does it because he's lived through a dozen or more major hurricanes. His house was destroyed in Hurricane Katrina. He barely made it out alive. He escaped out of one of the windows in an inflatable raft and was picked up in a helicopter. He lost his dog in the flooding. So he moved closer to the rest of us and bought a little house and filled it with freezers.

Of course, when hurricanes come, the power goes out, and what he'll probably have are eight freezers filled with rapidly decaying old food, but that's not the point. I don't know what he saw when the waters rose around him, but whatever it was, it made him want to get eight freezers. Some things are so bad that once you've been through them, you don't have to explain your reasons to anyone.

I was thinking about this as our big black cab pulled into the Wexford square, bumping up along the cobblestones in front of Hawthorne. I could have let my parents go and get my things for me—I could have left London and never looked at the place again. But that felt wrong. I would go to my room. I would get my own things. I would face this place and everything that had happened here. I might get stares, but I didn't care.

Anyway, I could tell from a quick look around and a check of the time that that wasn't going to be an issue. It was seven in the morning on a Saturday. The lights in Hawthorne were mostly off. Aside from two people crossing the green and walking toward the refectory, I saw no one. Everyone was still in bed. There were two news vans around, but they were packing up their equipment. The show was over.

Claudia opened the door as we approached. I would leave as I had arrived just ten weeks before, with Claudia in the doorway, waiting for me.

"Aurora," she said in her softest voice, which was the same

kind of voice most people used to bark orders over malfunctioning drive-thru microphones. "How are you?"

"Fine," I said. "Thanks."

She introduced herself to my parents with one of her mighty, bunny-crushing handshakes. (I'd never seen Claudia crush a bunny, to be fair, but that's the approximate level of pressure.)

Claudia had been fully briefed on the situation, and mercifully, she wasn't going to belabor things.

"There are boxes upstairs," she said. "I'd be more than happy to help you."

"I'd rather do it myself," I replied.

"Of course," she said, with what I took to be a nod of approval. "Mr. and Mrs. Deveaux, why don't you come through to my office? We'll have some tea and a little chat. Aurora, you take as long as you need. We'll be right here if you need us."

"Remember," my mom said, "no lifting, no bending."

This was because of my stitches. My wound wasn't that bad—just a flesh wound, as they say—but I still had a large trail of stitches across my body. I'd been given a set of instructions on how to move around for the next few days while it all healed up. I hadn't actually *seen* my wound yet—it was under lots of bandages and tape. But from the size of the bandages, and from what I could feel, it was about a foot and a half long. I would, I was assured, have a wicked scar that ran from just under my ribs on the left side to the top of my right thigh. I'd been ripped by the Ripper. I was a walking T-shirt slogan.

Hawthorne really felt empty during the day. I could hear the heat whistling in the pipes, and the wind outside the windows, and the creak of wood. Maybe it felt more empty than normal because I was leaving. I was no longer part of this place. There was the familiar smell of my floor—the leftover sweetness of shampoos and body washes floating out of the steam of the showers mixed with the strangely metallic smell that always emanated from the dishwasher in the kitchenette. I touched the doors as I walked down the hall until I reached our room.

The promised boxes were stacked on my side of the room; some were piled by the closet, and more were on the bed. It looked like Jazza had started the packing process—some of my books had been carefully packed into one box on my desk, and my uniform shirts and skirts had been carefully folded and placed in another box.

I wasn't here to do any heavy packing—I was here only for a few personal items and some clothes for a few days. I decided to do it as quickly as possible—a handful of underwear from the top drawer, my two favorite bras, some sweats, the contents of my small dish of jewelry, and my Wexford tie. The last item I clearly didn't need, but it was a symbol of my time here. I would have my tie. I shoved all of these things into a small bag. The rest of my Wexford life would come later—the books I hadn't finished reading, the labels I never used, the sheets and blankets and uniforms.

The last thing I took was the ashtray shaped like the lips from Big Jim's. I put this on Jazza's bed, along with a few Mardi Gras beads. I took my little bag and left our room.

I walked down the Hawthorne stairs for the last time. On the last step, I hesitated. I stared at the flyers on the bulletin boards and the recently filled pigeonholes full of mail. Claudia's voice was fully audible, even though her office door was closed. She was telling my parents about hockey opportunities in Bristol.

" . . . once her injuries are healed, of course, but the padding does cover quite a lot . . ."

I turned in the direction of the bathroom. I could leave now and never see that room again, but something drew me toward it. I walked down the hall. I reached out and ran my hand down the wall. I passed the common room, the study rooms . . .

The bathroom door was gone. From the way the hinges were bent, it looked like it had been smashed down. The glass of the mirrors was completely gone; only the silver backings remained. There was also a crack in the floor—a long one, at least five feet, and maybe a quarter of an inch wide at points. It ran jagged from the center of the room in the direction of the bathroom stall, breaking every tiny tile in its path. I walked along it, up until the point where it slipped under the door. I pushed the door open.

There was a woman standing there.

Maybe I still had some of the painkillers in my system or something, because I should have jumped or screamed or registered some surprise. But I didn't.

This woman was old. Not in age—she looked like she was maybe twenty or thirty or something, it was hard to tell—but in time itself. She wore a rough blousy shirtdress.

Over that, she had a heavy, rust-colored skirt that went to the ground, and over that, a stained yellow apron. Her hair was as black as mine and was drawn away from her face with a scarf. But it wasn't just her clothes that told me she was old—it was the way light reacted to her. She was there, she was solid and real, but there was a strange cast about her, like she was standing in a fog.

"Hello?" I said.

Her eyes widened in terror and she backed up into the corner, squeezing herself between the toilet and the wall.

"I won't hurt you," I told her.

The woman pressed against the tiled wall with her hands, which were worn and red and marked with cuts and strange patches of black and green.

"Seriously," I tried again. "It's okay. You're safe here. My name is Rory. What's yours?"

She seemed to understand this, because she stopped clawing at the wall for a minute and looked at me unblinkingly. She opened her mouth to speak, but only a rasping sound came out. A slow hiss. It wasn't an angry hiss. I think that was just what her voice sounded like now. It was a solid conversational start.

"Do you know where you are?" I said. "Do you come from here?"

In reply, she pointed to the crack in the floor. Even the act of pointing to the crack distressed her again, and she began to cry . . . except she couldn't cry. She just heaved and made a noise like air slowly leaking from a bike tire.

"Aurora?" Claudia called. "Are you down here?"

I had absolutely no idea what to do about this situation. But the woman was clearly distressed, so I did what I had seen Boo do—I reached out to her to try to calm her down before Claudia came into the room and this conversation was over.

"Come on," I said. "It's okay—"

As soon as I made contact, I felt a crackle, like a static shock. I couldn't move my arm. Something was running through it, something that felt like a current, something that made me stiffen in position. I had a feeling of falling, like a lurching elevator dropping between floors. The woman opened her mouth to speak, but before she could say anything, there was a rush of air around us and a roaring noise.

And then, there was the light—impossibly bright and filling the senses. It consumed us both. A moment after that, it blinked out. I fell backward, stumbling through the open doorway of the stall and just managing to catch myself before I fell over.

"Rory!" That was my mother's voice, urgent. Claudia was saying something as well. My eyes were still adjusting. I could just make out shapes at first—the stall door, the window, the pattern of the tiles. The smell was already there, sweet, floral, almost like a scented candle. The unmistakable smell of a ghost departed. And as my eyes came back into focus, I saw that the woman was gone. I looked at the empty space, then at my hand.

"Rory?" my mother said. "What happened? What was that noise?"

That was not a question I was prepared to answer.

# ACKNOWLEDGMENTS

I HAD THE IDEA FOR THIS BOOK ONE VERY HOT SUMMER'S DAY IN London. I shoved everything else aside and worked on it like a mad working thing. I talked about it a lot. I dragged people to dark alleys in the East of London to stare at walls and sidewalks. I made some of the same people watch hours of footage taken from the driver's compartment of a Tube train ("Hey! This one is forty-five minutes of driving the Northern line tunnels! Grab a snack!") I have depended on the following people in various ways, and they are all owed thanks.

First, to my agent and friend Kate Schafer Testerman—there is no me without Kate. I will always fondly remember how you answered e-mails about this book while you were in labor, and I asked you why you were answering e-mails while you were in labor, and you said you were bored and between episodes of *Buffy*.

To Jennifer Besser, my editor, who believed in this book from the word go—I don't think the term "fairy godmother" is out of place here. To Shauna Fay, who is always there with a helping hand. And to everyone at Penguin for all of your support.

To my friends Scott Westerfeld, Justine Larbalestier, Robin

Wasserman, Holly Black, Cassie Clare, Sarah Rees Brennan, John Green, Libba Bray, Ally Carter . . . who read drafts, walked me through plot problems, and talked me off ledges. (Not that I was ever going to jump, but like a cat, I find myself in high, precarious places sometimes.) You are wise and long-suffering, and I am lucky to know you all. Believe me, I know it.

Andy Friel, Chelsea Hunt, and Rebecca Leach all served as advance readers. Mary Johnson (RN, CSNP, MOM) served as the medical consultant and got very used to me calling up and starting conversations with things like, "So, say I was sawing off a human head . . ."

Jason and Paula allowed me to marry them in the middle of all of this, and went with my idea of rolling a twenty-sided die in the ceremony to determine the success of the marriage.

And thank you to all my online friends who listen to my ramblings every day as I merrily roll along.

Without all of you, I'd be nowhere. Or, I'd be *somewhere,* but it would be the wrong place.

Turn the page for a preview
of the second novel in
the SHADES OF LONDON series . . .

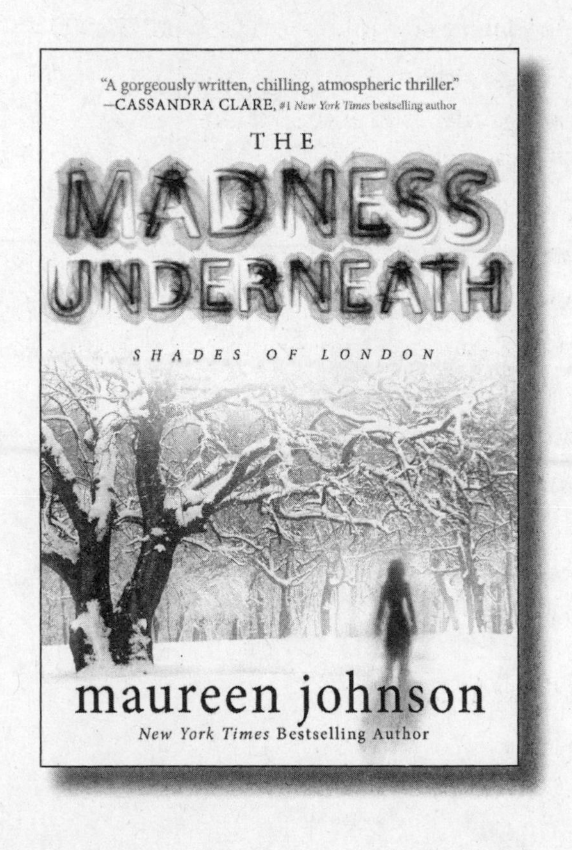

I wasn't going to be able to cope with many more of these sessions.

I like to talk. Talking is kind of *my thing.* If talking had been a sport option at Wexford, I would have been captain. But sports always have to involve running, jumping, or swinging your arms around. You don't get PE points for the smooth and rapid movement of the jaw. Three times a week, I was sent to talk to Julia. And three times a week, I had to *avoid* talking to Julia—at least, I couldn't talk about what had really happened to me.

You cannot tell your therapist you have been stabbed by a ghost.

You cannot tell her that you could see the ghost because you developed the ability to see some dead people after choking on some beef at dinner.

If you say any of that, they put you in a sack and take you to a room walled in bouncy rubber and you will never be allowed to touch scissors again. The situation will only get worse if you explain to your therapist that you have friends in the secret ghost police of London, and that you are really not supposed to be talking about this because some man from the government made you sign a copy of the Official Secrets Act and promise never to talk about these ghost police friends of yours. No. That won't improve your situation at all. The therapist will add "paranoid delusions about secret government agencies" to the already quite long list of your problems, and then it will be game over for you, crazy.

The sky was the same color as a cinderblock, and I didn't have an umbrella to protect me from the dark rain cloud that was clearly coming in our direction. This was Bristol, my new home. It was a big city, bustling, with a massive university. I understood there were many interesting things happening in Bristol—lots of music, theater, comedy. All sorts of stuff at the university. I didn't actually go to any of those things, but I had heard they were around. I had no idea what to do with myself, now that I was actually out of the house. I saw a coffee place. That's where I would go. I'd get a coffee, and then I'd walk home. That was a good, normal thing to do. I would do this, and then maybe . . . maybe I would do another thing.

Funny thing when you don't get out of the house for a while—you come back into the outside world as a tourist. I stared at the people working on laptops, studying, writing things down in notebooks. I flirted with the idea of telling the guy who was making my latte, just blurting it out: "I'm the girl the Ripper attacked." And I could whip up my shirt and show him the still-healing wound. You couldn't fake the thing I had stretching across my torso—the long, angry line. Well, I guess you *could*, but you'd have to be one of those special-effects makeup people to do it. Also, people who get up to the coffee counter and whip off their shirts for the baristas usually have other problems, ones much deeper than my injury.

I took my coffee and left quickly before I got any other funny little ideas.

I walked along the waterside, away from the shops and restaurants. I would walk. I would walk and walk and walk, and maybe I would walk right out of Bristol to a new city. Maybe I would walk all the way to the ocean. Maybe I would swim home.

God, I needed to talk to someone.

I don't know about you, but when something happens to me—good, bad, boring, it doesn't matter—I have to *tell* someone about it to make it count. There's no point in anything happening if you can't talk about it. And this was the biggest something of all. I *ached* to talk. I mean, it literally hurt me, sitting there, holding it all in hour after hour. I must have been clenching my stomach muscles the whole time, because my whole abdomen throbbed. Sometimes, if I was still awake late at night, I'd be tempted to call some anonymous crisis hotline and tell some random person my story, but I knew what would happen. They'd listen, and they'd advise me to get psychiatric help. Because my story was nuts.

The official story:

A man decides to terrorize London by re-creating the murders of Jack the Ripper. He kills four people, one of them, unluckily, on the green right in front of my building at school. I see this guy when sneaking back into my building that night. Because I'm a witness, he decides to target me for the last murder. He sneaks into my building on the night of the final Ripper murder and stabs me in the downstairs bathroom. I survive because the police get a report of a sighting of something suspicious and break into the building. The suspect flees, the police chase him, and he jumps into the Thames and dies.

The real version:

The Ripper was a ghost of a man, formerly of the ghost policing squad. He targeted me because I could see ghosts. His whole aim was to get his hands on a terminus, the tool the ghost police use to destroy ghosts. The termini (there were actually three of them) were diamonds. When you ran an electrical current through them, they destroyed ghosts. Stephen had wired them into the hollow bodies of phones, using the batteries to power the charge. I survived that night in the bathroom because Jo, another ghost, grabbed a terminus out of my hand and destroyed the Ripper—and in the process, herself.

The only people who really knew the whole story were Stephen, Callum, and Boo, and I was never allowed to talk to them again. That was one of the conditions when I left London. A man from the government really had made me sign the Official Secrets Act. Measures had been taken to make sure I couldn't reach out to them. While I was in the hospital after the attack, knocked out cold, someone took my phone and wiped it clean.

So I was in Bristol, alone, walking the riverside in the drizzle and occasionally scratching at my abdomen. The stitches were out, but I swear I could still feel them sometimes—ghostly twinges at my middle. Sometimes, when it got dark (and it got dark so early) and I was alone in my strange new bedroom, I wondered about myself. Because it couldn't be true. Maybe I had had a total break from reality.

I was so preoccupied in my wallowing that I almost walked right past him, but something about the suit must have caught my attention. You don't see many people who are probably in their twenties just sitting around in a suit, looking lost. And the cut of the suit . . . something was strange about it. I'm not an expert on suits, but this one was somehow different, a very drab gray with a narrow lapel. And the collar. The collar was odd. He wore horn-rim glasses, and his hair was very short, but with square sideburns. Everything was just a centimeter or two too long or two short, all the little data points that tell you someone isn't quite right. That the clothes you're seeing aren't quite the ones you're used to.

He was a ghost.

My ability to see ghosts, my "sight," was the result of two elements: I had the innate ability, and I'd had a brush with death at the right time. It was not magic. It was not supernatural. It was, as Stephen liked to put it, the "ability to recognize and interact with the vestigial energy of an otherwise deceased person, one who continues to exist in a spectrum usually not perceived by humans." Stephen actually talked like that.

What it meant was simply this: some people, when they die, don't entirely *eject* from this world. Something goes wrong in the death process, like when you try to shut down a computer and it goes into a confused spiral. These unlucky people remain on some plane of existence that intersects with the one we inhabit. Most of them are weak, barely able to interact with our physical world. Some are a bit stronger. And lucky people like me can see them, and talk to them, and touch them.

This is why in my many, many hours of watching shows about ghost hunters (I'd watched a *lot* of television in Bristol) I'd gotten so angry. Not only were the shows stupid and obviously phony, but they didn't even make sense. These people would rock up to houses with their weird night-vision camera hats and cold-spot-o-meters, set up cameras, and then turn off all the lights and wait until dark. (Because apparently ghosts care if the lights are on or off and if it's day or night. Isn't that supposed to be vampires?) And then, these champions would fumble around in the dark saying, "IF SPIRITS ARE HERE, MAKE YOURSELVES KNOWN, SPIRITS." This is roughly equivalent to a tourist bus stopping in the middle of a foreign city and all of the tourists getting out in their funny hats with their video cameras and saying, "We are here! Dance for us, natives of this place! We wish to film you!" And, of course, nothing happens. Then there's always a bump in the background, some normal creaking of a step or something, and they amplify that about ten million times, claim they've found evidence of paranormal activity, and kick off for a cold, self-congratulatory brew.

I edged around for a few minutes, taking him in from a few different angles, making sure I knew what I was looking at. I wondered what the chances were that the first time I came out and walked around Bristol on my own, I'd see a ghost. Judging from what was going on right now, those chances were very good. A hundred percent, in fact. It made a kind of sense that I'd find one here. I was walking along a river, and (as Stephen had explained to me once), waterways always have a long history of death. Ships sink and people jump into rivers. Rivers and ghosts go together.

I crossed in front of him, pretending to talk on my phone. He had a blank stare on his face, the stare of someone who truly had nothing to do but just *exist.* I stared right at him. Most people, when stared at, stare back. Because staring is weird. Ghosts are used to people looking right through them. As I suspected, he didn't react in any way to my staring. He didn't look over or acknowledge me in any way. There was a grayness, a loneliness around him that was palpable. Unseen, unheard, unloved. He was still existing, but for no reason.

Definitely a ghost.

It occurred to me, he could have a friend. He could have someone to share this existence with. Something welled up in me, a great feeling of warmth, of generosity, a swelling of the spirit. I could share something with him, and in return, he could help me as well. Whoever this guy was, *I could tell him the truth.* He was part of the truth. No, he didn't know me, but that hardly mattered. He was *about* to get to know me. We would be friends. Oh, yes. We would be friends. We were *meant* to be together. For the first time in weeks, there was a path—a logical, clear, walkable path. And it started with me sitting on the bench.

"Hi," I said.

He didn't turn.

"Hi," I said again. "Yes, I'm talking to you. On the bench. Here. With me. Can you hear me?"

Still no reply, but he did turn to look at me, his eyes wide in surprise.

"Bet you're surprised," I said, smiling. "I know. It's weird. But I can see you. My name's Rory. What's yours?"

No answer. Just a wide, eternal stare.

"I'm new here," I said. "To Bristol. I was in London. I'm from America, but I guess you can tell that from my voice? I came here to go to school, and—"

The man bolted from his seat. I mean, he shot out of it like the thing had fired him. Ghosts have a fluidity of movement that the living don't know—they remain solid, yet they can move like air. I didn't want him to go, so I bounced up and reached as far as I could to catch his coat. The second I made contact, I felt my fingers getting pulled in to his body, like I had put them into the suction end of a vacuum. I felt the ripple of energy going up my arm, the inexorable force linking us both together now, then the rush of air, far greater than any waterside breeze. Then came the flash of light and the unsettling, floral smell.

And he was gone.